LOVERS AND USERS

ERNST—The playboy who can't get enough of all the wrong things.

PRINCESS SOLANGE—His wife, forced to find satisfaction where she can.

GERRY—War hardened, worldly wise, but still hungering for romantic love.

HEINRICH—The tough, brooding hustler.

HANK—The good looking, all American hunk.

MARIA—The procurer of drugs and boys.

NOW LET'S TALK ABOUT MUSIC

By the acclaimed bestselling author of AN IDOL FOR OTHERS, THE LORD WON'T MIND and ONE FOR THE GODS.

Other Avon books by
Gordon Merrick

The Peter and Charlie Trilogy:
FORTH INTO LIGHT
THE LORD WON'T MIND
ONE FOR THE GODS

AN IDOL FOR OTHERS
THE QUIRK

GORDON MERRICK

NOW LET'S TALK ABOUT MUSIC

AVON
PUBLISHERS OF BARD, CAMELOT AND DISCUS BOOKS

NOW LET'S TALK ABOUT MUSIC is an original publication of Avon Books. This work has never before appeared in book form.

AVON BOOKS
A division of
The Hearst Corporation
959 Eighth Avenue
New York, New York 10019

Published by arrangement with the author
Library of Congress Catalog Card Number: 80-69901
ISBN: 0-380-77867-x

First Avon Printing, June, 1981

Printed in the U. S. A.

10 9 8 7 6 5 4 3 2 1

FOR NESTA

who is real, thank heavens,
with much love

JUST OFF THE SOUTHERN TIP of the distant land called Ceylon, more recently Sri Lanka, within plain sight of the old Dutch port of Galle, a luxury yacht skewered on a coral reef has been slowly disintegrating since 1975. Every year, pounded by the heavy surf of the Indian Ocean, buffeted by the gales of the Southwest monsoon, it settles deeper into the sea. It has long since broken in two, evident from the wide inverted V of its profile, both bow and stern pointing into the deep. Within the first year, it was stripped of everything of use or value by the efficient fishermen based in Galle, several of whom sacrificed their lives to their arduous quest.

Many stories circulate about how it came to be there. Legend proliferates like mildew in tropical climates; fact melts easily into fancy in the heat. Everybody remembers the night it happened, a relatively clear calm night before the monsoons had really set in. Some of the more prosperous shopkeepers leaped to the prosaic conclusion that it was run in on purpose for the insurance, probably thinking of what they would do if they possessed such a craft. In view of the owner's vast wealth, this version appears to be at the least an oversimplification. Others maintain that it is there due to a navigational error. This school holds that the lighthouse in Galle Fort failed that night, as it is known to do periodically. The official log shows that it was operating normally. Various forms of skulduggery creep into other accounts—murder, piracy, smuggling, a plot to overthrow the government. Scandalous gossip clings to the four handsome young men who came ashore and lingered briefly among the townspeople before they too disappeared. There was something definitely odd about those handsome young men.

Everybody agrees on two indisputable facts: the owner of the yacht was the notorious Baron von Hallers and its name was *Hephaistion.* Hephaistion. An odd exotic murmurous sound. Hephaistion, the lifelong comrade-in-arms and lover of Alexander the Great. History recounts that Alexander reached India in the course of his conquests. How natural to assume that, being so close, he came on to visit the fabled island of Ceylon, like any intelligent tourist. In fact, there is a large indentation in a rock up in the high country that is said to be Alexander's footprint. Or perhaps it is the Buddha's. No matter. They lived within a couple of thousand years of each other.

The heat plays its part in the conjectures of those who are captivated by the mythic rather than the material aspects of the disaster. Surely it is a curious coincidence that the yacht bore the name of the great Alexander's lover. The four handsome young men come into it somehow. There is a tendency to nudge the story toward the miraculous: the reincarnation of Alexander and his beloved Hephaistion as they sought to return to the most beautiful land they had visited in their brief mortal lives. It is unlikely that this will acquire the echoes of legend and get a grip on the local imagination until the wreck slides into the sea forever, as it is bound to do in the next few years, leaving no visible evidence of what actually happened.

He moved through gold and ivory and turquoise light under the ornamental dome, past lushly elegant jungle foliage imprisoned in beaten brass. Responding to his surroundings, he eased the straps of his knapsack and shrugged it off and carried it dangling from one hand.

The end of the trail. In fact, it had ended some days ago when he had crossed the Mekong River from Laos and made his way to Chiang Mai in the north. The journey down to Bangkok last night had been in the considerable comfort of a first-class railway compartment. Farewell to the sad funny horror of Saigon. Farewell to Jack. He would be home by now, lying in a hero's grave.

He paused at the edge of the emerald lawn that stretched to the bank of the wide river. Gleaming temple trees were grouped around the pool at the far side of the hotel compound. Smart garden furniture was set out along the riverfront—canvas chairs, tables impaled by gay umbrellas. There was no streaked or flaking paint, no chipped masonry or shattered woodwork, no trace of war or poverty. Was this what the real world looked like? The contrast to the life he had been living was so great that he felt unreal, dreamlike, invisible.

He was seen, however; his arrival didn't go unnoticed. A trim youngish man stylishly dressed in appropriate tropical clothing leaned against the reception desk, waiting for the mail to be sorted for Baron von Haller's party, and watched the tall spare young stranger cross the gold-and-ivory lounge whose glass dome and turquoise silk upholstery gave it a cool underwater look. The young stranger swam across it. His knapsack, serviceable boots, worn khaki pants and shirt gave him a vaguely military look; the elegance of the way he moved—a hint of a sexual swing in the hips—belied the costume. Rich silky chestnut hair. The face stripped down to the bone, gaunt but cheerful-looking. The features were easy to forget but they left an appealing impression. Definitely not a hippie. What Ernst would call a gentleman.

"A new arrival?" the Baron's secretary asked of the receptionist behind the desk, nodding toward the vanishing khaki figure.

The receptionist leaned forward briefly. "Yes, yes. Mr. Kennicutt. A client sometimes. He arrived without booking and no luggage. He asked for a room but we have only the Conrad suite. He will be there across the way from the Baron."

"He's in business here?"

"Who knows? These young men who come and go. There's much money in the drug trade."

"That's what he does?"

"I not say so. Who knows?"

The secretary nodded. Just as well to have asked a few questions. He would have to alert the bodyguards. Ernst liked to know who was in the adjacent suites. In this case, the occupancy was apparently fortuitous but one couldn't be too careful these days. "Kennicutt, you say? Where from?"

The receptionist picked up the registration card that had been filled out only a few minutes before. "Gerald Kennicutt. Of New York City."

"An American. Of course," the secretary murmured, flipping through the packet of letters that had been put before him. The Baron liked Americans. He would mention the newcomer to him.

The subject of this brief interrogation was sipping his third iced beer out on the river terrace when he was approached by the jaunty young waiter who had been flirting with him in a playful Oriental way.

"Mr. Kennicutt, sir?" the waiter asked, smiling into his eyes.

"Yes," Gerry said with a responsive smile. He wasn't interested but had never been able to casually dismiss an attractive flirtatious male. The waiter offered him an envelope on a platter. Gerry took it, saw his name on it and withdrew a heavy sheet of crested stationery.

> Dear Kennicutt,
>
> Is it possible that I know your mother? A charming lady in New York has talked much of her son Gerald who travels in the East. Will you have drinks and lunch with us on the river? The boat is just beyond the hotel restaurant. About 1:30.
>
> Cordially,
> Ernst von Hallers

Gerry stared with astonishment at the signature. Mum knew the damnedest people. Like the rest of the world, he had read a lot about Ernst von Hallers, most of it scandalous. Von Hallers had flaunted his boyfriends in the face of the world press. An hour after his wedding he had eloped in his own plane with his best man. Gerry had seen a number of photographs of Ernst on his yacht in the Mediterranean, always surrounded by beautiful boys, Ernst the most beautiful of them all. He was the result of a dynastic conjunction of Krupps and Schneiders and Creuzots, much as if Du Ponts and Rockefellers and Fords had somehow come together to produce a single heir. His father was said to have managed and manipulated all the wars of the earlier decades of the century; the fashionable lip service paid to social conscience after World War II and the shift in political and economic power had changed all that.

By the time Gerry had become aware of him, Ernst was no longer the heir to a great industrial empire but a footloose playboy cloaked in the legend of his extraordinary background. Gerry had always felt a special affinity for him because he was just discovering the joys and perils of his own sexuality when Ernst had first become the delight of the gossip columnists. There was a difference of only a few years in their ages. Gerry had found it thrilling that someone so young and prominent could so brazenly defy convention. All this had been long ago. He hadn't heard of Ernst von Hallers for years.

The waiter was still standing beside him. He looked up into eyes that were waiting to meet his. "Where did this come from?"

"The lord Baron, sir. He's in the Maugham and Coward suites."

"I thought I was in the Maugham suite. No. Some other writer. Conrad. Much more distinguished. OK. I'll take care of this at the desk." He glanced at his watch. Not yet eleven. "You can bring me one more of these freezing beers if you will."

The waiter bustled off to obey. Gerry sat back and tossed the note onto the table. He looked out along the riverbank and saw a bizarre but luxurious-looking boat, all teak and carving, moored to a jetty beyond the pavilion where tables were being laid for lunch. The craft was an odd shape, sitting high in the water with a pagoda-like structure on the deck, an Oriental Noah's Ark. It looked like an amusing place for a social event, but had he traveled through the East for five years in order to have lunch with Ernst von Hallers? He doubted it. Von Hallers was no longer a fantasy hero; he was part of a dead past. Why *had* he traveled through the East for five years? It was a question he could very nearly answer. Almost. He suspected that the answer would grow clearer as he headed home. If that was where he *was* headed. He had almost become a holy man but had found that the role didn't suit him. He had shaved his head and worn the saffron robes of a Buddhist monk, but the disguise hadn't altered the fact that he was irrevocably bound to a materialistic Western concept of his own individuality. He had found peace and solace in yoga and meditation but he didn't want to lose himself in a Universal Soul or achieve higher levels of Non-Being. Nirvana was not for him. He wanted to *find* himself in the world of men. Was that the sum of his discoveries on his five-year odyssey? There was more of course, but even if that were all, it was a great deal.

The playful waiter put another beer in front of him. He forgot their flirtation and only nodded and muttered his thanks while his thoughts continued to drift.

A search for self? It sounded rather pretentious but it

had started out as something of the sort in a fairly negative way. The succession of shocks five years ago had ended in depression rather than aspiration. At thirty, he had been faced with the conviction that he had led a silly and useless life, with no glimpse of how it could have been or ever would be otherwise; he was a silly and useless person. Events had piled up and fallen on him in a way that seemed to call for some sort of heroic reaction, but he doubted if there was anything heroic in him. His mother, who knew him better than anybody else in the world, had chosen that moment to make him rich; that is, she had given him an income of forty thousand dollars a year.

"Will that be anything like enough, darling? It's all I can manage. Your father—" She looked uncharacteristically flustered and almost girlish. "Well, he *thinks* he's your father. He'd never approve, so it has to be a bit of a secret. I can't make a secret of more than forty thousand, more's the pity."

"Really, Mum, you're quite mad," Gerry had pointed out. "Do you have any idea what I make? Barely more than a third of that."

"Poor lamb. Did Walter know? Why didn't he give you some money?"

"Why should he? More to the point, how could he without spilling the beans? I wasn't his lover, you know. We can't count those few weeks twelve years ago. Still, I did have an affair with my father. We're all very incestuous, aren't we? I wish I'd given him more reason to be proud of me."

"Don't talk about yourself like that, darling."

"It's all right, love. I may have been a screaming eighteen-year-old queen but I'm not a screaming *thirty*-year-old queen, mostly thanks to Walter. We have that to be thankful for. Can you really spare all that bread?"

"I should think so. We're frightfully rich. It's really yours, in a way. Walter made a great deal of money for us, you know, when he first started out as a producer. I don't know how many hundreds of thousands. Think what it must be now, properly invested all these years. It wouldn't have happened if—if I hadn't wanted him and he hadn't wanted my money. It was a lovely exchange and you're the heavenly result. Walter wouldn't have wanted his oldest son to be proverty-stricken. He quite naturally expected me to do something for you. Very well. I shall. Dear me. How sad. He was *the* great love of my life, you know."

"Mine too, probably. I wish you'd known Tom. Such a beautiful guy. He was the great love of Walter's life, I think. So there we are."

"Yes, darling. There we are."

"I think I'd better go away for a while, Mum. I'd been thinking about it before I knew I was going to be a millionaire. Try to put myself together again. Well, you see, I really haven't had all the pieces until now. Where to go? I don't know. Nowhere in particular. Somewhere new. I might find out if there's anything good enough in me to be Walter's."

"Walter was a genius, darling. That's often a handicap for the sons, but it shouldn't matter to you since you didn't know he was your father until a few days ago. Still, it's a bit of a tangle for you. You're his oldest son, which would ordinarily make you the leader, the crown prince. You're my youngest, the baby of the family, the coddled and sheltered one. And of course you're my beloved bastard, which makes you my particular joy. Remember all those things when you're fitting together the pieces. Is there no lovely boy in the offing, darling?"

"I haven't stopped looking, Mum. Perhaps now I'll find one who'll love me for my money."

Five years later, he was still looking but hope had taken a nearly fatal beating in the last weeks. He had come so close with Jack but he knew that his death had probably saved them both from disillusionment. Before Jack, he had learned to live in and for himself, a strength acquired in the East. He had learned from yoga simple ways to direct and control his sexual urges if he should find himself leading a monkish life once more. Perhaps freedom was what he was after. In one orgiastic Hindu community, because of the dimensions and capabilities of his sexual equipment, he had served as stand-in for a god. Ritualized worship at last. He hoped that it had finally cured him of his prolonged infatuation with his own cock. Jack had helped. He hadn't paid much attention to it.

He glanced at the note on the table. If Ernst von Hallers hadn't changed his ways he might have a retinue of pretty youths, but Gerry wasn't greatly tempted. He might go to lunch, he might not. He had long ago lost all sense of time's urgency. He would decide when he went to the desk to pick up his key. They would probably press him to name a departure date, as they had earlier. Another decision he would have to make without any compulsion. A day. A week. What difference did it make? The idle rich.

As it had turned out, the money had made very little difference to him. A good three-quarters of the last five years' income was earning interest in a bank in New York. Perhaps that should be the next step—a binge of spending to mark his return to the bloated West. Except that he couldn't think of anything he wanted. He needed some clothes, but then what?

He finished the beer and signaled for the bill and gave the waiter a dutiful wink when he signed it.

As he was conducted to Conrad, up the ornamental double staircase, past Maugham and Coward, his eye was caught by a striking-looking woman, smartly dressed in white, with great popping eyes, deep in conversation with a round little Oriental. He heard them exchange a few words in Sinhalese, a language he had learned to stumble through in Ceylon. He recognized the words without remembering their meaning. He glanced across the hall and wondered if Ernst von Hallers had received his note of acceptance. Now that he'd written it, he was intrigued by the impending meeting.

The Conrad suite was agreeable, such a change from the accommodations he had grown accustomed to that it seemed almost overwhelmingly luxurious. There were a few handsome Oriental pieces in the sitting room and a good-sized bedroom with the usual twin beds pushed together to suit every taste. He tipped the elderly roomboy who installed his knapsack ceremoniously on the baggage rack, and made sure the ceiling fans were working before sending him away.

He sat on the edge of the bed and removed his boots and the socks he had washed threadbare during the last weeks' rugged travel. Not a high price to pay for getting out of Vietnam alive—tramping through steaming jungles, riding in bullock carts, crawling for hours through tunnels. He hadn't had a very clear idea where he was going. The bartender at the café he and Jack had frequented told him he'd better get out before the news of Jack's death spread. Strangers had taken charge of him. He had passed through many hands, apparently part of a well-organized transport or communications system. He supposed he had been in danger at times, judging from the precautions that had been taken. He had been given ragged coolie clothes to wear, including a big conical straw hat that shadowed his face. He had sometimes been instructed to go barefoot. His knapsack had been wrapped in leaves or straw matting to make it look like a peasant bundle. He was heavily tanned so his color was not conspicuous.

He had made it, which was more than could be said for Jack. The last papers and magazines he had seen from home were filled with news about the vast forces that were going to be flung into the war to finally turn the tide, which made him wonder if everybody in Washington had gone mad. Anybody with eyes could see that the war was over. The Communists had won. *Finito.* He supposed the news would reach the press eventually.

He stripped off his shirt and tossed it aside. He stood and started to unzip his fly when there was a knock at the outer door. He pulled the zipper up and called, "Come in."

A youth in hotel uniform came trotting in and stopped in front of him with a little bow. "Good morning, sir. I'm roomboy. Special for here. I do everything you want. You ring. I come."

"An excellent arrangement." The boy was attractive in a harmlessly wolfish way, with the attractive body common to all in this part of the world, slight and shapely, despite the statistics about disease and malnutrition. His tight trousers betrayed no sign of male attributes, a less happy characteristic of the East.

"No lady, sir?" the boy asked with a glance around the room.

"No. I'm alone. This was the only thing they could give me." He was so aware of having all this comfortable space to himself that he felt a need to apologize for it. Thinking of the woman in the corridor, he tried a few words in Sinhalese about laundry. The boy beamed. "That Ceylon language. What you tell?"

"I was asking if you could take some laundry. Is that your job?"

"Yes, sir. Laundry. Which?"

"Everything I've got on." He unzipped his fly again and at the risk of offending the boy's Oriental modesty, peeled off his pants and shorts. Finding himself naked with an attractive youth was mildly titillating. The boy's eyes dropped in a frank examination of him. He had never minded showing himself off. He gathered up his clothes and rolled them into a ball and presented them to the boy. Their hands touched as he did so and he realized that the youth was available. He didn't want him, but going without sex for so long made him look increasingly as if he did. It was getting to be a considerable display, of evident and gratifying interest to the beholder.

"You wish massage, maybe?" the boy suggested cheerfully. "Very nice. You wish? I good massage you. Only ten bahts. Many gentlemen like. Lie down please."

Gerry laughed. "Not now. Maybe some other time."

"You very much big, sir. Every extras, twenty bahts. You like sure."

"It sounds great but I'm expecting a friend." Gerry caught sight of the boots and poked them with a toe. "You can take those if you know anybody who can use them. I won't need them anymore."

"Very fine, sir. Someone pay many bahts. This every laundry?"

"That's it. I don't have much with me."

The boy dropped to one knee to pick up the boots, but his eyes remained for an unnecessary moment on Gerry's evenly tanned midriff. He rose and they exchanged a knowing look. "Very fine, sir. More big and more. Your friend comes soon? A misfortune. My name Lee. You ring. I come. Anytime."

Gerry waited while he trotted out, impressed by the hotel's service, and then headed for the bathroom to have a look at what he'd been displaying. He stood in front of the mirror and uttered a brief little gurgle of laughter. Like this, not certifiably aroused but at a stage that invited conjecture, it looked as if it might turn out to be a yard long. His Majesty. He hadn't had a good look at himself for a long time (the cracked scrap of mirror in Jack's little apartment in Saigon) and his eyes strayed up over the rest of his body, noting the striking changes of the last few years. Before, it had been somehow expensive-looking, slightly soft and blurred and vaguely effeminate, which had given his extravagant masculinity the added emphasis of incongruity. Now, pared down, it looked tough and hard, the lightly developed muscles firmly defined under dark sun-ruddy skin. His shoulders looked wider, his hips narrower; if he lost any more weight he might begin to look scrawny but he still had a couple of superfluous pounds on his well-rounded bottom that he didn't want to lose. The concavity of his abdomen and belly delighted him. It was an amazingly young body, a slim kid's body, and without having grown more than a couple of hairs on his chest, it was finally wholly male, much more suitable for carrying around His Majesty's grandeur.

He nodded approvingly as he saw the display for Lee shrinking. Now that he was safe and getting rested from his journey, he was only beginning to realize what a big adjustment he still had to make to Jack's absence. Showing himself off to roomboys wasn't going to get him anywhere, nor was an aging playboy with a reputation for surrounding himself with pretty young hustlers likely to offer any great new hopes for the future. That's what it was all about finally: the last five years had been a preparation for living according to the values that had perhaps been bred in him but which he had been painfully slow to recognize. Why bother to meet von Hallers? His initial indifference to the lunch invitation had been tempered by the men at the desk being so impressed by it and he had let curiosity get the better of him. Would Jack approve? Belonging to a man for almost a year, as he had belonged to Jack, had left him uncertain about even something so trivial as lunch. Jack had made all the decisions right from the start.

He had picked Gerry up beside the pool at the old E and O Hotel in Penang, literally and physically picked him up in his arms and carried him inside. "You know I'm going to fuck you, don't you?" he said as he started down a vast and endless corridor. They were almost the first words exchanged between them. He had been at the pool barely five minutes and Gerry had been trying to lay the old eye on him without much hope of success. He was speechless with delighted astonishment. "If you don't want it, you better say so quick and I might let you down. Once I get you to bed you won't have a chance. I'll rape you if you make any trouble."

"It sounds heavenly."

"Yeah?" They were laughing now. "You're such a fancy-looking piece I wasn't sure you'd know what fucking is. You're for guys?"

"What else?"

"That's what I figured. Same here."

Gerry was being carried by a tall rangy kid with unruly straw-colored hair, a dashing straw-colored moustache and the fresh good looks of a country boy. He had known immediately that he was an American but it took him a few more hours to learn that he was an Air Force colonel stationed in Vietnam and only twenty-six. Jack took him without preliminaries and kept his wonderfully substantial cock in him all afternoon, driving one orgasm after another into him until there wasn't a corner of Gerry that hadn't surrendered to him.

"I don't know what it is about you," Jack said when they suspended operations for dinner. "I guess maybe I've always wanted a guy who looks sort of like a girl and has the biggest cock in the world. I don't particularly want to *suck* cocks often, but I sure like to look at them and feel them when they're standing up wanting me. With you, it's like being wanted by a baseball bat. I mean, if I don't watch out, it's apt to knock me cold. Now that I've got you, I guess I better keep you."

He did. Gerry had been waiting for friends who were due to arrive at any moment but the next day Jack put him in a private plane he had wangled somehow and flew him to Singapore where he transferred them to a military plane and continued to Saigon. Gerry felt as if he were losing his mind but you couldn't argue with Jack. He had a keen sense of the world's madness and was determined not to let it do him in. He acted on the assumption that anything he did was bound to be more reasonable than anything laid down by the established order. There was no possible way for Gerry to get into Vietnam, but here he was. His status was clear from the beginning; Jack introduced him to all his friends as "my missus." By taking for granted that Gerry belonged to him, he made him belong to him. They never talked of love but nobody except his mother had ever made him feel so treasured and cared for. He wiped out the eight years' difference in their ages by establishing himself as his protector in all matters. Their sex life was more robust, their roles more clearly defined, than in any relationship Gerry had experienced. Jack treated His Majesty like some precious, almost feminine adornment; Jack's somehow became the dominant male organ.

"I've got to shove off for a few days," Jack said after they'd been living in his apartment for less than a week.

"I'm not going to tell you much about where I go and that stuff. The whole deal out here is a fuckup. If I say I'll be back Thursday and don't show up, you'll worry. I don't want that. You know your way around now. I'll be back. Don't worry."

For some reason, he didn't. He couldn't imagine anybody stopping Jack from doing what he wanted to do and he knew Jack wanted to be with him. Jack was totally, incredulously, inarticulately in love with him. He had never seen so much naked love in anybody's eyes. When he was home, the place was usually filled with friends. Gerry served them drinks from an apparently inexhaustible supply of liquor and cooked for them and felt oddly at home in this tough male world. At thirty-four, he wouldn't have been surprised if the younger ones had made him feel like an old man but they all treated him like a helpless child, with shy solicitude and in some cases with suppressed desire. From their brutal jokes and the stories they told of their missions, Gerry acquired a weird, nightmarish vision of meaningless devastation eroding the foundations of the crumbling but still macabrely elegant city.

When Jack went away, their friends evaporated with him, even the ones Gerry knew wanted him. He found it odd and asked Jack why nobody came to see him when he was alone.

"They wouldn't dare. I don't want those cats prowling around you. I know your cock. There's so damn much of it that it's bound to get restless. When we get out of here, we'll take some of that money of yours and set ourselves up someplace and see people together and all that stuff, but I'll be there to keep an eye on you. I don't like it when I'm away. Why should you?"

He loved Jack but much as he wanted to, he couldn't fall in love with him. For the first time in his life, he was undeviatingly true and faithful because he couldn't imagine being otherwise with him, but he knew it wouldn't last except under these very special circumstances. There was too much that was basically incompatible in their natures. Jack was too straight and clear and extroverted to even imagine the depths of what Gerry used to think of as his triviality, but with the growth of self-respect had come to recognize as a failure to give direction to his deepest feelings. He had failed at the beginning with Ned. He had failed at the crucial moment with Tom. He had never felt guilty, any more than Jack, about his deviant sexuality, but his colonel's wholesome unimaginative confidence in the future had made him feel unworthy. The big experience of love had eluded him again, as it always had, but this time at least he had held himself ready for it, all his perceptions geared to receive it. He had done nothing to betray it.

Thoughts of Jack, the longing he could still feel on his skin for the touch of his body threatened to arouse him much more thoroughly than stripping for the roomboy, and he turned away from the mirror in favor of a calming shower. His unaccountable ability to retain an erection almost indefinitely, the trick that had made him so popular with those nutty Hindus, was often a nuisance. He didn't want to have to jerk off in order to get into his pants. He luxuriated in hot water and scented soap and felt a world away from the life he had just left.

He smiled to himself as he put on his only change of clothes, remembering what it would have been like five years ago preparing to meet Ernst von Hallers—the fuss with his hair, the time-consuming but almost imperceptible accenting of his eyes, the choice of just the right thing to wear from closets and drawers overflowing with clothes. He pulled on the matching beige shirt and slacks he'd had made in Saigon, and was ready.

He crossed the gangplank to the boat just after 1:30 and found nobody on board but servants. He was asked his name and a list was checked and he was assured that the Baron would soon be there. An iced drink was put into his hand while he wondered if he should go ashore and make another entrance. A table gleaming with silver and crystal was set for ten or twelve under the roof of the odd craft. Waiters passed to and fro across the gangplank between the boat and the hotel restaurant. Being removed and water-borne created an atmosphere of vast luxury. He wandered to the rail and looked out along the broad river dominated by the great white Temple of the Dawn on the opposite bank. He couldn't think of anywhere in the world quite like it—the chaotic city beat at the hotel walls barely a hundred yards away. After Saigon, the serenity of it made his throat ache.

He was aware of renewed activity behind him and turned to see a group advancing across the gangplank. His initial impression of massed elegance made him feel that he wasn't properly dressed and then he saw Ernst. For an instant, the time it took him to blink, he thought it was Ned and almost let out a whoop of recognition. The same golden hair, the same stunning head, the same superb physique. He was dressed in an exquisitely cut dove-gray costume with a stand-up collar, like a very stylish uniform, and wore some sort of ceremonial medallion on a chain around his neck and another pinned to his breast. He looked like the ruler of a fairy-tale kingdom. He handed pale-gray gloves to an attendant who walked a pace behind him as the group stepped aboard and took animated possession of the deck. He advanced to Gerry with a charming smile that remained slightly aloof. He moved with light unhurried grace. Gerry saw with a small shock of distaste that his eyes were undisguisedly made up.

"Gerald Kennicutt." He pronounced each syllable slowly. His voice was lively but subdued, as if he had no need to raise it to make himself heard. "What delightful surprises New York always has in store for us." He held out a hand but the gesture turned into not so much a handshake as simply holding hands. It was frankly sexual and Gerry responded instantly, suddenly caught up in the excitement of what he felt might be a momentous encounter. He had recovered from the shock of the makeup.

Ernst looked down at the hand he held. "Magnificent. So *big*, my dear." His eyes moved up for a thorough examination while he enumerated Gerry's good points. "Beautiful hair. Charming looks. *Très racé*. One can't say refined, can one? But how did your mother manage to have you? She told me herself she was seventy. Even American ladies don't usually have children at fifty. I was expecting an old gentleman of forty-five with nice safe gray hair at the temples, not a disturbing stripling. You threaten to complicate my life quite beyond endurance." He made a slight gesture to the attendant.

Gerry laughed. "That's the most marvelously complicated flattery I've ever heard. If I remember correctly, there's only two or three years difference between us."

"You? Over thirty? I don't believe it. You mean we're *both* going to suddenly shrivel up and turn into old hags? How ghastly." The attendant held out a jeweled cigarette holder with a cigarette already in place. He waited with a lighter. Ernst turned his head for a light and waved smoke away. "This is Paolo, without whom I couldn't move."

Gerry nodded to Paolo, a dark thin sharp-featured young man with a pencil moustache, dressed as casually as he was but more expensively. As a member of the fabled retinue, he was a disappointment. So much the better. The coast was clear. He felt absurdly as if Ernst had been waiting for him. "I'm sorry to be looking so shabby," he apologized. "This is all I have. My luggage was stolen."

"The devils. I heard you arrived with nothing. Pay no attention to my sedate drag. We've been to an audience with the Queen Mother." He made a vague gesture at the medal hanging around his neck and Paolo removed it. "A minor order, but these Eastern courts are easily impressed. We were with the King in Chiang Mai yesterday. The poor pet was in a tangle of walkie-talkies the entire time. Keeping abreast. Rallying his forces. He's terribly exercised about Vietnam."

Gerry refrained from mentioning that he too had been in Chiang Mai yesterday. He had decided that it would be wise to obliterate all traces of the last year. "What's happening in Vietnam?"

"Heaven knows. Do you understand anything about it? The Pathet Lao. The Khmer Rouge. Who are they all? You Americans haven't clarified matters. The dear little King is terrified of being toppled. I do hope he isn't. He makes our stays here so agreeable." He passed a gleamingly manicured hand over the immaculate golden hair. "I have a dreadful feeling I'm forgetting something. Of course. You must be introduced. I can't keep you all to myself, more's the pity." He took a fastidious puff on the cigarette and blew the smoke away and handed the holder to Paolo. He spoke a few muffled words through scarcely moving lips and the indispensable attendant withdrew. Gerry was adjusting to the difference between his preconception of an aging playboy and the fairy-tale reality that his busy eyes were bringing into focus. Ernst was classically handsome, with cleanly modeled features that were sensually stirring, but something was slightly out of key aside from the aggressively superfluous eye makeup. It wasn't age. There wasn't a line or a wrinkle. He too could pass for under thirty but the good looks that should have had a constant vibrance seemed to retreat intermittently behind a toneless layer of mystery. The smile charmed but died just as it was about to seduce. There was humor in his eyes, laced with self-mockery, the humor of despair. Gerry was stirred by renewed curiosity and a determination to plumb the mystery.

He was going to have an affair with Ernst von Hallers, of all people. His battered dream of a big complete love had amazing resilience; why shouldn't it happen with Ernst? They had been waiting for each other.

A waiter presented two glasses of champagne on a tray and Gerry disposed of the glass he'd been holding. Ernst looked up at him over the rim of his. Gerry noted that he was slightly taller than his host. "Yorgo will get a handsome reward for finding you," he said. "I want to hear everything. Where have you come from?"

"Penang," Gerry said, wiping out Jack.

"Really? That's where my yacht—here you are, my dear." A willowy girl stood beside them. Ernst performed introductions. "This is *la baronne*, Princess Solange. My sweet little wife. Look, my dear, look at my reward for behaving so perfectly in New York. If I hadn't listened to a lady talking about her son, without even a spellbinding photograph to hold my attention, I would never have met this delicious creature. Gerald Kennicutt."

Reverting to his Paris manners, Gerry bowed and lifted her hand to his lips and looked down into softly mischievous eyes. She was dressed with great chic in formal summer daytime wear but he had the impression that she would look the same no matter what she wore; her slight lovely physical presence would make any clothes right. She wasn't beautiful and certainly not pretty. Her long narrow face was too intelligent to qualify for any of the usual words. She was subtly appealing without any apparent sexual wiles. Her dark hair was combed out softly around her face and she wore less makeup than her husband. Her unguardedly friendly smile melted him. He knew that she was almost as old as Ernst, but with these two age had no meaning.

"Shouldn't we give our friends the pleasure of meeting him?" she asked. Her voice was gentle and husky and her English was blurred by a slight accent.

"Carry on, my dear. You at least will remember their names." Paolo had resumed his position at Ernst's elbow and the Princess tucked her hand under Gerry's arm and they were absorbed into the group. Waiters circulated with champagne. Gerry was introduced to a French couple. He gave a small start of recognition as he was presented to the popeyed lady he had seen in the corridor little more than an hour ago. She was an American called Maria Horrocks with a husband called Trevor. There was an exquisite Oriental lady with a European escort. The men were all dressed in elegant resort attire and the women with a chic to match the Princess's except that he suspected they would fade away if robbed of their expensive clothes. Solange was the fairy queen of this fantasy realm. Her feet twinkled when she walked.

He saw a dark trim stylish young man briefly engage Ernst's attention. Paolo produced a notebook from the leather carryall that seemed to contain all Ernst's immediate needs, and handed it to the newcomer who wrote in it and returned it. A *maître d'hôtel* approached and presented a large card that Ernst glanced at and waved away. He was like a general conducting a battle at a safe distance from the front. Gerry was drawn irresistibly back to him. Ernst smiled at his approach and put a hand on his arm and drew him closer, as if for support or protection. Gerry found it curiously touching and was suffused with a warm flush of pleasure. A current of desire was transmitted between them every time they made physical contact but wasn't always reflected in Ernst's eyes. Every time he spoke, Ernst added little hints that he already took for granted that they belonged in each other's lives. "I *am* so pleased we found you. You add a much-needed touch of youth and charm to the scene. Aren't you going to want some clothes?"

Gerry laughed. "I am indeed."

"You must go to Smiling Sam." He waved at Paolo, who produced the notebook and tore out a sheet and handed it to Gerry. "Yorgo is arranging for you to go to him after lunch. It's just up the street. He'll come to you for fittings but I thought you'd want to go to the shop first to see his fabrics. He has some lovely ones. If you go to him by four he'll have some things for you this evening. You'll have dinner with us."

"I was going to ask when you could have dinner with me."

"That will be another time, Gerald darling, preferably just the two of us. Oh dear. This is Heinrich, my new husband." A dark stocky youth had appeared beside them. Ernst spoke to him rather sharply in German. He had a sullen sexuality that Gerry supposed might make him attractive to anybody who went in for rough trade. He had known plenty of guys who liked rough trade, but they'd never been interested in him. Was Heinrich a momentary aberration who could be easily swept aside? The impression was growing in him that Ernst was waiting to be released from some sort of imprisonment, like Sleeping Beauty. Everything in Gerry rallied to the call; he would be Prince Charming. He was intrigued by the challenge; perhaps he could kindle a fire behind the ornate but somehow chill façade.

"Have you been in Bangkok long?" Gerry asked Heinrich, to be polite. He was answered by a dull stare.

"If you don't speak gutter German," Ernst explained, "there's no way to communicate with him. Actually, he's just arrived. It couldn't be less convenient, could it?"

"Am I being too obvious?"

"You couldn't be, as far as I'm concerned, darling."

"You know where my room is. That's pretty convenient." They exchanged a look that was finally direct and unequivocal, a look suggesting that the fire might be banked but could be stirred to flame. His Majesty was beginning to ache with confinement.

The popeyed woman swept up to them. "Ernst lamb, you must tell me what I should do about missing the audience with the dear little Queen Mother. I've never been so mortified. Should I send flowers? I've been out rushing around this infuriating city all morning and then lost my car or the driver lost me. I didn't get back until after one and then it was too late. Will she ever forgive me?"

"I think so, Maria," Ernst said dauntingly. "I'll send Her Majesty a pretty jewel and all will be forgotten."

Gerry looked at her with amusement. She was as big a liar as he, but she had the sort of theatrical style he liked. Her staring eyes were the most prominent feature of a dramatic face that included a beaky arrogant nose and ripe lips. She looked like an Italian actress. Everything was on too grand a scale to allow room for humor, but the intensity with which she spoke was almost comic.

"I know your parents, Mr. Kennicutt," she announced as if it were a privilege for both of them.

"Oh please. We're both Americans. Call me Gerry."

"Of course, now that I know your name. Somebody said it was Harold. I wouldn't want to call anybody that. Mine is Maria."

"Yes, I know. Not Mary?"

"My parents were Italian. The Prince and Princess Torrolonia. Where are you staying, you adorable lamb?"

"Here. Right across from Ernst. I'm in Conrad."

Her brows contracted briefly. "Really? I thought I knew everybody in our party. Ernst didn't tell me. Have you been at the audience with the dear little Queen Mother?"

"No. I just met Ernst a minute ago. He knows my parents too."

"Of course. We were all in New York together."

"I see. Do you know Sri Lanka?"

"Who?"

Gerry released an explosion of laughter that the whole occasion inexplicably provoked in him. Nerves? "I mean Ceylon. The country."

"I hear it's divine. In fact, I've told Ernst we should go see it."

"But you speak Sinhalese?"

"Dear me, no. I speak seven languages when I remember which ones they are, but I haven't tackled the East."

A liar, but so was he. How many lies had he told? The stolen luggage. Penang. Two to two. They were offered more champagne and he heard Solange's surprisingly robust laughter rising above the hum of conversation. He saw her talking to Maria's husband Trevor and moved toward them, leaving Maria talking in German about some yacht with Ernst and Heinrich. He wanted a moment's respite from Ernst's potent physical attraction. Perhaps it would pass as such things sometimes did. He knew a lot about the vagaries of desire but had never felt such instant power over anybody except with Tom, and that had been a case of mistaken identity. Perhaps he was imagining it; Ernst was obviously a practiced charmer.

Solange offered him the sweet friendliness of her smile and took his hand like a little girl. The flush of pleasure he had felt with Ernst spread through him again. There was something childlike about both of them, children playing very sophisticated games.

Trevor had faded, boyish good looks and an effete manner and Gerry saw in his eyes that he needed no encouragement to make a pass at him. His tongue was wittily bitchy and in a moment Gerry's laughter joined the Princess's.

There was soon a general movement toward the table. Ernst's hushed voice carried above the others. "This is a very impromptu affair. We can dispense with protocol. Everybody sit where they wish." He caught Gerry's eye. "You're our special guest, darling. Come sit with me and protect me from my terrible husband." Maria moved in on his other side and they all sat.

The others had sorted themselves out in the conventional fashion of alternating sexes, the dapper young man who had written in Ernst's notebook among them. Yorgo? Yorgo, who had been rewarded for "finding" him, whatever that meant, and was in charge of his tailoring? A very pretty girl he hadn't seen before was sitting next to him. He began to feel that he was hallucinating. Everything on the table—silver, glasses, linen—bore Ernst's monogram surmounted by a coronet. Nobody still traveled with their household goods.

Conversation flowed around the table in French and English. Gerry had no trouble with the former. He heard snatches of talk about yachts and cruises, about grand hotels and the proper seasons to stay in them, about the best places to buy expensive goods. Maria spoke to Ernst about the chores that had supposedly kept her out of the hotel all morning. She sounded like his housekeeper. "I took care of the brandy. It'll be flown down this afternoon. The emeralds will be delivered tomorrow. Yorgo says the Ban Thai asparagus has been taken care of."

She sounded warmly solicitous and very competent. While the first course was being cleared away, Ernst moved his hand to Gerry's where it lay on the table and casually caressed it. Gerry was so stimulated by it that he forgot to worry about what the others would make of it and returned the caress with pressures of his fingers. Ernst turned to him and they exchanged another inflammatory look. They both shifted in their chairs so that their knees nudged each other. Gerry went through the rest of the meal in intense discomfort and dangerously close to orgasm. He wondered if he would get to the tailor that afternoon; their physical contact was so urgent and overt that bed seemed their immediate destination. They had finished the second course when Ernst dropped his hand onto Gerry's lap and almost made him leap out of his chair.

"Oh, darling," Ernst exclaimed, trailing his fingertips over what he had discovered.

"Don't, for God's sake," Gerry murmured. "Something's apt to give." Ernst removed his hand with purring laughter.

As the meal was coming to a close, Ernst directed a signal to Paolo, who hovered behind him. Fifteen minutes later, the party broke up as swiftly as it had gathered. The handshakings and bows and farewells were performed with finesse and dispatch. Gerry remained at his host's side, prepared to leave with him. Ernst turned to him. "I'll be waiting for you at 7:30, darling. Don't be late. I've planned an amusing evening. We must have time together. The question is, when?" He leaned forward and brushed Gerry's lips with his mouth and departed with precise deliberate steps. Gerry stood looking after him as members of the party fell into step around him, as frustrated and bewildered as if he'd been initiated into a secret society without having been given the rules. Why had they worked themselves up to such a pitch if there wasn't time to do anything about it? So much for romantic fancies. They wanted each other. That was what it boiled down to. When Ernst could fit him in, they would add each other to their respective rosters of casual bedmates.

Yorgo was waiting for him at the gangplank. "The Baron wants to be sure that you're satisfied with the tailor. Should I go with you?"

"I don't see why." He pulled the slip of paper out of his shirt pocket. "I have the address."

"It's very simple. When you leave the hotel, it's on the corner at the first turn on the right. Hardly three minutes away. They're expecting you. The Baron said that if there's anything at all I can do for you, just ask at the desk for Yorgo, the Baron's secretary. That's me." He smiled with smooth ambiguity.

The Baron's secretary could be had too. Ernst wasn't lonely. Why had Gerry supposed that he might have some importance for him? He smiled and thanked him. He stopped at the desk and collected the thousand dollars' worth of traveler's checks he'd been carrying with him as long as he could remember. It was time to get rid of them before they fell apart.

Outside the hotel, he was thrust brutally into a big modern town. It was hot. It was noisy. Traffic was heavy, moving at breakneck speed. The slacks and shirts and dresses of the passersby looked like cheap Western products. Only the small pretty people in them reminded him that he was still in the East. He found Smiling Sam without difficulty, and was welcomed by a phalanx of bowing Orientals.

After being shown heaped bolts of gorgeous fabrics, he decided to outfit himself entirely in white silk. It would set off his dark hair and heavy tan. He ordered the sort of clothes he would wear at any resort, with exotic details, and a couple of dressing gowns. When he offered to pay something in advance, hands were thrown in the air with horror. A friend of the Baron's? Never. He asked about shoes and was directed to a shop down the street.

There, he found white slipper-shoes of such soft leather that he could wear them without socks. The sandals he had on would do if he ever wanted to walk again. He took the only pair that was big enough for him and ordered a couple more. Back in the street, he passed a jewelry shop and saw a heavy gold chain with a chunky piece of worked gold hanging on it. He went in and came out wearing it around his neck. Another shop offered an array of silk scarves and he picked up a selection.

He was outfitting himself for Ernst. He knew it might be for only one evening, but the more he thought about him the more convinced he became that they could be more than casual bedmates. The impression lingered that Ernst was somehow locked away waiting for a touch to restore him to life. He knew that he was too rich, too surrounded by ceremony to be easy to get at, not in a physical sense (they could grope each other as lecherously as street boys) but on an emotional level that might have real meaning for both of them. Something had happened between them that filled him with a growing determination to try. Aside from his physical attraction and the enormous glamour of his legend, Gerry was stirred by the power he had felt he could exercise over Ernst. He found that he was jealous of Maria for seeming to be so firmly in charge of him. He didn't want to leave him in her hands. Ernst had aroused in him an aggressive unfamiliar masculinity.

Passing two burly men who were apparently on guard in the corridor in front of Ernst's suites, he got back to Conrad with an hour to spare before Smiling Sam and his merry men were due to fit him for his evening costume. He thought of the notice Ernst had taken of his hands and decided he could use a manicure. A pedicure, too, after his tramp. What the hell. The sybaritic life. He considered ringing for Lee and having a massage but his mild attraction paled further beside his lust for Ernst. Just as once he had enjoyed swelling the total of his conquests, he now took greater pride in the encounters he avoided. Today he already had quite a list of opportunities gladly missed—the waiter on the river terrace, Lee, Yorgo, even Trevor. Not bad for a thirty-five-year-old who even at his best could never claim more than passably pleasant looks.

He called down to the desk and found that there was a lady manicurist in residence. At the end of an hour, his extremities were gleaming. The fitting was a great success. Smiling Sam had done wonders with shoulders and hips. He actually looked as if he had a physique rather than just a body. The tailor was a genius in the crotch department. Snugly fitted, his basket had never looked more scandalous. His behind was a smoothly rounded delight. A dressing gown was ready and he put it on and let everything else be taken away for final stitching.

By 7:30 he was ready. He had experimented with scarves and decided he looked sexier with an open shirt and nothing but the glitter of gold against his brown chest. He arranged his hair with soft bangs on his forehead the way Leslie had taught him in the summer of his sixteenth birthday. It no longer made him look girlish, only ridiculously young. He lingered approvingly in front of the mirror. He was a very different figure than he had been six hours ago, as expensive-looking as any member of Ernst's court. His face was still his face but at least it was tanned enough to look as if it might have some character. He had much more excuse for making up his eyes than Ernst. Beady little things. With makeup he could do wonders with them, but he knew Ernst wanted him to look like a potential husband.

Yorgo opened the door of the Coward suite to him and

stepped back, his eye traveling over him admiringly. "Hey there. Smiling Sam? Terrific. What beautiful material."

Paolo approached, his eyes also roving over him, and asked if he wanted champagne. He accepted and greeted Trevor, who was seated at the end of the room.

"I must say, you're looking ravishing this evening," Trevor commented. "I'd marked you down for my special attention. I thought a dozen passionately red roses might do for openers, but perhaps I'd better make it diamonds. You *like* diamonds, don't you?"

"Sure. I'm crazy about diamonds," Gerry said cheerfully. He must have looked awful at lunch to be causing such a sensation now. He had a moment to feel quite pleased with himself and then Ernst appeared in the bedroom door. He took a quick breath.

He was wearing a transparent collarless natural silk shirt, cut so that most of his broad shoulders were bare, with full sleeves caught at the wrists by jeweled clasps. A tangle of chains hung around his strong smooth neck and several big-jeweled pendants lay against his marble chest. He was a statue. The open shirt was cinched by a belt of solid square gold links that sat low on his hips so that his navel and several inches of flat hairless belly were bare. The definition of the pelvic area was worthy of Michelangelo. Below the massive jeweled belt buckle was an intricate arrangement of buttons outlining a flap fly that had the effect of a codpiece, presenting his genitalia in a bold curving package. He had had his golden hair done; it was fuller and fell around his handsome head in soft waves. His eye makeup was more subdued, or appeared so in artificial light, so that he looked almost boyish, but it was the opulent display of his body that left Gerry feeling weak in the knees. Had he actually exchanged physical intimacies with this superb creature?

Their eyes met and held as he approached at his deliberate pace. Gerry had time to set down his glass, wanting his hands free for him before he came to a halt in front of him. He searched Ernst's eyes for the yielding desire he had seen earlier, but caught only a deranged glitter in them and a slight lack of focus. He was stoned. Five years in the East had taught Gerry all the symptoms. Momentarily disconcerted, he dropped his eyes to the glorious torso.

"You're looking utterly enchanting tonight, darling," Ernst said. "Where did you get such beautiful clothes? Are you ogling my baubles?"

"I'd like to get rid of your baubles. I'm ogling your body. It's breathtaking."

"How sweet of you. I hoped you'd like it." Ernst reached for his hands and placed them on himself inside the open shirt. He lifted his arms and put them around Gerry's neck. As he did so, Gerry saw that his armpits were shaved. Ernst tilted his head up to him and his lips parted, inviting a public embrace. Gerry felt a moment's reticence at being observed and a stubborn reluctance to be unfaithful to Jack and then control snapped. He forgot where he was. He forgot the others. Their mouths opened to each other and the impression he had had of vital fires banked and barely smoldering was swept away in the blaze of Ernst's response.

Their mouths parted and their eyes met incredulously. Gerry eased himself away and Ernst dropped one arm from him and trailed a hand along the taut confining fabric of his new slacks. Gerry was surprised that he still had them on.

"I can't believe it. *Quel mari étonnant que tu serais,*" Ernst sighed.

The drumming in Gerry's ears subsided and his consciousness of place returned and he found himself once more in Ernst's hotel living room, breathing heavily. Paolo was busy at the drinks cabinet, Yorgo was shuffling through some papers at the desk. Trevor looked self-consciously detached. Heinrich entered from the bedroom and Gerry ran a hand along Ernst's bare shoulder as he approached. Ernst had given himself to him. He intended to protect his rights.

"Give him a kiss, darling," Ernst said as the surly boy stopped in front of them. "He wants you, too."

Gerry did his best to conceal his reluctance as he followed directions but firmly withdrew when the youth tried to prolong it. Ernst reached around for the glass Gerry had left on a table and lifted it to him and held it while he drank. He withdrew it and put it to his own lips and drained off what was left. Gerry felt that pledges and promises were being exchanged between them that he hoped they were both prepared to honor. His hand returned possessively to the naked shoulder. Ernst looked up at him with unreliable eyes but despite their slight madness, they seemed to see him and accept him. Gerry drew Ernst closer and felt his body melting to him again. He took a deep breath to relieve the tightness in his chest. He had plunged into the unknown, staking out his claims as the dominant and aggressive partner in a love affair, much as Jack had claimed him, and the possibility that he might succeed took his breath away. Could he hope for Ernst to prove as docile as he himself had been?

Yorgo joined them holding a sheet of crested paper on a leather portfolio. He handed Ernst a gold pen. "It's the letter for His Excellency in Goa. I think that takes care of everything." Ernst filled the bottom of the sheet with a splendid imperial scrawl, hardly glancing at it.

Gerry wanted to snatch the pen away, wondering if Ernst should be allowed to sign anything in this state. He felt an irrational sense of responsibility for him. He wanted to protect him from imagined dangers. He wanted to know how far he was into drugs, and which ones. He wanted to get rid of Heinrich and anybody else who might challenge his claims. The love of a lifetime? Ernst made him feel that it was up to him to make something of it.

The room was suddenly crowded. A bell sounded and a clever-looking middle-aged man entered who looked so familiar to Gerry that he thought he knew him until he realized it was Ralph Farr. He had just been introduced to the legendary movie star when he heard the bell again and turned toward the door. His eyes were filled with beauty. A vision was making a diffident entrance. Gerry immediately decided that it was the most beautiful boy he had ever seen, a Botticelli beauty, delicate yet coolly voluptuous. His brows arched superbly away toward his temples. His wide-set eyes were enormous—green, heavy-lidded, fringed with an inch of lashes that swept his gentle cheeks. His nose was modeled with infinite care so that the bridge was the perfect accent for the aristocratic tilt at the end. His mouth looked as if it had been made to bite into ripe peaches. His fair hair had none of the metallic highlights of Ernst's but was pale and long and fell poetically over his forehead and ears. He was slight and shorter than Ernst and wore his clothes like a schoolboy, haphazardly, with no attempt at style. He greeted Ernst, who kissed the devastating mouth. A fierce flash of jealousy seared Gerry but it passed when he saw that the embrace was passionless. Ernst introduced the vision as André de St.-Hubert. Gerry refrained from the kiss that would have been acceptable under the circumstances and briefly took a shapely hand, glad that Ernst already commanded all his attention. Young beauties generally made fools of their admirers. They liked to lead you a merry chase and give you a brush-off at the end. This one looked as if he wouldn't even be aware of being pursued. He was removed, otherworldly, contained in some private dream. Gerry resolved not to look at the boy again, no matter how purely aesthetic the urge to study him might be.

The room was a babble of voices. There was much talk of arrivals and departures, delayed flights and distant destinations. Gerry slowly gathered that they were all talking about some expedition they were about to embark on. He was rather hurt not to be included but supposed it was something Ernst wasn't in charge of. Farr raised his glass to toast "All shipmates, past, present—and those who will come." The way he said it made everybody laugh. The star moved from one guest to another with urbane assurance. Gerry saw that he and Trevor appeared to know each other and that he was instantly entranced by André. Good. Let him do the chasing. He had heard a lot of stories about Farr and knew that he had lived with his mother all his life. He had had a long and brilliant theatrical career. Hollywood had adapted his highly sophisticated talents to turn him into a folk hero of monumental and iconoclastic bad temper. He had been at the height of his success when Gerry had left the States. He wondered if he still was. He also wondered if this was to be an all-male gathering. He stood close to Ernst, wishing he could rush him across the corridor. Their bodies touched with every move they made and their eyes met constantly to reaffirm the pledges that bound them. Gerry didn't see how he could get through the evening without expressing in words whatever they had discovered in each other, savoring and defining it together in order to make sure that neither was deluding the other or missing any of the nuances behind the explosive sexual attraction. He exerted pressure on the naked shoulder and Ernst turned in to him and slowly moved the back of his hand up along the front of his slacks before joining both hands on his glass.

"Still?"

"God, yes. Don't we have time to get away from here? Even fifteen minutes would be better than nothing. We should've torn each other's clothes off when we had the chance."

"I'm thinking of it too, darling, but I'm afraid fifteen minutes would make it worse. Fifteen hours, perhaps, but our guests might miss us."

"We could always invite them in to watch."

"What a delicious thought."

Ralph Farr intruded. "What are you two mooning at each other about?" he demanded in his famous irascible tones. "Isn't it a bit late in the day for puppy love?"

Gerry laughed and swung them both around to face him. "I've been wanting to talk to you. You knew my father." He took himself by surprise. This was something he'd never mentioned to anybody.

"A great many young men are saying that these days. I wish they'd stop. Who is it this time?"

"Walter Makin."

"Nonsense. I distinctly heard Ernst say your name was Connecticut."

"It is, more or less. I'm Walter's bastard. My mother backed one of the first shows you were in. Faye Kennicutt."

"Good heavens. Faye and Walter? How naughty of them. Is this generally known?"

"My father—my legal father, I mean—had a stroke about a year ago. He doesn't know who he is anymore. It doesn't have to be a great secret now." He felt himself acquiring a new identity, a suitable preparation for new experiences.

"Darling Walter. I was mad about him, of course, but so was everybody else. It was one of *his* first shows too. We were both three at the time but everybody said we showed great promise." He turned to Ernst. "Do you realize that this charming young man's father was *the* greatest genius of the American theater?"

"Everything about him is remarkable." He edged in closer against Gerry. "How adorable of him to be a bastard."

"Oh God, Ernst. If you tell me you've fallen in love again, I'll scream."

"Have you ever known me to fall in love with anybody like this?" Ernst retorted ambiguously.

"You have a point." His sharp eyes gave Gerry a careful scrutiny. "Walter's hair. Lovely stuff. You look quite sensible for your tender years. You'd better be."

It was good to hear that Ernst wasn't averse to falling in love although Farr didn't make it sound like the great romantic event Gerry would like it to be if it happened to them. The bell sounded and Solange and Maria were admitted, accompanied by the pretty girl who had materialized at the lunch table and a woman who looked so much like Farr that she could have been his older brother in drag. Gerry moved slightly away from Ernst, prepared to behave with more decorum, but Ernst put a hand on his arm and moved with him, keeping him close. Mrs. Farr flung herself on her host with raucous laughter. Solange made a charming fuss over Farr. He saw Maria and the young beauty embrace and for a moment he wished very much that he was Maria. He allowed his eyes to feast for a moment on the exquisite profile and then forced them back to the extraordinary Mrs. Farr. She greeted him before Ernst could introduce them.

"Of course. How delightful to see you again. You're looking younger than ever. You know how stupid I am about names. It'll come to me in a minute."

"Gerry Kennicutt." He managed to keep his laughter under control.

"Naturally. I know how much you've always admired Farr. You must've been so pleased to see him. Did darling Ernst tell you we were coming?"

They were launched on a series of non sequiturs that had Gerry rocking with glee. Her cackling laughter joined his. She waved a glass in the air, spilling a large part of her drink. "We're going to have such fun. What a darling boy you are. I've always said so to Farr."

They were friends for life. He liked feeling Ernst's friends becoming his friends. Perhaps he should make an effort to establish friendly relations with Maria. She was still with André, who was looking more animated than he had on arrival. Such beauty lighted with pleasure was almost more than he could bear. He turned to the pretty girl and learned that her name was Sally and that she was English. He found himself with Solange. She tucked her chin in and looked up at him with mischievously smiling eyes.

"Isn't Ernst stunning? I told him he would be in that shirt."

"He is. You're fairly stunning yourself. Who's the sublime André?"

"Sublime is the only word for him. I think Ernst is fond of him, but nothing more. You know? He's shy but you'll love him when you get to know him. He's a very sweet boy." There was apparently going to be time for all of them to become friends for life. Solange glanced at Ernst, who was still heavily embroiled with Mrs. Farr, then moved closer to Gerry and lowered her voice. "You know, you're the only one who counts tonight. Ernst is terribly excited about meeting you. I've never seen him like this with anybody. He's fascinated by you."

"That's wonderful. I feel the same way." The man at the desk had pushed him into fixing three days as the length of his stay. He would find out how long the von Hallers were staying without seeming to be moving in on them and adapt accordingly. He had found something to motivate his decisions.

She took his hand and looked up at him over her glass with uncomplicated affection. "You're a breath of fresh air. You may have guessed that his judgment about people is sometimes erratic."

Her accent wrapped around the last word and gave it all sorts of comic implications. She delighted him. "He didn't go wrong with you," he said, giving her hand a little squeeze.

"But I'm a girl, darling. I didn't rob him of his critical faculties."

When half an hour had passed without any new arrivals, Gerry assumed that the party was complete. He found them all much more fun than the crowd at lunch. He and Ernst remained a constant in their midst; the others drifted into changing combinations around them. Maria spoke to Ernst about arrangements that had been made for the evening, to do with cars and restaurant reservations, secretarial details that she transformed into intimacies, dramatizing her usefulness. Gerry's resistance to her stiffened. She wasn't to be trusted. Why had she lied about such apparently trivial matters? His own lies had been social conveniences that he was anxious to clear up at the first opportunity. There should be no secrets with people you cared about.

At a signal from Ernst, Yorgo shepherded them all out and, escorted by guards, down to the driveway in the back of the hotel where three enormous chauffeured limousines were drawn up in the hot night. Gerry saw the guards head for a fourth smaller car at the end of the line. Ernst touched his arm and got into the first car. Gerry followed while Yorgo sorted out the others. Heinrich got in beside Gerry and Paolo took the seat beside the driver.

As soon as they started moving, Ernst and Gerry turned to each other and in spite of the dark, their eyes were full of questions and invitations. At the risk of making a public spectacle of themselves again, Gerry wanted to consolidate whatever hold he had established over his host before he escaped into drugs or his own private mystery or another's arms. A sense of their joined destiny was growing more pronounced in him. Perhaps all his life had been leading up to this moment; it was possible. They looked into each other's eyes and an irresistible force flung them into each other's arms.

Ernst lay back in the corner with Gerry half on top of him, their mouths joined. Heinrich shifted about beside them. Gerry dismissed him from his thoughts. Ernst's heavy belt was gone and the flimsy shirt fell away from his shoulders. He freed his arms and lolled back half naked, offering himself. Gerry pushed the chains out of the way with a clatter of precious stones and made love to the perfumed torso with his tongue and teeth while Ernst gasped and whimpered and uttered little moans of pleasure. He put his hand inside the top of Ernst's tight trousers and tugged them down. His fingertips barely brushed crisp hair and a firm curve of flesh before Ernst twisted away and seized his wrist and held it.

"No, darling. We mustn't. I don't want to make Heinrich jealous."

All Gerry's pent-up passion exploded in a great burst of laughter. He lay against the naked body while his tension drained away in hilarity. "What we've been doing won't make him jealous?" he asked with a final spurt of laughter.

Ernst was laughing with him. "Perhaps. A little. But he might kill me or you or both of us if I let you do things there." He tugged at Gerry's wrist.

Gerry withdrew his hand and ran it up caressingly over his chest, marveling at being allowed to hold the superb body. "I know a lot of you. I can wait for the rest. It's going to be a long evening." Gerry touched Ernst's hair and smoothed a stray lock into place. He straightened his chains and restored order among the pendants. He gathered him into his arms again and took his mouth with loving gentleness. He could feel him yielding touchingly to his tenderness. They had achieved some sort of public union.

Gerry was aware of the car slowing and he released Ernst and looked into his eyes. Light fell into the car from somewhere and he could see that they were clearing. He touched his cheek and found his shirt behind him and helped him put it on. "Fasten your belt, darling," he ordered.

Ernst did as he was told. "Am I all right? I don't look as if I'd been raped by a regiment of Cossacks?"

"You're stunning as usual. That's your wife's word. I agree with her."

"Isn't she marvelous?"

"Too good for the likes of us, I imagine. I love her."

"She loves you. That will make it easier for us if we go on falling in love."

"Is that what we're doing?" He knew that neither of them could answer that until they had made love and could see beyond sex. He would have him tonight; tomorrow they might know.

"You heard what I said to Farr. I haven't known anybody for years I would want to really fall in love with. I told you you were going to upset my life hopelessly."

"Not if we fall in love with each other. That shouldn't be upsetting."

"I wonder. You have money, of course. I wouldn't know how to behave with a lover who wasn't after mine."

"You mean somebody you can't order around?"

"Yes, darling, that's exactly what I mean."

"I wouldn't let you order me around. You need somebody to take charge of you. A real husband. I'd probably be good for you."

"I know you would be, darling. That's what frightens me. I don't know what would become of me if I let myself go with you."

"Nothing bad. I can promise you that. It's rather wonderful that we can even think about falling in love. To tell you the truth, I'm not sure I know what it's like."

"I think I remember. It certainly isn't what Farr was talking about. The best thing about it, if I'm not mistaken, is that you can't help it. It saves you from having to make up your mind. I think you can die of being rational. I'd like to be in somebody's power. Do you want me in your power, darling?"

"I've thought about it. I haven't thought about much else but you since lunch. No. Not unless I'm in love with you." He raised a hand to Ernst's face and touched his short straight nose, the hollows of his cheeks, his square chin, and traced the curve of his full firm mouth. "Such a handsome guy. I'm ready to fall in love with somebody. I'd like to find out what it's like. Yellow hair always turns me on and as for your body—God, it's a work of art."

"You, quite simply, are the most attractive man I've ever seen in my life."

The car slowed further and turned. They had entered a garden drive and in a moment came to a stop in front of what looked like a large private suburban house except for a modest sign over the door announcing the name of a restaurant. The smaller car pulled around in front of them and the guards spilled from it. Ernst took Gerry's hand as they descended and the party reassembled around them. Yorgo led the way into an elegant candlelit dining room where only a few tables were occupied. A big center table had been set for them. Nobody disputed Gerry's right to be seated at his host's side. He was filled with mirthful happiness. Big words had been spoken. It remained to be seen what they would lead to.

Ernst placed Mrs. Farr at his right and they all sat. Farr and André faced each other on either side of Solange. Gerry wouldn't have traded places with anybody but he envied Farr his view. If everything turned out as he thought it might, he wouldn't glance at a hundred Andrés: Heinrich was back with Maria and they immediately fell into a muted conversation in German. He wondered if they were talking about what had happened in the car. If he didn't tell her, Trevor could be counted on to be indiscreet about their first embrace. He wondered if she would resent a new favorite.

As the sumptuous meal got underway, Mrs. Farr asked Ernst about the "dear Duke and Duchess" and this led to reminiscences about other royalties he knew. His knowledge of the subject proved encyclopaedic. To him, a King was a King, regardless of how long ago he had lost his throne. When his talk widened to include heads of state he said interesting and intelligent and amusing things about people who were obviously familiar to him but Gerry noted the special respect with which he spoke of the royalties, even the most inconsiderable, and wondered where he could fit into the life Ernst was sketching. Did he want to spend the rest of his days paying calls on dispossessed monarchs?

"Tell them about when you turned twenty-one," Maria urged, breaking off her conversation with Heinrich.

A curious look of repressed hostility settled over Ernst's face and the sharp note Gerry had heard him use with his "husband" crept into his voice. "It's not much of a story. My father was in prison at the time. He doubtless belonged there, if not for the reasons officially given. He hadn't seen me or my mother since I was five. It was easy enough for them to strip him by inventing new laws and charging him with crimes that had never existed, but I despised him for not resisting. He had bargained away a great deal. I was an inconvenience. I was the sole heir and the family had always taken care to protect the heir. Legally, I could have brought the industry of half the world to a halt while the case dragged on for years, perhaps decades. They all came to me—delegations from England and Germany and France and Italy, begging me to make a settlement. President Eisenhower wrote me a private letter telling me that the future of the world depended on the industrial revival of Europe. I told them I'd sign anything if they let me have my grandmother's inheritance intact. They were delighted with my reasonableness until I told them that I also wanted all taxes waived for my lifetime. They howled but they had no choice. I have a safe full of secret protocols that would be an acute embarrassment to a number of important people and their governments if they ever became public. I have the world by the balls—a lesson I could have taught my father." The story had brought general conversation to a standstill. Gerry had time to be shocked by his own audacity. This was the man he wouldn't allow to order him around? His tentative thoughts of a future with him were madness. His ruthless glamour made Gerry feel insignificant. Ernst turned to him.

"If I ever start to tell that story again, stop me. It's vulgar and unpleasant and boring. No friend of mine should encourage me to tell it."

It was a slap at Maria. It made Gerry his social arbiter. The great could lift you very high or drop you very low. "It's interesting because it shows you haven't always had everything handed to you on a platter," he said quietly, leaning to him as conversation resumed around them. "I suppose that's why she wanted you to tell it."

Ernst looked at him with astonishment. "Are you really that much interested in me?"

The question touched him. He had once more the sense of a spirit trapped, doomed, waiting to be rescued. "Yes, definitely. Even *your* body isn't everything. I keep hoping I'll meet somebody who'll let me have all of himself and will want all of me. I don't quite know what that means but I'll know when it happens."

"I don't want to let anybody have any of myself. Isn't that the point of my story?"

"What about wanting to be in somebody's power?"

"Ah, that's the other side of the coin. I'm a creature of extremes. Perhaps I want it because I know it's so nearly impossible."

"Self-sufficiency? At times I think I'm almost there. But what about desire? You wanted me the minute you saw me as much as I wanted you."

"I want you, the way I want anybody, on my own terms."

"You could've had me once upon a time. I was an undemanding lover. Not anymore. Certainly not with you." Their eyes were fixed on each other during the exchange. They were sparring without hostility, with a touch of wonder, even of love. Gerry's happiness bubbled to the surface and he chortled. "We're getting in deep, darling."

"Possibly, but I'm not frightened at the moment. It's extraordinary. Already, I automatically turn to you when in doubt, as if I take it for granted that you'll be there. I wasn't aware this morning that I needed somebody like you. Not *like* you. Exactly you."

"Does that have anything to do with falling in love?"

"It sounds rather like it, doesn't it?"

The meal wound to its mouth-watering conclusion. "I imagine we should go," Ernst said after coffee and brandy had been disposed of. "I'm going to take you to a rather fun nightclub."

"Oh dear. I had a foolish hope that we might be going home."

"It's early, darling. We must give our guests a jolly time. You see? When I say 'we' and 'our' I mean you and me. Do you know that?"

"It sounds nice, but it isn't real unless I pay half the bill. That's one of the things you'll find out if I take charge of you."

"Oh darling, never fuss about money. You haven't a glimmer how rich I am. I don't even know who pays for everything. Let's just say it's you and forget about it." They looked at each other and laughed, although Gerry doubted that they were laughing at the same joke. Ernst had turned into a child again, a child in need of protection. The childlike quality combined with his pronounced streak of callousness had a sort of comic incongruity, difficult to assimilate until it occurred to Gerry that children were inherently callous. It was what made them children. The greatest joke of all would be if it turned out that neither of them knew what love was, if this elaborate courtship were leading to nothing but the roll in the hay he had been ready to settle for after lunch.

The drive to their next stop proved short and uneventful. The car and the company were too confining to permit them to explore each other any further than they had already and they managed to limit themselves to holding hands.

The nightclub had lavishly cushioned and silk-draped alcoves and an all-girl show that on closer inspection turned out to be an all-boy show. Only one nearly naked boy was undisguised. When it was over, half a dozen of the pretty performers swarmed around them and as if following instruction, selected Farr and Gerry and André for their advances. Ernst watched with amused approval while Gerry patted behinds and was showered with kisses and caresses. He saw that André, looking charmingly flustered, was coping with similar attentions. Farr shrank back and waved his arms about as if he were being attacked by hornets.

"Ernst, stop this nonsense instantly," he commanded, with harsh bad temper. "I'm not amused. There might be photographers. Do you want to ruin me?"

"My men don't allow photographers," Ernst announced coolly. "Do you see any?"

"You must have taken leave of your senses. In front of Mother. It's an outrage."

"Don't be tiresome. Your mother is old enough to know that you sometimes find amusement with boys."

"One of the blessings of my life has been knowing that Farr would never make a fool of himself with a woman," Mrs. Farr proclaimed proudly.

"Do you want to keep any of these adorable children?" Ernst inquired. "Gerald, darling? André? How unappreciative you all are. It must be time to go." He rose abruptly.

The Farrs were guests at some embassy so a limousine was detached from the convoy for them. Yorgo joined Paolo in the front seat of Ernst's car and they set off once more. Now that he had had time to think about it, Gerry was growing almost as indignant as Farr about the performers. Did Ernst seriously think he could be tempted by whore boys after all that had been said this evening?

"What was the idea of turning those little harpies loose on us?" he asked, choosing to keep it light.

"I'm known there. The management always offers its wares to my guests. It's put on my bill." He sounded sulky. "My friends are often pleased to take advantage of the opportunity."

"It's very thoughtful of you." Perhaps it had been an attempt to find out how lax his sexual habits were. Sticking to the same person all evening might be considered quaint in his set, especially after they had explored each other's bodies quite thoroughly. He mustn't become a difficult husband so soon. "What would you've done if I'd wanted all of them?"

"I'd have thought it a trifle ostentatious of you but there would have been no difficulty. Transportation is provided. They would have been sent to your rooms."

"And a happy orgy would've been had by all. Wouldn't you have been a bit upset?"

"How do I know? We're just getting to know each other."

"That's true. Well, now you know I'm not interested in dancing boys and if I were, I wouldn't want you to know about it. I want *you* right now. Nobody else." As far as he could see, the only place where there would be time for them to get to know each other was bed.

There had been talk about a lunch they were going to tomorrow—the Summer Palace, the Prime Minister, something of the sort. He hadn't been included nor did he expect a stray guest to be imposed on such exalted circles at the last minute. Tomorrow night would doubtless be swallowed up in additional festivities. He could imagine days passing with only snatched fleeting encounters to appease his hunger to push things to a conclusion, one way or the other.

They drove through busy late-night streets. Huge neon signs flashed past them. He knew they were getting near the hotel. He put his arm around Ernst and gave him a little hug to rouse him from his sulks. "How'll we work it when we get back?" he asked in an undertone. "Will you come across to me?"

Ernst put a hand on his lap where everything was quiescent for a change. "I can't do that, darling. The guards wouldn't allow it without tearing your rooms apart."

"Oh. That's a thought. Why am I getting involved with a —well, whatever you are. With a Personage. I guess I'll have to come to you. So long as we don't have an audience of more than fifteen, I suppose it'll seem quite intimate."

"Don't be cross, darling. It's all rather unexpected. I want to arrange everything so that it's right for us."

"When will that be?"

"In the next day or two."

"Yeah. Well, in the meantime, I guess we'll have to settle for something a little less than right. I'm not cross, darling. You're not exactly a kid I picked up in the street. All I know is that we have to be together, tonight most of all."

"But, darling, tonight isn't possible."

"What do you mean?"

"Just what I've been talking about. There are things to be worked out."

Gerry withdrew his arm and sat forward and looked at him. Ernst was eerily, youthfully handsome in the shifting light from the street but Gerry could see that the curtain of aloofness had dropped around him again. Sleeping

Beauty. "Now listen. I know you lead an elaborate life but there're a few complications we can get rid of right away. Such as our friend next to me. You worry about making him jealous. What about me?"

"You're a civilized human being, which is one reason why I adore you. I brought him here. I have a responsibility."

It was a point Gerry didn't want to argue; he liked him for making it. "All right, but he can see what's happened to us. Let him see more if that's the way it has to be. Or put him in my room, for God's sake."

"You don't know what he's like. I have to handle it very carefully. Maria will be helpful. She understands him."

"That's nice. I hope she'll understand me. I'm supposed to go quietly to my celibate bed when we're both longing to be with each other? You're playing with something that might be important for both of us."

"But darling, that was the point of the dancing boys. I thought you might want company until we get things reorganized."

"Jesus Christ. You can't be so dumb. You must've known I expected to be with you. I don't need you to provide dancing boys. I want us to be together. Is that so very uncivilized?"

"It's very fastidious of you, darling, and I imagine it's quite depraved of me to be thinking of your pleasure."

"Oh God." Gerry was close to tears of rage and frustration. "You make me ashamed of what we did. If I'd known that was all there was going to be, I wouldn't've touched you. Necking in a car with people watching. Jesus."

"It was much more than that. You gave me something I craved. You made me feel how much you want me. You must make me belong to you. That's the miracle I'm playing with."

"Oh darling." He put his arms around him again and searched his empty eyes. "When?"

"Don't fret about tonight. Please don't," Ernst begged with a hint of panic in his voice. "We're going to be together constantly for the next month."

"Are we?"

"Well, of course. You know that, darling."

"Thanks for telling me." Their kiss was a long reconciliation. Gerry's hands moved ecstatically over the almost naked body. Free yourself from the bondages of the flesh. That was salvation. It was all just a matter of breathing right. For one who had taken a tiny step toward Nirvana, he remained lamentably sex-oriented.

The remains of the party assembled once more in the hotel lobby and were escorted upstairs by the guards. The Horrockses disappeared somewhere along the way. As they milled about in front of Coward and Maugham, Gerry saw André trail off along the corridor and was tempted to follow him. Sally slipped off in the other direction. Ernst gave him a brief kiss on the mouth. A door closed. He and Solange were alone with the guards. It was such an anticlimax that he felt like lying down in front of the door and howling. He looked at her, feeling lost and helpless.

"You're not going in with Ernst?" She took his hand sweetly. "Would you like to come in and have a nightcap with me?" She led him along to the Maugham door. A guard opened it and closed it behind them. The living room they entered was more lavishly furnished than his or Ernst's. His trained eye spotted a couple of good French pieces and he wondered if they were part of the von Hallers household equipment. Why not travel with your own chairs and tables? He shrugged off his silk tunic and draped it over a chair. "May I?"

"Please do, darling." She tucked her chin in and looked up at him in that way she had. It shortened her long intelligent face and gave her an endearingly playful look. In spite of it, he realized that her dark eyes were touched with melancholy. "What shall we have to settle all that wine? More champagne? Not for me. I think a nice sensible whiskey."

"Same here." He followed her to a table laden with bottles and glasses and an ice bucket. "Let me," he suggested.

"Please." He mixed drinks. She took hers to a sofa and kicked off her shoes and sat with her legs tucked up under her. He sat in a chair near her. "How was the evening?" she asked in a way that made it clear that it wasn't intended as polite chitchat.

"Fairly exhausting."

"I was afraid so. We all could see that something extraordinary was taking place. Are you going to fall in love with him?"

"I don't know. The trouble is, it's a possibility. It made me very happy at moments."

"I think I hope *not*, for your sake, but I can tell you the things you did wrong. You let him have all of your attention. You mustn't. You should've taken one of those boys even if you sent him away after you got back here. He's a masochist in his way. He would've imagined you having a night of blissful debauchery and would've been quite desperate for you in the morning." Her voice was low and melodious and she spoke loosely and unemphatically, with none of the mannered flourishes her entourage had adopted. "Don't you find André attractive?"

"Terrifyingly."

"Then why didn't you pay any attention to him?"

"I did my best not to. Too young. Too beautiful. Leaving Ernst out of it, it's so silly to get carried away when you know you're going to be turned down. I'll leave him to Farr."

"You're wrong about that. He could hardly take his eyes off you all evening. Have you been through some crucial period in your life recently?"

"Yes," he said, taken aback. "For the last few years, really."

"I feel it. I don't think you know what it's done to you. You're attractive in a quite magical way. You know? It's a curious combination of simple good nature and toughness and something intensely physical that bursts out of your clothes. Everybody's felt it."

"My goodness. Have another drink and tell me more."

She tucked her chin in and a slow smile spread across her lips and sprang up into her eyes. "You also make it very easy to like you, which doesn't necessarily go with the rest of it. I like you so much that for once I care terribly about how it works out with Ernst. I'm afraid he knows very little about serious emotional situations."

"So I gather. How did you happen to marry him? Good Lord, what an awful question. I'm sorry. I like *you* so much that I feel as if we'd known each other forever."

"I'm glad. It's a question I'm sure a lot of people ask themselves. It's quite simple really. My family is one of the oldest and grandest in Europe and hasn't a bean. Ernst had to have a suitable wife in order to lead the sort of life he likes. Consorts are obligatory in court circles. It was a very satisfactory arrangement. And then there's the other thing that people often don't think of—I was very much in love with him. You can understand that."

"Of course, but I should think that would've made it difficult. Are you ever alone with him?"

"Almost never."

"I wonder if I ever will be. I might as well go ahead and ask everything. Are there other men in your life?"

She uttered her curiously hearty laughter. "How could there be, darling? Can you imagine a plain ordinary man attaching himself to us for long? That's what I'm telling you. Observe us, be amused by us, but don't get involved with us. There hasn't been anybody like us for a hundred years, more likely not since the little eighteenth-century Middle European princelings. Any modern man who was serious about me would want to take me away and that's out of the question. There's Sally. Haven't you got the point of her?"

"Oh, I see. I'm sorry. Are you expecting her? Should I go?"

"No, darling. She's out of action for the moment."

He put his glass on the table beside him, pushing a small parcel wrapped in brown paper out of the way as he did so. He saw that it was addressed to Madame Maria Horrocks as if it were intended for the mail, but there were no stamps on it. She saw him looking at it.

"That's something I found in Ernst's room. I picked it up absentmindedly. I get terribly absentminded when I'm curious. I'm trying to decide whether to give it back to her or open it."

"What's in it?"

"I think I know but I'd like to make sure. Are you clever with your fingers? Can you open it and put it together again without its looking as if it's been tampered with?"

He picked it up. It was unexpectedly heavy for its size. Emeralds? It wasn't the neatest package in the world, held together by coarse string. "Do you want me to?"

"Yes, please."

They smiled at each other like naughty children. As he worked at the knots he felt a nice little glow of pleasure in performing a service for her. When he'd untied them, he opened the paper carefully so that it would fall back into the same folds, and withdrew a cardboard box. It contained a block of some dark substance. He sniffed it and detected a faint odor. He looked up at her. "Opium?"

"Exactly. I found wrappings like that in his room last week, also addressed to her. Why?"

He thought of the round little Oriental he had seen Maria with that morning. "I suppose she's getting it for him."

"Yes, but why? It's so unlike him. If he wants something, he has his people get it. Why use her as a go-between?"

"It does seem rather pointless here. You can get all you want by the case. Is he heavily into drugs?"

"He was at one time. It became quite a problem. There was some trouble with the police in Paris. As he told you at dinner, he's very powerful so they couldn't really touch him, but it was unpleasant and expensive. He even took a cure. We agreed not to have anything with us when we're traveling. You know? Where there's staff we can't be sure of and all that." She looked thoughtfully at the box he held. "Why that?"

"He was on something tonight."

"He has been recently. Quite seriously. You'd better do it up again."

He did so. "Who are the Horrockses anyway?" he asked while he reknotted the string.

"I don't know. They know all the right people. That is, all the people we know. They've turned up everywhere we've been for the last year or two. He amuses me. He's quite a well-known poet. He's given me a couple of his books. You haven't heard of him?"

"Trevor Horrocks? No, but that doesn't mean anything. I'm not very strong on poetry."

"Maria has made herself useful in a number of small ways whenever she's had the chance. A court requires courtiers. She's rather a sycophant but that's never bothered Ernst." He held the package out in the palm of his hand for her inspection. "Well done, darling. Thank you. I can only suppose she's giving it to him. An unsolicited gift, as it were. So long as he's not getting it for himself, he'd think he's living up to our agreement. I suspect she's almost as expert at playing on people's weaknesses as he is. I'd better put it back and have a word with her."

"If I ever get a chance, I'm going to have a word with *him*. Not about this of course, but drugs generally. I don't like them. If he made any sense of his personal life, he wouldn't need them. Heinrich. Really."

"I know, darling."

They looked at each other with growing affection and understanding. He felt a quick sudden solidarity building up between them. Their small secret act had created an agreeable air of complicity around them. It pulled him out of his chair and carried him to the sofa. He perched on the arm and took her hand in his and looked down into her eyes. They were playful and gentle and deeply intelligent. It was the intelligence that touched them with melancholy.

"I like you so *damn* much," he said, speaking the truth but thinking, as Ernst had suggested, that it might be easier for them if he established this secondary beachhead.

She looked at the hand holding hers. "Doesn't it sound old-fashioned? Nobody we know likes each other anymore. They're all *mad* about each other or *adore* each other. You know? Detest each other is more like it. Your hands are part of your magic, darling. If you wore gloves, I'd want to tear them off you."

They burst out laughing. "You're a dream. I'll borrow a pair of Ernst's so you can strip me. Goodness, how sexy." Saying it carried with it the incredible thought that he was attracted to her, not only in a friendly way, but actively, sexually. He felt stirrings he would have expected with a boy. He had never felt them before with a girl. He glanced down at her body. The tender swell of her breasts was just visible at the top of the silken sheath she wore. She was slender and slim-hipped and lovely. To test himself, he thought of her with nothing on and something in him recoiled from the image. He stood and swirled the ice around in his glass.

"Am I making a nuisance of myself or can I have another drink and make a night of it?"

"Please do. Me too." She lifted her glass with a graceful arm and he imagined it sliding around him. He bounced back from his brief distaste. He mixed drinks and returned to his chair.

"How strange all this is," he said. "I appeared out of the blue this morning and now look at us. Entanglements within entanglements. Shall we clear everybody out and start a new life?"

"Easier said than done, darling. First of all, you're going to have to make Ernst feel that he has to woo you."

"OK. It'll be pure playacting but I'll try to convince him that I'm hard to get. I don't have to pretend with you. Is there any faint chance you'll let me spend the night here?"

"Why, darling? Your room is just across the hall. We're not marooned in a snowstorm or anything."

"Worse luck. Thanks for not throwing me out for suggesting it. If you were a boy, I'd like to stay and talk and have a few drinks and have sex or not, as the case might be. It's not the same with a girl, is it? It turns into a heavy pass."

"Oh dear. That's my fault. Let's be marooned in a snowstorm."

"Can we be? Just two people liking each other? Even going to bed together needn't be a big sex scene if we don't want it."

"I could hardly feel all those things about you without sex being very much a part of it, darling. How do you think I know who André was looking at all the time? I was trying to be less obvious about it. It's impossible to look at you without wanting to see you naked."

"You'll let me stay? What I'm trying to say is, something very unusual has happened to me. I'm attracted to you. I think I want you. I've never been attracted to a girl in my life. I can't think why that should make you want me unless you're interested in scientific experiments."

"Why didn't you say so, darling? You want to find out if it's true? Shall I put on something seductive and see if you go mad with desire?" Her eyes sparkled with fun.

"Yes, I'd like that. Don't laugh at me. It'll probably end in disaster but it might work if you want it to."

"It can't be a disaster, darling. You mean you might not get hard for me? What difference does it make? It would be thrilling to have you in bed with me even if it turns out you're not interested. Just a moment." She rose and floated out of the room on feet that didn't seem to touch the ground.

He waited, filled with curiosity shadowed with uneasiness. He tried to reason the uneasiness away. As she had said, the worst that could happen was that he wouldn't be able to get it up. And if he succeeded in undoing the habits of a lifetime? Heaven knew what it would do to him but the possibility of succeeding seemed to add a new strength to him. He thought of Tom. Without Tom, he would never have dared even contemplate what he was doing, any more than he would have dreamed of assuming the role of husband with Ernst. Tom had taught him how to be a man. Perhaps the process would be completed with Solange. To him, being a man didn't necessarily mean wanting girls. Being a man was a reinforcement of his masculinity to balance the feminine element that had always been so strong in him. Jack was the most complete man he had ever known and he too claimed that he had never been attracted to a girl.

His eyes remained on the bedroom doorway. Solange reappeared in it, looking small and very naked in a diaphanous robe under which her small deliciously rounded breasts were visible. His heart began to beat rapidly with excitement and anxiety. He realized that her having removed all her jewelry and makeup was what made her look so naked. Her hair was brushed out softly around her face. She tripped into the room on bare feet with her chin tucked in, looking at him teasingly.

"Do you still want to spend the night?" she asked.

He rose slowly, wondering. "Your breasts are beautiful," he said, surprised that he meant it.

"My tits? You like them? That's a good sign."

"All signs seem to be amazingly favorable."

"In that case, let's go into the next room and see where they lead. I'll try not to fling myself at you in a frenzy of passion."

They laughed as she preceded him into the bedroom. Her bed was placed lengthwise against a wall and was elaborately draped in netting. She dropped onto it and pulled a pillow up behind her and sat propped up against the wall.

"What's the usual thing now?" he asked, standing facing her in the middle of the room. "Do I take my clothes off?"

"Oh yes, darling. It starts with a naked man, especially in your case. Like everybody else, I'm dying to see you with nothing on. You can undress me afterward if you're sure you want to."

"Well, here goes. If you were a boy, I wouldn't necessarily have a hard-on right away. We mustn't forget that." He turned from her. He was going to have Ernst's wife. If that thought didn't stir him up, nothing would. Pulling off his shirt and starting to unzip his slacks reassured him. His Majesty reigned supreme. He quickly removed the rest of his clothes and turned back to her. Her eyes unabashedly followed the swing of his erection as he approached.

"Good heavens, darling. Isn't it rather staggeringly big? Does Ernst know about it?"

"He has a rough idea."

"I don't see how he could let it out of his sight. I've heard him talk about big boys. Surely this counts as big." She lifted a hand to it and drew him down and laid him out flat on his back. She held it upright with both hands and lowered her mouth to it. The memory of his mother's lips on him came rushing back to him and the splendid edifice slowly collapsed.

"Oh dear. Have I done something wrong?" she asked.

He burst out laughing. "You're the first person who's ever managed that. There's a perfectly good psychological reason for it but we needn't go into that." He reached for her and brought her down beside him. He was inexplicably confident that it was only a temporary failure. "If you don't mind waiting a minute and we can dispense with the oral trimmings, would you like to try it in the plain old-fashioned way?"

"Are you going to be able to, darling?"

"Oh yes. I'm already recovering from the initial shock." He lifted himself on an elbow and opened her robe, exposing all of her slender body. He kept his eyes on her breasts. They were the most exquisitely formed flesh he had ever seen, plump and soft, so delectable that he wanted to bite into them. He ran his fingertips lightly over them and felt the nipples harden. He leaned down and drew them into his mouth and ran his tongue around their gentle curves while his hand strayed down over her and his fingernails made tracks across her belly, stopping short of the mysterious area between her legs. He shied away from the emptiness there. He felt excitement gathering in her body and his own potency being restored.

"The old-fashioned way often leads to babies, darling, in case you haven't heard." She spoke with a little catch in her voice while she held his head against her breast.

He lifted it free and looked down at her. "What about you and Ernst? You haven't had any babies, have you?"

"Ernst has never done anything old-fashioned in his life."

"I see. Well, I don't want to insist—yet." His erection was completed with a hard thrust against her. Her hand went to it and ran along its length. He shifted so that she could do anything she liked with it and she lifted it onto her belly and held it and stroked herself with it. It was something a boy might have done. "You see? I'm ready if you are. I've heard that ladies don't like them big."

"I can see why a lady might hesitate about this. It's the most intimidating thing I've ever seen in my life. I'm almost afraid to look at it, as if it might turn me into a frog or something. You know? It's magical."

His hands felt oddly empty at not finding a matching erection and he wanted to take her before he began to miss it too much. She drew his head to her and their mouths met. Hers felt small and confining, with none of the lusty generosity of a boy's. Her hands urged him up over her. He lifted himself and straddled her. She pulled up her knees and freed her legs and flung them around him. She sat up and her arms encircled him and she held his erection against her breasts. "Will it stay hard now if I kiss it?"

"It'll stay hard no matter what you do. I'm so pleased you like it."

"I do. I want to make love to it." She covered it with eager kisses.

"God," he gasped. "You're fantastic."

"I want you to know how much a lady can like it. I've never known anything about phallic worship but maybe it's in all of us."

"What do we do now? You want me to come like this?"

"No, darling. You make me feel very old-fashioned."

"You're not afraid of babies? You want me to fuck you?"

"Yes, darling. Please. I'll worry about it later. Put it inside me." Her legs slipped away and she held it with both hands and guided it to her. "It's big. Oh darling, it's so big. Yes, slowly. It's heavenly having so much of you in me. Oh darling, you're in me. You're so hard and gentle. Yes, now, all of it."

He drove deep into her welcoming moisture and experienced a moment of breathtaking revelation. A revelation of what? He was fucking a woman. He was finally doing what nature had intended. There was a marvelous sense of uncomplicated physical union, a feeling that everything fitted easily. Her desire for him and his ability, as he found her rhythm, to satisfy it was rewarding and somewhat obscured the fact that his tenuous desire for her was already abating. The compulsion he felt with boys was lacking. He was in masterful control of both of them and could stay in her as long as she wished, finding pleasure in her ecstasy, but it was a mechanical act, unnatural, a perversion of all his deepest instincts. His love of boys was his normality. This was the revelation, although it only confirmed what he had known about himself all his life.

"You're glorious, darling," she crooned as he felt her shaken again by what he recognized now as orgasm. "You're gigantic but it doesn't hurt. I didn't know I wanted a man to take me so completely. I wish you could stay hard in me all night."

"I probably could if you wanted me to."

"We mustn't wait too long. I feel as if you could make me come forever. Come with me now, darling. If I don't wash soon, it'll be too late."

"I'll pull out of you at the last minute if you want."

Her arms tightened around him. "No, that wouldn't help now. You may've already given me a baby. Come in me, darling. I want the whole bliss of you."

He drove her to paroxysms of ecstasy as his own body was charged with the approach of the orgasm that he felt had been accumulating all evening. When it came they both cried out and thrashed about together, but there was none of the power in her that he was accustomed to capturing and absorbing into himself. They lay together, waiting for his presence to diminish. When it had finally done so, she stirred.

"Quickly, darling. Let me up. You'd better go. I'll have to spend the rest of the night trying to wash you out of me. What a waste."

He withdrew from her and she scrambled up and was gone. She darted back in a moment with a towel. "There, darling. Put that around yourself if you don't want to bother to dress."

He pulled himself up and stood and kissed her mouth,

feeling grateful to her for the initiation. She lingered in his light embrace and looked up at him with grave eyes. "Is anything wrong," he asked, feeling suddenly wary.

"I don't know. If I'd known what it was going to be like, perhaps I would've tried not to let it happen. No. I wanted you to take me even though I didn't think you'd want to. You did, a little bit. I'm glad. I'll try not to let myself want it again."

"You understand about that."

"Of course. I've never competed with Ernst. I'll tell him about it. He'll be wild for you in the morning. Be careful. I've tried to warn you but we must find out for ourselves in all the important things. You mustn't trust me anymore. I'll be doing everything I can to keep you with us. Don't trust anybody but yourself and try to be more sure of yourself than you ever have been before. You know?" She put a hand caressingly on his chest and her expression brightened. "Such a lovely man. A woman who has just been fucked as gloriously as I've been is in a highly emotional state. I'll try to be your friend again tomorrow. Go quickly." She slipped away from him again.

He wrapped the towel around him and gathered up his clothes and pulled his key out of a pocket. He was eager to wash too; the smell of her was troubling. Somnolent guards indifferently watched him cross the corridor and let himself into Conrad. He stood just inside and took a long breath and slowly exhaled. A smile played around his lips. He had fucked a girl successfully and acquired an ally, regardless of her warnings. He felt a quiet pride and the new strength he'd expected to find with her. He had paid his debt to society; nobody could accuse him of willfully refusing to go straight.

He crossed the living room with long strides and hung up his clothes in the bedroom and tossed aside the towel. He was ready to tackle Ernst. Out with Heinrich. Out with opium. Out with Maria if she represented a threat. He had found Walter in himself. His father, the reformer. He laughed out loud as he headed for the bathroom. He would follow Solange's advice and make his own tough terms. He felt the hum of happiness in him.

What if Ernst insisted on his own terms? Was his strength great enough to resist him? He stopped in front of the shower and stood motionless while a lump knotted in his throat. His imagination was captured by the man. He touched and infuriated him and he loved him. He wanted him. He wanted to take him and make him belong to him. He realized that falling in love didn't mean much unless there was time to give it concrete expression in daily life. He would make the time for both of them. The prospects were far from perfect but the day had restored to him the sense of excitement and discovery that he associated with the shining promises of the summer of his sixteenth birthday.

He washed and stretched out on the bed. The day was finally over but he doubted if he would fall asleep quickly. His mind was crowded with plans for the future and reminders from the past, searching for clues to the present. Ned, Leslie, Walter and Tom, Alain, Richard, they had all marked him. Two of them were dead but were alive in him. Ned was probably an old married man. Leslie had frittered his career away. Alain had survived as a minor Hollywood star and given him a taste of what he faced with Ernst. Richard? Poor Richard. The summer of his sixteenth birthday.

He was still only fifteen when it started but with his sixteenth birthday approaching, he was beginning to think of himself as an adult and his virginity was a source of increasing dismay. He had already reached what proved to be his full height of six feet. Whatever his height, he hoped that his cock would go on growing until it was at least a foot long. That had been his principal concern ever since he had begun to suspect that it was bigger than average. All his time alone was spent experimenting with stretching devices of his own invention, keeping it hard for as long as he was able, measuring it. It was still a few inches short of his goal but recent developments gave him grounds for optimism.

He had never had any doubt about his sexual desires. When he first heard about homosexuality, everything about himself became clear; he wanted to make love with boys. Because it was such a dark and unmentionable subject, apparently something that happened to damned souls somewhere but never with people you knew, he supposed he never would, but his dreams were growing increasingly explicit.

Summer on Long Island where his family had a baronial holiday mansion was a pleasant round of country-club dances and beach picnics and swimming parties but it wasn't very exciting. He found the boys and girls he ran around with pretty boring and often wished he were at home engaged in his ambitious project, although his opinion of a number of the boys might have altered if he'd known how to lure them home with him.

The excitement that he missed was suddenly provided when Ned burst upon the scene. From the moment Gerry set eyes on him he became the sole partner of his dreams. They made love in every way he was capable of imagining. When he first saw him in swimming trunks he thought his heart was going to stop. The part of him on which all his thoughts centered was magnificent, surely matching or surpassing his own. He didn't dare follow him into the showers at the tennis club for fear of what the sight of Ned's cock would do to him, so he kept adding to it in his imagination until it became a monument of phallic fantasy.

All of him was beautiful; beautiful fair hair, a beautiful face with big wide-set eyes and a bold mouth, a body that was both athletic and elegant, with none of the clumsiness of most well-developed boys. His skin was the most beautiful he had ever seen, smooth and honey-colored by the sun, with no disfiguring hair. He was as charming as he was beautiful—quick, vivid, gay, with an enchanting smile that he bestowed on anybody who crossed his line of vision.

Gerry tried to stay near him everywhere without appearing to do so, devouring him with his eyes whenever his attention was sufficiently engaged elsewhere for him not to notice. Ned was dedicated to his pursuit of girls, with whom he obviously made a big hit. He was practically a grown-up, about to start his last year of college, and for this reason alone Gerry knew he couldn't hope for him to take any interest in him. Gerry was content to intercept the smile from time to time and gaze at him with wonder, storing up impressions of beauty that he could take home with him and incorporate into his forbidden dreams. He couldn't remember afterward whether his mute worship lasted weeks or only days.

It was at a standard country-club dance that he noticed a difference in his fantasy lover, nothing specific, just a difference in the way he looked at him, more friendly and aware of him personally. Maybe his hero was a little drunk. As the evening progressed, their eyes met constantly, whether they were dancing near each other or just standing on the sidelines. Gerry broke the contact instantly so as not to give himself away, but after it happened a number of times he grew bolder and let his eyes seek Ned's and linger in them briefly. He thought he detected a question in them. His skin began to prickle with terror and longing. He knew it couldn't mean what he wanted it to mean. He told himself he should leave. He wasn't ready for it, whatever it was. He wouldn't know how to behave. The eyes were prodding him to declare his passion. Ned would despise him. He would have to kill himself.

When he next caught Ned's eyes on him, they contained a look of such urgent summons that his breath stopped and his head swam. He saw Ned turn and head for the wide doors giving onto the veranda. He struggled for breath and waited for the beating of his heart to subside. Surely the look had commanded him to follow. His vision was blurred and he didn't know how to move. He stumbled forward, bumping into people. He couldn't see Ned anywhere. He burst through the crowd at the door and his momentum carried him almost to Ned's side. He was standing at the edge of the veranda looking out into the night. Gerry stopped in his tracks as Ned turned and offered him his enchanting smile. He looked quite normal, loose and cool and easy, with nothing urgent in his eyes. Gerry had imagined it all. His face was burning with shame and embarrassment.

"Hi there. Looking for me?" Ned asked paralyzingly.

"No. I just—I just—" Gerry couldn't make his tongue work. People in groups and couples were moving around them in the semidarkness, so he was spared the agony of being alone with the partner of his outrageous dreams. Realizing that he was blocking traffic, he forced himself to ease in closer.

"I hoped maybe you were," Ned said lightly. "It's hot in there."

"Yes," Gerry blurted. He found himself standing beside the beautiful figure, almost touching him.

Ned laughed, thrillingly soft and gentle laughter that Gerry had never heard pitched to just that tone. "Don't worry. I like being followed by a cute kid. There's not much point in flirting if it doesn't lead to anything. Girls don't understand that." Miraculously they were close enough for their shoulders to touch.

"Flirting? I, uh—I thought—" Searching wildly for something to say that would give legitimate purpose to his being there, Gerry peered into the night and caught dim sight of the small lake at the foot of the lawn. "It's usually cooler down there if that's what you want." He was amazed that it all came out as a complete sentence.

"That's an idea. Shall we go find out? At least we'll be alone. I have a feeling that's what we're both thinking about." Ned uttered soft laughter again and placed a hand on Gerry's arm.

Gerry couldn't believe that his ears were working properly. He must have invented Ned's words in some fantasy. He was aware of being led to steps and then they were in the dark, walking down the gently sloping lawn. He stayed close to the boy at his side so as not to dislodge the hand that guided him. Their bodies brushed against each other. Gerry's heart was beating so violently that he wondered how long he could stay on his feet. A rail appeared out of the dark and they came to a halt against it. Gerry saw the edge of the lake at their feet. A small open pavilion stood nearby, dimly lighted by a lamp under the overhanging roof. He remembered it and wondered why he hadn't seen it until now. He couldn't trust his ears or his eyes.

"You're right," Ned said close to his undependable ear. "It's much cooler here." The hand moved from Gerry's arm up over his shoulder blades and came to rest on his neck. Fingers caressed the back of his hair. He clutched the rail to control the trembling that seized his whole body. Risking disgrace, he nudged his hand up against Ned's hip and moved his knuckles against it. Miraculously, it appeared to be the signal Ned was waiting for. He heard a soft chuckle and Ned's fingers spread out on his neck and circled it. Gerry saw his other hand drop. He heard the ripping sound of a zipper and the hand withdrew, revealing a long pale indistinct form jutting out against the dark.

"I guess that's what you've been waiting for. It's all yours." Ned's offer was casual.

A sound like a sob broke from Gerry's throat while his eyes stared incredulously. Trying to make out details blinded him. Blindly, he reached for it with a trembling hand and found it. All his senses staggered and churned at the warmth and weight of it, and its satin smoothness. It felt enormous but he was indifferent to its size. It was Ned's. His head whirled. He felt as if he had been lifted to the stars. It slanted downward and he could feel some flexibility in it still but it seemed to come alive in his caressing grasp. He wanted to make it as hard as his own.

Without conscious will or really knowing what he was doing, he dropped down and drew it into his mouth. He heard a little cry above him and flesh instantly swelled and lifted and hardened. He had never wondered how his mouth would encompass the gigantic creations of his imagination. This sublime reality stretched his jaws until they felt as if they would crack and he quickly improvised movements of his lips and tongue to compensate for his inability to contain all of it. Additional little sounds of pleasure and approval reached him from above and Ned's hands in his hair urged him on. It was happening at last. He had broken through the forbidden barrier to share in hard male ecstasies.

In a moment, Ned leaned down and gripped his arms and pulled him up. Gerry's hands clung to the erection and he let himself slump forward, longing to be gathered into strong arms, to feel a mouth on his. Ned held him firmly in front of him. Gerry stared into his face to assure himself that he was still the most beautiful boy he had ever seen, not a monster who had tricked him into defiling himself.

"You certainly know what you're doing," Ned murmured with a hint of laughter in his voice. "Girls always say it's too big for that. Boys like you never have any trouble. Come on. We'd better go in there." He put his hand on Gerry's neck again and turned him and moved him toward the lighted pavilion.

They were almost running when they reached its shelter. They jostled each other, arms and hands held and embraced each other and they laughed breathlessly as they entered. They found themselves in a big bare room that was in shadowy darkness except for an area in the middle that caught the light from outside. They faced each other and Ned ran his hands over Gerry's shoulders. His eyes were glowing. His smile was an enchantment of complicity. He moved his face closer. Gerry's lips parted, preparing for a kiss.

"Shall we take all our clothes off?" Ned asked in conspiratorial tones. "It's more fun that way. You've been wanting to see me naked, haven't you?"

"I'll say," Gerry admitted, amazed that Ned knew so much about what he wanted and seemed to accept it as natural.

Ned dropped his hands and folded them over Gerry's and disengaged himself slowly. "You can have it back in a second," he whispered.

A bench ran around the wall and they followed the path of light back to it and dropped their shirts on it. Gerry's confidence faltered at the prospect of exposing his undeveloped body, and he reminded himself that Ned had seen most of it and still had chosen him. Perhaps he had been intrigued by what had been concealed. He needn't be shy about that. He had seen Ned's in the light and knew that his was a good deal bigger. He was afraid he might have come already but found no traces of it. He felt as if it would happen at any moment. He was out of his clothes in seconds, to allow no time for reticence. He stood aside out of the light, careful not to cast a shadow on the marvel he was witnessing.

Ned lifted first one foot and then the other onto the bench to remove his shoes and socks. He bent to pull off trousers and shorts and straightened and turned to the light. Gerry's heart stopped. Without the shorts his nakedness was a supreme revelation of grace and power. Gerry shook off enthralled paralysis and took a step toward him. Ned dropped back onto the bench and spread his legs and put a hand around his erection. He looked up with an inviting smile. Gerry fell to his knees and put his hands on Ned's thighs and moved in between them. Ned fed him the coveted flesh. "There it is. Suck me off. You're the best ever."

The words banished for a moment his growing awareness that there was something oddly one-sided about it all.

Ned had demonstrated no interest in his body or that much-exercised part of it that was his particular pride, nor had he allowed the kiss he understood to be essential to true lovemaking. The best ever. He wanted to demonstrate that he had already learned how to be even better. The thought of holding all of his body against Ned's shattered him. He lifted his head with a shout and dropped it again while he seemed to explode and dissolve. His shoulders heaved. His breath came in hoarse gasps. He welcomed ecstatically what felt like total destruction. It took him a dazed moment to realize that he had never known what an orgasm could be.

Ned ran his hands over his hair and down to his back. "You came. That's sweet. You've almost got me there."

As soon as he could breathe, his body still shaken by recurrent spasms, Gerry began a display of his newfound skills. In seconds, he had brought Ned forward to the edge of the bench, gasping and writhing with excitement. He drifted in a trance of revelation—the driving demands of lust, the sounds of ecstasy, the straining muscles, a beautiful body quivering with desire under his provocative hands—it was all a dream coming true. No dream had prepared him for the bliss that transfused him as his mouth was flooded with Ned's precious essence. He swallowed it avidly and welcomed the additional jets that filled his mouth again. The taste of it intoxicated him—thick and spicy and slightly sweet. He heard him moaning as if he were stricken. He brought him down to the floor and pushed him back and spread his legs without relinquishing the diminishing flesh in his mouth. He continued to suck on it until it was small enough for him to draw all of it in and he buried his lips deliciously in soft curly hair. His hands continued to learn the delights of the beautiful body. Silence enveloped them.

"God," Ned murmured at last. "I could lie here all night and let you play with me." It aroused Gerry to greater activity. He rolled the soft flesh around in his mouth and felt it stirring. Ned tugged at his hair. "No. It's too soon. I can't—" Gerry cut him off with a gentle pressure of his teeth and felt flesh beginning to fill his mouth again. Ned's hips gave a little leap under him. "Jesus. I guess you *can*. Oh God, baby. Why didn't we do this sooner? You're fantastic. God yes. Don't stop. You're really doing it."

Gerry's spirits sang. He was learning how to make Ned want all of him the way he wanted Ned. He had a feeling that there was some sort of resistance he was slowly overcoming. The big cock was getting bigger. Ned's hips jerked about in a little dance of participation. A final throbbing surge brought complete erection and Gerry laughed and lifted himself over him on his hands and knees and looked down at him. The fair hair was tumbled about on his forehead. His face was alight and expectant. He put his hands on Gerry's shoulders, holding him near yet keeping him at a distance.

"You really like my body, don't you?" he asked with satisfaction.

"Oh God. I worship it. Your face. Your beautiful cock. All of you."

"Why don't girls ever say things like that?" he said with his gentle chuckle. "How old are you, anyway?"

"Eighteen." Gerry hoped he could get away with it.

"Is that all? I thought you were closer to my age. I better look out. Corrupting a minor. You're awfully damn sexy."

Gerry felt the restraint in Ned's hands slacken. He dropped onto him and arms slid up around him. He saw Ned's lips part and a great cry of joy was strangled in his throat as their mouths met and opened to each other. Their bodies locked together. They pitched and thrashed about on the floor, grappling with each other. Ned wrestled him over onto his stomach and lay on him. He thrust his erection between his thighs and worked it back and forth so that Gerry was immediately afire with an image of it entering him. He eased his hips up and brought into play muscles he didn't know existed in order to hold it, sobbing with excitement and desire. Lips moved against his ear.

"This is wild. I want to fuck you. You know what I mean?"

"God yes. Everything," Gerry begged. He struggled to his hands and knees, offering himself. Ned lay on him with his arms wrapped around his chest, swaying his hips so that his erection lightly nudged his balls.

"We can't here. You want me to take you home with me?"

Gerry answered with a choked and passionate yes.

"Is it all right? You won't have trouble with your family?"

"No. Nobody knows if I'm there or not."

"OK. I'll take you home and we'll really do it."

It wasn't until several hours later that Gerry finally received the attention he had thought his size would automatically command. After a shower, they lay together in Ned's big bed with a light on beside them and their arms thrown loosely across each other. "You're really amazing," Ned said. "You know, I don't really go for guys. I mean—well, for one thing, I've never paid any attention to cocks. I've never thought one was beautiful like you say mine is. I look at them like everybody else and check for size and all that, but that's all. Do you realize how amazing yours is?"

Gerry was sore where Ned had entered him and he gloried in the pain. He knew now all the rewards that sex could offer him. He was stunned that in only a few hours, everything in life had opened up to him. "I wasn't sure you'd noticed," he said with cheerful mockery. "I want you to tell me. Is it really amazing? I've never been with a boy before."

"You're kidding. Really? You mean it? I'm the first? How do you know how to do all those things?"

"Doing what comes naturally, I guess." They both laughed.

"It hasn't happened to me all that often," Ned added carefully. "Usually it's girls, but they always make so many difficulties. Well, you know how it is. Every now and then when a cute kid comes along and looks at me as if he really wanted it—well, what the hell. I've never gone after a guy myself."

"Is that the way I looked at you?"

"Boy. The way you've been looking at me, it was driving me crazy. I kept getting a hard-on. I was going to follow you into the shower at the club but you never came around. Tonight I decided we'd better do it before it got to be a big thing. Then you produce *this*." He moved his hand down to it and held it. "It makes me want to do things with it."

"I wish you would."

"No. There're certain things I won't do even if I might want to sometimes. I'm not going to be that way. I hate queers. If a good-looking guy wants to give me a blow job, OK. It's fun and that's all there is to it. Most guys feel the same way. There've only been a couple of times when—well, you know. Kissing and everything. Really making love. Nobody's ever turned me on the way you do. I've got to watch it."

"If you like girls, why worry?" Gerry propped himself up on one elbow over Ned and looked down into his wide blue eyes. He already felt older and wiser and more experienced than his first lover. He was such a pushover, with his talk of not liking boys. He knew all the ways to excite him. He lowered his head and kissed his mouth, drawing the soft lips between his teeth and biting them. Ned began to whimper breathlessly.

Gerry was astonished by how noisy lovemaking was; all the grunts and groans and shouts were thrilling tributes to a successful performance, like applause. He drew back just enough to speak against his lips. "I want you to fuck me again." He lifted himself to his knees and straddled him with his hands on his hips so that his cock stood free and towered over him.

"My God," Ned gasped. "It's incredible, baby. I guess maybe it is beautiful in a way. It's so sexy." He reached for it but Gerry seized his hands and placed them on his thighs.

"Look at it. Nobody's ever seen it like this before. It's still growing. I want it to be a foot long."

"It looks it already."

Gerry laughed. "Not yet, but it's bigger tonight than it ever has been." He lowered himself and worked himself along with his knees against Ned's sides, snaking his cock over his body until it touched his chin. He stroked his neck and ears with it. He could feel Ned's chest heaving and the rapid beating of his heart under him. He lifted himself slightly so that it hovered above his face. Ned's lips trembled. "You want to do things with it," Gerry whispered. "Suck it. You're going to give me my first blow job. That's what you get for corrupting a minor. I'm still only fifteen really. Open your mouth. Quickly. It's going to happen."

Ned did as he was told. Gerry felt his tongue on him and then was sliding into a velvet mouth. An enormous orgasm crashed through him, more devastating than ever. He felt all his strength draining away in great waves into

Ned's welcoming mouth. He toppled over and lay in a lethargy of victorious satisfaction. He could still feel Ned's hands fondling him and his mouth moving over his body as he was rolled over onto his stomach. Was this the beginning of a real love affair? It had been a very complete seduction.

By making no claims on him, Ned launched him on a life of carefree promiscuity. He lost overnight his fear of rejection or of being classified with the damned. If it could happen with Ned, it could happen with anybody. He discovered that several of the boys he had looked at before with interest and dread were susceptible to a smile or a touch. He remembered Ned's blithe acceptance of blow jobs and the clue he had dropped about the club showers. Ned proved to be a good guide.

Once, he followed a tennis foursome of attractive youths into the locker room during the deserted lunch hour and undressed with them and let them gape at his erection and teased and taunted them into taking him one after the other in a shower stall. It was more a bawdy roughhouse than lovemaking but one of the four handled him with furtive tenderness and later proposed that the two of them should have more of the same. They did whenever the opportunity arose. One thing led to another. There was a handful of such regulars, but Ned wasn't one of them.

Showing off his cock became something of a party trick. A couple of times, at night at a beach party, in a bathroom at a private dance, a group of boys surrounded him and urged him to produce it. He was glad to oblige and it gave him an erection, which became the object of much wonder, accompanied by obscene comment. By watching their eyes, he could spot the ones who wanted more than just to look at it and he noted them for future pleasure. The years of single-minded application were paying off.

He didn't find a clearly defined homosexual set in the world he frequented so he might have taken refuge with Ned in the pretense that everything he did was just for the hell of it, but he knew it was much more than that. Some instinct, perhaps being the object of male desire, led him to develop effeminate mannerisms and turns of speech. He discovered he had a sharp tongue. When he was jeered at as a faggot, he gave as good as he got. He felt as if he had had a ready-made personality tucked away somewhere that Ned had helped him bring out into the open.

Ned made a point of ignoring him. His smile was still brilliant, but without enchantment when directed at him. He wasn't surprised—once seemed to be the rule of the game except for the four or five regulars—but he still looked at him with longing, thought of him when he was having sex with others, wished it was possible to have a love affair with a boy. Whenever he had the opportunity and the courage to suggest their getting together again, Ned snubbed him coldly.

Beach barbecues had become his favorite kind of party because they offered so many opportunities for sneaking boys off into the dark. One night on the beach he found a new boy who immediately became the object of his pursuit. Ned was there, drinking quite a lot. He remembered thinking he'd been drinking the first night and wondered if it would make him more receptive. Meanwhile, he was intent on isolating the new boy.

He saw his chance when the boy was returning his plate to the folding table. He moved in beside him. "Geting enough to eat?" he asked.

"Yeah. Thanks." The new boy looked him over with a knowing smile. "How about you? I hear you're a ter—"

Ned suddenly pushed in between them. He seized Gerry's arm and dragged him across the dunes to where the cars were parked without giving him time to protest. He pushed him into his car and went around to the other side and got in behind the wheel. Gerry was thrilled and frightened but he was with Ned again. From the violence with which he had been handled he had a feeling that it might end with his getting beaten up, but he didn't care. They were together. Ned started the car and drove off with a roar.

"Where're we going?"

"Home."

"How wonderful."

"Goddammit," Ned burst out. "I've done things with you I swore I'd never do with anybody. That makes you sort of belong to me. You better know it. I won't have you running after every guy you can get your hands on."

"I haven't done all the running. If anything, it's been the other way around."

"Everybody's heard you have a huge cock. It's just curiosity."

"Word *has* spread, rather. I don't understand. You like girls. I'm gay or queer or anything you want to call me. Where've you been the last few weeks? You haven't wanted me. What am I supposed to do?"

"You wouldn't be thinking of doing *anything* if it weren't for me."

"That's true. You did a pretty thorough job of corrupting me. Oh God, I've wanted you so much."

"How many of your boyfriends suck your cock?"

"Not many. None, really."

"I do. Think about it."

"I—" He started to explain that most of them had fucked him but decided that the less he said the better while Ned was in this mood. He appeared to be intent on his driving which was just as well because he was going much too fast for safety. They didn't speak again until they were in Ned's room. He followed Ned's lead in getting quickly out of his clothes. They stretched out in bed and reached for each other eagerly. He almost broke into sobs of happiness as he felt the magnificent body against his again. They kissed at length. Ned pulled back.

"All right. I've got to tell you something," he said, somber and hesitant. "It's crazy but—oh dammit, I'm in love with you. I've tried not to be but there's nothing I can do about it. I'm madly in love with you."

"But darling, that's beautiful." Calling boys darling was part of his new flagrant persona. Bursting out, it befit the occasion. He gazed up at him with awe. Everybody agreed that falling in love was the supreme experience of life. He was barely sixteen and somebody was in love with him. Ned was practically a grown-up so he must know what it meant and how to do something about it. "Why haven't you had anything to do with me? Why haven't we been making love together?"

"I tell you, I've been fighting it. It's impossible for me to be in love with a boy. It doesn't happen to normal guys. Just now, when I saw that guy after you, it was more than I could take. I wanted to kill him. You belong to me. You're mine."

Gerry pressed himself closer to Ned and stroked his broad back. "But you haven't been paying any attention to me. You know you can have me whenever you want me. I won't fuss about what you're doing the rest of the time. I mean, if you want girls . . ."

"That's not the point. Something's happened to me. I'm in love with you. Don't you understand what that means? I can't stand for either of us to be with anybody else."

"That sounds sort of selfish, darling." They were in Ned's bed. He held Ned's body against him. For the moment, it was all he could possibly want but he couldn't imagine turning away from lively young eyes when they singled him out. He looked into the troubled passionate beauty of Ned's and was aware of a sort of dislocation in himself, a yearning for whatever was being offered him and an impulse to protect himself from an exclusive passion. He drew Ned's mouth to his and kissed him voraciously, plunging his tongue deep into his mouth, performing the tricks that excited his lover most. He could feel all the passion and need blazing up in the body he held, and was stunned that it was all for him. He drew back slowly and kissed his face with a darting tongue. "Make me belong to you if it's possible, darling," he urged, daring to let the endearment become a habit; Ned had really let his hair down. "If I belong to you, I ought to be with you all the time. That first night, I didn't even know if it was something that could happen a second time. I love being in bed with you more than anybody else. I love your body. Your cock is bigger than all the others. You know how much that means to me. I keep hoping to find a bigger one but so far, no such luck. I'm not complaining. What if it had been tiny like Phil Blair's?"

"I'm insane. I know it," Ned said helplessly. "You're not even sixteen yet, for God's sake. What do I expect? We're going away together tomorrow, baby. I've got to have you all to myself for a few days. You can tell your parents we're going to that theater in Montauk—I've heard the show's good—you can call them later and tell them we're staying over for a party or something. We'll shack up somewhere and I'll fuck you silly so you won't want anybody else for the rest of the summer."

"If you had more ideas like that, nobody else would have a chance. How marvelous." Ned would do anything for him. Maybe jealousy would make him even more in love with him.

The night passed happily, as did the three days they spent together in a motel at the end of the island. They met a young golden-haired actor from the show on the beach with friends of Ned's, and Gerry was gripped by instant desire. His name was Leslie. Gerry directed a long unguarded look at him when he rose to go for a swim. Leslie came plunging after him. They splashed about together, laughing and flirting. They made a grab for each other's trunks and pulled them down and Gerry found what he'd been hoping to find for weeks. It was a beauty, not much less impressive than his own, and they hurriedly arranged for Leslie to come stay with him the following week on his way back to New York. He hadn't the slightest idea what he would tell Ned when Leslie turned up, but hoped he would think of something when the time came. Ned was proving touchingly easy to manage. He loved having him in love with him.

A day or two after the excursion, his mother came to his room one morning just as he was waking up. He had his usual morning erection, but a glance at the rumpled covers assured him that it was sufficiently disguised and he let her come in and sit on the edge of the bed beside him. She was wearing some sort of negligee that made her look very smart. It was the thing about her that made her different from other mothers. She dazzled him. He knew she had to be almost fifty because his brother and sister were a good deal older than he, but she still had a light bright youthfulness that made her fun to be with.

"I've been wanting to have a talk with you, darling," she said. "I've been hearing a lot of gossip about you recently."

Something in her tone made his heart stop. He knew with appalling certainty, as if he'd just fallen out of a tenth-story window, that his life was over. He couldn't live without her approval. He was going to have to kill himself after all. He reminded himself that it had started with Ned; nothing Ned did could be bad. "What about? About Ned?" he blurted, amazed that he could still speak.

"Ned and others," she corrected him.

She said it without sounding like the herald of doom. His vertiginous terror passed. Could he bring it all out in the open so that it wouldn't come between them? He was her pampered baby. She had always underlined the difference between him and the other two. She would surely defend and support him now. He gathered his courage to speak. "That's just it. There's nothing special about it. It just happens. You'd be amazed how many boys do it."

"Not amazed in the least. It seems fairly widespread these days. I imagine it always has been but people didn't use to talk so much about it. I gather you feel no need to be discreet."

"If that's the way I am, how can I be? Guys aren't discreet about chasing girls."

"I'm sure that's a very healthy attitude, darling. I certainly wouldn't want you to be consumed by guilt. Still, there *is* a difference. Mothers expect boys to chase their daughters, not their sons. They don't know what to do about it, which makes them angry. I don't want you to be a social outcast. Don't you think you might be a little young still to go into it quite so enthusiastically? It might be just a passing phase, as the saying goes."

"It might be, but I don't think so. Ned's the most popular guy around and he likes me. It's what I've always dreamed about as long as I can remember. I've never thought about girls."

"Don't you think you might want help? I've heard of psychiatrists who specialize in this sort of thing."

"Oh no, Mum, please. I don't want to be cured, if that's what you mean. It's the way I am. I'd be terrified of being cured of being me."

"I see what you mean. Very well. My only real concern is your happiness, darling. I'm glad you're enjoying yourself." She put a hand on his erection. He let out a yelp and briefly levitated. When he had dropped back onto the bed, her hand was still there.

"Hey, Mum. That's supposed to be private," he protested.

"Don't be absurd, darling. When you were a baby I used to play with it and give you the sweetest silliest little erections." She tossed the covers aside and pulled her spectacles out of a pocket and put them on her nose. His body gave another leap and then he lay still as she studied him. "My word. So that's what all the excitement's about. I'm beginning to understand. It reminds me of someone I knew once long ago. I suppose one looks back at the past with rose-colored glasses but I do believe his was bigger."

"Mine's still growing."

"Really? You must show me when it stops." She put a hand on it and lifted it upright and caressed it lightly with her fingertips. "I've always been fascinated by incest. Don't worry, darling. I'm speaking purely of theory, not practice. I'm rather pleased with myself for having equipped you so handsomely for life, though I can't claim to have done it all by myself."

His glazed eyes watched the hand moving lightly on himself. He was bewildered and frightened but above all grateful. By committing this sin, she was sharing his guilt. He felt comforted and protected. It seemed an approval of whatever he did with his body, an absolution. He knew that he shouldn't allow it and that he wanted it. For an inconceivable moment, he even wished she would make him come. He flung both arms over his face and waited to be consumed by the flames of Hell. The hand withdrew and he felt himself being covered and he slowly calmed down. "I don't understand," he said when he could speak. "Why did you do that?"

"I was trying to find out something about you, darling. It's the most natural thing in the world." Her voice was cool and healing. "We're made of the same flesh and blood. You've lived inside me. There's no part of you I can't touch and know." He dropped his arms away from his face to his sides and lay with his eyes closed. She took a hand in hers. "I just want you to remember that if you ever find a girl you like, there's no reason to assume that she won't please you. You'll meet lots of girls who would be very happy to satisfy you in any way you wish. And now I want you to promise me two things. You must promise me not to have anything to do with boys you don't know. I mean boys you might pick up in the streets. I've heard of toughs who lead boys like you on and then turn nasty. I won't have you hurt in that way. I also want you to promise me that you'll never again flaunt yourself in public. It cheapens you."

His cheeks were burning with shame. How could she have heard about his displaying himself? "I promise, Mum," he blurted.

"Very well. You understand now that you can come to me if you find that being a homosexual is more of a problem than you think."

He opened his eyes and gave her hand a squeeze. "How

could it be with somebody like you around?" He saw a glitter in her eyes as she pulled off her spectacles and returned them to her pocket and straightened her shoulders.

"I love you, darling. I want very much for you to have a good life. I don't care about your being brilliant or famous but I would like you to be happy. Perhaps you should give me an idea of what's been happening. You've had much more freedom this summer without your brother and sister here to keep an eye on you. I hope it hasn't been a mistake. Ned's mother thinks you're having an affair with him."

"It seems to be turning into one. That's why we went away together, but it was his idea. He thinks he's in love with me. He's the most beautiful boy I've ever seen but that's not being in love, is it? He knows about the others. I don't think I *can* be in love yet. Puppy love, maybe. I'm still finding out what it's all about."

"You sound quite reasonable, darling. How does this boy Leslie fit in?"

"Not very well, I guess." They exchanged a look and she burst out laughing. To his amazement, Gerry found himself laughing with her. "Ned doesn't know about him. How could I tell him I'd made a date with another boy when he was acting as if we were practically on our honeymoon? If he comes, I'd like him to stay in here with me, not in a guest room. Is that all right?"

"Of course, darling. Boys room together. Except that this house is so big that it might look a bit odd. I'd better have the bed made up next door and you can muss it at appropriate intervals to give the maids something to do. Do try not to be a heartbreaker, darling."

"I don't want to be. It's all so new to me. God, I wish we'd talked about it sooner. A month ago, I thought I was doomed. I couldn't see any hope except to kill myself. I didn't think it was something I could talk about to anybody, least of all you. When it happened with Ned, I began to think it couldn't be all that bad. I mean, there's nothing wrong with *him*—popular and having girls and everything. Then I discovered that quite a lot of guys went in for it, too, and I realized I'd probably been in a state about nothing. You've helped more than anything. I was a bit nervous about having invited Leslie here."

"Well, darling, I don't think it would be fair to you to let you feel quite so complacent about it. I'm more civilized about it than most people you'll run into. It *is* forbidden. It *is* unmentionable, although a good many people mention it quite a lot. I understand your feeling that a boy like Ned gives it a sort of sanction but you're mistaken. The fact that you've found other partners doesn't mean very much either. I believe it's usual for boys your age to find substitutes for girls when they aren't available, but most men end up following what seems to be nature's plan, finding a wife and having children. You *are* doomed in a way, darling. You've got to be prepared for a lifetime of concealment or sink into an unhappy half-world where everything is accepted. We mustn't let your father find out about this. A life sentence to Siberia would be the least of it. We'd have to go trudging off into the snow together. I wouldn't let us starve to death but it's not somehing I look forward to. Remember that anything you do will affect me, too, at least for the next five years. I won't have you killing yourself, but please don't give up on girls. Not yet. Not until you fall in love with a boy and are absolutely sure. If you do, I'll welcome him into the family as if he were your wife or your husband or however these things work, but you'll have to be very very discreet so your father has nothing more than suspicions to go on. Thank heavens the other two are about to get married. That'll distract him for a while. I must say I never expected you to be like them, darling. We both must have our secrets."

She left him on this cryptic note and he lay where he was while his gratitude grew for everything she had said. He didn't see how he could make so much of himself invisible, as she was suggesting he should, but he resolved to do his best. His mind grappled with her extraordinary act. Maybe it was as insignificant as she claimed it was. Maybe he should drive from his mind the impression that his mother had made love to him, however briefly. Whatever it had meant, it seemed to give him an extraordinary hold over her. They were partners in crime.

On the day Leslie was expected, he arrived at about noon in a sporty little MG with a great deal of luggage. He was even more attractive than Gerry remembered—laughing eyes, a pert nose, a mouth as luscious as a girl's. Gerry was slightly taller, which made him less shy of the older boy. He raced him up the ceremonial staircase and hurried him along the corridor.

"You looked like a rich boy," Leslie commented, "but

I didn't know you lived in a castle. It's what you might call a real fairy tale." They veered closer and threw their arms around each other and laughed. "I'm glad you're in a rush too, darling. It'll make it seem as if we hadn't been interrupted six days ago. I've never felt so frustrated. All that time to think we might've made a mistake."

"I know."

"You too?"

"Sort of. Not now."

"We'll soon see. I mean, I assume this house stops somewhere."

Gerry gave Leslie a little push into his room and closed the door behind them. They looked at each other for a breathless moment and then they were in each other's arms and their mouths were open to each other. Gerry had come in from the pool and was wearing only trunks. They were peeled off him and hands explored his erection and closed around it. Leslie withdrew from the kiss and dropped down to it. He put it in his mouth and closed his teeth on it. He released it and moved his hands to Gerry's hips and gazed at it. "Oh, oh, oh," he crooned happily. "I'm trying to make sure I'm not dreaming. I've been looking for you for twenty-five years. I knew *somebody* had to have a bigger cock than mine."

Gerry laughed and ran his hands through the golden hair and gave it a tug. "I don't want to get too worked up before your bags arrive. Come back up here."

Leslie sprang up and put a forefinger on his nose and pushed it like a button to emphasize his words. "Never interrupt me when I'm looking at your cock. Hey. It's a song." He improvised additional lyrics and set them to music. They held each other and rocked with laughter. He was so cute and saucy, as pretty as a picture. Gerry dropped his hands to the thick ridge that rose across Leslie's belly to his hip. "You're allowed to get it out," Leslie said. "It won't turn to dust if exposed to the air."

They collapsed with laughter again. "You don't understand. I'm trying to lead up to it slowly," Gerry protested through his giggles as he removed his light cotton jacket and tossed it onto a nearby chair. He unbuttoned his shirt and Leslie pulled it off. His body didn't have the perfection of Ned's but it was very sexy—slim and smooth and nicely developed. He had already discovered he had a weakness for blonds, probably because they usually weren't hairy. He unbuttoned the top of Leslie's trousers and pulled down the zipper and held what he'd been hoping for. He uttered an exclamation of delight. It was much bigger than Ned's; he hadn't been wrong about that.

The rest of his clothes were quickly disposed of and he straightened with his hands on Gerry's hips and held him so that their erections lifted side by side, swaying against each other. Gerry's was longer and more bulky but the difference was slight; they made an imposing pair.

"My God, there we are, darling," Leslie exclaimed. "At last. Look at us, honey. We're fantastic together. I've never seen so much cock in my life. It's staggering. I've been to bed with three hundred and forty-six guys and I had to wait for the three hundred and forty-seventh to meet my master. What's your guess, sweetheart? An inch difference?"

"Not that much, I'll bet. I've been looking for you too." He wished he'd kept count. He knew it must be getting close to twenty.

"We'll find out later." They both put their hands on them and pressed them together and made gleeful sounds in their throats. "Let's—"

There were footsteps outside and a knock on the door. They were still standing just inside it. Gerry backed up hastily to it, drawing Leslie with him, and answered.

"Here's the luggage, Master Gerald," a cheerful female voice sang out.

Leslie had him pinned against the door. Their bodies writhed together and their hands were all over each other. Gerry had to take a deep breath before he could speak.

"Just put it all in the next room. We'll take care of it." They were shaken by smothered laughter.

"Master Gerald," Leslie gasped. "*King* Gerald. His Majesty in person. Everybody should kneel and pay homage. That's what I'm going to do."

They made a rush for the bed and fell on top of each other. Gerry cried out with the sheer wonder of what was happening—he was making love with a boy in his own house. His mother knew. He abandoned himself to the marvels of Leslie's uninhibited body. He had done all the basic things with Ned or others but this new lover introduced thrilling variations that aroused all the eroticism that had hitherto been confined to acts of his imagination. He realized that he had been on his best behavior with Ned.

When it was time to join his mother for lunch, he was a bit on edge and self-conscious at her seeing him for the first time with somebody who had been his partner in unnameable intimacies but, thanks to his talk with her, he at least felt no shame. They put on swimming trunks and crossed the sloping lawn down to the pool house. This was Faye Kennicutt's creation and her special pride, a wide, luxurious and luxuriant indoor–outdoor garden with inviting, brightly upholstered patio furniture set about in it and out around the pool, the whole enclosed in a high yew hedge for total privacy.

They found her at the bar mixing a drink, wearing a smart beach robe. Gerry performed introductions and knew immediately that Leslie was going to make a hit. She offered him a drink while Gerry helped himself to a watered-down vermouth and within moments they were chatting and joking together. Leslie called her "darling" and "Mum." He called Gerry "darling" too, which made him blush with delight. He sat on the arm of Gerry's chair and kept putting his hands on him almost absentmindedly, displaying his possession of him, stroking his chest or ruffling his hair.

Gerry slowly relaxed and began to revel in his new status as a grown-up with the right to a life of his own. He wished he and Ned had started off like this. It was so difficult to fall in love if you had to hide it all the time. If his father never came home, he could live forever with his mother, a lover at his side, basking in her approval. She wasn't a very large public but she was enough to make him realize how much he longed for public acceptance. He supposed he wasn't strong enough to be secretive and alone. He wanted to be open with everybody. A lifetime of concealment, she had said. He didn't think he could stand it.

When the happy lunch was over, Mrs. Kennicutt announced her departure. "I must run. The hairdresser in half an hour and an afternoon of utterly boring good works." She looked at Leslie with amusement twitching at the corners of her mouth. "My husband will be home this evening. If you meet him, try not to call him 'darling.' "

"Oh dear. I'm sorry. We pick up these habits in the biz."

She laughed. "I like it but he's rather old-fashioned. Actually, we had quite a lot of theatrical connections once upon a time. I'll remind him what it's like in case you make a slip."

"They practically gave Walter Makin his start," Gerry pointed out with pride in his mother's unconventional side.

"Really? That's right. He worked out here at the beginning, didn't he? All those fabulous shows he was doing when I first started going to the theater. His pictures make him look like a raving beauty."

"He was the most extraordinary young man I've ever known, even younger than you when I first met him. The Boy Wonder. Dear me." She gave herself an odd little shake. "Well, off I go." She rose briskly and put out a restraining hand as Leslie shifted in his seat. "Don't get up. You can swim down here with nothing on if you like. Nobody's allowed in without calling down first. I like my privacy too." She kissed him on the top of his golden head and came around to Gerry and gave him a hug and was gone. Left to their own devices, they were soon out of their trunks, with predictable consequences.

Later, back in Gerry's room, Leslie dropped a bombshell. He and Gerry could obviously have something terrific together, he pointed out, the sort of thing that didn't happen often. Nothing would be going on in New York till after Labor Day. Would Gerry like him to stay on for a month or so? Gerry was incoherent with delight and amazement until he remembered Ned. An overnight visit could be explained away somehow, but what would Ned think if Leslie stayed? Would he believe it if Gerry told him that nothing was happening between them?

Confronted with the possibility of Leslie's staying, he couldn't imagine letting him go but he couldn't imagine losing Ned either. It wasn't fair. If Ned was in love with him, why didn't he insist on their being together all the time, the way it had been in Montauk? Leslie was proposing a real grown-up affair, being together all day and all night, the way he had dreamed it might be someday. Gerry was already beginning to feel a change in the way Leslie treated him; he was becoming solicitous and tender and protective, as if a real connection were growing out of their lovemaking. Ned always maintained a certain distance between them; except when they were in bed, they remained just buddies.

Leslie was the first avowed homosexual he had ever known and he was relieved at not feeling any of the guilt in him that Ned forced him to share. He loved the way Leslie took him, as if it were natural and normal, not a substitute for what they should really want. Leslie simply eliminated the awkward problem of girls.

"What should I tell Ned? I mean, about your staying. You remember Ned." Gerry was wondering about the party that night. He had thought that if they skipped it, Ned might never find out about this visit. He could hardly keep Leslie's presence a secret for over a month.

"The beauty you were with in Montauk? Is something serious going on there? Will I be in the way?"

"Of course not." Gerry's only wish was to dispel the slight cloud that had crossed his new friend's merry face. They were both naked again; Gerry wanted to make love some more. "It's just that—well, there's a party tonight. He'll probably be there. We don't have to tell him right away how long you're staying, do we? Why not say it's just for a day or two and let him slowly get used to your being here? You wouldn't mind if I went off with him sometimes, would you?"

Leslie winked at him, his face once more full of fun. "Of course not, honey. *I* certainly wouldn't say no to him. Resisting temptation is bad for the complexion. Maybe all three of us should try some tricks together."

"You're kidding." Gerry laughed as he imagined Ned's reaction to such a suggestion. "He'd never do anything like that. He's not like us. He won't admit he likes boys. He says he's in love with me but he doesn't understand how it happened. He's always liked girls."

"Everybody has their little peculiarities. Come on, sweetheart. If we're going to a party, I want to make you pretty for it." He got out his stage makeup box and went to work on Gerry's eyes. He rearranged his hair. It became an act of more complete possession than anything Gerry had experienced during sex. The brush of Leslie's body against him, the fingers moving lightly on his face, the flow of concentration directed toward him flooded him with warmth and caused odd little flutterings around his heart. Ned claimed that he belonged to him but he hadn't made him feel like this.

"There. Fantastic. Come look." Leslie took his hand and led him to the mirror. He stood a little behind him and held him. Gerry gazed at himself with wonder. His eyes were soft and luminous and twice as big as they'd been before. The hairstyle turned him startlingly feminine. "My God," he exclaimed. "I'm almost beautiful. I wish I could go out like this."

"Why can't you? Nobody'll know. I'll teach you how to do it so it's impossible to guess. Look at it close-up. You can't see it's makeup."

"But everybody'll think I'm a girl."

"You're my baby bride. What a darling. You're urgently wanted between our nuptial sheets."

When they finally got to the party, Ned was there. As soon as Gerry saw him, he said a word to Leslie and they both went to him. Gerry watched Ned's eyes fix on him and widen with astonishment and desire and then shift to his companion and turn cold. Gerry launched into his prearranged explanations but Ned didn't seem to hear them. He looked contemptuously at Leslie.

"You've come to stay with him, have you? I wondered if you'd had time to fix something. You're fast workers, both of you." He turned abruptly and left them. Leslie looked momentarily at a loss.

"It doesn't matter," Gerry said in a voice he scarcely recognized. He was stricken, but Leslie was taking possession of him so thoroughly that he was able to curb his impulse to go after him. He told himself that he would only risk a public scene. "As soon as he gets used to the idea, he'll want me back," he said to reassure himself. "He always does."

Leslie was a great success with both the boys and the girls but Gerry couldn't enter into the party spirit. He wanted to talk to Ned alone, to convince him that he was wrong, that Leslie's visit wouldn't interfere with their being together whenever Ned wanted them to be.

He remained on the lookout for him for the next few days but didn't run into him anywhere, and when he finally inquired about him he was told that he had gone away. It was a frightful shock but he was sure that he was bound to come back soon. Being in love was for a long time, almost like being married. They hadn't even discussed the winter or made plans for seeing each other. He felt a sharp pain of loss that didn't go away, but he had Leslie.

Their lovemaking remained inventive, unflagging and mirthful, peacefully free of any emotional stress. Spice was added by Leslie photographing him naked in extravagantly erotic poses. "How will you get them developed?" Gerry wondered.

"Don't worry. I have a friend. You'll be a celebrity before you get back to town for your Christmas holiday."

Leslie told him about his life in New York and dispelled whatever lingering fears Gerry might have had about the future. Although a native, he knew nothing about the city Leslie described. It sounded as if it had been created especially for him, a place where there was no concealment but a lively fraternity studded with famous names waiting to welcome him. He wanted to tell Ned about it to prove to him that there was nothing strange about boys being in love with each other. If only school were out of the way, life promised to be dazzling. He already had a resident lover. His ideal of male beauty was in love with him even though he had momentarily disappeared. The one person who might have turned it all into a nightmare had given him her blessing.

Leslie's famous playwright friend Edgar Seibling had a summer house in a neighboring Hampton and as his first week drew to a close, he called him from the pool house and came out to report that they had been invited for the following evening. "It may be a bit wild, darling," he said. "To be perfectly truthful, he's rather partial to orgies. From what you've told me I doubt if it'll shock you. After all, being fucked in the shower by four beefy tennis players is not exactly kid stuff."

"You mean I'm going to be fucked again by four beefy tennis players?" They shook with laughter. "Tell me. An orgy? Do you mean we'll have sex with other guys?"

"If we want to. I take it you like the idea."

"I was just worrying about my complexion."

Gerry wasn't as sanguine about the orgy as he pretended but he was eager to widen his experience. The next evening, Leslie spent more time than usual on his eyes and hair. "We don't have to be so subtle for Edgar's crowd. Your face is amazing. It's made for makeup. You look like

Hedy Lamarr. We'll have to be careful nobody sees you on the way out. We can use the back hall door."

He walked him to the mirror. Gerry was getting used to the beautiful girl he could be turned into. He *did* look like Hedy Lamarr. Leslie turned him and looked him over. "You'll lay them in the aisles. You needn't take that literally, darling. It's an expression."

They dressed informally and made their escape without being observed. When Leslie pulled up in front of a big house, they found several other cars parked in the drive. He stopped Gerry as he was about to get out. "Wait a minute, darling." He produced a small pot from his pocket and dipped his forefinger in it and applied it to Gerry's mouth. In the light from the house, Gerry could see that it was rouge. "It's supposed to be indelible. If it gets kissed off, I'll fix it up. Now you *are* Hedy Lamarr. Let's see how it works." He gave him a hungry kiss, running his tongue over his lips, and drew back. "Perfect. God, you're beautiful, honey. I certainly married the right girl."

Their entrance created a stir. Gerry was dazzled by an assemblage of good-looking young men. He heard Leslie's name called out from several directions. Everybody seemed to be embracing everybody else. He was passed from youth to youth. Mouths opened to his. He was held at arm's length and told that he was fascinating. He ended up in front of their host who, to his relief, gave him only a peck on the cheek. He was old, probably almost fifty, bald, and wore glasses. Leslie appeared beside him and they put their arms around each other.

"You're a sensation," Leslie said, his eyes gloating on him.

"My God," Gerry exclaimed. He was in a whole roomful of his own kind. Nobody was concealing anything. Nothing suggested that they inhabited a half-world of lost souls. He couldn't wait to tell his mother. As he recovered his balance, he saw that he was one of about a dozen and that although the level of good looks was extraordinarily high, only four or five of them were able to draw his eyes away from Leslie for long. He saw hair spilling out of several open collars, which he didn't like. Once they had all settled down to drinking again, it could have been any gathering of well-heeled young men except that their hands were frequently in places one wouldn't ordinarily expect to see them and their voices had odd intonations and emphases. Leslie remained close to him, interposing himself slightly between him and the others, retaining a proprietary hold on him.

They were joined by a youth called Benjie who wasn't good-looking at all but had a curiously sensual face, dissipated and provocative, emanating a powerful animal magnetism. Leslie put an arm around the newcomer familiarly and ruffled his hair while Gerry exchanged a long speculative look with him that ended with mutual acquiescence. He could see that orgies presented particular problems. He was surrounded by young men who excited him and he didn't want to exclude any of them by paying too much attention to one.

Soon, there was a general movement toward the dining room and sex play was suspended while they all ate. There was the usual milling about after dinner while people went off to pee and drinks were replenished. Gerry had some more wine even though he had already far exceeded the amount he was used to. He had the impression that casual dress had become more casual. Nobody was wearing a jacket anymore and several shirts were unbuttoned to the waist. Bodies were beginning to fall into indolent poses and entangle themselves with each other, and hands roved more openly. He didn't think it would be long before some of them started to make love on the spot.

He left Leslie with Benjie and a couple of others and wandered off down a corridor looking for a washroom. He found one and relieved himself of some of the wine. He admired his new mouth in the mirror. It looked wonderfully voluptuous. He was making some small adjustments to his hair when the door opened and Benjie appeared in the mirror.

"Sorry," he said, drawing back.

"It's all right. I was just coming out," Gerry said, not wanting him to go. He'd been waiting for the chance to make a real play for him. Their eyes met in the mirror and transmitted blunt invitations to each other.

"Actually, I was looking for you," Benjie said. "I had to knock Leslie down so I could be the one to tell you that they're all going upstairs. They're expecting us."

Gerry looked at the debauched face in the mirror and decided that it was good-looking after all, dissolute, hinting at unimaginable depravity. Dark eyes bored into his.

"Upstairs?" he asked, his heart beginning to accelerate. "What're they doing upstairs?"

"Fucking, I guess, or getting ready to."

Gerry forced a tense little smile. "Are we all going to bed together?"

"After a fashion." Their eyes held for a long silent moment, Gerry's heart pounded. Benjie spoke at last. "I love the way you look at me, as if I'm Svengali about to hypnotize you. You're all ready to let me take you away with me but Leslie would never forgive us." He took a step into the small room and closed the door behind him. "We shouldn't be here. It's against the rules. The action's supposed to be upstairs." He took a few steps closer and put his hands on Gerry's behind and moved them over it, following its curves. "The prettiest ass I've seen in years."

As if obeying orders, Gerry unfastened his pants and let them drop and pushed down his shorts. The hands on his bare skin gave him goose bumps and his buttocks began to quiver. He reached behind him and unzipped Benjie's fly and withdrew a slim erection. Benjie stepped in against him and ran his hands up under his shirt and pulled his shoulders back. Gerry's cock lunged up over the washbasin. Benjie looked down at it over his shoulder. "Yes. Even more amazing than Leslie's. I've maybe seen a bigger one but I was probably drunk. Take your shirt off. Turn on the water. Give me the soap."

Gerry followed each command as it was issued. Benjie worked up a lather in one hand and pulled a towel from the rack beside them with the other and stepped back. Gerry clung to the edge of the basin, his heart bursting out of his chest. The slim erection entered him and began a long gliding penetration. It was so deliberate and passionless that he couldn't believe it was happening. He was being taken like a piece of equipment that had been installed for this strange boy's convenience. He was shocked by the suspension of his own volition and thrilled by being used so cold-bloodedly. It was degrading and yet it excited him. It revealed in him depths of surrender that he hadn't known existed. He propped himself on the basin and worked his buttocks to stir Benjie into action. Benjie gripped his cock with both hands and pulled him in hard against him and held him impaled and motionless.

"It feels good, doesn't it?" he whispered.

"Yes. God, yes. Take me. I mean, do it. Fuck me. Oh

God, please." He wanted to shout his surrender but he kept his voice pitched low to match Benjie's.

"Look at my hands on your cock. You like me to hold it, don't you? You're so damn young I could cry. They're all going to be grabbing for you in a minute. Don't move." His hands moved slowly back over his cock and across his groin and up to his chest, barely touching him, his fingers fluttering against him. Gerry began to tremble from head to foot.

"Oh please," he begged. "Please. Please."

"Boys who like to be fucked have to learn to take it the way they get it. Look at that cock. God Almighty. You're about to come." His hands fluttered up around his neck and out across his shoulders and exerted barely perceptible pressure. "That's right. Like that. Not too much. Feel that? You like it, don't you?"

"God yes. It's fantastic. Oh Benjie. Please."

"You better look out or you're going to turn into a men's room queen."

"But you're making me," Gerry gasped, tears starting to his eyes.

"Of course, but there're plenty of Svengalis around. That cock is going to get you into enough trouble without your being so easy to hypnotize. OK. Come when I tell you to and then I'll have to throw you to the wolves. I wanted you first."

Gerry cuddled down against Leslie as he started the car and turned it into the drive and headed for home. His senses were still reeling from the shocks and discoveries of the evening. The mirrored room with its low cushion-strewn divans with towels and cigarettes, lubricants and drinks laid out in liberal profusion, and the mirrored shower room next door—both had been centers of activity and there had been constant traffic between them. He had witnessed scenes that he had found beautiful as well as some that made him want to avert his eyes, which wasn't always easy because of the mirrors. He had been surrounded by vistas of naked writhing young males, multiplied to infinity.

He had been looking forward to telling his mother about his first gay party but he wondered now how much he could tell her. That wasn't good. He didn't want to have secrets from her. He hadn't broken his promise. He had flaunted himself but nobody could consider that secret gathering "public." He had flaunted himself at the beginning, with Leslie as a partner, to excited applause. In that experienced and shameless gathering, it was thrilling to discover that he could provide a new thrill. Could he tell her that he had made love in one way or another with six other boys? They had all wanted him. Leslie had known how to keep off the ones he didn't like. Thinking of telling her about it gave him an erection.

Leslie dropped a hand onto his lap and found it and laughed. "You're impossible. After all that, you're still ready to go. Everybody was amazed by the way you can keep it up. Get it out so I can hold it." Gerry did so. Leslie caressed it gently. "It's come home to mother. You enjoyed it, didn't you, darling?"

"Yes. Doing it with people watching is exciting. Why is that?"

"You're a natural-born performer, darling. The smell of the greasepaint, the roar of the crowd."

"Maybe so. I know now how much you like to be fucked. I was amazed."

"I like it both ways. I told you that. You weren't jealous, were you?"

"No. I'll never want to do it that way so I don't care who fucks you so long as you go on wanting to fuck me. Jealousy is silly." After tonight, he didn't think he'd ever be jealous. His cock was supreme, a phenomenon even to guys who'd seen hundreds of them, a supreme embodiment of the masculinity he worshiped. It was intoxicating to display it for everybody's wonder and envy. The thought of its being confined or concealed made it shrink.

"I guess nobody's jealous if they're not in love," Leslie said. "That's why I hope it doesn't happen to me, not even with you. Not yet, anyway. I'd like to go on being a loose lady for a while."

"I don't know much about it yet. Is there a big difference between the way we are and being in love?"

"Not as much as I'd like, as far as I'm concerned. Shall I tell you I'm in love with you, honey? I will if you promise not to believe me."

"Sure. Let's tell each other we've fallen madly in love with each other and see what happens."

"We can be in love until Edgar's next party. He says he's having another crowd out from New York soon. OK, sweetheart. I'm—oh Christ." He swerved the car over to the side of the road and brought it to a jolting halt. He sat with his head bowed over the wheel in the sudden silence. Startled, Gerry leaned in close to him with a hand on his shoulder.

"What is it? Are you all right, darling?"

"No. Your butch sister's finally gone around the bend. I can't joke about it. I *am* in love with you."

"What *is* this?" Gerry drew back with uncertain laughter. "You made me promise not to believe you."

"Well, don't believe me, but it's true." Leslie turned to Gerry and gathered him fiercely into his arms and plunged his tongue into his mouth. His hands worked on his clothes until all of Gerry's body was exposed.

Cries of pleasure choked in Gerry's throat. His heart sprang up and pounded in tune to his lover's passion. Leslie's hands on him made him feel as if he belonged to him. Briefly, Benjie had made him feel as if he belonged to him. One or two others, too. There was apparently something in him that made it easy to feel as if he belonged to a lover who seemed determined to have him. Leslie drew back. His cheeks were damp with tears but he was laughing. "Do you feel it, honey? Do you believe me now? I want all of you for myself—this wild cock, your pretty ass, your sweet girl's face. It's all mine. I want to take you home and make you forget anybody else has ever had you."

"Maybe it's the same for me but I don't see what we can do about it," Gerry said soothingly.

"No. It's nuts. School, for God's sake. I didn't want it to happen. You're not ready for just one guy. Why should you be? I haven't been until right now. I thought tonight would fix it but I was wrong. I was going crazy with jealousy. I kept busy so I'd get over it but it didn't work. We can't go through another evening like that."

"Not if you don't want it," Gerry said dutifully. He was prepared for the prohibitions that apparently accompanied declarations of love. Ned. Leslie. Perhaps lots of boys would fall in love with him. The possibility was just beginning to figure in his thoughts of the future. He wished something would happen to him that would make him feel sure that he knew what it meant. "We're so wonderful together," he sighed, moving Leslie's hands over his nakedness.

"You feel it too, honey?"

"Of course. Being with those others made me want you even more." If nothing else, he felt as if he were learning how to handle love in others. "We can do anything as long as we're together."

"I don't think it works like that, darling. We'll see. I want us to be just for each other."

"That's just it. I don't know what'll become of me when we have to be apart. That's what scares me. You've got to help me not to get too dependent on you. I already feel as if I'll go out of my mind without you."

"My own baby. I'll be with you, thinking about you all the time. We're married, remember."

Gerry's birthday finally arrived two days later. The red Thunderbird he had more or less expected was waiting in the drive. He and Leslie whooped with joy over it and made plans for him to take the test for his driver's license the next day. He found the party for him that evening very boring. He wished Ned had come back for it. There was a marquee set up on the lawn and a band, but he wasn't even interested in flirting with the attractive boys. After his experiences at Edgar's, and with Leslie as a constant bed companion, the little sexual adventures that a few weeks earlier had provided the excitement at the parties now seemed childish. He felt much older than the sixteen years the party was celebrating. It wasn't until late in the evening, as he became aware that a charming blond youth who had been brought by friends was pursuing him, that things began to get interesting. It took only the exchange of a few glances to tell them that they both knew what they were after. Suddenly, everywhere Gerry turned, Nicky was beside him.

"Is there any chance of our getting together?" the newcomer asked quietly.

"You've met Leslie, haven't you? He's staying with me."

"So I understand. I guess I better go."

"Why?" Gerry interjected hastily. "Don't you think he's attractive?"

"Lord, yes. I just—oh, I see. Both of you? I don't know. I want you. I guess I can try anything once."

"You'll stay? I want you to."

"I'll make myself scarce until everybody's gone. Whatever we do, I'll count on ending up with you."

"I'll say." Gerry's arm was squeezed deliciously and Nicky left him. His heart was racing with anticipation. He was sure Leslie wouldn't object. They hadn't talked any more about their being only for each other and, anyway, sharing one boy was different from being handled indiscriminately by a crowd. He looked for him and drew him aside and broke the news. "He wanted me to go off alone with him but I wouldn't. I said we were together."

Only a faint cloud crossed Leslie's merry face. "Count your blessings," he said with his customary little swagger. "What about having you all for myself, honey? Never mind. It's your birthday. He'll be my birthday present to you. You sure know how to pick 'em." The way he swayed forward and laughed into his face made it clear that he'd had a lot to drink.

The last guests had departed and Gerry had a bleak moment wondering if he had lost Nicky when the boy appeared around the corner of the marquee. Leslie welcomed him effusively. Nicky's first move was for Gerry; he put his arm around his waist and hugged him.

"Shall we stay down here?" Gerry asked Leslie, beginning to feel as if he belonged to this fascinating stranger.

"Definitely. It offers scope. The theater of the absurd."

They went down to the pool where Nicky unveiled a body as breathtaking as Ned's. Leslie interposed himself more effectively than ever between Gerry and his conquest, monopolizing him with his practiced wiles. Nicky was visibly spellbound by their almost equal majesties but Leslie thrust his to the fore as if he were the champion. Gerry discovered what jealousy was like; it made him angry, so angry that he decided to fall in love with Nicky. He let Nicky give him a quick orgasm with his mouth and withdrew from the contest. Damn both of them. He washed and dived into the pool, trying to shut out the yelps of pleasure issuing from the couple entangled on a chaise longue. Perhaps there was some point in fidelity; it was awful knowing that two guys who supposedly wanted him could enjoy themselves so much without him.

He hadn't been swimming long when Nicky's thrilling body knifed into the water toward him and his spirits lifted. He came up beside him with his fair hair plastered to his skull. It accentuated all the planes and hollows of his charming face. His lips were parted in a gentle smile. "He's asleep," he reported. "Passed out cold is more like it. I didn't think a threesome would work. I went along so we could finish with it and I could be with you."

"You seemed pretty happy with him." They kicked themselves to the side of the pool and held on while their bodies drifted in against each other.

"He's great but you—you're absolutely devastating. There's something about your being so young and knowing. I've never fallen in love but I'm feeling something very strange with you."

Another. The unique experience of a lifetime could apparently be his for the asking practically every day. He let himself drift closer and took Nicky's hand and placed it on his revived erection. "I've been waiting for you."

"God. It's fantastic. I have to leave today. It's probably just as well. I don't want to make a complete idiot of myself."

"How could you? I've never been in love either—almost with somebody a lot like you. Maybe it'll really be you. You've got to come back after Leslie goes. I'll have a couple more weeks before school."

"We'll work something out. We have to."

Having triumphed over Leslie, he forgave him. He put his hands on broad shoulders and an arm encircled him and drew him close and their lips met and opened. They exchanged a long exploratory kiss, in which tenderness vied with hunger. They drew apart slowly, breathing rapidly.

They swam swiftly to the end of the pool and climbed out and skirted Leslie's slumbering form and devoted themselves to a thorough discovery of each other on the big sofa at the back of the pavilion. In Nicky's possession of him Gerry felt a fervor and intensity that was new to him, like Ned but with more authority. Perhaps it had something to do with emotional maturity. Responding to it made him feel mature. The evening was turning out to be a big advance in his erotic education.

"It's so tremendous," Nicky murmured. "I'll write you

and try to tell you. It's something in you—something fresh and unspoiled and giving. God, the way you make love. I feel as if I could never get enough of you."

They continued to make love with word and deed until the sky was paling. In the half-light, after Gerry had devoured it with a thousand kisses, Nicky's face was the most fascinating he had ever seen, surfeited and defenseless with love. They relinquished each other with an effort and Gerry walked him up to his car in the still dawn. They exchanged a final lingering kiss when Nicky was behind the wheel, after having agreed that he would come back for a weekend. As he waved him off down the drive, Gerry's heart sang with the birds that were beginning to herald the new day. He was in love with Nicky. He was in love again with Leslie. He was in love with all the beautiful boys who would fall in love with him. Life was too marvelous to be true.

Leslie's stay, which at the beginning had seemed like an endless block of time, suddenly began to rush to its conclusion. He had Nicky to look forward to but Gerry was seized with panic when he let himself think of the days ahead without his guide and protector.

The promised letter arrived and he was amazed that he could inspire such sentiments in a boy as coolly elegant as Nicky. It made him almost ashamed of his simple lust for Nicky's body. He considered showing the letter to Leslie but decided it was too personal to share. He had learned that it was advisable to keep lovers out of each other's sight.

He and Leslie made love without sleeping throughout their last night and grew tearful occasionally and Gerry gave him all the cash he had on hand in the morning, a little over twenty dollars.

"This'll go into my special fund, for a love nest," Leslie promised. "I'm going to find someplace decent where you can stay with me over Christmas, even if I have to get a regular job to do it. We don't have to promise not to have sex with anybody else, baby, but I can't imagine wanting anybody without sharing with my little sister. Don't let it stop growing, lover honey. A foot long, remember. I'll expect to see big progress when we have our night on your way through town."

He was gone. Gerry went down to the pool and stripped, expecting his mother to join him. She had always insisted that the kids should keep themselves covered up till the moment of diving in but the regulation seemed rather pointless after what she had seen. It was cooler since the last thunderstorms; there might not be many more opportunities for them to be here together. Now that Leslie was gone, he felt a void that he sensed his mother could somehow fill. Without understanding it, he knew that something had happened between them that he wanted to enlarge and incorporate into their lives. Thinking about her finding him here naked aroused him and the memory of her hand straying on him brought him to complete erection.

He went to the edge of the pool and stood, prepared to dive, and looked down at himself with satisfaction. He had been sunbathing without his trunks and he was evenly tanned all over. He thought he heard somebody at the gate and dived in. When he came up she was there.

They waved to each other and she settled into a chaise longue and put on her spectacles and opened a book. He waited to find out what effect her presence would have on him. The thought of showing it consolidated his erection until it ached. He swam to the steps nearest her and climbed out.

She looked up over her book. "My word," she said with no change of expression.

"Is there any reason I shouldn't let you see me this way?" he asked. He looked at her without moving, briefly daunted by his boldness.

"I can't think of any, darling. Some people might find it indecent, but I think you're rather superb. Do you know why it's like that?"

"I'm not sure. Probably the idea of letting you see it again." He approached her and picked up the towel at the foot of the chaise longue and began to dry off, moving his body so that she would see it from various angles.

"So that's it." She removed her spectacles and closed her book. "Well, if I don't like it, I have only myself to blame, haven't I? Actually, I find it quite thrilling. It makes me feel young. I think I told you, it reminds me of someone I knew once. I'm really rather glad you're not interested in women. It might be quite difficult to resist."

"Leslie's going to try to come back next weekend. Can he be naked down here with you?"

"What an extraordinary suggestion." Girlish laughter

burst from her. "I've seen just about all of him there is to see. I don't suppose a bit of cloth makes much difference. But, darling, don't you think we should talk about things?"

"I want to," he burst out in a rush of enthusiasm. "It's been wonderful having him here and your being so sweet to us and knowing we were lovers and everything. That's what I mean. I want it like that with you, not caring if you see how we feel about each other. I didn't want to tell you about Nicky Chalmers while Leslie was here. Did you notice him with the Edgertons at my birthday party? He's in love with me. He's coming to stay for a weekend as soon as you give the OK. None of this could happen if it hadn't been for what you did that morning."

"Very well, darling. Let's go back to that." She hitched herself up in the chair and tucked her legs under her and arranged her beach robe around her. Nothing could ruffle her impeccable chic. She lifted a hand to him and drew him down so that he sat facing her, one foot on the ground, the other leg doubled under him, his erection lifted between them. She laid her hand on it and stroked it slowly. "Yes, let's begin with this."

He closed his eyes and choked back a sob as he was flooded with an ineffable contentment. It was happening again. She belonged to him forever. "Oh God," he gasped. "It feels so wonderful when you do that. I've been wanting you to. I'm almost coming."

"Do you want to?"

"Yes, but not yet. I want it to stay like this. It feels so good."

"I think we must be very careful not to get into a tangle about this, darling." She spoke with an uncharacteristically gentle note in her voice. "I've always had this idea stuck away in the back of my mind about how fascinating a son would be as a lover. There's nothing very original about it. It goes back to the beginning of time, just as homosexuality may have to do with some hermaphroditic folk memory about when we were one, male and female combined. I'm really a very conventional woman. The thought could never be father to the deed. I'm quite stunned at my allowing myself this much with you. It's heavenly knowing that your nature could never let it lead to more. I don't completely understand why you're so ready to show me yourself in the full glory of your manhood. Perhaps there's some little urge in you to seek feminine contact. If it's that, let's encourage it. I suspect that you're a very vicious boy, darling. I'd like to help you find releases that won't hurt you. Watching you with Leslie has convinced me that your love of boys is much more than just a phase."

Her hand was doing what he wanted it to do, holding him exquisitely on the brink of orgasm. "You've accepted me the way I am, Mum. That's what's so wonderful."

"Up to a point. You're surely aware that Leslie is very effeminate. You've picked up a lot of his mannerisms. Do you want to be effeminate too?"

"I wouldn't mind being like him. Everybody loves him."

"He's an actor and clever and bright and makes people laugh. They think it's an act. You're a different type. When you let yourself be girlish, you're very, very girlish. It's odd when this is so gloriously virile. There's something else. I haven't wanted to mention it while you were so happy with Leslie. Have you heard any rumors? Ned tried to kill himself."

"He what?" Gerry seized her hand and held it motionless on himself.

"Unsuccessfully, fortunately. That's why he went away. He actually wrote a note that they found while they were bringing him around. There was apparently nothing very conclusive in it. If he did it because he was unhappy in love, he's too silly to think about. The first thing we all have to learn is how to cope with normal emotional upsets. The tragedy is that he might've done it because of what he was finding out about himself. With you. When I think about it, I realize that the truly great blessing is that you've simply refused to be tormented about yourself. It's very courageous of you, darling."

He let his hand fall away but left a finger pointing at himself. "He may have done it because of this, Mum. I wasn't his first but he'd never paid much attention to this part of a boy before. He thought the way he'd fooled around was normal. I think he was shocked to discover how much this really meant to him. It's awfully big. I've been with enough boys to know that now. Lots of them say it's the biggest they've ever seen."

"I've only seen five or six men in my entire life, darling, so I'm no judge, but it's difficult to imagine anything much bigger. I gather it's rather a special attraction for boys like you, more so than for girls, although I think most women would be excited by it, if rather alarmed. If you're going to be—what do you and Leslie call yourselves? Gay? Since you're gay, I'm glad you're so well equipped to attract the boys you want. I'll never knowingly do anything to undermine your happy adjustment to yourself but I think you can afford to steer a very careful course between what you are and what you let the world see. For your sake, I don't want you and Leslie playing around naked together in front of me. It's going too far and you don't need that sort of encouragement. There's another reason. I haven't been entirely truthful with you but I will be now. I don't have to hedge what I say the way I would with a normal boy. Grotesquely enough, the funny idea that's been in the back of my mind all these years has finally borne fruit. I love you physically. If you wanted me, I might have let you have me."

Delivered in her cool cultivated tones, it took a moment for the words to ricochet through him, setting up a riot of responses—fear, ecstasy, repugnance, incredulity, joy. He planted his hands behind him and dropped back on the support of his arms and eased his hips up toward her. "Oh God, take me, Mum." His voice came out as a hoarse supplication. "For God's sake, take me." He felt her mouth on him and he uttered a strange shout of terror and triumph.

Leslie wasn't able to come back for the weekend because of auditions, so Nicky came instead. His mother pronounced him "a real gentleman" but didn't warm to him as she had to Leslie. He was reserved and very guarded about his inclinations in public. His visit brought the summer to an end with passonate declarations of love.

At school, Gerry set about making life tolerable by seducing quite a few of the more seductive seniors and organizing an enjoyable vice ring. His own classmates were beneath his notice except for one young beauty who spurned him. Perhaps they all would ripen in a year.

He wrote Leslie everything, and his mother quite a lot. Thoughts of her were with him constantly, comforting and yet somehow tinged with terror. His mother had made love to him. When he forced himself to put it into plain words, it turned him to ice. His hands and feet went numb. He felt as if he would never have an erection again. He learned to disguise it in his mind as "something special," the "funny thing" that had happened between them. It had happened only once but he had let her see him with an erection several times in the last days before school. He was driven to commit her fully.

"Let me say another word about this, darling," she had said one day at the pool when he was drying himself in front of her, "and that will end it. I've made love to your manhood but somehow I've been able to go on thinking of you as my baby. Now that you're going away, that'll change. When I see you again, you'll have become a man, a man who wants men. You know you can count on my sympathy and understanding, if a woman of my generation *can* fully understand, but fortunately it'll change the way I feel about your body. My love won't change. You know that, darling."

No matter what she said, it had happened. It absolved him of all guilt. There was nothing he could do that she could condemn. Perhaps that was what he found terrifying. The abhorrence he felt at the thought of her wanting more of him convinced him that whatever faint chance there had been of his being attracted to a girl was gone forever.

With his mother's connivance—she couldn't refuse him —he was allowed out of school for a number of weekends, which he spent with Nicky in a nearby town. Nicky introduced odd little quirks into their lovemaking, including binding his wrists and undressing him slowly, but his tenderness could still bring tears to Gerry's eyes.

As Christmas approached, he was reduced to praying for something to happen that would extricate him from the dilemma of having promised to spend the holidays with both Leslie and Nicky. In November Leslie got a job that would take him out of town and for a few weeks it looked as if the problem had solved itself, but the show folded and Leslie was back in New York, writing about the apartment he had found for them. Gerry was at least able to tell his mother that he wouldn't be spending much time at home.

His first few days back in the city were spent juggling dates and lovers and inventing stories about family obligations. The stylish apartment Leslie had found on Beekman Place was borrowed, so Gerry was spared the guilt of having caused him to waste his hard-earned money. It never occurred to him to make a break with either of them; they were both in love with him.

He never found out where he had slipped up. Leaving Leslie to meet Nicky at his place late one afternoon, he was confronted with disaster. Without any waste of words, violence finally erupted. Nicky beat him and tore his clothes off and bound his hands and feet with strips of his tattered shirt and took him mercilessly while he struck and cursed him. The thought crossed Gerry's mind that perhaps he hadn't been caught in a deception but that this was what Nicky had wanted all along. It was strangely exciting and he might have accepted further developments along the same lines, but Nicky ended by throwing him out in his ripped and ruined clothes.

He had no choice but to return to Leslie and confess, to explain his bruises and black eye and the condition of his clothes. Leslie seemed to forgive him. Gerry wept with genuine misery and swore not to let anything ever come between them again. The immediate effect was to simplify his life enormously, but he was soon suffering a real sense of loss. He had cherished Nicky's love. He wondered when he would again find somebody who would love him with Nicky's passionate intensity. He longed for his body and the small exciting perversities that had become a part of their lovemaking and the sense he had given him of acquiring insights into the complexities of adult emotion. Meanwhile, he didn't want to miss any of the fun and, with Leslie's guidance, he discovered the gay city he intended to inhabit.

When they were reunited for the Easter holiday, he found that Leslie was drinking so much that many evenings ended with Gerry sitting alone with an unconscious body. When he remonstrated, Leslie seemed inclined to throw him to the wolves, as Benjie had once expressed it. Multiple sex, or gang bangs, became their way of life, with Leslie not always a very active participant. They remained devoted companions but love had somehow been diluted beyond revival. Among the army of hungry youths he found no one to fill the emotional vacuum, but three grown men had fallen in love with him in little more than the same number of weeks so he expected somebody would come along soon. In any case, he concluded sensibly,

New York wasn't as conducive to romance as the soft summer nights of Long Island and it would take a very romantic atmosphere to make anybody get really serious about him until he had finished school.

In his final year, he was reluctantly obliged to accept the fact that His Majesty had stopped growing without having attained his goal, and he sent out the melancholy announcement to a host of devoted subjects.

He was expelled from college in his freshman year as the best way out of a nasty situation. He had picked up a handsome town boy, in violation of his promise to his mother, but it hadn't been the boy who had made the trouble. A door was left carelessly unlocked. Irate parents, intent on revenge or recompense, took the matter to the college authorities. Expulsion silenced them and left them no grounds for further action. His mother covered for him at home, as he knew she would, so it caused no major drama in the family.

At loose ends for the rest of the school year, he had a chance encounter with his mother's old friend, the celebrated Walter Makin, when he was out on the town with Leslie and some friends, and decided quite irrationally that he had met his fate. Walter was obviously interested in him and having no other points of reference, Gerry assumed that it must be sexual. It turned out that Walter was bent on reforming him, for reasons he couldn't fathom. It gave him the opening he wanted; he promised to do anything requested of him if they became lovers. Despite his reputation as a model family man, underlined by the fact that he had just been named by somebody as the Father of the Year, Walter took him in a way that made it clear that such pleasures weren't unknown to him. Like Leslie, Gerry was enraptured to discover a majesty greater than his own. Knowing of their old friendship, he wondered if this was the one his mother had compared him to. He was ruled by an exclusive love at last. He told her about it, of course, but for once she didn't seem to want to hear. She simply warned him with unusual severity not to get involved with older married men.

Walter, too, was severe with him, treating him like a recalcitrant child, and he backed out of the relationship as soon as Gerry gave signs of paying attention to his teachings, which boiled down to being a man among men regardless of sexual inclinations and saving one's body for those who had more to offer than a night's titillation.

Later, he came to feel that Walter had somehow broken his spirit. He had weaned him away from many of the habits he had picked up with Leslie (the makeup, the camp jargon, the assumption of a totally feminine personality known as Geraldine) while withholding the love that might have made the reformation worthwhile. He hadn't developed any talents or any dominating interests pointing to a particular career. He thought he'd probably enjoy being a decorator because he had a lot of gay friends who were decorators. He and his mother agreed that there wasn't much point in his going on with college and decided to spend a while in Europe, where he could take some courses in the decorative arts.

In Paris, he met a young film star (blond) called Alain Lescaves and they fell obsessively in love with each other. He tried to remember Walter's words about the importance of love, even homosexual love, but Alain hadn't had the benefit of Walter's teachings and they both had many admirers. Their relationship was stormy. A contract with Hollywood was in the air and Gerry's lover was determined that he should go with him, but this would have meant leaving his mother who had set them up in a comfortable furnished apartment in the Avenue Henri-Martin. Gerry was skeptical of the contract in terms of the young star's professional future. They quarreled over it. Their parting was violent and destructive but his mother was there to help him through it.

Back in New York, he found quite a good job in an important decorating firm and at twenty-one embarked on his adult life. Walter's influence had dimmed and flaunting himself became routine. There were frequent parties at which His Majesty was the star attraction. It was great having a big one but nobody was much interested in anything else about him.

He was plagued by a sense of opportunities missed. Ned, Leslie, Nicky, Walter, Alain, the dazzling life that had seemed to be opening up before him five years earlier —none of the promises had been fulfilled. When he thought of happiness it conjured up glimpses of a past beyond recall. Nothing seemed much fun anymore. He felt useless. Only his mother remained constant and he cherished and adored her. Whenever his vague longings became so acute that he felt he had to do something about his life or go mad, take any action no matter how ruinous so long as it offered change, she was always there to restore his confidence in himself and the way things were.

He had been doing well at his job for about two years when he fell peacefully in love, or believed he had, with a nice young man who was a few years older and worked in Wall Street. They set up housekeeping together and soon his mother was including Richard in all the family events. He had apparently settled into placid domesticity and it lasted much longer than he had expected, almost six years. When he was caught once too often in one of his numerous infidelities, the parting was painless. Thinking of the storms of his Paris passion, he wished he could at least shed a tear.

He drifted to San Francisco for a better job. A useless life, but on the whole harmless. In San Francisco, Walter came back briefly into his life, bringing with him, fatally, Tom. His persistent triviality killed Tom.

It wasn't any wonder that he credited his five years of wandering in the East with his new recognition of the importance of enduring values and a new strength of character that made him feel almost worthy of being Walter's son. There had been so little there when he had set out.

He awoke slowly, trying to remember where he was. He didn't panic when the answer continued to elude him; the bed was unusually comfortable and smelled unusually clean. There was no one in it with him; Jack was away again. As soon as he remembered the train from Chiang Mai, the rest immediately fell into place—Bangkok, the von Hallers, the huge excitement of Ernst and his abrupt abandonment, his first girl. Sober and rested, he didn't find it surprising that he'd been left in the hall. He had expected to take Ernst as he had taken or been taken by all the others in the past—the acknowledgment of mutual attraction and the straightforward arrangements to satisfy it. He had failed to take protocol into consideration. He laughed out loud as he untangled himself from his sleeping position and rolled over, lifting his morning erection with one hand to bring it comfortably with him. He lay out flat on his back and remembered his resolve to tackle Ernst head-on. Solange thought he should put on a show of independence and play hard to get. Which would it be?

He grabbed one of the down pillows beside him and threw it into the air and let it land on his face. He lay smiling into it. Just thinking of Ernst existing nearby exhilarated him. Saying his name to himself filled him with curiosity and lust and a sense of challenge. As it progressed, he remembered, the evening had seemed full of storm and stress but now it possessed in his memory a marvelous clarity. He must have been fairly drunk. Quite clearly, he had been struck by thunder, as the French put it. He was nuts about the guy. The problems were nothing compared to what they might have been—lack of time and money were usually the big enemies. He had established himself in the household through the Princess. Thinking of her fondly, he almost wished she were here. The von Hallers' stud. Every court needed one.

He pushed the pillow aside. He was bursting with anticipation of the day, although his watch told him that quite a lot of it was gone; it was almost noon. Ernst would be getting ready for his lunch or had already gone. They wouldn't see each other till evening. As far as he could remember, they hadn't even made a date for then, though Ernst probably took it for granted. He wanted him to take it for granted but would try to remember Solange's counsel if he took too much for granted.

He pressed a button beside the bed. He must remember to arrange for money to be wired from New York. They could probably take care of it downstairs. He had more fittings in the late afternoon. The rest of the time he would spend beside the pool. Waiting. In a moment, Lee came trotting in and he greeted him and ordered breakfast. He watched him go, wondering how he could have considered playing around with him even for a moment. He was after big game.

He threw the covers off and sprang out of bed and went to the bathroom. He put on his new dressing gown and admired the way it emphasized his tan, but there was a limit to his admiration for himself. He had thought he would be wearing it for Ernst by now.

He found Lee in the sitting room laying out his breakfast. Two orchids and a white hibiscus decorated the tray. Life here was wonderfully soft and beguiling, meant to be shared by lovers. Who needed orchids if you were alone? He made a mental note to get some books. He rang for Lee again and asked him to bring up whatever new French and English and American magazines he could find. He returned with a glossy pile of periodicals.

"I bring laundry, sir. You no forget massage?"

"No. This afternoon maybe." Maybe Lee would get him yet.

When he was ready to go, he put his trunks on under the dressing gown and stuck the hibiscus over his ear and picked up a couple of magazines and his key and took the stairs down to the garden. The sun was blazing, striking reflections from the glossy temple trees. There weren't many people at the pool. He glanced over at the restaurant pavilion and saw that it was filling up for lunch. He found an isolated deckchair and an attendant brought him a towel. He ordered a beer from one of the pretty, crisp little waiters and dropped his dressing gown and settled down to freshen up his tan. A shadow fell across him and he glanced up, expecting his beer. It was the pale-haired young beauty, wearing brief trunks and trailing a towel.

"Hello. I'm André. Remember?" he said with a tentative smile. "We met last night."

The explanation was so superfluous that it made Gerry laugh. He sprang up, still rather daunted by the youth's perfection, and shook his hand, French fashion. "I seem to remember your ugly face from somewhere. How come you're not having lunch with Ernst?"

"I was going to ask you the same thing."

"I wasn't invited."

"Neither was I." They laughed and their eyes met for an instant. The boy's beauty struck Gerry like a thousand hands caressing him everywhere. He had assumed that the beautiful head was attached to a body, but in simple justice it might have been deformed. It wasn't. It was lovely, slim and graceful and beautifully proportioned with the fine modeling of breeding. He made a quick check of the brief trunks. Everything in proportion. Nothing grossly conspicuous.

"So much the better for us," he said. "I don't like dressy official lunches."

"Yes, but—I mean, I should think you'd do everything together. Aren't you in love with each other?" It came out with forced bravado and he blushed while his eyes flew about for somewhere to land.

Gerry laughed. "Ah. That's the big question. We just met yesterday. I don't think you can be sure that quickly."

"I can be. I—" He blushed again. He was full of stops and starts. This wasn't the spoiled beauty he had been prepared to flee but a sweet shy kid, just as Solange had said. Was she right about the rest of it or had she been exaggerating to deflect him from his preoccupation with Ernst, as had seemed to be her purpose at first? He had no intention of pursuing the boy but if he were pursued, he doubted if he would be very hard to catch. Why should he be? Ernst had given him every reason to take what he could get. If Solange could be trusted, a little fling with André might stir Ernst's interest. There was no question in his mind about his priorities.

"You what?" he asked encouragingly.

"I just—uh. I don't know. Is this your beer?"

Gerry turned and found the waiter beside him. "Oh yes. Thanks. Do you want something?"

"Could I have a beer too?"

"Of course." He ordered it. "Where're you sitting? Why don't you pull a chair over here?"

"You don't mind?"

"Far from it. I've been feeling lonely."

"I'll get my suntan lotion. That flower looks wonderful in your hair."

"What?" Gerry had forgotten the hibiscus. He reached up and found it and pulled it out and looked at it and put it back. "I've gone native. Be careful not to get burned. This sun is fierce." André's skin was pale with only the beginning of a tan. He found it difficult not to touch him.

"Your color is magnificent. I'll be right back." He turned and Gerry's eyes fell on a bottom that was enough to make strong men weep, twin globes of exquisitely compact flesh. He sat and took a long swallow of beer. He had enough on his hands without being distracted by the most beautiful boy in the world. There was a dreaming poetry in his face that was uniquely unsettling.

A flurry of activity announced his return. An attendant placed another deck chair beside him, the beer arrived, and André himself, carrying a toweling robe and the suntan lotion. Gerry told himself that he didn't have to look at him. Yesterday, if he had found himself practically naked with the boy, he would have leaped on him. An indication of how far his commitment to Ernst had progressed.

"Tell me about yourself," he said. "Have you known Ernst for long?"

"Quite long. Almost two years. Did you—I mean, you're lovers, aren't you?" There was the forced note of bravado again. André was obviously trying to overcome his shyness. Preparing to pursue? Gerry could at least give him fair warning.

"Not yet. I hope we will be soon."

"It certainly looked so last night. I hoped the same thing when Maria introduced me to him."

"Maria Horrocks? Who *is* Maria?"

"She's some sort of relative of mine. My mother hates her. She says she's wicked but that's because she introduced me to Ernst. My mother thinks he corrupted me. I can't make her understand that I was with boys long before that." He spoke with no accent except the impartial mix of English and American characteristic of bilingual Europeans. Only an occasional awkwardness of phrasing indicated that he wasn't speaking his native tongue.

"*Were* you lovers?"

"Ernst and I? Not really."

"How do you mean?"

"Can I tell you? I mean, can I say private things? I don't want to shock you."

Gerry laughed. "I doubt if you could. You can say anything you like. I don't want to know any secrets."

"No, not secrets. Just a little private. I've been naked in bed with him but he didn't want to do anything, just look and touch. It was strange. I didn't make him get all the way hard. We didn't have orgasms so I don't think it counts as being lovers, do you?"

"It doesn't sound so. That happens sometimes but I shouldn't think it would often with you."

"I've been with ten boys, always the same way. Ernst wants it the way I do. I think that was the trouble. Do you understand?"

"I think so. That happens, too. At least you stayed friends."

"Oh yes. Do you imagine everybody will share cabins on the yacht?"

"What yacht?"

"Ernst's yacht. The yacht we're all leaving on tomorrow or the next day."

"You're all leaving tomorrow or the next day? *Ernst?* This is the first I've heard of it. For how long?" Gerry turned his head to look at him, waiting for him to say something that would make sense of it. A day cruise on the river?

"For months. We're going—" He stopped short and turned to Gerry and his great green eyes widened and filled with dismay. "I think I've made the most frightful *faux pas*. Ernst is probably keeping it a secret to surprise you."

Gerry sat forward. "You'd better tell me more."

"Yes, but don't tell anybody I told you." André sat up and they leaned toward each other against the arms of their chairs. "I know you're expected. That's why we're all here. We're going to Penang on Friday. That's where the yacht's waiting. I think we're going to Goa first and then fly to Kashmir and pick up the yacht again in the Mediterranean. We're going to be together for months."

Gerry was so fascinated by the lips forming words that he found it difficult to listen. He had to try to put it together. He remembered Ernst making a remark about a yacht in Penang. He'd said something inexplicable last night about their being together constantly for a month. André might be right but how could you know where you stood with a guy who was high all the time? Was Ernst waiting till the last minute to make sure he was worthy of an invitation? Fuck Ernst. He shook his head and sat back. "You don't understand. I'm not part of your group. I turned up yesterday by accident. There might not be room for me." Ernst would make room of course, but he was growing increasingly indignant at not having been consulted. Ernst was treating him the way he said he was accustomed to treating all his lovers—like paid attendants.

"But I know they're expecting you," André insisted. "I asked Maria. Well, naturally. It was the only thing I could think of as soon as I knew I'd fallen in love with you."

Gerry stared. "You did what?"

"I—in love with you. The minute I saw you." André was blushing furiously and his mouth was working, but his great eyes, fringed with the incredible lashes, gazed unflinchingly at him, limpid with what Gerry recognized now as adoration.

"Oh for God's sake," he muttered. This vision was his for the taking? The mouth alone, lips parted while he searched for words, was enough to unhinge him. He didn't know what was holding him in the chair. He wanted to leap up and take him in his arms. His trunks were suddenly much too small.

"I thought you must know," André finally managed. "That's what I was trying to tell you. You don't have to worry. I don't expect much of love, do you?"

"Yes, I guess I do. God knows why." Gerry slowly pulled himself forward again and leaned against the arm of the chair and exposed himself to the full blaze of adoration in the glorious eyes.

"But it's so unlikely that it could ever happen right." André had found his tongue. "How can I hope that somebody will fall in love with me at the same time I fall in love with him? I suppose it happens sometimes but the odds are all against it. I *had* to go after you. I realized that if I didn't I'd never have anybody I want. I've never done it and I don't know how, but I had to try. When Maria said you couldn't be included in the lunch, I said I wasn't feeling well. I've been waiting and hoping for you." André shifted around once more toward him and gripped the arm of the chair with both hands.

"You *were* invited." Almost without knowing it, Gerry adopted André's position. They had only to straighten their fingers to touch.

"Yes. I had to see you. I don't expect anything with you. Honestly. It's obvious what's happened with you and Ernst. I just had to tell you. I called you last night after we got back to the hotel, on the chance that you wouldn't be with him. I'd drunk quite a lot of wine. It made me brave. I wanted to call you this morning but I didn't dare."

"I almost followed you in the hall last night." Gerry watched all the beauty of the face in front of him become incandescent with youth and love. "Don't make too much of it," he added hastily. "Ernst had just ditched me. I was feeling a bit lost. I had a nightcap with Solange instead. I guess I was with her when you called. It's probably just as well." He was applying all his brakes. Fidelity hardly entered into it yet, if, judging from Ernst, it ever would.

He could accept an offer of dancing boys. He could get the most beautiful boy in the world on his own. So be it, but it didn't seem fair to take advantage of young untried passion when all his thoughts and feelings were directed toward a man he wanted to make a part of his life. Was there anything to spare for this angel? He looked at him, his body tensed and straining toward him, and was deeply moved. He wanted to hold him and tell him that he mustn't fall in love so devastatingly until he'd had time to find out if it could lead to anything. He was so amazingly modest, as if he hadn't looked at himself in the mirror.

"What will you do if you don't go on the cruise?" André asked apprehensively.

"Oh, I'll probably go—assuming you're right and I'm invited—but I won't go quietly. It all depends on how he puts it to me."

André's face lighted up again. "Then everything's all right. That's why I asked Maria right away. I didn't see how I could go if you didn't. I would've stayed with you if you'd let me. What about sharing a cabin? Ernst might put you in his but he usually doesn't. I mean, he doesn't let anybody spend the night with him. If you have to share with anybody, I hope it'll be me. I don't mean that the way it might sound. I mean—not, uh—well, you know—not sex or anything." The charming blushes suffused his face once more. "I'd just like to be with you as much as possible since we're going to be together for the next month or two anyway."

"That's nice, baby. Let's see how it works out. I might have a word to say about who Ernst spends the night with. Tell me about yourself. I said that hours ago and we've been talking about me ever since. Let's start with how old you are. Twenty? Twenty-one?"

"Almost twenty-two."

"Only thirteen or fourteen years between us. A mere trifle." He still hadn't adjusted to the fact that there were young adults in the world who could almost be his children. "You seem to have a weakness for old gentlemen. Ernst is even older."

"I can't believe you're that old. I guessed twenty-five. Ernst seems much older. Not his looks exactly, but something about him. Almost like my father. I probably need somebody older to teach me about everything."

"That sounds as if it's going to be more about me. Come on. Tell me about you." With considerable prodding, he learned that André wanted to be a painter but was training as a dress designer in one of the big Paris couture houses. He'd been given three months' leave of absence before going back for the fall collections. He'd also studied interior decoration and had no money. He was traveling as Ernst's guest, including the trip to Bangkok. Gerry's knowledge of the Paris artistic world overlapped sufficiently with his, despite the gulf of time, so that they found a great deal to talk about. They even discovered that they had some friends in common. They had more beer and became simply two people getting to know each other. Gerry began to be able to look at him without swooning. He had the feeling that André was also beginning to take his infatuation in his stride. The more they talked, the more he liked him. He would be a pleasure to be with on a cruise.

Was he going on a cruise? No matter how cool he tried to play it, he knew he'd go in a flash if invited. Everything Ernst had said last night became sheer insanity unless he was to be included in all his immediate plans. Gerry hadn't checked at the desk for messages; perhaps the invitation was already waiting for him. The thought made him restless. He wanted to find out but he didn't want to discover that there was nothing; the rest of the day would be a misery of waiting and wondering.

"Are you planning to see Ernst later?" he asked the boy at his side. André remained turned toward him, leaning forward against the arm of the chair in an obvious and endearing effort to get as close to him as the chairs allowed. Gerry could almost feel his body nestled against him.

"I don't know. There was something about a party. Are you going?"

"Listen. Everything that's happened between me and Ernst happened in a few hours yesterday. We haven't had time to make plans. I arrived out of the blue when he's obviously got a lot on his hands. I don't know anything about tonight's party or the cruise or anything else."

"Do you know a lot of other people here?"

"No."

"Well then." André's amazing eyes glowed with innocent candor. "You said you were lonely. I'd like to be with you as much as you'll let me until everything is straightened out, about the cruise and everything." His smile was melting but lighted with humor. "My illness could turn out to be lingering. I mean, we do like each other, don't we?"

"Of course, baby. How could I help liking you? You're sweet to take pity on a lonely old man, but just remember —if Ernst suddenly gives some signs of life, I'll go running."

"Oh, I understand that. Anything you do is all right with me. That must be part of being in love with you."

The boy's tranquil declarations of love rendered Gerry speechless. "Let's go for a swim," he suggested abruptly.

"I don't know how to."

"How to swim? Really? That's easy. I'll teach you." He rose.

"I told you I want you to teach me everything." André scrambled up beside him and Gerry became aware of his own height. He didn't exactly tower over the boy but he was considerably taller. For some reason, it made him want to put an arm around him and hug him, but he refrained. "I'll meet you at the shallow end." He ran off and dived in.

He shot up out of the dive and took a deep breath and swam hard to loosen himself up. Resisting the irresistible was a strain. He emerged where André was standing cautiously in water that reached to his knees.

"OK. Let's see what you can do," Gerry suggested. André lowered himself into the water and launched into a violent splashing that would have disgraced a retarded dog. Gerry burst out laughing. "Stop, for heaven's sake. You're going to drown in six inches of water." He took his hand and led him out to where the water came up to their waists. Their bodies bumped against each other as they got in deeper and Gerry was excited and touched by the hand clinging to his. "Now. We'll start with the breast stroke." Gerry demonstrated. "You see? Arms and legs together." He stood and put his hands out palms up under the water. "OK? Just lie out flat. I won't let you sink. Relax." The water floated André up against him and Gerry's hand brushed against an unmistakable erection. André's body contracted violently and he immediately sank. Gerry grabbed for him and got him to his feet, his hands freed to find out what the boy felt like. Wonderful. André spluttered and spat water and was shaken by a coughing fit. Gerry kept an arm around him and moved him toward the steps. His own erection was about to burst from his trunks. He glanced around the pool but there were only a few people left at the far end.

"I can't help it," André gasped as his coughing subsided. "Don't pay any attention. Please." He broke away and climbed out and ran to their chairs. Gerry broke into a jog and grabbed his towel and sat with it across his lap and dried his hair. André sat huddled under his towel, his head averted, breathing heavily.

"We'll have another lesson later," Gerry said in an effort to relieve the boy's embarrassment.

He lifted his head and looked at him with his unflinchingly expressive eyes. "I'm not going to be tiresome. I promise."

"You're anything but tiresome, baby. A bit too much the opposite, whatever that is. Do you go in for big lunches? How about having a bite here and then you should go in. You've had enough sun for today."

"Are you going to stay out?"

"I don't know. Do you feel like a siesta?"

"You mean, with you?"

Gerry laughed. "I said a *siesta*."

André was only mildly flustered as he reverted to a favorite topic. "Well, sure, I know. I was thinking of if we're going to share a cabin. I'm not like Ernst. I like to sleep with somebody I really like. I mean, it feels good to have someone around, don't you think?"

"Of course, but we're not sharing a cabin yet." He signaled a waiter and ordered an exotic equivalent of sandwiches while he battled with himself. Eating gave them a respite from personal contact. He thought again of the Solange Solution: drive Ernst mad with jealousy. Something in him balked. He had pinned his hopes on Ernst. If it was important to him, he should play it straight and true and be ready to take the consequences. He wanted to propitiate all the gods who governed such matters; he wanted to deserve to be a little lucky for a change. Decision reached. Calm and cool-headed. Stick to it.

When they had eaten, the waiter brought a small stack of chits and Gerry signed them all, remembering that when he settled with Smiling Sam and the hotel he'd be broke.

If André's yachting timetable was correct, there would be no time to send to New York for money. If he was left behind, he'd have to work something out with the hotel while he waited. He could afford to delay till tomorrow.

"Thank you," André said. "If you'd keep count, I could pay you at the end of the cruise."

"Don't be silly, baby. I haven't told you yet that you're the most beautiful boy in the world. It gives old gentlemen pleasure to buy you lunch." They laughed and their eyes met and became impossibly entangled. "Jesus, baby," Gerry said in an undertone. Despite his desire to possess this unique beauty, he knew that in a couple of days, a week, even a month he would be able to go on his way unscathed, which he doubted would be so with Ernst. The Baron had his hooks in him. He looked into the limitless beauty of André's eyes and saw depths upon depths of adoration. He cleared his throat and hoped that the gods were watching and were prepared to hand out fat rewards. "We'd better look out, baby," he said. "Let's stick to what you say you know. You're in love with me and I'm in love with Ernst. It may not be true but the possibility should help us make sense. If it were just a matter of being attracted to each other, we could go to bed and that would be that. I can't play around with love."

"I told you I didn't know how to go about it. I probably shouldn't have said anything about being in love but I wanted you to know. Well, it seemed only fair, especially if that's what's stopping you from taking me. I didn't expect you to want me in any case, not after seeing you with Ernst last night. I'd better go. I'm beginning to feel a little burned. What about later? Would it give an old gentleman pleasure to buy me dinner? I haven't any money." They laughed together and the emotional atmosphere cleared.

"Let's call each other. I'm going to try to get hold of Ernst in a little while. I've got some new clothes coming later. Let's see how the land lies at about seven. I don't want to keep you away from your parties."

"You know I can't think about parties until we can go to them together." Their hands touched and their eyes held for a beat longer than Gerry intended. André was shaken by a small shudder that ended with a gasp and then he gathered his robe around him and stood quickly and left, sparing Gerry another inflammatory glimpse of his behind.

Gerry lay back and relaxed at last. He was worn out with good intentions. He breathed deeply and congratulated himself on his successful struggle. Avoiding sex with people you weren't particularly interested in was nothing to pat yourself on the back about but in this case he deserved a medal. He waited until he was sure that he wasn't going to change his mind and follow the boy before he allowed himself to get up and go for another swim. He dried off in the sun and put on his dressing gown and steeled himself for the verdict of the desk.

There was nothing for him. No note. No telephone messages. This was his reward. The pleasant hours by the pool were effaced by shocked disbelief. He told himself to forget it once and for all while he was torn by anger and what felt strangely like grief. He rejected a dignified withdrawal and asked to speak to the Baron.

"We're not allowed to put a call through to him directly, sir. Do you wish to speak to his secretary?"

He went to the house phone and was told in Yorgo's smooth tones that the Baron wasn't to be disturbed until eight. "Is there anything I can do for you, sir?"

"I wanted to speak to him personally," Gerry said, trying not to sound abject. "He didn't leave any message for me?"

"He mentioned that he wanted to get in touch with you but he didn't give me any specific instructions. He's not very good about using the telephone."

"I see. Well, tell him I'll call again after eight. Tell him I won't be leaving the hotel until about nine."

"Very good, sir. I know he won't want to miss you. We have a dinner tonight and a boat party at midnight. He's very busy."

Gerry hung up, anger overcoming self-pity, if that was the word for what made him feel so hurt. Damn Ernst. Why should he suppose that he was going to sit around and await his pleasure? Patience, he warned himself. They had more or less agreed that that was the way it was going to be for a day or two. What he had said to André was true—he couldn't expect Ernst to drop everything just because of his unexpected arrival. Why not? Gerry was prepared to drop everything for him, except that he hadn't much to drop. André. What else? He had to make an effort of imagination to get a sense of what Ernst's life must be like: guarded from the world, surrounded by buffers to fend off all of life's little annoyances, committed to a round of formal social occasions. Not to mention Heinrich. He thought of calling Solange but decided it would be too humiliating to ask Ernst's wife's assistance.

The guards were on duty across the hall when he returned to Conrad. He felt like beating the door down but the guards were more than a match for him. Sleeping Beauty. Do not disturb until eight. Why wouldn't this have been the perfect time for them to be together, exploring what they thought they had discovered in each other last night? Because he was a disturbance? Yes, that too. He was a threat to the smooth order of Ernst's ornate existence. He intended to be as big a disturbance as possible.

He stripped and settled down at the desk in the living room and wrote his mother the first long explicit letter in a year, telling her everything he'd been doing; he'd written only short notes pretending to be in Singapore all these months. From time to time, he got a semi-erection thinking and writing about Jack, about Ernst, about André. He couldn't help thinking about what a lovely time he could be having right now if it weren't for his scruples. Still, he was glad he had them. It was about time.

He spent some unhurried time in the bathroom getting ready for his fittings and the blank evening that lay ahead. He still thought it possible that Ernst might ask him to join him somewhere along the way, if not for dinner at least for the midnight boat party which sounded as if it would have room for one more.

He was in his dressing gown once more when the outer doorbell rang and Smiling Sam's henchmen came swarming into the room, shaking out clothes and picking threads off them. They had done their usual expert job and except for some buttons here and there that had to be moved, no alterations were required. Gerry couldn't help admiring himself in the creations; he was Bangkok's best-dressed man. He hoped he would soon be able to show himself off to the person his finery was intended to impress. The tailors bowed their way out and he checked the time. A little after seven. Too soon for Sleeping Beauty. Time for a drink. With André.

He picked up the phone to call him and for a dreadful moment couldn't remember his last name. He managed an approximation of it and was corrected by the operator before being put through to him. The delight in his response to Gerry's greeting was balm to his anxious spirit. "You want to have a drink with me?" Gerry asked.

"Oh yes. Wonderful. Have you talked to Ernst?"

"Not yet. His Highness isn't to be disturbed for another hour."

"I've talked to Maria. I can't wait to tell you."

"You sound happy."

"I am. I think you will be too."

"Can you meet me in a few minutes?" Gerry considered asking him to his rooms, but listening to his eager young voice convinced him that he wasn't quite ready for such potentially combustible intimacy and they agreed to meet in the bar downstairs.

The guards were still in place as Gerry left Conrad. André was already in the bar; wonder filled his eyes as he watched Gerry's approach. "You're absolutely stunning," he exclaimed. "Are those new?"

"Yeah. I've decided to have all my clothes made in Bangkok from now on. Aside from everything else, they're so cheap."

"You'd look marvelous in anything but they're beautifully made," André said, sounding a professional note. His beauty made ornaments of his nondescript schoolboy clothes. His shy diffidence was gone. Remembering his first impressions the night before, Gerry was still amazed that the boy had fallen for him. They had become devoted friends in an afternoon. He felt he could safely put a hand on his shoulder as they settled into ornate wicker chairs in a private corner.

"I've been dying to talk to you," André burst out. "I had to check with Maria about the cruise to make sure I hadn't misunderstood. She says he's definitely expecting you. She knows because she's been helping with the arrangements. She doesn't understand why he hasn't spoken to you but it seems he's had a busy day."

"So I gather, except for the last three or four hours. Unless he's been closeted with the King. I hadn't thought of that." As he spoke, he realized that it had been childish of him to assume that Ernst had been idling away the afternoon in secret pleasure. He might easily have had urgent business. The thought made him feel much better. A waiter approached and André waited until Gerry had ordered an exotic vodka drink and then asked for the same.

"Are we just having drinks or are you buying me dinner?" he inquired boldly.

"Are you still sick?"

"Frightfully." He giggled. "I'm going to stay that way until Ernst decides to take you away from me."

"I doubt if he does for dinner. It's a bit late. I hear there's some sort of a boat party afterward."

"Yes, that's the one I'm supposed to go to."

"Maybe I'll be included when I talk to him. We could go together. Meanwhile you're stuck with an old gentleman for dinner. What would I do without you?"

"I'm sure you'd know how to find plenty of company. I'm the lucky one. Aren't you excited about the cruise?"

"I might be if I knew more about it." Looking into André's radiant face, Gerry felt obliged to do better than that. "I'm sure I will be as soon as Ernst tells me about it. It's good to know you're going. Do you know who else?"

"Everybody from last night and two more boys who're waiting in Penang. We go there day after tomorrow. That may be why Ernst didn't think there was any rush about telling you."

"It's sweet of you to make excuses for him but you must admit he's got his own rather peculiar rules. I know one thing. If he doesn't make me feel awfully damn wanted the minute I get through to him, the game's canceled."

"Of course he will."

"OK. You'll save me from a galloping case of paranoia." He resisted an impulse to give the boy's hand a squeeze. Tall drinks were put in front of them and they drank.

"What were you planning to do after Bangkok if you hadn't met Ernst?" André asked.

"Nothing in particular. I don't remember. I'm more or less heading home. I think my mother would like to see me soon. Time's passing." He told him about his travels in the East, omitting Saigon. André made a rapt and avid audience. They ordered more drinks and continued to reach out to each other in ever-widening circles of intimacy, but Gerry was acutely aware that they hadn't yet reached the cool plateau of platonic friendship. Every word the boy uttered, every glance, every movement was tremulous with adoration and desire.

"I think I'd be scared wandering around alone for so long," André commented.

"I was learning things."

"I meant what I said about not going on the cruise without you, now more than ever, only I haven't much choice. I'm probably going to say all the wrong things but I want to tell you everything. I know you and Ernst are going to arrange everything but if by some chance you don't and you'd like me with you for company, just to have somebody you could do things with, I'd go with you in two seconds. At least until we got back to Paris. I could pay you back slowly when I'm working again."

"Thank you, baby." Gerry was more touched by the speech than he wanted to show. "I didn't know anybody so beautiful could be so nice. I'm sure we could have fun together but don't let's think about it now. It makes me jumpy."

"I'm sorry. I knew I'd say something wrong. It obviously can't mean anything to you but it means a lot to me to tell you. I never dreamed I'd be able to talk to you like this."

"I understand, baby." This time, he let his hand go where it wanted to go. André gripped it as if his life depended on it. Gerry had never felt such passionate need conveyed by a hand. He stroked it soothingly with his fingers. "We've got to make sense, remember. It's almost time for me to call Ernst." They let go of each other and finished their drinks and Gerry ordered another round. It was just eight fifteen when he pushed his chair back. "OK. I'll be right back. Maybe then we'll know where we stand."

He asked for Yorgo on the house phone in the lobby and let the number ring for a long time before accepting the fact that it wasn't going to answer. He signaled the operator. "I've got an appointment with the Baron this evening," he lied. "I'm trying to reach him. It's urgent. Can't you call his suite and tell him Mr. Kennicutt is waiting on the line?"

"The Baron, sir? He's already left the hotel for the evening. He left word that he wasn't to be disturbed until eleven in the morning."

Gerry felt as if he'd been slapped in the face. It numbed him. He somehow put the phone down and stood in a trance of frustration. Left the hotel? It wasn't possible. He wasn't to be disturbed until eight. That didn't mean that he'd planned to leave at eight. Was Ernst trying to avoid him?

He was appalled to discover that his eyes had filled with tears. More threatened to flow. Was he so desperate for love? Why did he suddenly feel so alone when he had long since come to terms with solitude? Was it a delayed reaction to the loss of Jack? He wasn't alone. He could console himself with the boy who was waiting for him. Pride intervened. He wasn't going to allow Ernst to virtually dictate how he handled his sex life. He would battle it out with him man to man, with no hidden resources to fall back on. But how could he battle an invisible adversary? He had to drag him out into the open somehow.

He knuckled tears from his eyes and turned abruptly and made a dash for the stairway. He ran up to the corridor that led to the suites. It was deserted. No guards were posted in front of Coward. Ernst was gone. That much had been true but he still felt as if they were victims of a conspiracy to keep them apart, a conspiracy in which the entire hotel staff had joined. What had Prince Charming done to get at Sleeping Beauty? Hacked through some brambles? He would much prefer tangible brambles to the amorphous wall of inaccessibility that had sprung up around Ernst. If he was stoned, he might not even be aware that they had been out of touch for almost twenty-four hours.

He returned to the house phone and spoke to the operator. "I want to leave a message for the Baron. Please tell him that Mr. Kennicutt wants him to call as soon as he gets in tonight. It doesn't matter what time. It's urgent. Have you got that?"

That was all he could or would do. He didn't want Ernst to think that he was laying siege to him. All he would know was that Gerry had told Yorgo that he would call at eight and hadn't, and that he wanted to reach him urgently tonight. That wasn't overdoing it but he was already running out of cards. If he hadn't heard from him by tomorrow morning, he would write a note saying that he was leaving and that would be that.

The tears sprang to his eyes and again he was appalled by them. Nobody had ever made him cry. Perhaps this was it. Perhaps it had finally happened. Perhaps he really was in love. He laughed out loud and choked on his tears and made a determined effort to get a grip on himself before he returned to André.

He leaped up with delight to welcome him back and Gerry shook his head as they seated themselves again. André had the kindness to look crestfallen. "I missed him. He's already gone out," Gerry explained.

"But you said he wasn't to be disturbed until eight."

"I thought that's what Yorgo said. Maybe I misunderstood. It seems to me Ernst makes us all feel as if we'd misunderstood quite often. He's running a world of his own."

"I'm sorry. I honestly am. It must be awful not to know what's going on with somebody you care about. I'm sure there'll be some reasonable explanation, but that doesn't help until you know what it is."

They finished their drinks and went along to the river terrace for dinner. The food was good, they shared two bottles of passable French wine and didn't lack for conversation, but it wasn't a happy evening. Gerry appreciated André's sweet devotion but it also got on his nerves. He didn't want to find escape with a substitute; the boy should be directing his passion toward somebody who could respond to it properly. He felt he was cheating him by accepting so much of his time and attention.

"Won't you please go to that party without me?" he urged after they'd had coffee and were finishing the second bottle of wine.

"I'm too sick," André said with a ravishing smile. "Honestly. It's been such a perfect day. I don't want anything to spoil it. If you want to be alone, don't worry about me. I'll go to bed and think about everything that's happened."

Gerry didn't linger for long. Lulled by wine, with waiters no longer hovering over them, they were too vulnerable to the treacherous magic they both obviously felt in each other. André avoided an awkward parting in front of a bedroom door. He stopped in the lobby to say good night.

"You go that way. It's easier for me to take the lift—the elevator. Thank you for everything. It's been wonderful. Can I call you in the morning?"

"Of course, baby. Or I'll call you. We'll see who wakes up first." The great eyes briefly devoured him with longing. Gerry held his hands firmly at his sides and watched the boy turn from him and go. He'd evidently made it almost too clear that pursuit wouldn't lead to anything. He supposed it was a mark in his favor but the way he was feeling now made him wish that he'd left a little room for doubt. He mounted the stairs with dragging feet. The corridor remained deserted. He let himself into his empty suite and undressed and prepared himself for bed.

He put on his dressing gown and settled down in the living room with his magazines, hoping to read himself to sleep, but the questions that had plagued him all through dinner and ruined his evening continued to pursue their dreary round. Was Yorgo reliable with messages? Had Ernst tried to reach him? Was Heinrich plotting with Maria to get rid of him? Was he really going to be invited on the yacht? Had he frightened Ernst off by acting possessive too quickly? His mind was in a rut that he supposed might be a condition of being in love. What good was he doing anybody sitting here alone, wide awake but unable to concentrate on the page in front of him? He wanted to assure himself that he was doing no good at all, but he knew better. It was good *for him* to hold himself to his commitment to Ernst until he had some definite reason for breaking it. It was as clear and simple as that, and the other question that was waiting to divert his thoughts from Ernst was irrelevant.

He let his mind frame it to help him out of a dead end. Would it have been kinder to André to take him to bed and help the boy get over him? He thought of his boyhood obsession with Ned and how paralyzing it had been. A few hours in bed had done wonders to liberate him. André was a good deal more mature than he had been but his infatuation was probably similar. So maybe he could do the poor kid a kindness? Damn decent of him. He'd think about it tomorrow when something had been resolved with Ernst.

It was just about time for the boat party. He hoped everybody was having a good time. He pushed the magazines away and rose and rang for Lee. He got a little old man instead and ordered ice and a bottle of local whiskey. He'd have his own party. He wondered how long boat parties lasted. He felt as if he'd still be awake no matter what time Ernst got in. When the whiskey arrived, he poured himself a stiff drink and returned to his magazines. By the time the glass was empty, he was actually able to read, thoughts of Ernst relegated to the back of his mind like an aching tooth. He fixed another drink and began to feel as if he might eventually get to sleep. He was going for a third when there was a gentle tap at the door. He put his glass down and swung around, not sure that he'd actually heard it. It was repeated. Ernst? He made a joyful rush for the door and flung it open. It was André, looking small and forlorn.

"Oh, for God's sake," he exclaimed, too surprised to conceal his disappointment.

"I— You're not asleep?" He attempted a smile that was so timid that it died before it got started.

"No. Neither are you, I gather."

"I didn't— The wine's made me brave again. I thought—"

Gerry glanced over his shoulder, aware of something amiss in the corridor. The guards were in place outside of Coward, staring at him dully. Ernst had returned. He hadn't called. Gerry's spirit surged up in rebellion against such lack of consideration. He reached for André and pulled him in and shut the door behind them. Somehow, they were in each other's arms, their mouths joined. For a tumultuous moment, Gerry was aware only of his tongue exploring a soft welcoming mouth and of the feel of a slim body in his arms. He drew back gently.

"Oh God. Oh my God, Gerry," André said out of a daze of incredulity. "Are we— You don't mind? I can stay?"

"Of course, baby."

"Are we—going to bed together?" It came out on a breath, his lips barely moving. Color flamed up into his cheeks.

"God yes. That's what you want, isn't it?"

"I can't believe you want me."

Gerry chuckled. "We can easily dispel any doubts about that." He shrugged off his dressing gown and tossed it onto a chair and stood motionless before him, his erection lifting vigorously between them.

André lowered his eyelids, his lashes sweeping his cheeks like miniature brushes. "Oh, Gerry," he murmured. He turned his back hastily and threw off his clothes so quickly that he gave the impression of being afraid that Gerry would change his mind and, still with his back turned, he hurried toward the bedroom. Gerry followed, his eyes fixed on the intoxicating behind. He was apparently so self-conscious about any frontal display that it hadn't occurred to him that his buttocks could incite to riot. Gerry's heart beat with amorous rapidity. Every step André took was a licentious provocation. He dropped down on the nearest bed and stretched out on his stomach. Gerry made a quick detour to the bathroom and then prepared them both and took him slowly.

André cried out once and his body leaped convulsively and he subsided into a crooning ecstasy of surrender. Gerry held him while the jangling excitement of possessing his sweet beauty cleared and focused and joy seeped through him. He felt the enormous need in the young body and the timid inexperience that held him back. He tested him and felt his acquiescence. His body was so light and lithe and supple that he quickly mastered it and lifted it to him and moved and shifted it to satisfy its need. He stirred the boy from somnolent surrender to clamorous participation and led him to an impassioned climax.

He withdrew from him and left him sobbing quietly and went to the bathroom. He washed thoughtfully, shaken by the depth of the need he had been called upon to satisfy. He hadn't felt anything like it since Tom. If he had exercised more fully the masculinity that Tom had uncovered in him perhaps he would have learned to take it for granted. Thoughts of Tom made him uncomfortably sensitive to his sudden responsibility for André, the responsibility inherent in demanding and accepting his surrender. He had failed Tom fatally.

Walter had brought Tom into his life. At the time, he had still thought of Walter as the glamorous figure who had been the object of his erratic passion some twelve years earlier. He heard that Walter had turned up in San Francisco with the celebrated young writer Tom Jennings and that they had set up housekeeping together. He was surprised and pleased when Walter looked him up and his pleasure and surprise were even greater when all three of them had ended up in bed together. It had been a slightly drunken occasion but Tom had remained in firm control of it, as if it were some sort of test; Gerry had never encountered a homosexual couple who seemed more totally dedicated to each other. They were the embodiment of everything he had missed in life.

In the following weeks he heard that plans were going ahead for Walter's production of Tom's new play and that it was to be rehearsed in San Francisco before being taken to New York. He assumed he'd see them again when the play was out of the way; nothing had prepared him for a call late one night from Tom. His speech was rambling but Gerry gathered he wanted to see him. He supposed he was drunk. He had acquired some scruples about getting mixed up with established couples but he remembered how exciting Tom had been in bed and couldn't say no.

When Tom arrived, Gerry's first thought was that he'd been in a fight or a car crash, although he saw no signs of bodily damage. It was the way he moved that suggested some physical disaster. He fell against Gerry and hugged him without speaking and went lurching off around his stylish living room picking things up and putting them down. Drink was the obvious explanation but he looked more injured than drunk. His clothes hung on him strangely, as if the body under them were broken. Fear of having to cope with some terrible catastrophe made a cold hollow in Gerry's chest and he hurried to the bar and poured a stiff drink and took it to Tom. Tom drained off half of it without looking at it and stood with the glass hanging at the end of his arm. His wonderful healthily sensitive good looks had collapsed. His long fair hair was tangled and unkempt. Gerry knew he was in his late thirties, seven or eight years older than himself, but he'd looked much younger when they'd met. He didn't now.

Tom turned to him abruptly and stared into his eyes. There was none of the drunk's vacancy in Tom's. They were fixed with terrifyingly deep startled anguish, as if he'd just been shot and knew it was fatal, the look of a man who was about to die. "Gerry," he said in a rough voice. "Oh my God. You haven't heard?" He tangled his strong fingers in Gerry's hair and yanked his mouth to him and kissed him violently. He jerked his head back and his eyes seemed to falter and go dead. "Walter's left me." All the muscles of his face and body contracted and Gerry caught him and dragged him to the sofa. He grabbed his glass and dropped down with him and held his head in his lap while his body was contorted by wracking spasms. Terrible animal sounds were torn from him. Gerry had never seen grief or known that it could be so devastating. He tried to soothe him by stroking his hair while his body pitched about as if it were being torn limb from limb.

The terrible sounds were suddenly cut off and he lay motionless. Gerry's heart stopped. The cold hollow of fear grew in him.

Tom stirred and sat up and gripped Gerry's hand and turned a tear-streaked face to him. "It's all right," he said in a strangled voice. "Seeing you—you're part of Walter too." He pulled his arm away and began to repeat an odd gesture with the flat of his hand, a quick sweeping gesture as if he were trying to calm Gerry. "OK, OK, OK, OK, I'll tell you. Yesterday. He left a fake letter saying he was going back to your mother. I mean, his mo—oh shit. Whatever she is. His fucking wife. David's here. You know David? David Fiedler, the Hollywood producer, Walter's oldest friend. He won't tell me anything except that Walter wants me to go on with the play. You've heard about that? My play. He walked out just as he was about to start directing rehearsals of my play. I'm going mad but he wants me to go on with it. I'm going to, too. I'm going to do everything he wants me to do. When he comes back, he'll see that I didn't believe a word of that stupid letter. I'm going mad, darling. Try to help me."

Gerry caught the hand that was still making the quick calming gesture and held it in both of his. He was appalled and frightened. Tom had been so keen and sure and full of laughter. "I don't understand any of this," he said helplessly.

"That makes two of us. You're Walter's. We belong together."

"What do you mean? You don't think I've been having an affair with him, do you?"

A ghost of a smile crossed his lips. "We've been together every fabulous minute of every fabulous day ever since that night you spent with us. I don't mean anything. How can I when nothing means anything? David's been trotting out a stable of studs for me. Christ. I'm Walter's. Walter's mine. You're the only person I can be with. Yesterday, I was too numb to know anything. Then suddenly I realized it was a nightmare. I know I'm going to wake up soon. If I don't I'll go mad."

"You mean, he just left? You didn't have a fight or anything? He says he's going back to his wife?"

"That's what he said in the letter. We made love yesterday morning." His head dropped back and his mouth opened and he doubled his fist and lifted it over his face. Gerry held his breath, waiting for a scream. He could see all the sinews of his hand straining as if they would break. He slowly relaxed and lifted his head again. "Give me a drink, darling. Have one with me." Gerry jumped up and threw two drinks together and returned with them. Tom drank with growing signs of control. "We had a lot of things to do about the show so I let him go to the doctor's appointment alone. He sent a message telling me to meet him at the office. When I got there, I found the letter. He was gone."

"But if you think he's gone to his wife, why don't you call?"

"He told me not to. I'm not going to. We'll play it his way. I just wish I knew what we're playing. I'm going to act as if nothing has happened. I've got to. If I believed a word of his letter, I'd kill myself. What else could I do? It would be better than going mad. I can't live without him. He can't live without me. He knows that. Remember what I told you on our big night? I could never do anything I wouldn't want Walter to know about. That still goes. He knows what happened with you and me and he understood when I explained why it had to happen. There's something even you don't understand. Take me to bed, darling. Let me stay. It's the only thing that'll keep me going."

"What don't I understand?"

"Why I love you. Why I need you. It doesn't matter. Just take my word for it."

Gerry was alarmed by the thought of going to bed with somebody on the edge of total collapse. The smallest unwanted move or ill-judged word might bring on an irreversible crisis. He wanted to comfort him but he wondered if sex was the right way. He thought of Tom's lean hard body taking him and put a hesitant hand out and touched his knee. "I'll take your word for it but please be sure. Don't you think it might make things worse?"

"No. It's the one thing in all this I know. That's the part I can't explain. I am sure." Tom lifted his legs onto the sofa and dropped over against him and lay his head on his chest and burst into tears. His sobs were more like normal weeping and Gerry held him close and felt his grief easing. His heart swelled with love and compassion for both the parted lovers. If this was what being in love did to you, he should probably be glad that he was only a bystander. His role in life.

Tom's sobs grew quieter and trailed off. They both drank. "That does it," he said. "I'm where I belong. You're going to get me through it, darling. Can I stay with you when it gets too bad to handle? You're not tied up with anybody?"

"Nothing worth mentioning. You know I'm fairly mad about you—both of you."

Tom lifted himself and their mouths met in a kiss that deepened and intensified until they were putting all their longing into it, Tom's the longing of desperation, Gerry's the familiar longing for someone who could make his life seem important. Gerry drew back to speak. "We'd better go to bed now. You're knocked out."

"Yeah. I haven't slept since night before last."

They finished their drinks and rose and Gerry took his hand and led him to the bedroom. He was moving normally now with the springing stride of an outdoorsman. He went immediately to Gerry's dressing table and combed his hair. "I've got to keep myself pretty for him," he said. It was extraordinary hair, shoulder-length and fair with red-gold highlights, a great tawny mane. Gerry's was as long, glossy and soft. Walter had made much of their hair. They used the bathroom together; Tom obviously didn't want to let him out of his sight. They undressed together and moved to each other, naked and erect. Tom's tanned freckled body was a marvel of graceful strength. His eyes were on Gerry's erection.

"God. That gorgeous cock. It's Walter." He dropped down and kissed it and put it briefly in his mouth. He rose and they put their arms around each other and hurried each other into bed. Tom put his hands on Gerry's cock and held it and looked at him with eyes in which torment was diluted by intimations of peace. "I want you to take me, darling," he said quietly.

"You know I can't."

"I was the same way. I told you. Walter got me over it. You've got to fuck me, darling. I need it. I need it now more than I've ever needed anything. Take me the way Walter takes me."

Gerry could feel his need. It seemed to beat at him like a fist. The thought that Tom's salvation depended on his satisfying it made him doubly incapable of the act. "I can't. You can feel what's happening just talking about it. It'll never be right for me. I'm dying to have you in me again."

Something almost like a smile fleetingly lighted Tom's face. "Yeah. I've taken him. He's seen me taking you. OK, darling. Get ready. We'll see about the other way later."

Gerry lay beside him in the dark until Tom's breathing told him that he was asleep and then slept himself. He woke up with the light on and a hand holding his erection. He felt himself sliding into moist warmth and he cried out as he was hit by a sensual shock unlike anything he'd ever known. He thought he'd had an orgasm and came fully awake as he slid deeper into warm confinement. He let out a shout and lunged with his hips and felt himself contained to the limits of his reach. He shouted again and pulled himself up on Tom's back and felt a huge unknown power gathering in him. "Oh God. Holy Jesus. I'm inside you. Christ. I'm going to come."

"You're taking me." Tom's profile was turned to him. Tears were streaming down his face but a little smile played around his lips. "You're fucking me, darling. Oh God, you're it. He'll come back. I know it now. Fuck me and bring him back to me."

Gerry hadn't known he had such power in him. The threatened orgasm receded and he applied himself to establishing his control over a man's body. He gripped his shoulders and pulled him to him. He held his hips lightly and guided him to move to his desires. The power Tom acknowledged in him made him feel like a god. He drove him to a quick climax. He lingered in him and felt Tom's body open to him completely and surrender itself to his satisfaction. His orgasm became a supreme expression of his possession of him. He lay on him, still potent, prepared to take him again, and felt an extraordinary shift taking place in his psyche. Tom had delivered himself into his care. The responsibilities of domination had been forced on him. He had lost the liberty of carefree submission.

The night inaugurated his rule. He kept Tom sober and in working shape. Tom couldn't bear not to go home at least a couple of times a day in case he'd find some sign from Walter there and Gerry considered moving out to his house across the Golden Gate Bridge to spare him so much driving, but decided it would add to a dangerous confusion of identities. Already, he was aware of moments when Tom seemed to transfer to him all his love and passion for Walter. He recognized it as part of the illusion they were creating together and he knew that too many unexplored depths had been opened up in him for him to remain satisfied as Walter's stand-in for long. Gerry's sole aim was to get Tom through his initial desolation so that he could reassemble himself as an independent being. Gerry was enabling Tom to live in a dream, no longer a nightmare but equally unreal, and he was eager to exercise his newfound prowess with somebody who wanted him for himself. There was no lack of candidates. Several attractive guys had recently begged him to take them in the way he had thought was beyond his powers. He knew how to reach them but he had to keep himself free day and night for Tom.

Several weeks had passed when Tom called him at work in the middle of the day and told him he wanted to see him at his place in an hour. He sounded unusually calm and very determined. Gerry felt his responsibility as a growing burden but agreed. He interrupted a job and went home.

The minute he let Tom in, he knew something important had happened. He was almost the Tom he had first met weeks ago, without the happiness but with his assurance restored. He was dressed more formally than usual in a jacket and tie. They kissed briefly and Gerry knew that he was finally at peace.

"I know all about it at last," he said as they moved into the living room. "He's sick. Very sick. I went to the doctor he saw just before he left. I had to practically beat it out of him. I don't know why I didn't do it sooner. It's taken me this long to think straight. I never would have without you." He put his hand out and Gerry took it and stood in front of him. Tom moved in against him and laid his forehead against Gerry's. "It's bad, darling." He gripped Gerry's arms for a long silent moment and then pulled himself up and turned away. "There's no time to break down now. I'm so—well, happy is a funny word to use, but yes, I'm happy. I can go to him, the idiot. I understand what he was thinking. He thought it might ruin my life, as if I had any life without him. I'm leaving in a couple of hours. I'll be with him in the morning. You've got to come with me."

"What?"

He took a few quick strides to Gerry and put his hands on his shoulders and gave him a little shake. "You've got to. I don't know what I'm going to find. Have you seen that house he lives in? It's a goddamn fortress. I have a feeling they'll try to keep me away from him. They may not even tell him I'm there. You could get through to him."

"How could I? I don't mean anything to Walter—a messed-up kid who was in love with him for a couple of weeks twelve years ago and a guy who had a crazy night in bed with both of you last month. Why would he bother to speak to me?"

"I happen to know you mean a lot to him but even if you didn't, so much the better. You're no threat to his wife. She knows all about me and what's happened between us. He left her for me. She hates my guts. You've got to help us."

Gerry was surprised by the resistance to the suggestion that was stiffening in him. He had tried to be someone he wasn't for too long now. Everything Tom said cut him out of their lives. Couldn't he hear his own words? "If you think I can let him know you're there, that's easy. I can call him right now. What time is it? It's afternoon there. What's his number?"

"Oh God, if you get him, let me talk to him." Tom looked suddenly drawn and haggard and a feverish light had sprung up in his eyes. Gerry went to the phone and dialed. He heard the ring on the other side of the continent and a brisk female voice answered.

"Mr. Makin isn't taking any calls for the time being," it said in reply to Gerry's request. "He's very busy with production plans. If you want to leave your name, he'll call back as soon as he can."

Gerry left his home number and the number of the shop. "Tell him it's urgent," he said and hung up. He looked at Tom and shrugged. "He's not taking any calls. If I mean so much to him, he'll probably call back. Don't worry. If you can't get through on the phone, you can send him a note once you're there."

Tom moved close to him and held his elbows. He was looking composed again. "I need you, darling. I'll get to him even if I have to blow the door in. I'm not worried about that. It's the rest of it. What if he's worse than the doctor here knows? I'm scared. Waiting around alone in a hotel room—you've got to be with me. I'll pay for everything, naturally."

Gerry felt the hands on him beginning to tremble. He looked into deeply intelligent, sensitive eyes. His fresh good looks and the habits of their lovemaking filled him with protective concern for him but didn't weaken his resistance. Tom was being unreasonable. He seemed to forget that he had a job. He was all in favor of reunited lovers but what about him? He wanted to be himself again. He wanted to be with Phil or Billy or Herb and find out what was waiting for him there. He knew how important he'd become to Tom but basically he was nothing but a big cock that could take the place of the one he wanted. He put his hands on his shoulders and gave him a brief hug. "You're still not thinking straight, darling. You'll be with Walter. There's no question about that. You'll be thinking only about him. You won't want to be bothered with me hanging around. Anyway, he might misunderstand. You've been apart. He might be imagining all sorts of things. He knows how much we like each other. You mustn't let him worry about things like that." He could see his words sinking in. Tom's eyes grew reflective.

"I'll tell him everything you've done for me, of course. He knows I could never be unfaithful to him."

"Aside from everything else," Gerry hurried on, "I'm in the middle of a very important job. I shouldn't even be here now."

"Of course. Thank God, you are." He dropped his hands to his sides and drew back. "I *will* be with him," he said thoughtfully. He lifted his head suddenly and his whole being seemed to be suffused with joy. It straightened his body and brought a young eager shine to his face. "Oh God, I'm going to be with *him*. What else matters? I may not be gone long. Once we've had a chance to talk, he'll probably want me to come back to the play. I might even bring him back with me. He'd like that. I won't let him die. We're going to be together always. Oh darling." He threw his arms around Gerry and held him. "I just automatically thought of you being there to get me through it but you're probably right. I shouldn't be thinking of anything but him." They kissed lovingly. Gerry was prepared to take him to bed if he felt he needed it, but the body he held was overflowing with strength and a drive to get on with his business. He didn't want to divert his attention back to him. Their lovemaking was over.

They broke apart with laughter. "Oh God, I *am* happy," Tom exclaimed incredulously, looking it.

"Is there anything I can do?" Gerry asked. Having won his point, he was ready to bend to Tom's wishes. He wouldn't let anything interfere with his responsibility but if his sexual usefulness had ended, he couldn't see that he had much else to offer. Tom and Walter needed each other, nobody else. "Do you want me to come to the airport with you? The hell with work."

"No. Everything's taken care of. I have plenty of time. All is well, the way it always is when you're around."

"Call me if anything goes wrong. I'll come if there's anything I can really accomplish. Let's have an illicit drink. Have you had some lunch?"

"I grabbed something."

"So did I." They had a drink and Tom talked excitedly about Walter and how they would arrange their life if he had to take it easy from now on. They kissed at length and Gerry let him go with an undercurrent of misgiving.

A few days later, there were headlines in all the papers announcing Walter's death. Gerry was frantic to get to Tom. He'd had sense enough to ask him for the name of the hotel where he was going to stay in New York, and immediately called it and was told that Mr. Jennings wasn't in. Gerry was at work, still in a state of agitated indecision, when a telegram arrived from his mother telling him to come immediately. YOUR PRESENCE REQUIRED URGENTLY, was the way she put it. It baffled him but he was glad to go. He called Tom's hotel again and still couldn't reach him but left word that he would be there by midnight. The minute he arrived, he called again and was told that "we can't give you any information about Mr. Jennings at this time." He left another message, including his parents' telephone number.

The next morning over breakfast when he opened the *Times* he found the brief obituary notice of Tom's suicide and the world fell in on him. Chronology blurred. Somewhere along the way his mother told him that he was Walter's son and he began to understand the role he had played in the tragedy. Tom's insistence that he and Walter were somehow one made sense at last and brought him close to total collapse. Why hadn't Tom told him? Why hadn't he grasped the mystic sense of union Tom felt with him, instead of assuming that it had to do only with his big cock?

He got through Walter's funeral in a daze. He wanted to be with Tom, wherever he was. The funeral was a great star-studded affair dominated by the stately figure of the widow, flanked by two charming-looking youths. His half-brothers. Gerry's attention quickened briefly as he recognized signs in one of them that he might be a kindred spirit. His father. His mother. Now his half-brother? He wondered if Walter had endowed them as handsomely as himself. The fact that he could even think about it made him feel that he had been cast forever into outer darkness.

He wanted to get away from everything he had ever known, escape himself, find himself, sink into oblivion. He despaired of ever erasing from his ears the sound of Tom's voice saying, "All is well, the way it always is when you're around." He never knew if Tom had managed to see Walter at the end but their nearly simultaneous deaths gave him a glimmer of hope. A suicide pact? He hoped so. Walter had apparently been so nearly gone that nobody inquired into the specific cause of his death. He hoped they'd had time to decide to go together. He couldn't bear to think of Tom learning of Walter's death unexpectedly, alone, uncared for, in the frenzy of grief that only he had known how to ease.

As he slowly recovered his balance and his senses, Gerry resolved that if he accomplished nothing else in life, he would train his ears to distinguish the difference between a cry for help from the soul and the trivial whimperings of the flesh. It seemed to him that it was a sin of omission of which not only he but a great many others were guilty.

Time passed. He listened. The flesh made a frightful din, but since Tom he hadn't heard the soul's clarion call. He thought he might have heard it with Ernst the day before, far from clarion, a faint sigh as if issuing from some deep, buried place. He would remain alert for it with André. He had been truthful with the boy. He would stick to the truth.

He found him as he'd left him, lying on his stomach but dry-eyed and breathing easily. Gerry lay down beside him and opened his arms for him and he nestled in against him, giving himself into his possession again.

"I didn't know it could be like that," he murmured. "You were right. It changes everything. It's never been like that before."

"It's almost never like that, baby. It was amazing. Everything was working as if we were made for each other."

"That's what I felt. Does that mean we're in love with each other?"

"No. It means that sex is beautiful for us. So good that you've got to get over being in love with me and let us enjoy it while we can."

"I certainly want that. I want to talk and hear your voice so I know it's really happening. Your—it's—I mean—well, you know. Isn't it very unusual?"

Gerry laughed, knowing that it was going to be good. If André was in love, he wasn't morbidly or hysterically in love. "What're you talking about, baby? You mean my cock? You can say it. It's awfully damn big. There's no doubt about that. Is that what made it good for you?"

"That, and its being yours. Everything. You—I can say it? Your huge cock. I've always dreamed of being taken like that. I didn't think it was possible. I mean, so big."

"We'll have to find you a bigger boy." He eased him over onto his back and propped himself on an elbow and surveyed him. He felt as if he owned his luscious mouth. His eyes roamed over the lovely slim body that he had possessed and wanted again. André's hands crept to his sex and covered it. He was going to have to get him over his shyness. He wished he could will himself to fall in love with him, now that his longing for the experience of love had revived with a vengeance. Aside from the age difference, they made a good pair, already perfectly attuned to each other sexually. They could tell Ernst to take his yacht and shove it and go off together as André had suggested at dinner. He could take him to Paris and find an apartment and make a home for him. That would be something he could do with his money. Perfect, except that what had happened only confirmed what he had known all day—Ernst gripped his imagination, whether he liked it or not. Their eyes met and melted into each other's. "Oh honey," he said. It was almost a groan. "What am

I going to do with you? Once Ernst and I get together, I'll be faithful to him. You understand that, don't you?"

"Of course. I never expected you to want me. I know *I'd* be faithful to anybody I was in love with."

"That's a start. We're going to have to take the mystery out of sex for you. Take your hands away from your cock."

"No, please. You don't want to see that. It's nothing."

"That's where you're mistaken. It's a lovely cock, maybe even a bit bigger than average. I'm going to make it hard for you again and show you."

"Can you? We've just finished."

Gerry laughed. "That's the best time to begin again. You're the most beautiful boy in the world with a lovely body and a cock that's in perfect proportion to the rest of you. If you're an artist you must be able to see that. You're such a sweet guy that I don't think anything I can say will make you vain, but I want you to appreciate what God's given you."

"He's given me you all of a sudden. I certainly appreciate that. Why did you wait when you knew you could have me whenever you wanted me?"

"I had my reasons, baby. It's been touch and go all day. When I opened the door and saw that Ernst was back and hadn't even bothered to call me, I decided it was ridiculous for us to miss something good together. It *is* good, baby."

"Oh yes, *mon amour chéri*. Is it all right to call you things like that? I told you not to worry about my being in love with you. I've never been attracted to a boy without falling in love with him."

"That's what I mean about mystery. You shouldn't have to fall in love to be attracted to somebody. You're a very sexy kid. You should learn to let it all out the way you have with me. You'll fall in love with a boy who's in love with you soon enough if you learn how to enjoy sex without expecting it to be a grand passion every time."

"You see? You're teaching me things I ought to know."

"Let's teach you how pretty your cock is. If you're shy about it people are apt to think you don't want them to take an interest in it." He slid down to it and felt André's body tense as he removed the hands that still hovered near it.

"I don't think I can yet," he said anxiously.

Gerry laughed. "You let me worry about that." He performed some tricks with his expert mouth and watched it surge up along his belly and lie rigidly motionless.

"My goodness," André exclaimed.

Gerry laughed again. "If there's one thing I'm good for it's making a cock look its best." He hooked a finger around it and pulled it upright. "There. Look at it, baby. How much do you think most boys have?"

"I don't know. I always thought it was small."

"Everybody else's always looks bigger than your own. That's one of the peculiar facts of life." He moved up over him again, kissing him everywhere, teasing him with his teeth and making him jump and giggle and playfully defend himself. He put his hands around his neck to feel the laughter in his throat. He made love to the thrilling sweep of his brows and the smooth lean jaw and ran his lips back and forth on the exquisite softness of his remarkable eyelashes and gurgled with delight. "I want to feel them fluttering like that on me everywhere. You could make me come with them."

"I want to do things with you I've never dreamed of. I don't even dare tell you about them."

"Don't bother to tell me. Just do them." He encouraged him to take all the liberties he chose and made him watch everything they were doing. He felt André's reticence and tension melting away until the boy was leading them on with abandon in a conscious pursuit of pleasure. When from time to time Gerry felt a twinge of guilt for enjoying it so much, rebellion flared. Ernst hadn't even treated him with common courtesy.

"I had no idea it could be such fun." André giggled as he performed a new trick. "I feel so sexy and happy. Maybe I'll start wanting everybody in sight to show off everything you're teaching me."

"That's the spirit. Have I taught you how beautiful you are? I want to buy you things. We'll go shopping. I want to heap you with rare and exotic gifts."

André burst into sunny laughter. "Why hasn't this happened to me before? I've never spent a whole night with a boy and waked up with him in the morning. How marvelous that I was brave enough to come see you. I wasn't going to knock loud enough to wake you. I don't know what I expected. This is the most momentous day of my life. Forget about those ten boys and being in love before and the rest of it. I didn't start living until today."

Listening, Gerry heard only a note of fulfillment. Even while so much of himself remained unengaged, he was so far able to give the boy what he needed. They made love. They slept. They made love. André greeted the dawn with love-choked laughter.

"I've spent the night with a man," he crooned. "I'm all grown up this morning at last. It's amazing to wake up in bed with you and start a new day. It makes it so different, as if we're really living together. You're as black as coal in this light. Oh yes, darling. Please. Hold me like that. Do you feel what you've done to me? My body takes your shape no matter what you do with me. We're going to be lovers for at least some of today. If Ernst takes you away from me later, you'll still be part of me. I know that now. What a wonderful way to grow up, belonging to you."

They fell into a deep sleep at last and didn't stir until nearly noon. Gerry almost sprang out of bed as he returned to consciousness with thoughts of Ernst uppermost in his mind. Had he been trying to reach him? He lay back and tried to relax. Of course not. He hadn't left word not to be disturbed. The phone would have waked him.

He didn't want to let André affect the way he handled the situation but there was little doubt that waking up with a beautiful boy at his side took some of the urgency out of settling the affair. He had already decided that he couldn't go on calling Yorgo and leaving messages, but he felt no need this morning to write the note of farewell that would serve as an ultimatum. Let the day take its course. He would make his final decisions this evening.

He rolled over and gathered André into his arms and they were enveloped in a rekindled blaze of passion. Eventually, they had breakfast in bed and decided to have another swimming lesson. Gerry lent the boy his dressing gown and he folded his clothes into a discreet bundle and went back to his room to get his trunks. When he returned, Gerry picked up a couple of magazines and they went downstairs together, passing the desk for Gerry to check for messages just in case. Neither mentioned Ernst although he was a presence they both clearly felt, casting a slight shadow on their enjoyment of each other, a shadow that might darken as the day progressed. They settled where they had been the day before and extended their physical intimacy by applying suntan lotion to each other and letting their arms and legs touch when they lay back. Gerry ordered beer for them again.

They hadn't had more than a few sips when they were approached by a boy in hotel uniform who pronounced Gerry's name questioningly. He instantly spotted the familiar crested envolope being held on a platter and his heart leaped into his throat. He snapped up into a sitting position and reached for it. His hands were shaking as he tore it open and was confronted with familiar handwriting. His heart began to hammer as he read:

> Gerald darling—
> How can I ever hold my head up again in civilized society? You have become so much a part of us that I assumed somebody had made arrangements with you for the cruise. I've just discovered that nobody has. The walls have been echoing with my rage on this side of the corridor. How horrible if you have heard of it and thought even for a second that you hadn't been included. You have appeared in our midst so suddenly and momentously that you must forgive a little disorganization even though I won't. I won't even ask if you will come. You and I know that you must. If there are any difficulties we will sweep them away or the yacht will leave without me. I was quite desperate to see you yesterday but the decks are being cleared. Please come see me at six before the multitudes gather. Please. I remember every word I said. We will make the miracle happen.
>
> All my love
> E

It was better than anything he could have hoped for. Tears welled up in his eyes, tears of happy relief as he felt the rapture of loving and being loved spreading through him out of the tips of his fingers and down into his toes.

Even if Ernst didn't mean it, being told that he wouldn't go without him was what Gerry wanted to hear. Blindly he handed the letter to André and took a deep breath and waited for the tears to subside.

"Oh darling," André said after a brief silence. "How wonderful. I'm so happy. So *that's* settled. I knew there'd been some mix-up."

Gerry let out a whoop of laughter. "Yes. It's all settled," he announced exultantly. "Maybe my whole life. You're right. Falling in love is ridiculous but it feels awfully good."

"I think so. I can have you till six. I'm grateful to Ernst for that. I mean, I can, can't I? You're not sorry you let me in last night now that you know it was all a big misunderstanding?"

Gerry blinked his vision clear and turned to André and looked deep into his bottomless eyes. "No, my darling. Something really good has happened with us. It's rare. I'm just grateful that everything worked out the way it did."

"Thanks to my being so shameless."

"Oh, you're the shameless one, you are." They laughed and leaned close and brushed each other's chins with their knuckles in lieu of an embrace. "Let's finish this beer and have that swimming lesson while we're waiting for another. I have a feeling we're not going to want to stay out here all afternoon."

André returned the letter and Gerry slipped it between the pages of one of the magazines. Six o'clock. Before "the multitudes" arrived. Was it possible that they were actually going to have a little time alone together? The thought did strange things to him; it clogged his mind and sent odd unidentifiable shocks through his system. Ernst's behavior yesterday had unnerved him and the ready tears suggested that he could easily be pushed close to breakdown. He had always sailed through life on a boringly even keel and he wasn't prepared for the sudden violent wrenches that his emotions had been subjected to over the last two days. He didn't want to collapse sobbing at Ernst's feet the minute he saw him, even though it might reveal depths of feeling in him that he hadn't known existed. A peaceful afternoon basking in André's adoration might help prepare him for whatever storms lay ahead.

After the first rush of euphoria, he'd had time to note that Ernst made no apology for not responding to his messages. Perhaps that was covered in the overall confusion of his not being included in the yachting party but he was going to have to be careful not to let Ernst slide through situations to suit his own convenience. Was Maria behind the whole thing for obscure reasons of her own? He didn't know why he kept mentally picking on Maria. He was going to have to be tough with everybody until he had a grip on all the strands of the tangle he was getting himself into.

He reached for André's knee and gave it a squeeze. "Come on, darling. I'm going to turn you into Johnny Weissmuller."

The swimming lesson was more successful than yesterday's because they no longer had to take care where they touched. They had more beer and ordered lunch. Their eyes told them that they both had the same goal in mind. When Gerry had signed the bills, they looked at each other and smiled slyly. "Is it time?" Gerry asked.

"I hope so. I've been wondering if I was going to have to make love to you out here. I might if we wait much longer."

"You *are* shameless. I love it."

Their eyes released each other and they gathered up their things and headed for the stairs that led up to the suites. They had started up them when Gerry missed his magazines.

"Do you have those magazines?" he asked, leaning forward to see if André was carrying them under his robe.

"No. I'm sorry. I thought you had."

"It doesn't matter." He started up again and stopped, thinking of Ernst's letter. He didn't want to leave that lying around. "What the hell. I'll run and get them. Here's the key, baby. I'll be right there."

"I'll go in?"

"Of course."

He ran downstairs and turned toward the bar to take a shortcut to the pool. As he hurried in, he had a head-on collision with a stocky Oriental who was hurrying out. Gerry stepped back and apologized and they went through the ludicrous little ballet common to such mishaps. They both took a step in the same direction and bowed and apologized some more. They both took a step in the opposite direction and once more confronted each other.

Gerry began to laugh. He put both hands out to direct traffic and they circled each other cautiously and hurried on. Although it was a widely accepted fact that all Orientals looked alike, Gerry was pretty sure it was the man he'd seen with Maria Horrocks the day before. Sure enough, he came upon Maria sitting near the far exit of the bar having what appeared to be a very late lunch. He paused to speak to her, casting his eyes about to see if there were any brown paper parcels in sight.

"Hello, Gerry lamb," she greeted him. "Going for a dip?"

"No. I've had one. Why aren't you having lunch with swarms of Excellencies and Highnesses?"

"I seem to be missing out on all the nobs these days. Today was intentional, at least. There's still so much to be arranged before we get off. I volunteered to skip lunch. Heads were rolling this morning when darling Ernst discovered that you hadn't been put on the yacht's list. I hope that's been straightened out."

"Yes, thanks." He wanted to ask if plenty of opium had been included in the ship's stores but decided that it wasn't quite time for him to take the offensive. He smiled and waved and went on.

He found the chairs where they had been sitting a few minutes before, but no magazines. He looked around to see if anybody had picked them up and was approached by the waiter who had served them.

"You wish, sir?"

"I left some magazines. You haven't seen them?"

"Yes, sir. Boy take to Conrad suite."

"Oh. That's very efficient of you. Thanks a lot." The service couldn't be beaten. He took the longer way back through the garden to avoid Maria. André let him in, unabashedly naked and erect.

"They brought the magazines two seconds after I got here," he reported, approaching with a frisky little spring in his step.

"Yes. They told me." Gerry's eyes rejoiced in the graceful priapic figure as André moved around him, taking his dressing gown off and folding it over a chair, returning to peel off his trunks, crouching to complete with his mouth the powerful thrust of Gerry's erection.

They made love and slept in each other's arms. When

he woke up, Gerry saw that the hour was approaching for the big moment. He was excited but determined not to get rattled. André had soothed all his nerves and reassured him. He felt love flowing easily in him, ready to be offered to Ernst if it turned out to be as simple as that. If decks had been cleared, there should have been a word about spending the night together. He was prepared for surprises.

He hugged the somnolent boy at his side and slid out of bed and went to the bathroom to spruce himself up. He returned and sat on the edge of the bed. André opened his eyes and stretched out his arms to him. He felt quite sure that André's sane and balanced nature would get him through the break that was coming but he wanted to make it as gentle as possible.

"We're supposed to go to Penang tomorrow?" he asked. "Why don't you move in here until we go?" André's face was made for angelic raptures and was so transfigured that Gerry gathered him up and held him against his chest and felt him stirring and hardening. He spoke into his pale hair. "Please, darling. Don't look at me like that. I don't deserve it. I might not be here tonight. Who knows with Ernst? I just thought it would be good to share when we can."

"I know, *mon amour*. That's all I want. I can't help the way I look."

"No, you can't, thank God. I'll buy you a mask."

"I get a hard-on every few seconds now, just like you."

"Yes. I want to do things with it. I've got to go, darling." He released him and they climbed out of bed and went to the living room hand in hand, André proudly erect beside him. Gerry dropped a hand to it. "Keep it that way for when I get back." He handed André his robe and put his own on. He had decided not to dress for his meeting. Ernst might be alone.

The magazines were on a console near the door and he skimmed them across to the sofa with the others as he passed. A sheet of paper fluttered from one of them to the floor. It wasn't Ernst's stationery. He went to the magazines and flipped through them and shook them out. Ernst's letter was gone. He turned back to the sheet of paper on the floor and picked it up and read a painstakingly printed message.

Honored Sir
If you will be good frend to his Lordship Baron
I have thing to learn you that will partake of your
interest. You are only American can, famous for
your good justice and very right. You will have
me in front of store where ordered shoes wait.
Tomorrow morning. Ten on the clock. I show
your magazine copy. It is very much. Important.

Your respectable sir
A Frend

"What in the world—?" He handed the sheet of cheap paper to André who was at his side. "What's *that* all about? It seems I'm going to have somebody in front of a store. That should cause a slight stir."

André giggled but his eyes were serious when he looked up. "You must show it to Ernst. He gets a lot of funny things like this."

"Really? Who brought the magazine up?"

"One of the boys. You know, he was dressed like all the others."

"Very peculiar. Ernst's letter is gone. There wasn't anything incriminating in it, but still . . . I wanted to keep it. If somebody wants to send me a note, why not leave it at the desk downstairs? I mean, I guess it's for me. I *am* an American, if not an American can." Deviousness was a way of life in the East. Complications could be created where least expected. He wondered about Maria's Fu Manchu—the timing fit—and shoved the paper into his pocket.

"I'll get my things if you're sure I won't be in the way," André told him. "I'll be right back if anybody else wants you to have them."

They laughed and Gerry gave him the kiss that his mouth always seemed to demand. "You have the key?" André held up two and they went out together and touched hands as Gerry crossed to Coward and André continued down the corridor. The guards were well placed to keep a log of everybody's activities. Yorgo opened the door for him. Maria was there and Ernst with his back turned. If this wasn't a multitude, it would do nicely until the others turned up.

His disappointment was sharp but vanished as Ernst swung around and their eyes met. Gerry felt himself lighting up. His heart sprang up with joy. He hadn't been mistaken; Ernst was his destiny. Magic. Real magic. Ernst von Hallers. The last playboy of the Western world. The wicked hero of his misspent youth. Ernst approached at his measured pace and Gerry felt a quick surge of guilt about André. He shouldn't have listened to his declarations of love and taken him for his pleasure when all his commitments were here. Everybody in the room was obliterated; only the two of them existed.

He wondered why his looks were particularly striking today and in the next moment noticed that he wore no disfiguring eye makeup. He had become a perfect unequivocal example of the Aryan Superman, blond, blue-eyed, heroically Nordic. It might betray a lack of subtlety of taste to find such a stereotype compelling but there was no denying that he did.

Ernst was also wearing a dressing gown, carelessly open to the waist and exposing a tantalizing portion of unadorned statuesque torso. He stopped in front of Gerry and their eyes searched, questioned and claimed each other. There were no barriers between them today; communication was thrillingly clear and open. They had reached a turning point. All that remained was to be together and accept each other completely in the way that could be achieved only by making love.

"How wonderful," Ernst exclaimed in his soft voice. He brushed Gerry's dressing gown aside and put a hand on his breast. Gerry plunged his hands into his pockets to prevent himself from escaping cover. "What a beautiful tan. Did you have a good day?"

"Wonderful. I spent most of it with André." If he felt guilty, the least he could do was confess and get everything clear between them. "Since just after midnight last night, to be exact."

Ernst's smile acquired modulations; it was sly, amused, perhaps pleased. "In that case, I won't ask if you missed me."

Gerry smiled in return, directly into his eyes. "I'll tell you. I did my best not to. I went all day yesterday without hearing from you. Can you imagine what that was like? If I go on waiting for you, it's because I don't seem to have any choice. I even had qualms about fidelity but I think I ought to know what I'm being faithful to. You seemed to think it didn't matter the other night."

"Fidelity? That's part of the miracle we're going to accomplish together." He shifted his hand to Gerry's arm and steered him toward the end of the room. Gerry held himself with one hand and moved the other around Ernst's waist. The light embrace made his heart swell with contentment. He felt shorts under the silk of the dressing gown and wondered how long he could stand the waiting game. There was nothing more to wait for except privacy. He was beginning to feel that it was the most precious luxury in the world. They stopped beside a high wing chair and Ernst stood in front of him with his back to the room.

"Thanks for your letter. You said the boat would leave without you if I don't go," Gerry said. "Did you mean it?"

"Yes, darling." They looked into each other's eyes. Neither was smiling. Gerry believed him. He felt as if the floor had shifted slightly under him. He put a hand on the back of the chair. Ernst covered it with his own.

The idiot tears started up in Gerry's eyes. He moved his hand over Ernst's and entwined their fingers and exerted pressure and swallowed with an effort. "You've got to find time for us to be alone together. Why is it so difficult? Did all these people *have* to be here?" He succeeded in not letting it sound plaintive. It was a cool straightforward question that demanded an answer.

"That's fair. If I try to tell you, will you listen to me carefully? I lead a foolish life. I want to fit you into what I've always known and find comfortable. If I could succeed, you would bring me no more than what I've found with many others. You excite and frighten me. For the first time, I have found someone who might free me from all the things I'm too lazy to escape by myself. I may be deluding myself. Will you enter into a pact with me to fight each other—*for* each other?"

"It's a pact I've already made with myself." His heart was beating with exultation; the battle was joined.

"Then I'm not deluding myself and I'd better be armed. I'm terrified to think what will happen to me if you win."

"You said that the other night. I'm going to win, of course. What about your foolish life? I don't even know where you live, if anywhere."

"Here and there. I have a château in France and castles in Germany and Ireland, and a cattle ranch in Argentina that I adore. I come to the East every year and spend a month or two on the yacht. That's about it."

Gerry laughed and shook his head at his own temerity. "I see. I know of people who live like that but I can't imagine what it's like. You can show me. I suppose it could take about a year. It doesn't sound dull, exactly, but maybe like more trouble than its worth. I think I'll want to stay somewhere long enough to do something, maybe breed a perfect bull in Argentina. We'll get rid of dancing boys and dope. That's the main thing that's going to happen to you. Are you still terrified?"

Ernst disengaged his hand and edged him back behind the chair and unfastened the tie of Gerry's dressing gown. Gerry kept his hand in the pocket, holding his erection upright against himself. Ernst ran his hands slowly down bare skin alongside it and circled his fingers around its hard base. Gerry's breath caught and he closed his eyes and made a strangled sound in his throat. He swayed toward Ernst, longing for them to be naked in each other's arms, thrilled by the caressing hand that was trying to slip through his guard. He allowed it to advance, revealing the proportions of his major attraction while keeping it under cover. He opened his eyes and glanced over Ernst's shoulder to check the room. Maria and Yorgo were absorbed in some papers. He saw Paolo's back disappearing into the bedroom. Was Heinrich in there? So long as nobody approached, the chair offered more privacy than they had had so far.

"How superb," Ernst said. "You really are a marvel, darling, quite aside from the magnificent thing you're holding. I couldn't imagine a body that matches more perfectly everything I feel in you. It's so young and charming and without brutality, and this to demonstrate your terrifying authority. I feel as if I were in very firm and gentle hands. You're taking rather an unfair advantage of me—to be utterly endearing, with a strength of character that can't be bought, and this awe-inspiring and invincible weapon. I had an idea, of course, but I'll have to see it before I can take it all in."

"It's not just for looking at." He was torn between his reluctance to carry this furtive schoolboy play any further and his hot desire to know the ultimate secret of Ernst's body. It was impossible to stand here listening to speeches about himself without taking action of his own. He drew him farther behind the chair and slipped his hand between the folds of his dressing gown and ran it lightly over sheer taut fabric. It was tightly confined but was all that he'd expected, a handsome appendage to the heroic body. From the curve of it and the stirrings he felt in it, he judged that it had not yet reached full erection. He longed to offer it his mouth's skills and watch it lift as tautly as his own but there were limits to what was permitted in a room filled with people. He was aware of an unexpected reticence gathering in Ernst, a physical withdrawal like André's when he'd first held him, that was at odds with his casual public embraces. He made a final effort of will and withdrew his hand and gathered his dressing gown around him and retied it. He returned his hand to the pocket.

"Enough of that. No more stripteases. I'm getting you bit by bit. I'll probably explode when I have all of you."

"Only a few more days, darling."

"I assume Heinrich hasn't been eliminated overnight."

"No, I explained about that. Maria thinks we can make the necessary arrangements in India."

"If I were in full fighting trim, I'd refuse to go anywhere as long as he's around."

"There is no need to fight about that, I assure you. We're in complete agreement."

"If you say so. I feel a bit mad letting myself be carried off on a yacht to God knows where. There's one little item I've got to do something about. I was planning to have money sent here. Now there's no time."

"That's nothing. Give Yorgo a check. He'll take care of it."

"It might be quite a lot unless I can arrange to collect some along the way. Maybe five thousand dollars."

"Anything, darling. Go over it with Yorgo. He'll give you the itinerary and the names of our agents in Cochin and Goa and Bombay. After that we'll be in Kashmir and we'll pick up the yacht again in Alexandria. Yorgo will arrange for your mail and all that."

"It sounds as if we'll have plenty of time to fight things out before we get to Alexandria."

"I told you. Just over a month, I think. I imagine you will have altered my life beyond recognition in a month."

"Are we talking about a lifetime? It would hardly be worth the effort for less."

"We're talking about a miracle, darling. Can we manage it? After seeing your body, all I can think about is giving myself to you forever." Their eyes met. Gerry felt his arms lifting to him and his erection escaped from cover and soared up between them. Ernst's hands were immediately on it. "Oh darling. Yes, a lifetime."

Gerry hastily pulled the dressing gown around himself and gripped the back of the chair for control. "Then let's go to bed for God's sake. Tell these people to go. You're driving me wild with frustration."

"Please, darling. Please. We want it to be right."

"Then talk about something. Anything. Quickly. Let go of me and talk about nothing. Cochin, you say? Why not Ceylon? It's between here and Cochin."

"No, darling. I don't like Ceylon. The boys are too dreary."

"We're not supposed to be thinking about boys, remember." Gerry had his erection under cover again, a hand controlling it.

"That's all very well for us, but what about the others? We mustn't be selfish."

"That's true; I forgot about them. But it must be quite a long way to Cochin. What will they do all that time?"

"Wait till you see the crew, darling. They've been very carefully selected."

"I see. A floating brothel. It sounds racy. There's also this." He pulled the anonymous note out and handed it over. Ernst glanced through it and the curtain abruptly descended around him. He turned from Gerry as if he no longer existed and took a few steps toward the others, holding out the paper.

"Yorgo. Take this," he ordered. Yorgo sprang forward to do so. Maria was beside him and snatched it from him and read it.

"It's obvious what you'd better do about that," she said, returning it to him.

Gerry moved out from behind the chair and held out his hand. It was trembling slightly. "Just a minute. As far as I know, that's mine. I'm planning to go tomorrow and find out what it's all about." Yorgo gave him the note and he put it back in his pocket.

"You're out of your mind," Maria exclaimed. Her staring protuberant eyes, her imperious aquiline nose, her operatic, Junoesque body made her a formidable adversary. Gerry had sensed from the start that that was what she was. He made a wrenching readjustment to his surroundings and to the others as they resumed their social identities. Maria was the lady that Solange had described as knowing how to play on people's weaknesses. She was Heinrich's protector. She was supplying Ernst with drugs. It was evidently her intention to keep Ernst in her debt, perhaps only to consolidate her position at court. As a newcomer who was being lifted close to the seat of power, Gerry doubtless represented the threat of the unknown. The situation struck him as absurd, although he sensed that the drugs might be sinister. Was there something more that he had failed to put his finger on, or was it simply Maria's manner that blew everything up out of all proportion? He felt a twinge of uneasiness but his own position was clear: he had an invincible cock. It was time to make its power felt.

"You have no idea what you're dealing with," Maria declared in her full-blown dramatic voice. "Do you wish to endanger Ernst's safety?"

"You didn't read the note very carefully," Gerry pointed out, advancing into the fray. "Whoever wrote it is offering to tell me something as a friend. Don't you think it'd be interesting to find out what it is?" He could see her reconsidering her course of action. Her manner smoothed out and she took a placating step toward him.

"You're a darling lamb and I understand your concern, but you haven't known Ernst very long. You have no idea the lengths people will go to get to him. We must all be careful not to let ourselves be used. What if you were kidnaped? Don't you suppose he'd want to get you back?"

"Are you serious?" Her overdramatic style made everything she said faintly ridiculous but he wondered if he were still underestimating the wide gulf that separated him from Ernst's world. He turned to Ernst and sought his eyes but there was nobody there. Ernst was armed with his own invincible defense mechanism. He simply disappeared. Gerry addressed Maria but kept an eye on Ernst to see if he could bring him back. "I think you're all nuts. Nobody has asked where this came from." He told them. He sensed something wrong in all their reactions, something that didn't quite fit with normal behavior. Either the note was some sort of joke, as Gerry was inclined to believe, or it was serious and should be handled in a serious organized way. He wanted to knock some sense into all of them. "If anybody wants to kidnap me why can't they just do it? Why all this cloak-and-dagger stuff? I'm going to find out what this character has to "learn" me that will partake of my interest."

A hard glint of determination lighted Maria's staring eyes. "Don't be a fool, darling. I'm sure you have Ernst's interests at heart, but don't you understand how easily he can be blackmailed? His people know how to handle these things. I'm sure he doesn't want you to interfere."

They all instinctively turned to Ernst. He stood like a general surrounded by his aides, remote but alert. "I'm bored by all this." He looked at Gerry. "Please don't make unpleasantness, darling."

"*Me* make unpleasantness?" He moved back to Ernst's side to illustrate the fact that if Ernst was a general, so was he—not an aide. "I didn't write the note. I think I have the right to make a small unpleasantness about another matter. I'd like to know why Maria thinks you should keep Heinrich with you."

"He wants him to stay," Maria cut in quickly. Her eyes rolled toward the bedroom. "It's no business of mine."

"I wanted him to stay because you said he could be dangerous," Ernst commented succinctly. "Isn't that what you said?"

"I was simply stating the obvious. You told me how much you were counting on his being with us."

"I may have said something of the sort a few days ago. I told you yesterday how much I was counting on you to get rid of him."

Gerry watched with fascination. Ernst was emerging from his isolation in disarray. The sharp note had crept into his voice. "We don't have to count on Maria for anything," Gerry asserted. "From now on, we'll manage our personal affairs together." Their eyes met. Ernst looked surprised to see him.

"Don't be rude to my friends, darling," he protested.

"I'm not being rude. I'm simply stating the obvious. I suppose it might be a bit rude if I asked her why she's giving you opium." He swung on Maria. "Why are there all those little packages with your name on them?"

"Do you understand what he's talking about, darling?" She addressed Ernst.

"Yes. He's talking about those little packages with your name on them."

"Really. You're impossible. Are you willing to let him spy on you?"

Gerry looked at Ernst again and found his eyes full of recognition and acceptance of the role he was claiming for himself. They had made a major connection. Gerry wanted to put an arm around him but knew that he had gained his momentary advantage by being tough and independent. "Shall I go see that man in front of the shoe store tomorrow?" he asked.

"I really do believe it would be better to let Yorgo take care of it," Ernst said.

"When are we supposed to be leaving here?"

"We're all flying to Penang tomorrow afternoon."

"OK. In that case I don't suppose it matters much, but if there's any more of this sort of thing I want to know about it." He turned back to Maria. "Do you understand? No more opium. If he's easy to blackmail, why make it easier? Having people like Heinrich around isn't any help either."

"Ernst darling, will you please tell this sweet lamb that you chose Heinrich for yourself?" Maria requested.

"Yes, darling, it's quite true," Ernst assured him. "He amused me in his primitive way. Actually, Maria is much more alarmed by him than I am. I think he's quite harmless, if treated properly."

"I certainly don't want you not to treat him properly." He couldn't resist giving his hand a squeeze.

"If new alliances are being formed that make me *de trop*," Maria said grandly, "I'd be delighted to know about it. I'm quite exhausted with all these arrangements."

It was the obvious thing to say but she carried it off with style and put both Gerry and Ernst firmly in the wrong. "You've been indispensable," Ernst assured her smoothly. "We would never have got away tomorrow without you. There was nothing personal in what Gerald said. Tell her, darling."

Feeling like a naughty schoolboy, Gerry spoke up. "Certainly not. There're just certain things that Ernst and I want to decide for ourselves. We've got to be very careful about dope. You probably didn't know he's agreed not to have it."

"Then you're planning to replace Heinrich?" she asked.

"Me? Replace Heinrich? What a funny idea. I'm not replacing anybody. Ernst and I are working out a strictly private arrangement between ourselves." He turned to Ernst. "If we can't be alone, I might as well go." Ernst was looking slightly bewildered but amused. "I want to whisper something to you in a corner," he said, drawing him back to the end of the room. "I don't want to go into it with the others, but in that mix-up with the magazines your letter got lost. Taken maybe. I don't know. There was nothing in it of any importance except to me. Is it something that should worry us?"

"I can't see why. I didn't even try to tell you how much I love you. That will be the next step."

"Bit by bit. Little by little." Gerry smiled a challenge and decided to test him on another front. "I've always liked a nice grope but I gather there's no chance of being together in a way that matters until we're on the yacht."

"How can we? All these arrangements and rather a big surprise tomorrow. Once we're on board, we'll all be on our own."

"OK, so long as we both know what's going on. André and I are having an affair. It started with his saying he was in love with me but I think we have that under control. He knows I intend to be faithful to you but that makes sense only if we're together. I told him he could move in with me this afternoon. We're staying overnight in Penang?"

"Yes. We go on board the next day."

"Then I'll probably keep him with me there, too." If Solange was right, that should drive him wild with desire. If it did, he was awfully good at hiding it. "You have no objections?"

"I want you to be happy, darling. Solange says he's spellbound by you but then, so is she."

"She said she'd tell you what happened. You approve?"

"I certainly expect people to be spellbound by you, darling. Please try to be careful about making her pregnant. I'm planning to have an heir in the next year or two. I would like it to be my own. On the other hand, perhaps not. It might be quite fitting for you to provide one for me. It's something we must discuss together, all three of us."

Ernst was winning this round hands down. Gerry was allowed to have a beautiful lover. He could assume paternity on his behalf. He was going to have to do more than show him his cock to make him jealous. He was robbed of most of his armament. Looking at him, he knew Ernst had no reason to be jealous. André's charm seemed frail by comparison. His handsome head was set imperiously on his strong neck. He wanted to touch him everywhere, his hair, his lips, the part that had so far been concealed from him. He was aware of the vulnerability in both of them that was going to make it difficult to strike a workable balance between them. He still had a lot to learn about being firm and forceful when everything in him longed to yield. "At least we have no secrets. The next time you ask me to come see you, I won't expect us to be alone."

"I'm making my plans, darling. Don't be too difficult."

"Why shouldn't I be? Isn't that what fighting's all about?" He spoke belligerently. Not being a fighter, he had to fake it, but the effect was visible and arresting. Their eyes met and Ernst's wavered and betrayed him. He was hiding something. He was afraid of something. He was on the verge of some revelation. Their bodies seemed to be propelled toward each other but Gerry lifted his hands in a panic of resistance and held him off. He mustn't make anything easy for him. "Am I going to see you later?" he asked lightly.

"Of course, darling. We're all having a quiet dinner together on the roof terrace. Don't be more than an hour."

The moment passed. Gerry nodded and headed for the door. Maria intercepted him. "Is it understood? You want us to decide about the note? You're not going to get involved?" she asked.

"Oh." He pulled it out and threw it on a table. "Not if Ernst doesn't want me to. I'm sure you're right. Whoever wrote it probably just wants some money. It's all too new for me to be very clever about it. I'll learn." He saw her pick it up as he continued toward the door. He let himself out with the impression of leaving a gathering of conspirators. Odd. The rich and powerful were engaged in a conspiracy these days simply to survive.

He crossed the hall and rang the bell and André admitted him, still wearing his robe. Gerry threw an arm around his shoulders and walked him back to the bedroom.

"Are you all moved in, darling?" he asked, spotting a battered suitcase.

"That was no great job. I didn't bring much with me so I could pick things up along the way."

"We'll go shopping for you tomorrow. We have all morning. I want to get you a chain like mine. Do you like it?" Everything that happened with André should have been happening with Ernst—undelayed lovemaking, moving in together without to-do, the exchange of small love tokens.

"Like it?" André exclaimed. "Oh darling, I'd love one like it."

"Good. They'll be our lovers' chains." Looking into the clear depths of André's eyes almost made him forget the last troubling moments with Ernst. God knew what complications still awaited him; there was probably a long way to go before he had felt his way around all the ramifications of Ernst's life and was equipped to come to grips with them. He felt the twinge of uneasiness again, the sense that he had missed something. "I'm using you shockingly. You know that, don't you?"

"You mean, you like having me here while you're waiting for Ernst? What more could I want?"

"Not just tonight. We're going to be in Penang tomorrow night. I told him I wanted you with me there, too. He's not ready for me to be with him yet. That's why I say I'm using you."

"I want you to. Did you show him that letter?"

"Yes, they were in quite a state about it—especially your cousin Maria. They don't want me to do anything about it. We shall see."

"What do you mean? Mightn't it be dangerous?" André put a hand on his chest and toyed with the chain.

"How? Still, I know what you mean. There's something about Ernst that makes you think of danger."

He felt tensions mounting in him while they prepared for dinner, despite the comfort of André's presence. Would he ever be able to share a bathroom with Ernst, play with him, laugh with him, feel as if he owned him? His deep-seated fear of blundering remained with him. What if Ernst changed his mind and asked him to stay with him tonight? He intended to refuse, to put André first until Ernst dared claim him fully. Was it a decision he would regret for the rest of his life? He had survived Ernst's closing the door on him the first night. Maybe it would be his turn tonight. Hang tough. It was an expression he and Jack had turned into a private joke.

To distract himself, he concentrated on making André look his best. His body seemed to have expanded to fill his clothes. The hours in the sun were beginning to cast a glow on his skin. Gerry hitched up his trousers for him and tucked in his shirt and put his own chain around his neck. He unbuttoned his shirt to expose his smooth chest. The transformation was complete; last night's beautiful schoolboy had become tonight's boldly ravishing beauty.

"I must be out of my mind," Gerry said, gazing at him with astonishment. "How can anybody *not* fall in love with you? Come on. Let's go show you off."

They crossed the corridor hand in hand and found the party assembled. The conspirators had given way to the carefree, fun-loving Beautiful People. A cork popped. A quick glance around revealed that only the host was missing. Laughter and the hum of conversation filled the room. Even Heinrich was looking quite cheerful. Solange had her back to Gerry as she talked to Trevor. The sight of her filled him with a nice glow of affection. A waiter approached with a tray of drinks.

Yorgo appeared and handed each of them a cardboard folder of the sort used by travel agents for plane tickets except that it was black with the single word "Hephaistion" embossed on it in gold. Yorgo started away and turned back. "Ah," he said, consulting a leather-bound portfolio, also black, also with "Hephaistion" stamped on it in gold. "*Monsieur le comte* will see that he hasn't been assigned a cabin number. Mr. Kennicutt was given the last double cabin. The singles are rather cramped. We try not to put anybody in them. The Baron thought *monsieur le comte* might arrange to move in with Mr. Kennicutt."

Gerry looked at André. His face was alight and he was blushing again. Gerry laughed. "Sure. That'll be fine." He read no particular significance into the arrangement. Ernst had said they'd be on their own once on board. Why put

André in an uncomfortable cabin if a comfortable one would be free soon after departure?

Yorgo handed each of them a small gold pin in the shape of an H. "A memento from the Baron. The gold is real but there is a better reason not to lose them. Everybody must have one in order to get on board. You'll also be able to use them for credit here and there along the way. Charged to the Baron, of course."

"Are you *monsieur le comte?*" Gerry asked when Yorgo had left them, laughing again at the happy excitement in André's face.

"Well, yes, I suppose I am. I don't much bother about it but Ernst insists on it when we're being formal. Everything's perfect now, darling. I was afraid it wouldn't work out that way. No matter if you're not in it often, it'll be our cabin."

Even while he longed to be with Ernst, Gerry couldn't imagine saying anything that would put out the light in André's eyes. "His Highness may allow me into his quarters through the back door, but I'll still be able to check up on you." He looked at the black folder. "What's 'Hephaistion'?"

"The name of the boat."

"That occurred to me, but what's it mean?"

"You don't know? How marvelous. I know something you don't. He was Alexander the Great's boyfriend."

"The boat is named for Alexander the Great's boyfriend? Good for Ernst. Hephaistion lives." He opened the folder and removed a sheet of paper and shook it out. It was headed:

Hephaistion
Spring 1975

Below was a printed form with handwritten amplifications. His name and cabin number were there, departure and arrival dates (tentative), the address of a shipping company in Cochin, another in Goa, a third in Bombay.

"All very shipshape," Gerry commented. "Is this all of us? No new arrivals today?"

"No. The two boys are joining us in Penang. They're American."

Gerry looked around to make a quick head count, nodding and smiling at anybody who caught his eye. "Two more? That's bad. We'll be thirteen."

"No, twelve, I think, darling. Are you counting Yorgo? He's staff."

"He eats with us."

"So does the captain, I think. That makes fourteen."

"That's better. Let's go talk to Solange. She likes you almost as much as I do." They touched hands and crossed the room.

As soon as she saw him, Solange tucked her chin in and looked up at him with dark serious eyes and a mischievous smile. "You're here at last, darling. I missed you so yesterday. I've been waiting all day to tell you what a relief it was to hear that there had been a misunderstanding about your being invited on the cruise. I was so puzzled about your not mentioning it when we were last together." She laughed naughtily. "We *did* have other things to think about."

He leaned down to her and brushed her lips with his. "You're a sweetheart."

"Have you been filled with regret for the wasted years spent with lovely men?"

"Well, let's say I found out that girls can be lovely too."

They laughed and her eyes lingered in his for a moment, softening with remembered pleasure, and then she turned to André. "Dearest André. You're very beautiful tonight."

"I've had a beautiful day." His eyes were on Gerry, innocently proclaming his love. Gerry put an arm around his shoulder.

She looked from one to the other and back to Gerry. "You've learned that I was right about him?"

"Very right. I still can't believe that anybody so beautiful can be such an angel."

André laughed enchantingly. "You promised you wouldn't make me vain."

Her smile broadened and she crinkled her nose. "How lovely. We're all going to have a beautiful time."

Gerry kept watch on the bedroom doorway. Ernst finally appeared in it and their eyes met and Ernst's slid past as he moved regally into the room. He was looking imperiously handsome, more decorously dressed than the first night, with only one great gold chain and pendant and a more formal shirt with a Byronic collar that exposed an expanse of statuesque torso. Gerry dropped his arm from André's shoulder. As he approached, greeting his guests, Gerry saw that his eyes were clear and still without makeup.

He came to a halt in front of them and Gerry could feel all of them encompassed in his enormous muted charm. "I'm sorry to have been so long. The King was on the phone in a talkative mood. He regrets our departure. He has a notion that as long as we're here, his throne is secure. I had no idea I had such a calming effect on the populace. It's the only place in the world where I do." He was very much in command this evening, more integrated as a personality than Gerry had so far seen him. There were no elusive or tantalizing loose ends.

Paolo was immediately at his side with cigarette and jeweled holder. Ernst turned his head to the lighter and waved smoke away. His eyes fixed on André. "Good evening, dear child. I heard you weren't well, but good heavens—you really *are* the most beautiful boy I've ever seen in my life. What do you say, Gerald darling?"

"As far as I'm concerned, there's no question about it."

"We agree, as usual." He turned to Gerry with a gentle smile. "Perhaps 'as usual' is an exaggeration, but I think we're getting there, don't you?"

It was a very personal remark but Gerry felt nothing personal flowing from Ernst. This wasn't his disappearing act but a startlingly new and unexpected move in their war of nerves. He was demonstrating that he was intact, that the splendid façade was the whole man, that he had no need of a prince to awaken him with a kiss. If he could keep it up, he was truly invincible. Only a look of strain around the eyes raised doubts. Meeting the challenge, Gerry returned his hand to André's shoulder and hugged him closer. "I'm told that getting there is half the fun," he said, looking levelly at Ernst.

Ernst didn't respond but turned to Solange and kissed her on the cheek. "I hope you've told Gerald how glad you are he's coming with us."

"I have, but I think he knew already." She said it in a way that made all three of them laugh.

Ernst addressed André again. "I wanted to apologize to you about the cabin. I can't bear to put anybody in those wretched little single cupboards but Gerald has priority, as I'm sure you understand. Are you going to share?"

"Of course," Gerry interjected. "We were going to ask to be put together."

"Excellent. Everybody is content. I should tour our shipmates to see if anybody has any questions." He moved on with Paolo at his heels. Gerry had been relegated to the rank of guest—an honored guest, no doubt, but no longer a treasured companion. The waiting game.

He made an effort to climb back up to the festive level where he had started. André turned adoring eyes to him, the long soft lashes making them bosky pools of comfort. They almost made him forget Ernst's snub.

"He seems to want us to be together," André said.

"Yes. He doubtless has his reasons. You can see why I don't feel much about fidelity."

"I don't understand it but I hope I fit in the way you want me to."

"All I know is that I'm beginning to worry about being unfaithful to *you.*"

"Oh darling." He turned his head away with a quick intake of breath.

Sally, Solange's companion, joined them. Gerry's interest in her had been awakened and he found her even prettier than before, a vernal, well-bred English prettiness that contrasted piquantly with Solange's more subtle physical appeal. She was slight, with a boyish, forthright manner, and as they all drank and chatted together, he sensed an easy intimacy between the two girls. The four of them created an island of interrelated affection in the conflicting currents that eddied around them. He heard Farr's clipped witty inflections giving point to a story.

"—never met her? She was a formidable old bird. She was a dyke, of course. She was always surrounded by gays and thought of nothing but music. She conducted a great *salon* in Paris before the war. Cocteau took me once. I was a child at the time. When Jeannot introduced me, she looked at me across that great dykey chin and said, 'How do you do? I assume you're a homosexual. Now let's talk about music.' "

He had caught the attention of the room and raised general laughter. The court jester. Gerry wondered what the party would have been like if chance hadn't led him here. Who would André have fallen in love with? Would Ernst have remained satisfied with Heinrich? Would he ever have had a girl? Shake the kaleidoscope and watch the pretty patterns change. Imagining the group without him helped him to look at his heavy involvement with a more amused and detached eye.

He found that he needed all the detachment he could muster. When they mounted to the roof, Ernst's master plan for the evening became clearer. Three tables had been set out in a tropical bower that had probably been created for them since it was well apart from the public dining terrace. Stars glittered above them, the great light-strung river snaked away through a garish urban landscape. When they were all seated with a bit of prodding from Yorgo, Heinrich had been restored to favor; he was at Ernst's side, with Farr and Maria. Gerry's foursome remained intact. Poor Mrs. Farr had been demoted to a table with Trevor and Yorgo. In terms of protocol, Gerry had nothing to complain about; he was with his hostess where, as a male and honored guest, he belonged. The hell with protocol. He had fucked up royally. His play for some measure of control had been a flop. André wasn't being offered to him—he was being forced on him. He looked across the candlelit table into adoring eyes and his heart was pierced with sweetness. Ernst had fucked up too. Nobody had to force André on him.

The food was exquisite, the wines superb. As the meal progressed, it became apparent that Sally was captivated by the French boy. They looked about the same age. She teased him boyishly and made a joke of her flirtatiousness. André responded charmingly, with much more aplomb than Gerry would have expected, but his eyes didn't stray from his love for more than a few moments at a time. They all laughed a great deal and held hands on top of the table between courses and vowed not to let anything break up their happy foursome during the cruise. One for all and all for one.

When a waiter leaned in front of André to clear the table, Solange darted her head to Gerry and whispered into his ear, "Oh, *please* fall in love with him. I can't bear to see such adoration go unrequited."

"I've tried to," Gerry muttered. "I know what you mean. I think I'd kill anybody who hurt him."

"No secrets," André and Sally chorused in unison.

"It's all right if they're loving secrets," Gerry assured

them. "There are certain people whose vanity must be curbed." André chortled and put his hand out to him across the table. He took it and held it and wished that touching him would eliminate Ernst.

When they had finished dessert and the table was finally cleared, Solange ducked her head to him again. "Change places with me, darling. He's dying to be close to you."

They made the shift and André looked up at him with such joyful welcome as he reseated himself that he leaned forward and gave him a light kiss. Briefly, he resented the eagerness of the exquisite lips that brushed against his. He wasn't going to settle for the wrong person.

"Crikey," Sally exclaimed. "That's what I've been wanting to do all evening."

They ordered more wine and when their glasses were being refilled Gerry saw Ernst rise, Heinrich at his side, Paolo hovering in the background. The other two remained seated. He advanced deliberately to the foursome.

"You must excuse me. I'm having an early night. Enjoy yourselves." He looked down into Gerry's eyes. "It's very beautiful to watch you." He laid a hand on his shoulder in a sort of benediction that permitted no response and went on to the other table. The war was on. It was going to be a real one. Gerry's heart was beating violently. He wanted to jump up and follow him. He wanted to make a scene, claim him in front of everybody, renounce him forever, knock Heinrich down. He crossed his arms on his chest and hugged himself and waited to calm down. Why did he let Ernst do this to him? Was he trying to prove that making love was unimportant? He thought of the simple delight of holding André in his arms and of all that had grown out of it. He wished the boy would stop looking at him; André made him feel guilty for wanting somebody else.

Yorgo appeared at his side and leaned down to him. "Excuse me. The Baron says you'd like me to take care of a money matter."

Gerry collected his turbulent thoughts. Money matter? Of course. He'd buy André everything in sight. He looked up at Yorgo and said, "Yes. I—"

"If you'd like to call me when you're up and about in the morning, I'm sure it won't take more than a minute."

"OK. Thanks." He saw Ernst and Heinrich headed for the exit, followed by Paolo. Yorgo hurried after them. If he hadn't made a point about André, would he be going with them? Whatever for? He'd made his point about Heinrich, too.

"I'm afraid that's not a very good sign," Solange said quietly at his side.

"How do you mean?" he asked, wondering if she were referring to Heinrich.

"Hurrying through a meal. It's what he always used to do. He wants to get to his pipe."

"Is that it? Damn. I raised a bit of hell about that earlier this evening."

"You did?" Her eyes widened. "That was very brave of you, darling. It's something he doesn't like to talk about."

"It's something I don't like, period. We're getting off to a fine start."

"Then this *is* the start of something, darling?"

"I think so but if you don't make love with somebody you think you're having a love affair with, everything stays sort of esoteric. If we can work out some sort of life that makes sense for all of us, I go on thinking we might have something tremendous. Are you still on my side?"

"No, darling, I'm on my side. I told you. You're planning to make a life with us, not just have an affair? He's awfully clever at winning everybody over to his side, but he hasn't known anybody like you for a very long time. There *was* a man once, older than he, before we were married. He almost won but he was against our marriage. Ernst ran off with him on our wedding day but—I think he wanted Ernst to give up everything he'd ever known. He didn't succeed."

"I've heard about that."

"Many people have. I'm afraid I wanted Ernst to get rid of him at the time, but that was long ago. You know? Things change. Things changed very much for me night before last. I discovered how much I want change. I'm being very selfish. Otherwise, I would go on warning you to run for your life."

He lifted her hand to his lips and kissed it and didn't let it go. They were speaking quietly but he was aware that the playful exchanges between the other two were suspended at moments while they listened to this peculiar conversation. He didn't mind if Solange didn't; he felt as if they were all in it together somehow. Privacy had been replaced by group solidarity. "It's probably too late to run. Maybe it was from the minute I saw him. Something started that has to finish. You're in it, too, of course. All this sounds a bit mad still, but he said today that he might not mind my being the father of his heir."

Solange uttered her wonderfully hearty laughter. "It is *quite* mad, darling, but I wouldn't mind either. I'd love to be part of your household if that's the way you work it out."

They toyed with each other's fingers. "What did you mean about his not knowing anybody like me?"

"I told you, darling. You know? The amazing force of your attraction, to begin with. Just as important, maybe more so, is that you don't want anything from him except important things. I think that's what makes you seem so much more real than anybody I've known since I married him. Real. True. I can't help wondering why you want him but in such matters reason doesn't often play a very large part. Also, I haven't quite grasped yet how ambitious you are. If you rescue him from the life we lead, you might end up with quite an interesting and good man."

He laughed uncertainly. "Tonight it looks as if I'm going to end up with nothing at all, but there's a lot going on under the surface. I think I'm going to get him, whether he knows it or not." He looked at the other two and laughed again. "How's that for no secrets, children? Come on. Let's have some more wine."

The Farrs and the Horrockses soon came over to say good night to their hostess. "We're going to be friends, aren't we?" Maria asked as Gerry rose dutifully.

She could afford to be condescendingly kind after what she probably considered his humiliating exclusion from the inner circle. "Let me know if you find out anything about that crazy note," he said noncommittally.

"It's quite utterly revolting to see people laughing as if they hadn't a care in the world," Farr snapped. "I don't think I can bear it for four weeks."

They finished their wine and Gerry and André kissed the girls good night in front of Solange's door and crossed to Conrad under the somnolent eyes of the guards. As soon as the door was closed behind them they moved into each other's arms. Gerry lifted his hands to André's hair and held his head and basked in the glow of his young desire. He wanted to make up for his occasional brief resentment of him.

"I love being with you," he said, "regardless of what else is going on."

"You make me feel it even though I know you want to be with Ernst. Oh God, to be with you like this."

They released each other and went to the bedroom and undressed quickly. Gerry hung up his clothes and turned to the bed. André lay sprawled out on it like a wanton offering to Eros, defenseless, inert but erect, unashamedly surrendering himself. What more could anybody want? He went to him and dropped down to him and their bodies slid around each other, finding positions that were known and necessary to them.

"*Mon amour,*" André murmured. "I'd like to stay like this all night and talk about everything. It was amazing hearing you talk about Ernst. Did you mean that people like us can have lives together like—well, like people who get married?"

"Of course, darling. I've just spent a year with somebody who treated me like his wife. I'd still be with him if he hadn't been killed."

"Oh." He allowed a moment of silence to pass. "I've always thought it would just be sex for a little while and that would be that. I suppose that's part of being immature. You expect to really live with him?

"I'd much rather fall in love with you and really live with you. Maybe I'm biting off more than I can chew but I don't see why just because you're Ernst von Hallers and have all the money in the world you can't have some sort of a reasonable normal life."

"Well, darling, I don't know if I should mention it—I mean, I've never thought it was anything against him particularly but it might make a difference in the way you're thinking—I know he likes it with more than one. You know, *des partouses*. Orgies. There's something else—I was afraid to tell you but I can now. When I was with him, there were two other boys. One of them took me—one of my ten."

"With the others watching?"

"Well, yes. That's what Ernst wanted. I wasn't paying much attention. It was only the fourth time for me and my boy was heavenly."

"I'm amazed. Not about Ernst but by you. You don't act as though you'd been into that scene. I know Ernst has done the lot. So have I. That's why we should be ready to settle for each other. We've both had enough experience to know what matters." Was Maria pimping for Ernst, with Fu Manchu as a go-between, as well as supplying dope? Gerry suspected that this might be the clue to his troubling sense of having missed something. The note from a "frend," addressed to a new and therefore possibly impartial recruit to Ernst's circle, could be fitted into the picture he was groping to fill out. He had had a feeling that whoever wrote it was young. A disaffected member of a troupe of whore boys? Heinrich the stud ringmaster in a circus of local talent? *Something* had been keeping Ernst awfully busy. Boys and dope—the two things he had told Ernst were to be banned. He might have bitten off more than he could chew but he wouldn't know until he started chewing.

"Don't forget we have a date at ten," he said as they slid indolently over each other into a new and interesting position. "We mustn't keep each other up all night again."

"You know me. I do everything you tell me. I'll even go to sleep if—oh my *God,* darling. What're you *doing?*"

"We're having an orgy. It's more fun if nobody's watching."

They were ready in good time for the day's business. Gerry called Yorgo and the efficient secretary appeared promptly and cashed a check for two thousand dollars. He offered to take care of the cable Gerry wanted to send to his bank so that more would be waiting with the shipping agent in Bombay. He had the feeling that he'd better assure his independence of movement.

He dashed off a note to the accommodation address in Singapore that Jack had arranged for him, requesting that mail be forwarded to the Bombay address, and Yorgo took charge of that, too. "Is anybody going to see my friend at the shoe shop?" he asked casually as Yorgo was leaving.

"No. Mrs. Horrocks thought it was better to let it go and I agreed, since we're leaving. By the way, if you let me have your passports before we go, I'll take care of all the formalities. Departure is at two o'clock sharp in front of the hotel."

"It's amazing to see you handling your business as if you knew exactly what you're doing," André commented after Yorgo had left. "I can't imagine your letting Ernst run your life, the way he does everybody else's."

"People have in the past, darling, but don't worry—I'm not going to let Ernst take over. You're giving me some much-needed practice in running things for myself but I *am* practically old enough to be your father. Incest as usual. Ready?"

They smiled into each other's eyes and kissed and left. Gerry stopped at the desk to ask for his bill to be prepared.

"Excuse me sir, but the Baron has left instructions about that."

"Has he? Shouldn't you've checked with me?" he protested. He was more annoyed than appreciative. He wasn't going to let himself be bought.

"We must do as the Baron wishes," the clerk pointed out. Oh no we mustn't, thought Gerry.

They emerged from the hotel into the stifling clamor of the city. Traffic was heavy and moved at a breakneck pace. They turned at Smiling Sam's corner.

"This is exciting," André said. "Do you know what you're going to do?"

"The shop's right up there across the street. We'll walk past on this side and see if anybody's standing around with a magazine. If there is, we can decide if he looks like somebody we want to talk to. It's just a couple of minutes past ten."

As they approached the shop, Gerry glanced across without breaking his pace. A well-built young Oriental was standing in front of it, holding against his chest like a placard a copy of the French magazine Gerry had had with him yesterday. He was dressed in Western shirt and slacks and reminded him of Lee. Lee didn't frighten him. "Did you see him?" he asked.

"Sure. He's quite attractive. Pretty tough-looking."

"Tough but not necessarily dangerous. I think we can risk it." He took André's arm and turned toward the curb to wait for a break in the traffic to make a dash for the other side. There was the screech of tires and a clash of metal. Two taxis had met head-on in front of the shoe shop. Traffic ground to a noisy halt. Horns dinned. Asiatic hordes spilled into the street. The drivers gesticulated and backed up and were away again. Traffic plunged into its headlong rush. When Gerry looked for him, the young man with the magazine was gone. An image remained in his mind of a man's silhouette in the back of one of the taxis. Maria's Fu Manchu? Perhaps. Perhaps not. All Orientals looked alike.

"Where'd he go?" André asked.

"Let's go see." They held hands and dodged cars and made it safely to the other side. Pedestrian traffic had returned to normal. Nobody was standing in front of any of the shops. He led the way into the shoe shop and asked for his shoes and the bill to be delivered to the hotel no later than noon, carefully checking the personnel as he did so. Several personable young men, none of them tough-looking. A funny coincidence? Possibly, but credulity had to be stretched pretty far to accept it as such. It partook of his interest but that seemed to be the end of the matter.

"Where do you suppose he went?" André asked when they returned to the street.

"Heaven knows. We've seen two taxis run into each other in the exotic streets of Bangkok. Our friend has disappeared. Is there a connection? Or did he just get tired of waiting for us? Read the next installment for thrilling developments."

André laughed. "Now what are we going to do?"

"Now we're going to tart you up a bit." They went to the jewelry shop where Gerry had bought his chain and found an identical one with a similar pendant. "There," he said, putting it around André's neck. "Everybody can see we're lovers." André's eyes were shining. He shook his head slightly and opened his mouth and closed it, settling for speechless gratitude. "Now I want you to pick one out," Gerry instructed him.

"For you?"

"No, for you."

"But—"

"Not really for you. I want you to keep it until you fall in love with a boy and he falls in love with you. It doesn't have to be at the same instant. When you both know and have decided to live together, then you can give it to him."

"You're too amazing." André was wide-eyed with acquisitive anticipation. He laughed suddenly. "If I'm thinking of somebody to replace you, it'll probably be the most expensive."

Several young clerks stood behind the counter holding up chains while they listened to the conversation and grinned toothily. Gerry glanced at them and smiled back. "I've sneaked a peek at the prices. All these are all right." André moved a hand lightly among the chains and stopped at one that was different from the others, shorter with chunky links and no pendant. Gerry laughed. "I can see just the type it'll look good on. OK. Put it on and cross your fingers. I hope you won't have it long."

They took a taxi to the Jim Thompson silk shop. There, choice almost paralyzed by the glory of colors and textures, he bought André half a dozen shirts of rainbow hues and two pairs of very tight trousers that made his bottom a scandalous invitation. His slim body was so beautifully proportioned that he didn't need Smiling Sam to show it off. The clothes he'd brought with him must have belonged to an older brother.

Gerry picked up a suitcase at a nearby shop and they headed back to the hotel. André lay back in the taxi and took his hand. "You don't want me to be in love with you but you find the most peculiar ways of stopping me. Here I am, hung with gold, swathed in silk, feeling as if my body is so saturated with love that it must be dripping out my pores, and you tell me not to be in love with you. I'll find a way to thank you. It may take me the rest of my life but I will."

Gerry leaned forward and kissed his lips and sat back. "Darling, I've told you. You're too beautiful to thank me. You've let me have you. What more could I want? Well, we know the answer to that but I don't want to think about it. All I want to think about is whether there's time to make love to you again before we have to go."

André lifted Gerry's hand and put it on his lap. "I'd gladly do without lunch. You're making me so bold. It's not vanity, is it? I certainly couldn't be vain about that."

"I am. The way it gets hard for me. I'll never forget touching it for the first time. You don't know yet what being wanted by such a beautiful boy does to a guy."

André pressed Gerry's hand against himself and giggled. "It's not very big but it's amazing how much desire is in there. More all the time. All for you. It might be a relief to be attracted to somebody else. You really want me to be, don't you?"

"Of course, darling. You will be. Don't worry. That's what that butch chain is for."

They were laughing as they pulled up to the hotel. Gerry

was informed at the desk that his things had arrived and been sent up and he was presented with bills. André went ahead while he paid and waited for change. André let him in, naked except for the chains, his cock lifted at a lively angle.

"My God," Gerry exclaimed, standing back against the door and gazing at him. "Gold suits you. We've got to get you lots of it."

André moved in against him and quickly undressed him. His hands and mouth moved over him with the authority of an established lover. Gerry stood motionless for a moment, wishing for some dam to break and sweep him up in generous young love. The dam held.

"We're in luck, darling," he murmured. He leaned down and pulled him up. "It's not even 12:30 yet. We have half an hour to love each other some more and then we better have our things taken down and get a bite in the bar. If we have lunch sent up we might stay forever." They stood naked together and reached for their identical chains and tugged at them to bring their mouths together.

At two o'clock, they all became heads of state. At least, that was the impression their departure gave. Air-conditioned limousines were lined up in the driveway and hotel staff bowed everybody into them. Gerry craned his neck for Ernst and saw him and Solange bringing up the rear surrounded by bodyguards. Not a moment for intimacy. A motorcycle escort popped and stuttered into action around them and off they roared, bringing traffic to a halt all across the crowded city. Gerry and André had a limousine to themselves. André collapsed in a fit of giggles.

"Oh darling," he gasped. "Isn't it heaven? Is this the way you're going to live when you get Ernst?"

Gerry was laughing with him. "This isn't nearly showy enough for me. I'm going in for gilded carriages and outriders carrying spears. No. Elephants for Bangkok. We'll tie up the town all day when we go out to lunch."

They rocked about together while they elaborated their fantasies, then gradually sobered. "Do you suppose you have to be born to this for it to make sense?" Gerry wondered. "I mean, maybe there's a reason for it."

"The King probably wanted to give Ernst a nice send-off." André sputtered with laughter some more.

"Where did you know him before? Is it always like this?"

"In the south of France and Paris. There were limousines but no motorcycles."

"I think I could cope with a few limousines. The motorcycles are a bit noisy. Anyway, you can see why I have moments of thinking I must be crazy to imagine having a pleasant little romance with him."

"You *are* crazy. I'm much more the type for romance."

"You probably are. You better check with me before you give that chain to anybody."

"I'll give it to you right now if you accept the conditions of the donor. He insists that whoever gets it must worship me and give me lots of gold."

Gerry drew him close and made love to his face in the way that had become a familiar joy. He traced the sweep of his brows with his fingers and moved his lips over his lashes. He explored the bridge of his nose with his tongue. He put both hands around his neck and felt him swallowing. He opened his mouth with his fingers and held his ears to place his head so that their lips were barely touching and slowly inserted his tongue and let it roam voluptuously behind his lips and over his teeth and back to his throat. André began to make small crooning noises. Gerry hugged him and gently drew back.

André laughed shakily and sat with his eyes closed, breathing deeply. "Goodness. I was about to come. My mythical lover is going to have to work hard to make me feel he really loves me if what you do is just liking me."

"Not just, darling. I hope you notice I call you darling. I decided I wouldn't because everybody calls everybody darling, but when I knew I really meant it, I couldn't call you anything else. Even if we stop making love, you'll still be my darling."

"I know exactly when you first called me darling. I thought it might've just slipped out until you kept saying it. Now I think my poor young heart would break if you stopped."

They shot through several gates manned by little men in uniform and bumped out onto an air strip, sirens screaming, and came to a halt beside two small sleek planes. Gerry seized the opportunity to speak to Ernst at last. He put a hand on André's shoulder and led him to the group that was forming around their host. He kissed Solange. Ernst was looking energetic and alert. He put a hand out and held Gerry's without looking at him while he finished some exchange with Trevor. When he turned, Gerry saw immediately that he was still playing the wholly integrated man, with a slight difference; he was so at ease in the role that he could now include in it some recognition of the claims they had made on each other, while maintaining a distance between them. He was enormously, confidently attractive but not at all the man who needed his love.

"Now that you're here, darling, we can go," he said. "We're in this plane." He turned to André. "Has Gerald told you that you're growing more beautiful every day? But truly. You are. It's quite striking." Gerry saw his eyes drop to the chains and then move from him to André before lifting to him again. "How very charming of you. You can give us all lessons in loving." There was kindness and understanding in the choice of words but no warmth in their expression.

"I've been meaning to raise a bit of hell about my hotel bill," Gerry said, meeting him on his chosen level of host-guest artificiality. "You shouldn't have done that."

Ernst smiled with complicity. "You know quite well that it means nothing between us. We have more important things to think about."

Gerry put an arm around Solange and gave her a secret hug to give himself confidence and at a signal from Ernst led her up the boarding stairs. The Farrs followed. He glanced back to see that Ernst had André in tow. Paolo, transformed into an air steward, bowed them into the small cabin. Gerry waited while Ernst and Solange and the Farrs settled into the front seats. Then he nudged André into the rear and moved in beside him and slid an arm around him. They looked at each other and yawned hugely and burst out laughing.

"I guess we haven't had much sleep, have we? Come here, darling." André nestled in close against him and laid his head on his shoulder and kissed his neck. Gerry unbuttoned André's shirt and laid a hand on his breast. "Comfortable, sweet darling?"

"Mmmm," André sighed. His eyes were closed, the lashes furring his cheeks. "Ernst understood about the chains, didn't he?"

"Yes, darling. Everybody will. We've tagged each other." A smile twitched André's lips and a brief bubble of laughter escaped him. Gerry could feel the peaceful beating of his heart. They slept.

The arrival in Penang was a repeat in reverse of their departure. Official greetings, limousines, motorcycles, a drive along a winding jungle road, the dying siren wail as they drew up in front of the grand old pile of the E and O Hotel. Seeing it jolted Gerry out of his torpor. Here he was again, flown in almost as abruptly as he had been flown out. It had all happened so quickly that he hadn't given any thought to how it would affect him. It affected him very strangely. Again, he was deeply grateful for the beauty at his side. He was afraid he might lie down in the middle of the ornate lobby and bawl. He glanced down a vast endless corridor and felt himself being carried off in the sinewy arms of a rangy young stranger. A boy approached with keys and, to Gerry's relief, they were directed to the opposite wing. They were ushered into a huge high-ceilinged room simultaneously with the arrival of their bags.

"Let's go cool off in the pool," Gerry suggested when they were installed. "Then we can have a real nap and anything else that strikes our fancy. I suppose somebody will tell us what the program is for this evening. It's sort of peculiar being here again."

"You've been here before?"

"Yes. That man I mentioned—the one who was my husband—we met here last year. He took me to Saigon with him."

"How wildly romantic."

"Yes, I suppose it was. There was nothing romantic about his getting killed."

"I'm sorry."

He remembered the deserted pool more vividly than he had expected and wished that he had avoided it. He had been standing here when— He dived in and did two fast lengths and climbed out. It was just a pool. He glanced across at where Jack had been sitting and turned hastily away. Jack stood before him. "Hi there," he said. "You better come with me." He was unceremoniously lifted off his feet.

A great sob broke in his chest and he was blinded by tears. He stumbled toward the balustrade that separated the hotel garden from the sea. He found it and leaned against it while his chest heaved and tears streamed down his face. He licked them from the corners of his mouth and a choking cry of grief was wrenched from him. He felt André at his side and was immediately calmed. In a moment, he was able to lift his arm and put it around his naked shoulders and hold him close.

"It's all right. We're a weepy pair. He was killed only about a month ago." Saying it shocked him. It was hard to believe that it had been so recent. Had Jack died so that he could drift across the Eastern seas in decadent ease with a drugged playboy and his dubious entourage? Jack would be amused by the emergence of his masculine side and would approve of André, might easily want him for himself. He would doubtless want to hit Ernst. He ran a hand over his face, wiping away tears. "He was such a wonderful kid. That's what he was really, a big, crazy kid, not very much older than you. I made him happy for the last year of his life. I have that to my credit." He squeezed André's shoulder. "Come on. Let's have a swimming lesson and then we can lie down. I'm tired."

They returned through the hotel lobby in their dressing gowns. Passing a reception room, Gerry was surprised to see Ernst, still wearing the casual costume he had traveled in, surrounded by what looked like a group of local businessmen in ill-fitting summer suits. Ernst caught sight of him and lifted his hand to detain him and came out into the corridor, followed by Yorgo.

"I'd like to speak to you, darling," he said. His manner was gentle and agreeable but there was a new undercurrent of hostility in it.

Gerry turned to André. "You go ahead. I'll be right there."

Yorgo crossed the corridor and pulled out chairs around a low table and they sat. He placed an American passport in front of Ernst. "You haven't been entirely truthful with us, darling," Ernst said, looking at him almost playfully, as callous as a child.

Gerry felt the steel in him and a little chill ran through him. Ernst could hurt. He looked at the passport and recognized it as his. He'd forgotten the irregularities in it. He supposed that was what this was about. If so, why not just ask him about it instead of acting as if he'd been caught in a criminal act? He had the feeling Ernst wanted to make something big of it, perhaps so that he could forgive him magnanimously, perhaps to establish some hold over him. He was fighting once more for the preservation of his elusive dream. "I doubt if either of us has been *entirely* truthful," he said evenly.

"You told me you had just come to Bangkok from here. Your passport shows that you left here almost a year ago and went to Singapore. It was stamped a few days ago somewhere in the north near Chiang Mai. The authorities questioned Yorgo about it when we were leaving but because you were with me they agreed to let it go."

"Damn decent of them. I wish Yorgo had told me. I paid a good deal for that stamp. I'd've raised considerable hell if anybody had suggested there was something wrong with it." So much for the implication that he needed Ernst's protection. He grudgingly admitted to himself that the dates definitely looked fishy. Although Ernst's manner made him wonder if he deserved it, he forced himself to offer an explanation, hating to share intimacies with Yorgo.

"All right. You want to know where I've been all this time? If we ever had any time to talk to each other, you'd know the story by heart. It's rather an important part of my life, something I'd want anybody I care about to know. I've told André about it. I was in Saigon having a very serious affair with an American Air Force officer. It was all highly irregular. If the war weren't such a pitiful fuckup, I'd never have got in, much less stayed on for months. I suppose I might have got shot as a spy or something. I thought it would save confusion and embarrassment all around if I tried to forget it ever happened. That doesn't apply, as I say, to people I care about." He looked into Ernst's eyes and felt sick and sad at the uneasy distrust he saw in them. Memories of Jack were guiding him. Jack wouldn't put up with distrust. He was clean and straight and demanded the same from others. "Is that my passport?" he asked abruptly. He reached for it and put it in his pocket. "Thank you. I might need it."

"You must admit it's rather a fantastic tale, darling. You haven't by any chance been working for the CIA?" There was a note of apprehension in the question.

"Oh God. Paranoia rampant. Sure. My latest assignment is to attach myself to you and pass on all the secrets of the deposed monarchs of Europe. They just didn't bother to make sure my passport was in order."

"It's not as farfetched as you might believe. Attempts of that sort have been made before. Using you would indicate unusual intelligence on their part."

"A bit obvious, maybe, but I don't want to think about it. I will not allow anybody to doubt my word. If you think being vague about my recent travels when I'd just met you constitutes a lie, so be it." That was laying it on the line. Tough and firm. He was close to tears but he wasn't going to let this monster get the better of him. If it was time to go, he'd damn well make a dignified exit.

"If it was a lie, it could have been a harmless one, I agree," Ernst said, still withholding his verdict. "I know your background. I want to convince myself that I have nothing to fear from you."

"You probably have plenty to fear from me, as you've said yourself, but not the way you're talking about now." A voice in him told him to cut it short, before he begged for forgiveness or something equally idiotic. "Look, I don't have to go on this cruise. I'll take André, since he wouldn't stay without me, and go. That's probably what I should do anyway if I had more sense. If there's any doubt in your mind about this nonsense, just say so."

"How can I help having doubts, darling, considering what experience has taught me? As usual, you make it very difficult to resist you."

"You make me sound like some sort of con man. I guess we have to make allowances for your experience. I'll think it over." Ernst's eyes softened. Apprehension was shading into a plea for some assurance that Gerry had no way of giving. He and André had already achieved such confidence in each other through their bodies' passions that this sort of groundless mistrust couldn't arise between them. Couldn't Ernst understand what he was denying them? He looked at him as uncompromisingly as he could.

"Come, darling," Ernst said with a touch of petulance. "I have the right to make sure that the people I travel with aren't going to cause trouble."

"You certainly do and I should've remembered that my passport looks a bit peculiar. It was a serious oversight but I don't like the way you called it to my attention. You haven't treated me as a friend. I feel as if I'd been through a police interrogation. Come to think of it, if I were some sort of agent, this is just the way I'd carry it off. Bluff my way through. Invent a story you can't confirm. If I were you, I'd take that into account. We'd both better think it over. I suppose we'll see each other later." He forced himself to his feet and left, seething with conflict. He was angry and hurt and close to abandoning the struggle. They came so close and then the chasm opened between them. Apparently there was no substitute for physical union but he knew that his longing for it with Ernst was being diminished by his satisfaction with André. He felt as if Ernst were pushing him to the verge of an irrevocable blunder. By taking André, Gerry had created exactly the situation he had intended to avoid; he had made it dangerously easy to slide out of the big commitment that he had learned was the only thing that could give his life meaning. He heard footsteps behind him and turned to find Yorgo hurrying after him.

"He asked me to give you this," he said, handing Gerry a card. "It's the invitation we sent out for the gala tonight. They haven't been given to the yachting party. He was planning it as a surprise for your last evening ashore."

"I see. Thanks." Gerry glanced at the card as he went on. It was a formal crested and engraved invitation to "a musical evening" in the hotel gardens. Was it supposed to mean that peace was restored between them? Ernst would have to do better than that.

André was asleep naked on the bed, stretched out flat on his back, his legs straight, his cock nestled in repose between them, his arms thrown up over his head in an attitude of trustful abandon, beautiful and moving. Gerry silently approached and looked down at him. He had accepted a certain responsibility for him; he was going to have to cut him loose as painlessly as possible, regardless of what happened with Ernst.

André's eyelids fluttered and slowly opened and his eyes moved up wonderingly over Gerry. "Oh my God," he murmured. He raised a lethargic hand to him. "Whoever this belongs to can have me."

Not long afterward, there was a knock on the door, but they were too ecstatically engaged for it to distract them. When they got up to prepare for the evening, Gerry found an envelope lying on the floor in front of the door. His name was on it and he pulled out a sheet of the familiar stationery. "Forgive me. These misunderstandings will end. I need you. E." His eyes remained on the last brief sentence. He couldn't ask for more than that. He was learning how to win and his will to win was instantly revived. He had never had a taste for fighting; his first impulse had always been to dissemble or give in. And all the important things in life had passed him by. Resist simple undemanding adoration. Struggle on.

The party was memorable and Ernst arrived stoned. He drifted through it radiating a serene amiability, charming, a slightly insane glitter in his eyes, untouchable. As soon as Gerry had spoken to him, he realized that he needn't bother to attempt any further contact tonight. Victory was hollow. Why go on struggling when the field had been abandoned?

The foursome of the night before was reconstituted as a threesome, Solange being occupied with her guests who, it turned out, had been gathered from far and wide, from Kuala Lumpur and Singapore and Hong Kong. It was a mixture of Occident and Orient, with ambassadors in the ascendant. The ladies were decorative in evening gowns. There were a number of white dinner jackets adorned with medals.

"Crikey," Sally exclaimed. "I should've worn a veil. I've already spotted three very grand cousins."

"I've bagged an uncle," André said, newly elegant in his new clothes.

"Somebody asked me if I was my father's son," Gerry contributed. "I said yes, even though I'm not."

"That's right," Sally said. "Solange told me. You're a bastard."

"So people have often said."

The setting was superb. The garden was strung with lanterns. The lights of Butterworth glittered across the strait that separated Penang from the Malaysian mainland. The night was soft and perfumed. A miniature and very luxurious version of the Car Park in Singapore had been recreated under the trees, each food stall serving its individual delicacy. The turtle soup was a special triumph. The choice of wines was impeccable. Chairs and tables were set out for the hundred-odd guests and the threesome commandeered a table for themselves. Solange, looking exquisite, joined them briefly. Gerry took her hand.

"How do you do it? Did you dream all this up?" he asked.

"Mostly Ernst. Wait till you see the rest of it. I've almost forgiven him for being in the condition he's in."

"If we can prevent our lady friend from giving him more, it'll all be gone soon, if tonight's any indication. He must've had a ton of it."

"Once we're off, maybe you can start throwing it overboard."

"You're assuming that I'll be admitted to the inner sanctum."

"You will be, darling. Whatever happened this afternoon left him in a state. You know? You've seen the result."

"Is that it?" His heart leaped up with hope. He had driven him to his drug; Ernst was human after all. Maybe the waiting game was wearing him down, too.

"What happened to our new shipmates?" Sally inquired. "Are they here?"

"The Americans? Haven't you met them? If I see them, I'll tell them you're over here. I still have to do my duty to seven Excellencies." She twinkled off.

Everybody had eaten copiously and was consuming brandies and liqueurs when there was a clash of cymbals and a tinkle of bells, followed by the pounding beat of massed percussion instruments. Voices were raised in excitement and there was a general surge in the direction of the music. Farther along the seaside garden a stage had been set up where an orchestra in colorful Eastern costumes was sitting on the floor extracting spine-tingling rhythms from an assortment of weird-looking instruments. Four rows of chairs had been lined up to accommodate the company. Gerry caught a glimpse of Ernst in the middle of the first row as they seated themselves. An engraved and crested program in each chair announced the performance of an orchestra and troupe of dancers from Bali. Sally sat between her escorts and André put his arm around behind her and gripped Gerry's shoulder.

A half-naked male chorus performed a fierce dance as electrifying as hand-to-hand combat, with a haunting vocal accompaniment. There was a comic dance with performers in monkey and demon costumes. A beautiful youth performed an extraordinarily expressive solo without rising from his knees. A series of numbers was danced by incredibly beautiful girls in gorgeous costumes, all swaying bodies and sinuous necks and flickering fingers. All the while, the orchestra pounded out its compelling rhythms, punctuated by metallic crashes and tinkling bells. It reduced the audience to a drugged, spellbound stupor.

Without allowing time for it to recover, the performance was followed by a staggering display of fireworks that seemed to soar up out of the sea and obliterate all of Malaysia. Everybody was on their feet uttering collective gasps of awe as one explosive miracle followed another. Gerry remembered Ernst's dynastic origins. Was he trying to show them that he still had the power to destroy the world? The earth trembled and the sky cracked with a final stupendous pyrotechnical extravaganza. There was a long stunned silence and then a burst of cheering and applause. Penang would know that Ernst von Hallers had been there.

The company seemed to have trouble pulling itself together. People wandered about dazedly bumping into chairs and bushes. André leaned exhaustedly against Gerry. "Being in love with you and all this going on at the same time is going to be a tough act to follow," he said against his ear.

"Anybody who could've planned it deserves our respectful indulgence." Gerry was awed by the tenacity and ingenuity that must have been required to put it all together. He had the sense once more of having pitted himself against a giant.

"That was a bit of all right," Sally remarked perkily.

The Car Park had been replaced by a long table laden with bottles of every type including a splendid array of champagne coolers. At the other end of the garden, a dance floor had been laid down and an orchestra was launched creditably into Western jazz. Solange came tripping up to them.

"So? What did you think of it?"

"I'm speechless," Gerry said. "The Balinese are marvelous. I can't wait to go there. Absolutely fascinating. Do you give parties like this often?"

She tucked her chin in but her smile was almost tender rather than mischievous. "He's awfully good at them. Will they be allowed under the new regime?"

"Definitely. I'm already thinking about a private recital by Nureyev for a few carefully selected friends."

"He's already thought of that. When Rudi was first in Paris, he tried to arrange it. I'm not sure that he was purely motivated by his devotion to the arts."

"Now let's talk about music," Gerry said, imitating Farr's clipped delivery. They all laughed.

She stayed with them for the last couple of hours of the festivities. All four of them danced together. They drank quite a lot of champagne. They wandered through the garden. They encountered two young men in the shadows and Solange introduced them as Hank Something-or-other and Ken Bales, their new shipmates. The foursome moved on without them, too immersed in their private fun to acquire followers. Sally had resumed her tomboy flirtation with André.

They were the last to retire. Ernst had long since disappeared. Gerry and André were both slightly unsteady on their feet when they reached the privacy of their room. They stood together grinning a bit drunkenly at each other and their hands moved about on each other as if to make sure they were both still there.

"Sleepy?" Gerry asked.

"Drunk." André giggled. "What an evening. I've kept reminding myself not to miss anything. I may never have another night like it as long as I live. For the last hour what I was thinking about mostly was going to sleep with you. I mean just sleeping. Not like last night. Going to sleep with you makes me feel almost more a part of you than anything else. It's like getting into each other's unconscious."

"What a lovely idea. Let's dive into each other's unconscious."

Their instruction sheets warned them to appear before 12:30 at a dockside address to board the *Hephaistion.* They were awake long before the appointed hour but they lingered in bed until the last minute. They were up and packed and down at the reception desk at noon. They were informed that everybody else had gone and that their baggage would be put on board and were escorted out to a waiting limousine. Gerry waved it away and asked for one of the bicycle-powered rickshaws that crowded the streets.

"I'm tired of feeling like a Chicago gangster," he said as they were pedaled away. "I've never been so uncomfortable in my life. I love it."

They were jostled through the heat and stench of the teeming old Conradian port, past food shops and ship's supplies and all the esoteric junk of Oriental sidewalk bazaars.

"This is the first time I've really known I was in the East," André said. "It's amazing."

"Air-conditioned hotels and limousines aren't very interesting. We should really see things." It was a speech he was intending to deliver to Ernst. It was confusing living with the wrong person.

They lurched past the Butterworth ferry landing and on a slight rise through a gap in the sheds along the waterfront they had a brief view of a majestic yacht anchored in quite close to the Penang shore. Gerry had the impression of a smallish ocean liner before the view was cut off.

"My God, was that it?" he exclaimed. "Did you see it?"

"Yes, it must be. I know *Hephaistion* has a black hull. Well, Ernst says it's dark blue but it looks black. I saw her in Cannes but didn't go on board."

They turned down an alley and stopped at the end of a pier and scrambled out. While Gerry paid, two handsome young sailors approached with HEPHAISTION stitched across their T-shirts. He paused to gaze across at the long dark hull with its sleek white superstructure. He could just make out a gold *H* on the single funnel. He felt for the gold *H* pinned to his shirt and checked to see that André's was in place.

The sailors escorted them out along the pier to a gleaming speedboat. They all jumped aboard, the motor started, lines were cast off and they were away, leaving a great plume of spray in their wake. Gerry was suddenly caught up in a sense of adventure. His heart was beating rapidly. All his personal preoccupations had blinded him to the fabulous moment that was now upon him. He was about to embark on tropical seas with India as his destination. The graceful craft that was to be home for the next couple of weeks dwarfed all the traffic in the busy waterway and looked as if it could carry them to the ends of the earth. He turned to André and found a reflection in the boy's eyes of the light he could feel shining in his own. He gave him an excited hug and could feel his laughter although the sound was drowned by the roar of the motor.

In another few minutes, *Hephaistion* towered above them. The boarding stairs were down. They made a wide curving approach and the motor was cut. Another handsome young sailor was waiting with a boat hook to pull them in. Gerry and André clambered up the stairs and were met at the head of them by an officer type, resplendent in a crisp white uniform, very good-looking in a different way from the sailors, blond and Nordic and clean-cut. A bevy of beautiful Oriental boys was lined up behind him wearing little jackets over their brown chests, and sarongs. Something for every taste. If every male in sight were available, as Ernst had suggested, the voyage might prove quite exhausting for the insatiable.

The officer was holding a clipboard. He glanced at their pins and asked for their instruction sheets. He checked the names on them against the list. "You gentlemen are sharing a cabin," he said in lilting English. He looked at Gerry. "Mr. Kennicutt? I believe you still have your passport. We should have it if you don't mind, sir." Gerry fished about in his pockets and handed it over, feeling as if he had finally surrendered. Ernst had him in his clutches.

The officer waved at one of the beautiful boys who stepped forward and bowed them aboard. Somewhere above them, a whistle sounded. Gerry noticed two sailors with guns on their hips patrolling nearby. They followed the boy. Most of the afterdeck was taken up by a swimming pool. They were ushered through a large drawing room where Gerry spotted several good French pieces and a Cézanne over the paneled fireplace. Why not travel with a museum piece? They were led down a long carpeted passage. The boy stopped in front of a door and bowed them into a large cabin with twin beds. It was the equal of the first-class cabins Gerry had seen on the two transatlantic liners he'd been on. Their bags were already there. The boy showed them a modern bathroom, smiled winsomely and left. They approached each other with gleeful smiles.

Gerry pushed a stray lock of pale hair back from André's forehead. "There must be a bar on this broken-down scow. Let's go exploring. I need a barrel of beer. You're very nourishing but you don't exactly slake the thirst."

"I'll unpack for us later. That's a wife's job, isn't it?"

They threw their arms around each other and headed for the door. They found an open companionway just across the passage leading up and they climbed it and came out on the bridge. Another intimidatingly armed sailor was standing guard and Gerry turned toward the stern and saw the pool below. He led the way down to it by a steep ladderlike companionway and found an outdoor bar being set up in the shade just aft of the main saloon. Trevor was already there with a drink in his hand.

"Ahoy," he greeted them amiably.

A handsome youth served them icy beer and Gerry downed half his glass in one gulp and let out a great "Ahh" of pleasure. "I may live."

"We all had rather a night of it, I imagine," Trevor commented. His eyes lighted on their chains. He put down his glass and lifted the pendants from their chests and held them together. "I see. The banns have been published, have they?"

Gerry glanced at André. He wasn't sure his young lover was prepared for this sort of banter; he was gazing into his glass, looking flustered. Gerry dropped a protective arm around his shoulder. "Hadn't you heard? The captain has the right to join us in wedlock at sea, hasn't he? Our parents are beginning to make trouble. They don't approve of us living in sin."

Trevor laughed and after an instant André giggled and looked up delightedly. "Papa will be so relieved," he said. Gerry uttered a shout of laughter and hugged him approvingly.

Trevor looked at Gerry, making his usual pass with his eyes. "I must say you've kept us guessing. We don't know which way you're going to jump next."

"Those near and dear to me find me tiresomely predictable," he said with a hint of warning. He looked out across the pool. "Do you have any idea what those things are?" He pointed to two bulky shapes swathed in tarpaulins mounted at either end of the after rail.

"The machine guns," Trevor explained.

"Machine guns?"

"Of course. The Straits of Malacca are teeming with pirates. Didn't you know? There's a mortar mounted on the bridge. Ernst says he can blow anything short of a warship out of the water. I think he's rather hoping to put on a show for his guests. We're pretty much out of the bad area here, thank heavens." He put a hand on Gerry's arm and pointed astern across the water. "Sumatra's over there. The pirates generally stay in the narrows to the east. We're heading west of course."

"That's reassuring." He turned away to tactfully remove himself from Trevor's hand and asked for more beer. Anonymous letters. Taxi crashes. Now pirates. A vague air of danger seemed to hover around Ernst wherever he went.

The party slowly assembled. Maria appeared, more relaxed, less theatrical than usual. Perhaps she had been relieved of the cares of office; there wasn't much organizing she could do at sea. Mrs. Farr made a bizarre entrance, looking as if she'd borrowed a yachting costume from her son, slacks, double-breasted blazer, gilt buttons and all. Gerry was rather sorry she didn't have a cap to complete the effect.

"Is everybody having a wee drinkie?" she cried. "Who has a wee drinkie for me?" She spied Gerry and beamed at him. "How nice to see you again. My, how you've grown."

Solange and Sally arrived with Farr and the group was given an immediate lift as he took over with his performer's tricks.

"Really, Mother," he said, shaking his head dolefully at her. "Have you asked the captain to assign you a regular watch?" He turned to André. "You're still with us? When I was leaving, everybody was in a great flap about whether you'd wake up in time. I believe Gerald was the crux of the situation. I've always found there's nothing like a good crux to keep me in bed." He went on gathering laughs with his manner rather than by anything he said.

The two new Americans joined them. They struck Gerry as oddly straitlaced and conventional for this crowd, tall and slim and unobtrusive. One of them was good-looking in a buttoned-down way; the other was balding and a bit lacking in the chin department, a scholarly type. Ernst and his entourage arrived and the deck between the bar and the pool was suddenly crowded. He glanced around and came directly to Gerry and stood in front of him, looking clear-eyed and affectionate and composed.

"At least you're here." As he spoke, a look of such intense and inexplicable pain came up behind his eyes that Gerry wanted to throw his arms around him and hold him. The pain of need?

"I'm sorry," he blurted. "Thanks for your note. I didn't mention it last night because— Everything's all right."

The pain passed. "We're clearing the decks, darling." He gripped his arm for a moment and moved on among his guests. Heinrich detached himself to speak to Maria.

Additional beautiful serving boys appeared to set up a buffet. An awning unrolled silently over the pool. There was a drift toward the chairs and tables set out around it. Gerry became aware of a throbbing under his feet. The engines had come to life. His heart accelerated with the sense of adventure. A very pampered adventure, but still . . . Several sailors moved about on deck fiddling with ropes as sailors had a habit of doing, their trim bodies molded in tight pants and T-shirts. A stimulating sight. The stern was swinging around against the land. The narrow strait between Penang and the mainland came into view, bustling with seaborne traffic. A whistle blew above. Ernst stepped forward and lifted a glass.

"The anchor is about to come up," he announced. "Welcome, everybody. Here's to all of us and happy sailing."

Mrs. Farr burst into song. "Anchors aweigh, my boys," she screeched. "Anchors aweigh—"

"Mother," Farr said wearily. "The ship's concert isn't until tomorrow night."

Everybody laughed and cheered and raised their glasses. Two sailors moved aft and removed the tarpaulins from what turned out to be, in fact, very lethal-looking guns cocked at the sky.

"—twenty very well-armed men," Ernst was explaining to the two new Americans. "We're prepared for trouble. I'm always a bit sorry when there isn't any. It might be jolly good sport sending a boatload of pirates to the bottom of the sea."

The callous ruthless note. Spoken in Ernst's gentle voice, the words made Gerry's blood run cold. He moved closer to André and Sally.

"Do you suppose those things work?" she asked.

"Let's hope we don't find out," Gerry said. He took

André's empty glass. "How about another? Food seems to be on the way."

The yacht had started moving slowly forward. There were three deep blasts from the ship's horn that echoed across the enclosed sea and the throbbing underfoot became more pronounced as they picked up speed. Gerry followed André over to the rail and they looked down at the water swirling away from the dark hull.

"This is the first time I've been anywhere on a boat," André said. "Is it supposed to make you feel sort of sad?"

"You mean a lonely feeling? I always get it. You'll see. Once we're out of sight of land, everybody on board will become more important to us than anybody we've ever known." The right atmosphere for embarking on a major love affair. The decks were being cleared.

A sumptuous buffet was served, featuring a mountain of fresh gray caviar, as they rounded the southern tip of Penang and set a course toward the westering sun. Ernst soon withdrew. Solange caught Gerry's eye and lifted her eyebrows. The others sat about drinking wine when they'd finished eating. Little by little the group thinned.

"I've got to go unpack before everything's ruined," André said eventually.

"OK. I'll come help."

Solange and Sally rose with them and they passed through the main saloon, which Gerry thought of as the drawing room, and parted where a passage crossed over to the other side of the ship. When Gerry and André reached their cabin, they found that their bags had been unpacked.

"We've still got the workingman's mentality," Gerry said. "We've got to start thinking of ourselves as the leisure class. Let's go for a swim instead. The pool's salt water. It'll help you stay afloat." They wandered around the cabin, rearranging some of their clothes, using the bathroom, putting toilet articles where they wanted them.

"I think Hank is attractive, don't you?" André remarked.

"The good-looking American? Aha. Have you started wanting everybody in sight?"

André giggled. "Even if I did, I still don't know how to go about it. I can't throw myself at everybody the way I did at you."

"You don't have to throw yourself at anybody. You're

the most beautiful boy in the world. All you have to do is stand still and smile encouragingly. Nobody'll ever get that chain if you don't give people a chance." He had some deck-clearing to do himself. Hank might do the trick.

André laughed cheerfully. "What if smiling doesn't work? Then what?"

"I don't know. Maybe I'll have to take a paternal interest in your sex life. I'll make sure you'll like it, whatever happens."

"I probably will, if you have anything to do with it."

Gerry had undressed and pulled on his trunks. He handed André his. "Wait till everybody sees you with nothing on but that. You'll probably be raped by all those jolly tars and that'll take care of that."

"Goodness, darling, that sounds sort of sexy. Maybe that's what I really want." He giggled as he adjusted his trunks.

The awning had been rolled back from the pool and the remains of lunch cleared away. Everybody had gone except the two Americans who were also stripped down to swimming trunks and were stretched out on deck chairs reading. They all waved and Gerry led the way to the opposite side of the pool. Big beach towels had been placed on all the chairs. The yacht was gliding through the water at what seemed like a good speed. The throb of the engines was regular and lulling. Every now and then, the boat gave a slight lurch that made them adjust their balance. They stretched out and André pushed his trunks down on his hips so that only his sex was covered.

"I want to get tan all over like you," he explained.

"Why don't you take that thing off? Solange says we can be naked around the pool. Give your boyfriend a treat. If he comes on strong, maybe you won't even have to smile."

"Are you going to take yours off?"

"I don't have a sexual block. I'll wait and see how much privacy we have. If one of those sailor boys comes along and catches my eye I might have a conspicuous reaction. Go ahead. You're not shy anymore."

"Not with you. I'm not sure about others." He laughed and peeled off his trunks. The sun was burning but the air moving around them kept them cool. Gerry sat thinking of Ernst. The decks were being cleared. He could take the pain out of his eyes, whatever had caused it, if given the chance. "I need you." They needed each other. That was what it was all about. André was ready to embark on a life of his own. Perhaps he could speed the process along.

He jumped up and dived in and swam back and forth, casting glances at the Americans. A devoted couple? They were enough alike in general type to suggest that they belonged together, both dark, both in their mid- or late twenties, with similar builds. They were both wearing dark glasses so he couldn't tell if they were paying any attention to him. They looked as if they were absorbed in their books. He climbed out and lay in the sun with André again and dozed. When he next opened his eyes, he saw that one of the Americans had left. A full head of hair told him that the remaining one was Hank. He checked André. His lips were parted. His sex was neatly tucked between his legs. He was beautifully asleep.

Gerry rose silently and made a smooth dive into the pool and swam slowly along close to Hank's side. He saw him shift restlessly, suggesting that he might be aware that Gerry was looking at him. Gerry sank and swam underwater toward the shallow end. When he surfaced, he looked back and saw Hank remove his dark glasses and put them between the pages of his book. He sat forward and slung a towel over his shoulder and rose. Gerry pulled himself out and adjusted himself in his trunks, stirring things up for show, and strolled toward him. As they approached each other, he could see that he had a very good body, lithe and athletic with a permissible scattering of hair on his chest. He glanced down at the trunks and found the view unusually promising.

"Hi," Hank said in a pleasantly deep voice. They stopped and faced each other from equal heights.

"Hello yourself," Gerry said with a playful smile.

"How's the water?"

"Fine. A bit chilly when you get out. You haven't been in?"

"I meant to but it's cool out here in the breeze. I got caught up in my book."

"What is it?" Hank held up a deluxe French edition of *Madame Bovary*. A mind as well as a body. He put a wet hand on the hand holding the book and turned it as if he were studying the binding. Contact established. Hank didn't seem to mind. "It's good," he said, letting go.

"It's about time I read it. Poor thing. She didn't get much fun out of life. You better warn your friend that if he goes on lying around like that, somebody's apt to leap on him."

Gerry chuckled. "I'm sure he wouldn't mind in the least if *you* leap. He said nice things about you."

"He did?" Hank looked surprised and pleased. "Aren't you together?"

"We're sharing a cabin," Gerry said, leaving André room to maneuver. In spite of the American's almost too regular features, there was humor in his face. Gerry found him unexpectedly likable.

"It figures. The two most attractive guys on board."

"Thanks, but you shouldn't mention me in the same breath with him. He's one of the great beauties of all time. We've got to choose our words very carefully around here. If we except our host and the officers and crew and all the cabin boys, you and I might be the two most attractive guys on board." He let his smile become mildly flirtatious. "Actually, I'd put you way ahead of the cabin boys."

Hank's answering grin was no more than friendly but nice. "You have a very scientific approach to these things."

"I like to get everything straight. I know you're Hank. I'm Gerry Kennicutt. I still haven't got your last name."

"It's Smallacre. The English probably call it Smollicker or something to make it sound even sillier."

"I like it. It sounds sort of cozy and old-fashioned. I know somebody called Smallcock. You can be thankful your ancestors were thinking about their land and not something else. I have the impression that in your case it would be a gross misnomer."

"You really get down to the nitty-gritty, don't you? OK. I'll admit I've noticed something fascinating about you too. It would be pretty difficult not to notice it."

They laughed and there was a beat of silence while their eyes felt each other out. The interest in Hank's was unmistakable and growing more explicit. He had a little twitch in his strong jaw that was curiously sexy. Pent-up passion? Gerry was beginning to understand André's point. "Do you know Ernst well?" he asked before the silence could force either of them to make a definitive advance or retreat.

"No. I just met him. My friend Ken Bales has known him for quite a while."

"How long are you going to be with us?"

"Until Bombay, at least. Ken hasn't decided yet. He collects Oriental art. He's waiting to talk to some people in Bombay before we decide whether to go on to Kashmir."

"I hope you do." Gerry was frankly flirting now, trying to overcome the caution in Hank's eyes. He was pimping for André but the emphasis had shifted somewhat. Hank's emanations were wholly masculine. The old familiar yielding was spreading through him and desire was gathering in his groin, desire to be used for a man's pleasure. Discovering that Hank had had him should break André's block. Clear the decks. "How about you and Ken? Are you a serious pair or do you cheat?"

"Only when I'm pretty damn sure I won't get caught."

"I *always* got caught. That's why I'm a lonely old bachelor."

"I'll bet there was plenty to catch you at."

"I always try to keep busy." This time, neither tried to cover the silence with small talk. Their eyes met and held and there was no doubt where their thoughts were leading them. They were in it together although Hank still needed a bit of prodding to assert himself. He tried to pull back with a burst of solicitude.

"Good Lord. Look at you. You're covered with goose bumps. Here. Take this." He gripped his book between his knees and swung his towel out around Gerry and settled it on his shoulders. As he did so, Gerry caught sight of a significant bulge in his trunks that hadn't been there before. Hank's hands lingered on him while he adjusted the towel. Gerry lifted his to them and covered them. Gerry felt His Majesty sliding up along his groin, barely contained by elastic. Their eyes pinned each other down, Hank's searching and intense. He opened his strongly modeled mouth and his eyes shifted to Gerry's lips and he closed it again. Gerry let his arms fall to his sides and he held the ends of the towel. Hank reached for his book and grasped one end of it with both hands and propped the other end against the top of his trunks. It was quite a natural way to hold a book and brought the back of his hands to within grazing distance of Gerry's crotch. Cautious but inviting.

"You don't want to catch a cold," Hank said, recovering his voice and trying to pretend that nothing was happening between them.

"I should probably get out of these wet trunks." Gerry made a small thrust with his hips and closed the gap. The hands remained motionless against him for a moment. Hank's eyes wavered and then fingers crept stealthily over him. Gerry twisted his hips slightly so that they would find all of it.

"My God," Hank muttered. The muscle in his jaw worked.

"Thanks. If you're as nice as you look, you'd do me a favor and set it free."

"I'd sure as hell like to. You mean now?"

"Sure. It's putting on this show for you." He moved his hands forward holding the ends of the towel to make a tent around himself. "Nobody will see. It can't be considered cheating. It's just so I don't catch cold." He felt a tug on his trunks and his erection swung out into a waiting hand. Hank looked down and moved his hand slowly along it.

"Jesus Christ," he said. "Man, that's a cock."

"Thanks again. I'll probably say the same to you if you give me a chance. Your hand feels lovely there but I don't want this to be a solo. Can I talk you into some serious cheating?"

"God yes. Where?"

"That's no problem. We'll be very discreet. Look up at the bridge." He twisted his head and looked up too while the hand continued to stroke him slowly. "That's where all the works are. We naturally want to see what's going on up there. A fifteen minute inspection should be very instructive." He turned back with a smile. "Much as I hate for you to let go of me, we'd better make a dash for it." He glanced across at André. He didn't appear to have moved. He drew away from Hank and closed the towel in front of himself and bundled himself back into partial confinement as he strode to the ladder that led to the upper deck. He glanced at Hank at his side. "You'd better keep that book in front of you. Jesus Christ indeed." He climbed the steplike rungs with Hank at his heels. They hurried across the open deck to the companionway where the armed sailor had been earlier. Nobody was there now. He went on and came to an open door that gave onto the bridge. A sailor was standing at the wheel. He smiled and nodded and beckoned them in. A young officer appeared from around a corner and welcomed them.

"Gentlemen. Come in. You wish to see if we know how to run the ship?" He smiled broadly.

Gerry smiled back. "We just wanted to make sure there was somebody up here. Can you show us how everything works?"

"Of course. That's the wheel. You know about that. This is the most interesting part." He opened a metal door into a small cupboard of a room filled with a bank of instruments with dials and switches. "The electronic equipment. Actually, we'd get along very well without anybody up here." The three of them crowded into the cupboard and the officer began to explain the various functions of the instruments with his back to them. Gerry took advantage of their being crowded up against each other in the cramped quarters to thrust his hand down the front of Hank's trunks. He took a quick breath. It was big.

"I'll tell you what," Gerry interrupted. "I didn't realize there'd be so much to see." He squeezed Hank's cock and heard choked laughter behind him. "It's fascinating. We'll come back when we have more time."

"Anytime. Anytime," the officer urged, turning his head to them with an inviting smile.

Gerry pushed Hank out and hustled him along the deck and into the companionway. They tumbled down it, jostling each other, half in and half out of their trunks, tugging at the towel for cover and laughing breathlessly. With Gerry leading, they flung themselves across the passage and into the cabin. Gerry pulled off his trunks as he closed the door and turned to his quarry. Hank was naked, still holding his book. All the power of his athletic body seemed to be concentrated in a massive shaft of flesh that lifted heavily toward him. A shiver ran down his spine. He had found a man, but the hesitation with which he held himself suggested that he was a man who wasn't fully aware of his manhood's power.

Gerry stepped over to him and took the book out of his hand and put it on the bureau. Hank reached for him and they closed to each other, stumbling toward the bed. They toppled onto it, their bodies tangling with each other while

Hank took his mouth. Gerry felt him subsiding into the simple pleasure of letting their bodies play against each other, as if Hank were unfamiliar with the act of conquest, and he goaded him by pretending to resist him.

He started up and let himself be overpowered, like an undecided girl, and felt Hank charging into action. Gerry's hand found the lubricant where he'd left it in the drawer of the bedside cabinet and he prepared himself while their bodies struggled in erotic combat. Gerry thrashed about, shifting his body to make the outcome inevitable. Strong arms gripped him and forced him to yield. The full weight of Hank's body was thrown into the fray. Gerry managed to reach him with the necessary aid.

"You want to fuck me," he gasped, as if defying him to do so. "You're big. Use this, for God's sake."

"Christ yes. You want it. I've never done it. I'm going to now."

Gerry was enthralled by the conflict he'd provoked. He enacted further resistance to arouse all his partner's aggression for this initiation. Strong hands flung him out on the bed and Hank was on him and made an enormous lunge into him.

"Jesus, I'm in you," Hank muttered incredulously. He gained confidence and his thrusts became a long smooth assertion of his possession.

Gerry hurtled back in time. He was once more Jack's missus. He was a thoughtless kid eager to give himself to any attractive man who wanted him. He was swept up in the ecstasy of being filled hugely and used again, startled by the intensity of his craving. Was this the call of his true nature? It seemed so now but he knew there was an emerging side of him that felt diminished by this passive suspension of responsibility. One last time, before he assumed his role of husband.

With an effort, he retained control over his orgasm; he wanted to save that for later. Hank's body was growing taut with accumulating pressure. He reached his climax with a shout and was tossed about on top of him by long shuddering spasms.

"God, Gerry," he murmured when he was still. "I've never known anything like it. Nobody's ever let me. You couldn't've stopped me."

"I wanted to make sure nothing would," Gerry said with a satisfied chuckle.

"It was good for you? I didn't hurt you? I'm sorry. I couldn't think about anything while it was going on."

"You weren't supposed to. Everything was just the way I wanted it. You fucked me silly."

"God yes. My first guy. I'm still almost hard. I could do it again in a minute."

"Mmmm. I want you to but we'd better not. I forgot to lock the door."

"You what? My God. We'd better—" He withdrew hastily and jumped up. Gerry rose, his erection lifting with unabated vigor. Hank looked down at it. "God, that cock. You didn't come. I thought so. I'm sorry. I'm a selfish bastard."

Gerry laughed and gave him a push toward the bathroom. "What's to be sorry about? I'm still raring to go. It wasn't easy but I wanted to hold back. I had my reasons."

They crowded into the shower together. Hank's cock still jutted forward but had lost its upward lift. Gerry soaped it and in a moment had it operational again. It was shorter than his own but greater in girth. "There. Who'd ever guess you'd just had your first fuck? There's hardly room for both of them in here." He stepped out and quickly dried himself. He had risked André's bursting in on them because he wouldn't lock him out. Discovering them would have been a shock for him but less wounding than being excluded. Now he was ready for him and he wanted to keep Hank with him. For André, he reminded himself, his eyes fixed on the glistening body. Hank turned the water off and took the towel Gerry handed him. "I wish André would hurry up and get here. If he doesn't show soon I'm going to come all over the place. I've been trying to save it for him, in case you wondered."

"What're you talking about?" Hank stared at him, bewildered.

Gerry was learning how expressive his regular features could be. His eyes were full of humor and intelligence, his strong mouth was marked with passion. The muscle in his jaw worked. Gerry touched it with his fingertips. "He's attracted to you. I want you to have him," he explained.

"I don't get it. Are you two having it off or aren't you?"

"Every five minutes. Wouldn't you?"

"God yes, I started to get hard just looking at him lying

there. I'm surprised he even noticed me. He never takes his eyes off you."

"He did long enough to look at you. He's shy about making a pass at you."

Hank was holding his towel at both ends drying his back. He let it drop to his side and stepped out of the shower. His eyes searched Gerry's. "What is this? You wanted me and you want me to have him?"

"That's the idea. We're sharing the cabin. That's why I didn't lock the door. I wouldn't cheat on him."

Hank flinched. "OK. I guess I deserve that."

"Come here, honey." Gerry put his arms around his neck and pulled his mouth to his. Their bodies moved in against each other and Hank's arms slid around him and his hands caressed his buttocks. He loved hands holding him there. Their tongues played together. Gerry drew back as his breath grew labored. He mustn't revert to all his feminine ways; this was supposed to be a farewell performance. He smiled into Hank's troubled eyes and touched the twitch in his jaw. "Tell me about cheating. Are you doing something wrong or is it wrong only if you get caught?"

"It's not as simple as that. Ken's paying for everything. If I don't stick to my side of the bargain, I'll be nothing but a hustler."

"What's your side of the bargain?" Their hands moved over each other, keeping their erections in working order.

"It's a long story. He's done a lot for me. We don't see much of each other except for vacations, but it's understood I don't fool around when I'm with him."

"I see. Have I made you feel like a hustler?"

"No. You make me feel that it's a bum bargain." They looked at each other and burst out laughing.

"Thanks. I'm glad I convinced you you wouldn't get caught. We haven't been too long yet. Stick around a little longer. André's all hung up on me. I think you'll give him a new outlook on life. Do you see what I mean, honey?"

"All I see is that there's not much more chance of my getting caught if I have both of you instead of just you." He grinned and a light of anticipation sprang up in his eyes. "Is that what you mean? You expect me to have him the way we did it, with you watching?"

"Don't get me wrong. It's not for kicks. I'm afraid he

won't let it happen unless he sees I want it. Does it bother you?"

"It might've if it had started out that way. Now that it's happened with you, I guess I can handle it." They let go of each other and Hank toweled his head briskly. Gerry led him to the washbasin and handed him his comb. He felt a nice easy comradeship in their having erections together. He stroked Hank's and watched it stretch imposingly and thought of how excited by it André would be.

"You're a regular battering ram. Imagine your having to wait for me to show you what you really wanted. I knew it the minute I started talking to you."

"I've known it but I'd given up expecting anybody to let me do it. I sure thought of it when I saw André. You amazed me. If André is—"

The sound of the outside door opening and closing was clearly audible in the bathroom. Gerry turned quickly. "Come on," he whispered. André's face lighted up when he entered and froze as Hank followed him. "We've been waiting for you, darling," he said.

"What—?" It was the only word André uttered. Gerry suffered a pang of jealous regret at handing over the beautiful boy but, to his astonishment, he was more jealous of the desire he could see driving Hank's body. He was also astonished by his embarrassment. Jack had made him feel that there was something sacrosanct about lovers' privacy. In observance of the rules of threesomes, he participated in André's climax but it made too many links with his disgraceful past and he was glad when it was over.

Hank returned to the bathroom and André rolled in against him and curled himself up into a ball. Gerry put his arms around him and found his face and kissed him on the cheek. André remained mute and motionless. He held him until Hank came back and stood beside the bed, looking down at them. Gerry looked up at him, admiring his body and his neatly balanced good looks and was no longer jealous of either of them. Their eyes met.

"You're really wild," Hank said with a little smile. He dropped down onto the edge of the bed and moved Gerry so that he could put his erection in his mouth. He sucked it knowledgeably for a moment. Gerry couldn't deny that he'd given him the right to do it but was glad when he stopped. Hank rose and pulled on his trunks and threw his towel over his shoulder and picked up his book. "I hope you don't expect it to end there," he said.

As soon as the door had closed behind him, Gerry unrolled André and laid him out flat on his stomach and entered him. "I've been saving it for you," he said.

"Oh God, yes. Everything's all right again."

"How do you mean, darling?"

"I was afraid you wouldn't want me again after he'd had me."

"I wanted him to have you, darling. I told you I'd find you a big one."

"You said bigger," André said with a quiver of laughter in his voice.

"Well, it is—bigger around. I didn't say longer. You liked it, didn't you?"

"It was thrilling but that was because you were here. I don't see how you know the things you do. You knew it had to be with you."

"I wouldn't have done it like that if you hadn't told me about Ernst and the others. I would've been afraid of shocking you. I knew you wanted him and I suddenly felt this great urge to be taken by a man, the way I have been all my life. It was sort of a final fling before I settle down with Ernst."

"It's all getting more complicated by the minute," André said with a little sigh. "I adore you. I don't adore him but the thought of his fucking you almost makes me fall in love with him. Or hate him. Does that make sense?"

"I think I understand. We've been unfaithful to each other. That's the main thing. You're free now to find out things for yourself."

"Maybe. Yes, I'll certainly let Hank have me again if he wants me. Fuck me, darling. Let me feel the difference."

They found a printed sheet of paper on the floor when they came out of the bathroom. It was a sort of ship's bulletin with the date on it and information about meal times and when the pool would be emptied and other odds and ends. It announced a showing, at eleven o'clock that evening, of a film they hadn't heard of starring Ralph Farr. Ernst thought of everything.

When they went along to the main saloon they found the party gathering and Ken Bales playing expert jazz on the grand piano. Hank was sitting beside him. They all exchanged smiles, Hank a rather distant one. He blushed.

Gerry's smile grew broader. A boy passed with a tray of drinks and he and André helped themselves. Farr joined the pair at the keyboard and Ken switched to a show tune that the film star had made popular years ago. Farr sang it in a light professional voice. The yacht lurched slightly from time to time.

Ernst appeared with only Paolo in attendance and installed himself in a chair that was slightly removed from the other furniture in the room so that nobody could sit close to him. Gerry tensed briefly and relaxed when he saw that he was stoned again. Another evening lost. He went to him and crouched beside his chair. Ernst turned to him with a happy smile and slightly unfocused eyes and put a hand on the back of his neck and began to stroke it. The touch made Gerry's breath catch and his throat ache with longing.

"Hello, darling," Ernst said gently. "I've been thinking about you this afternoon. "What would I do without you?"

"I'm waiting to see what you're going to do *with* me," Gerry replied, putting a hand on his knee to balance himself.

Ernst laughed softly. "I don't wonder. Tomorrow, darling? You've been very patient. All my business is out of the way. We'll be able to talk tomorrow."

Could he count on it? For the first time, Ernst had actually fixed a day. Tomorrow? Did tomorrow ever come? He set his drink down on the floor and put his hands on Ernst's arms and pressed them in a chaste embrace. "Any particular time?" he asked.

"After lunch, don't you think, darling? We'll talk about it tomorrow."

It was like talking to somebody in a dream but it was enough to make Gerry feel gloriously drunk. He wanted to do something spectacular to celebrate the occasion but Ernst was locked away in his private high. He pressed his arms again and burst out laughing, mirthlessly, as a form of release. Tears would have served the same purpose. "You're going to have to share some of that stuff with me. We'll fly together."

Ernst's eyes came into focus on him and his smile brightened. "Would you like that, darling? Of course I will."

If he could get his hands on it, maybe he *would* throw it overboard. He stood and looked down at Ernst, who didn't appear to notice that he was gone. He felt drunk. He might as well *get* drunk. It was perhaps his last night on the town.

A gong announced dinner in the traditional seafaring manner. The captain had appeared, bluff and hearty, also in the traditional seafaring manner. He was magnificent in white and a lot of gold braid. They all filed through a small library into a narrow but handsome dining saloon with more good French furniture. There were place cards and Yorgo moved about explaining that they would be seated differently at each meal. Gerry once more had the place of honor at Solange's right but André had been pried from his other side to be replaced by Hank.

"Is this pure luck or has word spread already?" Hank murmured as they seated themselves. Their knees pressed against each other. "Cheating isn't as simple as I thought. You've got me in an uproar. I've got to talk to you."

"We better cool it, honey. We'll get together after dinner."

Beginning with smoked salmon, a spectacular meal followed. Gerry continued to admire the organizational skills involved and Ernst's canny judgment in selecting his guests. The haphazard group was beginning to find its own cohesion. Farr and Trevor kept them all amused, with inadvertent contributions from Mrs. Farr. Hank and Sally and André represented youth and beauty. The rest of them fell into place around them. Poor Heinrich was the only sour note but he was rapidly becoming irrelevant.

When they all rose to return to the main saloon for coffee, Ernst was with them. A few minutes later when Gerry looked around for him he was gone. He took a cup of coffee from a passing boy and went to Solange.

"Again?" he asked.

"Ernst? Yes," she said unhappily.

"What would he do to me if I really got rid of it?"

A wry smile flitted across her lips. "Probably get rid of you, darling. You don't have to do anything quite so drastic. If you can get him down to two or three pipes after meals, he'll be all right. You know? It's when he's at it all day, ten or fifteen at a sitting, then it's bad."

"I'll start a campaign tomorrow."

She looked up at him with quick attention. "You're going to be more with him now?"

"I hope so."

"I'm very glad, darling."

He finished his coffee and went out to a washroom he'd noticed aft, where the buffet had been set up. When he came out, Hank was waiting at the rail on the narrow covered deck that led forward outside the saloon. Their eyes met and Hank's drew Gerry to his side. They stood at the rail looking out into the dark, the sides of their hands touching. The night was warm with a breeze frisking around the deck.

"What's up?" Gerry asked in a low voice. "Ken didn't suspect anything, did he?"

"No. That's all right—for today. I think I'm going to have to tell him. I didn't know what I was getting into. Can I come to your cabin later if I can work it?"

"Another threesome? André would probably like it. He seems to like threesomes more than I do."

"He's sweet but you really turn me on. It may not be exactly falling in love but it's the next thing to it."

"Let's keep it that way. There're enough crossed wires on this boat already."

"Yeah, I gather you have somebody on your mind. Ernst, I suppose."

"Good guessing."

"I'm not surprised. Where do I figure?"

"Maybe you'll figure with André, honey. I wanted you for myself, as well as for him. You know that. We've had it. We better leave it at that. I'm sort of drunk. Don't tempt me."

"You may be drunk but I'm serious. We still want each other. I can feel it."

Gerry chuckled and moved his hand against Hank's. "Maybe. You're pretty potent stuff. I think you've already made André forget he's in love with me. I like you. That's what you feel. I have a sneaky urge to cut you loose from Ken. You're too young to make bargains except with someone you love."

"That's what I wanted to talk about. I'm going to tell Ken the bargain's off."

"The movie's going to start soon. I don't think Farr would like us to be late. Do you have time to tell me the long story?"

"What long story?"

"You said Ken was a long story."

"Oh. So I did. Well, it's not all that long."

Gerry gave his hand another little pressure and stepped back from the rail. It was time to move around. The urge to do more than touch hands was building up between them. He started forward slowly along the deck. Light streamed from the big saloon windows. Hank talked while they strolled side by side.

"It's not even a story, really, it's just so you understand why I feel obligated to him," Hank said. "Three years ago, I was twenty-three and a hot-shot architect just out of school. Honors. Head of my class and all that. Everybody was offering me jobs and I took one with a big firm in Boston. I was put on important projects almost from the beginning. One of our big clients had a son and we fell for each other when I was just getting going on a job for Daddy. There was a big fuckup. Some of my letters were found. The kid panicked and said he didn't know what it was all about, that I'd gone off my rocker and was trying to seduce him. We'd been going to bed together for weeks but I guess you can't blame him. If I'd had a rich father who was about to throw me into the street, I might've done the same thing. The client threatened to take his business away from the firm if I wasn't fired. That was the end of that."

"God, it's incredible," Gerry commented. "When you're off with a crowd like this, it doesn't seem possible that that sort of thing happens. Just because we're all queer, nobody's doing anything that would disqualify him for an ordinary job. Well, no more so than a comparable collection of heteros. What's your sex life got to do with architecture? A conundrum. Because they both have to do with monumental erections."

Hank laughed. Their stroll had taken them to the wide sweep of the forward deck. A sliver of moon was sinking in the west ahead of them. The sky was full of stars. The yacht was gaily lighted, with a spotlight on the big gold *H* on the funnel. The deck was cluttered with gear. Two speedboats and a long open cutter were cradled under tarpaulins. A crane lifted against the sky, presumably for lowering the boats. There was dense shadow everywhere and movement in every shadow as the breeze snatched at loose ends of tarpaulin and lengths of rope and tossed them about. Gerry thought he could make out a figure slumped in the bow beside the elongated shape he assumed was another gun. They stood beside one of the speedboats.

The breeze darted in under Gerry's shirt and sent a shiver down his spine.

"Have you ever made a pass at anybody who didn't know what it was all about or wasn't ready to find out?" Hank asked.

"Not that I know of."

"Neither have I. That's what makes it so stupid. Because I was guilty of going to bed with a guy who wanted to go to bed with me, the firm wouldn't give me a letter of recommendation. I had a gap in my employment record that had to be explained. I began to feel that my only chance of getting a job was to tell everybody I liked to suck cock and beg for mercy. It was too much for me. I'd known I was gay for a long time but I always tried not to let it bother me. Nobody ever suspected anything unless I wanted them to. I was always one of the guys. It really knocked me for a loop. That's when Ken comes into it. I'd known him before and I knew he had a thing about me but I'd never paid much attention to him. When he heard I was in trouble, he came to the rescue. He was terrific. He got me a good job in Dallas, no questions asked. Nobody asks Ken questions. He's loaded. The sex part has never been very big between us except in the negative way I told you. He wants to keep me for himself when we're together even if he doesn't do much about it. He travels a lot and doesn't care what goes on when he's away. We're talking about getting a couple of partners together and starting a firm of our own. That's it. That's what I think I'm going to have to give up."

"Not for the sake—" Gerry's eye was caught by movement beside the gun in the bow. He had a glimpse of an arm lifting and falling and a fleeting impression of a figure crumpling. He heard Hank say something and then he too broke off and sprang forward. Gerry grabbed his arm and held him. "Did you see what I saw?" he asked in an undertone.

"I don't know. I think I saw somebody get socked and a body being pulled behind that thing up there."

"Yes, something like that. We may be mistaken. Look again. There's somebody still standing there." His blood ran cold. He felt his scalp prickle. He was assailed by a sudden sense of menace. It had been there all along, something nagging, something wrong, a vague intermittent dread. He had related it this afternoon to the sad loneliness of departure André had mentioned. He thought of Maria's trivial lies and heard the crash of the taxis and his body was gripped in a way he had never known before, a turmoil in his stomach and an ache of foreboding that stiffened his limbs. He supposed it was fear and wanted to relieve it with physical activity.

"Shouldn't we go up and see what it was?" Hank asked.

"No." Gerry held his arm more firmly. Was Ernst in danger? Ernst and opium. That was what had started his strange uneasiness. He looked forward again. A figure still slumped in the bow. The dark and lonely sea was dotted with lights. Fishermen? Pirates? Sea monsters with flashing eyes? He tried to laugh himself out of the dread that weighed on him. "Maybe it was just something flapping in the wind. Or the crew fighting. We'd better stay out of it. Let's go up to the bridge and tell somebody."

"Yeah, that's the best idea."

They retraced their steps and found a companionway and in a moment reentered the wheelhouse where they had been that afternoon. They were met by a paragon of handsome Nordic masculinity. He wore the gold-braided shoulder boards of an officer and towered over them, golden-haired, blue-eyed, with a ruddy complexion and a shapely mouth. Gerry was reassured by his splendid presence.

"We thought we saw something funny out there," he explained. Pointing, he saw that the lighted instrument panels around the wheel obscured the view of the deck immediately below them. "It looked like a fight."

"Ah? So?" The officer stepped to a panel and flicked a switch and the deck was flooded with light. A sailor with a gun on his hip in the bow straightened and looked up, shielding his eyes.

"If it was a fight, it's over now." After another moment's inspection, he flicked the lights off. "It was very sensible of you to come and tell us. Any irregularity while we are at sea should be reported. We will check the crew for black eyes and broken noses. A lovers' quarrel, perhaps." He smiled with a dazzling display of big white teeth. "You have heard about sailors."

"Do you know the one down there?" Gerry asked, not knowing what he was getting at but not quite able to let it go.

"Pedro, I believe, although his hand covered his eyes. As you may have noticed, the crew are unusually fine-looking boys. The Baron feels it gives the yacht a better overall appearance. Pedro has many suitors. I'll find out if he's been causing trouble. Gentlemen. Thank you for coming up." They smiled and bowed at each other and the two passengers withdrew.

"If I really saw what I think I saw, it didn't look like a lovers' quarrel," Hank said.

"No. I know what you mean. There was something frightening about it but that might have been the funny light. It scared me. I'm going to ask Ernst how he hires the crew. Aside from having a beauty contest."

Gerry found the companionway that led down to his cabin door and hurried Hank along the passage. He stopped at the entrance to the saloon and made a quick sweep of it with his eyes. André was tactfully talking to Ken. They hadn't been gone long enough to be missed. He turned to Hank, making sure they were both visible from within.

"Finish telling me about Ken," he suggested, trying to get his mind off the sinister, if perhaps imaginary incident on deck.

"There isn't any more about Ken. The rest is about me—and you. The business in Boston did something to me. That's what I was leading up to. I thought something had been killed in me but this afternoon made me wonder. What it did, it made me cautious—cautious about people and cautious about work. I lost my nerve. I haven't wanted to stick my neck out about anything. Certainly not about sex. When you came on strong with me, flashing your cock and enjoying the hell out of yourself, I realized how dumb I've been. You stick your neck out. That's what makes you so exciting. God, are you ever. I want more. I've got to get over playing it safe. Don't you agree?"

"Naturally." Having made love with him made Gerry want to give some physical expression to affection and understanding, while warning him not to include him in the recovery of his nerve. "Just don't stick your neck out *too* far. You said Ken's going to set you up in business. You don't want to lose that."

"That's the risk I've got to take. I owe him a hell of a lot and I want to stay friends with him, but not to the point of turning myself into a zombie. Doesn't that make sense?"

"Of course. It's good for people to help each other but you can't let it change who you really are."

"That's it. That's what I mean. If I try to turn this afternoon into a little case of cheating, it'll be the same old story—not being willing to stick my neck out. It was too tremendous for me to do that. That's why I've got to tell Ken that the way things are won't work."

"That's fair enough so long as you're not getting mixed up about me."

"I'm not remotely mixed up. I know exactly what you do to me. You make me want to design the goddamnedest building that's ever been built. You make me want to work again the way I used to. What's wrong with that?"

"It sounds great. If flashing my cock has made a major contribution to architecture, I'm delighted." They looked at each other and laughed.

"So how about it? Is there a chance of spending the night with you and André? It's pretty kooky—trying to set myself up with two guys at once, but that might give architecture even more of a boost. I've never done anything like it. Well, it's *all* new to me. That's what's so exciting."

Gerry looked at him and saw the excitement in his nice straightforward eyes. He felt the power in him and melted to it. The waiting game was coming to an end in the nick of time. "Maybe we should wait until you've had a chance to talk to Ken and work something out."

"Oh, I'm going to talk to him, of course, but I don't have to tonight. If I come to you, he doesn't have to know where I am. I can say I'm going for a walk. When he goes to sleep, he passes out cold."

"Wouldn't that just be more cheating?"

Hank looked crushed. "Yes, you're right," he agreed without any fight. "I guess it would be. I'd probably go on hoping he wouldn't find out."

"Think about it. And don't forget that André wants you. Let's go in. I need a drink. I'm still thinking about what's going on on deck. Don't tell anybody about it. OK? I may talk to that officer again tomorrow." Gerry finally had a chance to give his hand a squeeze as they turned to enter the saloon. A boy gave him a whiskey and Yorgo approached.

"Do you still have a large amount of cash with you?"

he asked Gerry. "I could have it put in the safe if you want. I've suggested the same with everybody's valuables. We think the cabin boys are dependable but there's no need to offer them temptations."

Gerry remembered that not having to pay his hotel bill had left him with a good deal of money and he agreed to turn it over in the morning. A few minutes later, Yorgo spread the word that the film was ready to be shown and they all trooped out into the passage and entered a miniature cinema auditorium with six or seven rows of deep upholstered armchairs.

"You're about to have one of the major cultural experiences of your lives," Farr announced while they were seating themselves. "You'll laugh, you'll cry, you'll shudder—I hope in the right places."

Gerry chose the back row, followed by André. Hank and Ken moved in beside them. They all sank out of sight in the deep seats. The film was a comedy-thriller in which Farr conquered the forces of evil with his tongue alone. There were scenes of violence that made Gerry uneasy, reminding him of what they had witnessed in the bow. He was aware of André's and Hank's hands lying on their thighs so close to each other that they might have been touching. He hoped Ken wouldn't take it amiss. Halfway through, he heard whispers and Ken rose and crept out. Gerry sat forward and looked at Hank questioningly. Jealous scenes already? Hank leaned across André. Hands joined on André's lap as he did so.

"It's all right," he whispered. "He saw it in New York. He's sleepy."

When he sat back, Gerry saw that their attention was no longer on the screen. Their hands moved on each other. There was the metallic whisper of a zipper opening. He was glad they had taken the initiative and were working things out on their own. As the film came to an end, they straightened and faced forward and adjusted their clothing.

"It was good," André exclaimed when the lights came up.

"I don't think either of you qualifies as a serious critic," Gerry said with a chuckle.

"Well, there were parts that didn't completely hold my attention," André admitted jauntily.

"I'm going to have a nightcap," Gerry said, prepared for them to go off without him.

"Me too. I'm thirsty."

"I'll go see if Ken's OK," Hank said. "I'll be right back."

In the passage they said good night to those who were retiring, and were followed into the saloon by the star of the film and Trevor. A boy was waiting to serve drinks. They complimented Farr and discussed the film and Gerry and André drifted off to the other side of the room.

"Why don't you go to bed with him?" Gerry suggested. "I don't mind sitting up for a while."

"Oh no. I don't want anything without you. Not yet. You started it."

"That's true, but I can't finish it. It's every man for himself now."

When Hank returned, he gave Gerry a big grin. "Sound asleep. That lets me off for tonight, doesn't it?"

"If you say so. We're not making any objections."

"Are you going to stay with us?" André asked him with a little catch of excitement in his voice.

"I guess I better." Hank put an arm around his shoulders and looked down at him. "We don't want to go on misbehaving at the movies. God, you're beautiful."

They drank and chatted. The two older men departed, leaving them in sole possession of the elegant floating drawing room, with the boy to serve them. Gerry wanted to convince himself that this soothing secure luxury was reality, that scuffles on deck were part of a sailor's life.

He tried to pinpoint what it was that had frightened him. He realized that he had superimposed on the brief shadowy moment all the scenes of skulduggery at sea he'd seen in films. Mutiny. Piracy. Villains swarming over the rails. Except that there had been none of the customary plot developments. He hadn't found the resplendent officer bound and gagged, with blood running picturesquely down the side of his face. They sailed on serenely over a calm sea. If he'd been alone, he would be ready to admit by now that he had imagined it. But Hank had seen something too.

Now that he was pushing André off on his own, all his sense of responsibility was being refocused on Ernst. Maria's dramatic warnings had had their effect. It wouldn't require a whole boatload of thugs to "get at" Ernst in whatever way she had intimated. He was going to have to get used to living with unknown danger. He thought of all the guns on board and decided he was making too much of it.

Hank and André discovered, through Gerry's intervention, many shared interests, painting among them. They examined the Cézanne together and decided that it was genuine. Gerry envied them, close to the same age, setting up points of reference and experience between themselves, finding an easy opportunity to become friends. He was determined to efface himself, but they made him the center of their attention. They kept turning to him for confirmation and guidance, finding excuses to put their hands on him, letting their eyes linger in his.

Gerry assessed the bar boy as he served them and decided on evasive action. Maybe he'd been too drunk after dinner to make himself clear but now that his drinks had settled, he knew that a threesome was out of the question. In retrospect, his unexpected embarrassment stuck in his mind as active distaste.

He excused himself to go to the toilet and gave the bar boy a wink and was followed out onto the deck. He turned to the boy, who waited expectantly with a smile so wide and dazzling that it obliterated his face.

"What's your name?" Gerry asked.

"Sunil, sir."

"OK, Sunil. I understand that there're some empty single cabins. Can you let me have one for tonight?"

"Most gladly, sir, but a secret? Me not allowed. We wake the purser?"

"Not if we don't have to. We'll keep it a secret." All the cabin boys were interchangeably graceful and winsome but this one had traces of individuality. His grin was inviting and his body looked tough and manly. Gerry was resigned to being misunderstood but he'd cope with that when the time came. "Does it have a number or something?"

"I show you, sir. My free time in fifteen minutes. We go then."

"Stick around. I want to get away from my friends. You can help by pretending to take a personal interest in me, if you know what I mean."

The grin didn't obliterate the hard lustful glint in his eyes. "Very personal, sir. No pretending."

"I see. Well, thanks, I'm not sure." He smiled at the boy and touched his shoulder. "I'm ready for another drink." He let Sunil return ahead of him. The evening had been a strain—Ernst's tantalizing promise for tomorrow, the incident on deck, his two young friends' efforts to include him in their sexual arrangements. Now he appeared to be headed for complications with a cabin boy. He sighed and shrugged. Better that than coming between Hank and André and cheapening the nice feeling that was growing up between the three of them.

He rejoined them and Sunil brought him a drink. Gerry kept the boy with them by asking about his work and his travels. Sunil was ostentatiously flirtatious.

"Isn't it time for bed?" Gerry asked the other two when he'd finished his drink.

"I'm ready," Hank agreed. They all stood.

"You two go ahead," Gerry said. "I'm curious. I want to find out if these boys are really up for grabs."

"You're coming, aren't you?" André asked anxiously.

"Of course. I'll be right there. I just want to ask the child a couple of questions and tip him for keeping him up so late."

Hank frowned but took André's arm and they left. Gerry congratulated himself for letting them go, with a slight gnawing regret for Hank. If he were where he wanted to be, with Ernst, none of this would be happening. Another boy had appeared and was collecting their glasses. Gerry turned to Sunil with a smile. "OK?"

Sunil grinned. "This way, sir."

They took the corridor that Solange used and entered a small cabin not much bigger than the single bed it contained. Sunil switched on lights and showed him the bathroom and stood in front of him with the lustful glint in his eyes.

"We undress now, sir?" he asked.

Yes? No? He shrugged. Tomorrow it wouldn't matter.

"Is it a service that goes with the cabin or do you really want to?" he asked.

"Oh yes, sir. Very gladly."

"Well then, you'd better stop calling me sir."

Sunil's body was brown and wiry and smoothly hairless, his cock small but erect, his mouth prodigiously accomplished. They spent an agreeable half hour together.

Alone, Gerry slept fitfully, plagued by fragmentary dreams of violence, mixed up with Saigon and Jack and flight. A sense of menace penetrated his semiconsciousness. He endured it until he realized that he was fully awake and that daylight filled the cabin. He found his way back to his own cabin and entered stealthily. Hank and André were asleep in each other's arms. He pulled on his swimming trunks, looking down at them. They looked very right together—androgynous beauty and masculine good looks, a slim boyish body protected by an athlete. They both had erections which also provided a study in contrasts. He offered them his blessing and left them.

It was only nine o'clock and the yacht felt deserted. He stepped out onto the deck into a blazing sun that was climbing the sky over the stern. The sea was glassy and there was no land in sight. He wandered aft and found the pool full and dived into it and swam several vigorous lengths, hoping that activity would clear his mind of thought. If he was going to think about anything, he wanted to prepare himself for seeing Ernst alone at last. He was more than ready to call a halt to his sexual adventuring and dedicate himself to the exclusive connection they had pledged themselves to achieve.

He stood in shallow water and saw a boy loitering near the door to the main saloon and waved to him. He approached and Gerry asked for some breakfast and the boy glided off to obey his command.

Gerry climbed out of the pool and saw a great deal of land just ahead of them to the south. The western tip of Sumatra, he supposed, in which case they were well away from the waters Trevor had said were dangerous. He looked aft and saw that the guns had been returned to cover. That was the end of that. The boat hadn't been taken over by pirates. He and Hank had been dreaming.

He thought of Ernst again and was aware of his growing sense of responsibility for him. He must learn all about the security measures that were normally in force to protect him and decide whether they should be improved upon. After last night's fright, he understood Ernst's ruthless quality better; he must have learned to strike out at the first sign of a threat and consider the consequences afterward.

He ate his light breakfast and, remembering that nudity was permitted, peeled off his trunks and lay out in the sun. He liked having a yacht. He wondered if it could cross the Atlantic. He'd ask Ernst.

He hadn't been there long when Solange and Sally joined him. He rose to greet them and gave Solange a kiss. He was aware of Sally studying him and was sorry that there was so little for her to see. They went to the end of the pool where there was a sort of reclining banquette facing aft. The girls were wearing voluminous gossamer garments like sheets with holes for the head. When they removed them, they were naked. Sally had a boy's body with small breasts and narrow hips, slight and charming, although an unequipped crotch still looked sad and amputated to him.

They talked lazily and took frequent dips in the pool. Eventually, André appeared alone. He approached, hesitated as his eyes took in their nakedness, and turned away. Gerry got up and went to get him.

"How amazing," he said, his eyes roving over Gerry's body. "You look so naked out of doors. Why did you leave us last night?"

"You know why. Wasn't I right?"

André smiled with private satisfaction. "Maybe. It was rather marvelous, the two of us."

"Come on. Take that thing off and come join us. We've started a nudist colony."

André's eyes widened. "With the girls? I can't be naked with them. It's not big enough."

Gerry laughed. "You know perfectly well all guys look practically the same when we're like this. You'll be—" He saw the golden-haired officer of the night before crossing the deck. "Just a minute." He snatched up a towel and wrapped it around himself. "Excuse me," he called, hurrying toward the officer. The latter stopped and turned and displayed his big white teeth in a smile of recognition. He wore a cap at a rakish angle.

"Good morning. Good morning," he said. "I am glad to see you. I have wished to thank you."

"About last night? Did you find anything wrong?"

"Not of the sort you described. No casualties." His smile broadened. "When we checked below we found a mistake had been made in the boarding tally. One man too many was clocked on board. A small matter but the captain is most particular. The guilty party has been severely reprimanded."

"You mean somebody's on board who shouldn't be?"

"No, no, no. That would be quite impossible. Somebody was counted twice. It's an error that can happen easily if the deck officer is not paying attention."

His mind seemed to wander during this speech; his eyes

kept sliding off to the side. Gerry glanced around and found that André was joining them. "Oh. This is another of the Baron's friends, Count de St.-Hubert," he introduced them.

The officer straightened and bowed with a casual little salute. "Axel Torberg, first mate." His eyes settled firmly on André. "Your friend has been most helpful. You must all come to me if you observe any irregularities."

André nodded, looking bewildered. "It's just about something that happened last night," Gerry explained. He addressed the first mate who made a valiant but brief effort to take his eyes off André. "If you're satisfied that it was nothing, we can forget it."

"Yes indeed. I trust you won't find it necessary to mention it to the Baron. We don't like him to catch us making mistakes. I hope you're enjoying yourselves. If any of you gentlemen would like a tour of the yacht, I'd be delighted to escort you." He bowed again, took a last lingering look at André and left them. Gerry burst out laughing.

"Well, darling. You've driven our first mate mad. It was love at first sight."

André smiled slyly. "He's frightfully good-looking. Where did you find him?"

"It doesn't matter where I found him. He has eyes only for you. He'll probably run us into Sumatra."

"He *was* looking at me rather pointedly. He's so big. Can you imagine having all that in bed? I'd be frightened out of my wits."

"Go join the girls. They'll take care of you." He had an irrational impulse to revisit the scene of the nonexistent crime. "It'd be very rude to wear anything when they're naked. You'll have a chance to get used to it without my being there. I'll be back in a minute."

"Where're you going?"

"Just up to the forward deck. Something to do with what your admirer was talking about. I'll tell you later."

He gave him a pat on the behind and set off along the deck. When he reached the speedboats, he stopped where they had been the night before and looked up at the bow. His view was unimpeded. There was nothing to create optical illusions. The gun was shrouded like the ones in the stern. There were no sailors in natty white about, only a few deckhands in work clothes performing housekeeping chores. He had no idea what he had come for. What did he expect to find? A body? A trail of blood? A few significant clues that would be useful to Sherlock Holmes? He settled his towel more securely around his hips and walked forward, a tactical error if he'd seen anything he shouldn't have seen. He was advertising the fact that his curiosity had been aroused.

There was an open hatch near the bow and he peered down it. Steps descended into the bowels of the ship. According to Hank, somebody had dragged something in this direction. The raised hatch cover would have screened it. He stood for a minute or two beside the covered gun, looking down at the bow cutting cleanly into the calm water and watching the swift approach of the headland of Sumatra. He turned back and looked up at the bridge. He saw figures behind the glass and lifted his hand in a salute to show that there was nothing furtive about his presence. A deckhand was crouched over pulling a cable across his path. He altered his course to avoid him and the man glanced up. Gerry tried to transform a start of recognition into a hasty rearrangement of his towel. He barely strangled an exclamation of shocked astonishment. He forced himself to move on with no break in his pace. His spine had turned to ice. Fu Manchu was on board.

He frantically checked his memory to see if he had any grounds for doubt. Perhaps. Orientals *did* look alike, damn them. His mind had just registered a small scar beside the man's eye. Was he sure he remembered it from when they had bowed and sidestepped to pass each other outside the hotel bar? What was a man he had last seen in a business suit doing as a deckhand on the yacht? It was impossible.

He became aware of the rapid beating of his heart and a weakness in his legs and as soon as he reached the narrow covered deck he stopped at the rail and tried to organize his thoughts. Maria and opium. The anonymous note. Maria's determination to keep him out of it. The taxi crash. The vice ring he had dreamed up. And always the ubiquitous portly Oriental. Was Maria using the yacht for a smuggling operation? Had she posted the man here to observe the comings and goings between the passengers and the sailors? Dossiers were always useful. Two vaguely possible explanations. He held them in reserve and searched for others. The man might have been in trouble in Bangkok and had wanted to make a clandestine departure, just as he had had to make a devious escape from Saigon. Maria could have arranged for him to slip aboard. The mistake in the crew list.

Menace oppressed him again, out of all proportion to any facts he possessed. He had seen something the night before that had suggested foul play. A businessman in Bangkok had become a deckhand on the *Hephaistion*. Always *perhaps*. He wasn't absolutely sure there was any connection with Maria. She had provided Ernst with opium but she could have got it anywhere. Something was fishy but there was no excuse for the dread that seemed to slow the blood in his veins. Ernst. He had to talk to him and make sure he was in no danger. He continued on his way, pursued by a premonition of doom.

The pool had become the scene of normal holiday activity. André and Sally were splashing around together in the shallow end, both naked and looking very sweet together. Ken and Hank were back where they had been the day before, Farr and the Horrockses on the opposite side, all wearing bathing costumes. Gerry dropped his towel and dived in, determined to shake off his irrational worries. Hank dived in after him and came up a foot away. They treaded water and laughed into each other's eyes.

"Hello, you stinker," Hank said. "You don't expect to get rid of me that easily, do you?"

"It was a step in the right direction. Why don't you join the nudists?"

"Ken doesn't like people to see me."

"He really is a dog in the manger. Is everything OK?"

"Yeah. He gave me a rough time when I went back this morning but he wants to keep up appearances while we're on board. I told him I'd probably go on to Kashmir with you and Andy so it's not cheating anymore. I feel great, better than I have for years."

"Good. Did you have a nice time without me?"

"Yeah." He grinned, giving his Brooks Brothers good looks a boyish appeal. "He's so beautiful that it makes me happy just to see him all lighted up and excited. We missed you."

"I'll bet." The flow of water everywhere against his unconfined body and the references to their intimacies were having a predictable effect. His Majesty was on the verge of putting in an appearance. "We'd better knock it off or I'll have to stay in the pool all day." They smiled knowingly at each other and winked and sank out of sight.

Gerry surfaced at the shallow end beside Sally and André. They climbed out together and André sidled up close to him. "We don't look at all the same now, darling," he murmured. "Do you want me to get you a towel?"

"It'll stop there. Sally doesn't mind."

She was frankly studying him. "Mercy. Isn't there rather a lot more of it? I'd love to see it all," she said in her forthright way. She looked at André speculatively. "Why don't you do something nice like that? All the bother of giving you a swimming lesson. I thought my dainty hands on his fresh young body might create a scandal down there but it always stays the same."

"It can't do anything very scandalous," André admitted.

"That's for me to judge. I'm quite easily scandalized."

"It's frightfully scandalous," Gerry assured her. Being with them made him feel better. Their wholesome sweetness made dark deeds seem remote and unlikely. They all put on their scanty garments to have drinks and mix with the others. The awning was rolled out to protect them from the midday sun and more succulent food was produced, including lobsters and stuffed crabs. Gerry was anxious for Ernst's appearance but before he could begin to fret about it, Yorgo arrived with a message.

"Ernst isn't coming out for lunch," he said. "He expects you when you're finished. Anytime after three, he said. Do you know his stateroom? It's past your cabin, forward, as far as you can go."

Gerry ceased to notice what he was eating. All the future depended on the next few hours. He felt as if he were about to penetrate the inner strands of some monstrous spider's web. Danger was everywhere. He might be devoured. He might never find his way back.

He tried for detachment by asking himself why this meeting had assumed such importance for him. Their intimate contacts added up to very little; he couldn't trust anything Ernst had said. He was powerfully attracted to him but there might have been cures for that if his imagination hadn't been caught by Ernst's challenge to battle. Why had he accepted the disappointments and humiliations if he hadn't been sure with all the strength of his intuition that winning would offer the recompense he now had sense enough to cherish, the recompense of enduring and requited love? Words didn't count; he had seen it in his eyes, felt it in his touch.

He sat with the party till just before three trying to calm himself with wine. If he went to the cabin to tidy up, he'd get to Ernst a deceptively casual few minutes past the hour. He rose and gave everybody a smile and a wave and left.

He stood in front of the mirror in the bathroom for a long examination of himself. He was looking as good as he ever would. The tan everybody mentioned was sensational. The rich food he'd been eating for the last few days had already rounded off a few of the edges but he wouldn't let it go any further. His glossy dark hair had benefited from being shaved during his monkish days but he hadn't worn it long since Tom and Walter had died. He looked surprisingly straight and ordinary—one of the guys, as Hank would say. It was safe to assume that Ernst had never been attracted to anyone like him. If it didn't work out, he would grow a beard and marry Sally.

He considered dressing so he wouldn't look as if he'd come with one thought in mind but they had gone beyond that sort of nonsense. He put on his dressing gown and followed Yorgo's instructions. He stopped in front of the obvious door and knocked, trying to adjust the rhythm of his breathing to quell the pounding of his heart. Yorgo opened it, which didn't come as a great disappointment. Much as he would have liked to find Ernst alone, he knew that it was unlikely that he would. Yorgo ushered him across a small sitting room to a bedroom so dark that he had to wait a moment for his eyes to adjust to it. Light seeped from behind heavy draperies in front of him and he assumed there must be windows behind them giving onto the forward deck. Air conditioning whirred as an accompaniment to the distant throbbing of the engines. The door closed behind him and he made out Ernst's figure on the bed propped up on pillows in a half-reclining position. Heavily shaded lamps flanked him and Paolo sat on a chair beside him at a table on which were laid out the paraphernalia of the opium smoker. Gerry's eyes ran over miniature scoops and scalpels and several ornate pipes. He was holding a heating ladle over a spirit lamp. Ernst lifted a hand and Gerry went to him and took it and dropped down on the edge of the bed.

"Hello, darling," Ernst said in a dreaming voice. "Paolo

is preparing a pipe for you. We'll have a few together and then we'll send him away. Stretch out here beside me and relax."

Gerry did as he was told. The abrupt shift from the sun-swept deck to this murky den of vice unsettled his mind. He had trouble remembering where he was. He held Ernst's hand and saw that he was covered from head to foot by a dark loose robe. A pipe was held out and Gerry took it and drew on it in the way he had been taught and held the smoke in his lungs until little was left to expel. Ernst puffed beside him. They finished the pipes in several long inhalations and handed them back to Paolo.

"At last, darling," Ernst murmured. "I so hoped you would smoke with me. Have you had it often?"

"Here and there over the last few years. It's never had much effect on me."

"Perhaps it wasn't good. Frequently it isn't. This is excellent. If you're not used to it, three or four pipes should do amazing things for you."

"I've always hoped for celestial visions."

"Not visions, darling, just a lovely loosening of the mind so that all its secrets are revealed and you discover how beautiful they are."

Refilled pipes were handed to them and they puffed again. Gerry was getting a grip on his surroundings and checking his reactions in case another pipe made him incapable of doing so. He was with Ernst at last, lying in his bed, but he couldn't feel that they were truly together as long as Paolo was there. He still felt suspended on the brink of some ultimate revelation, the revelation he had been waiting and yearning for since their meeting. He didn't mind smoking opium with him—it was one way of getting rid of the stuff—but it seemed a silly way to spend the time on a yacht crossing the Indian Ocean. You could do it anywhere. He had important things to discuss with him and he didn't want the opium to make them seem unimportant. If this were pot, he would be getting the giggles already and wouldn't give a damn who was crawling around the decks. Above all, he wanted to have him and hold him and arrive at a complete irrevocable union. He'd heard that opium could make you impotent. That would be the last straw. He moved his fingers over the hand he held and felt his hand pressed in return. The simple intimate contact sent an ecstatic shock through his system that he didn't think any amount of opium could curb.

They returned the pipes to Paolo and they were replaced. "I'm beginning to feel something funny," he lied. He wanted to get rid of Paolo.

"That's nice, darling. What's it like?"

"I can't say exactly. Nothing in particular. All just sort of vague and lovely."

"That's only the beginning. It will be much better in a little while. We'll have one more. I thought four would be right if you haven't had it recently. We can have a few more after dinner."

Was it too soon to make a stand against turning into a junkie? He puffed contentedly and felt, indeed, a slight blurring of his thoughts but nothing to justify all this effort. The dead pipe was removed from his hand and in a moment he was holding another. He drew on it and began to get sleepy. He wasn't aware of finishing the pipe or of its being taken from him. He heard the clink of metal against metal and a box closing. A door opened and closed. Gerry sensed that they were alone but he felt no need to look around to make sure. He felt the contact of the hand he held flowing into the roots of his nerves; only the two of them had any significance in an ever-expanding world. Witnesses lacked eyes to penetrate the mystery they were enacting. He turned his head on the pillow and found Ernst's eyes on him. Their eyes could see into the hidden depths of each other's beings. Gerry saw the place in Ernst that was waiting to be completed by him. They simultaneously moved to each other and their mouths slowly consumed each other. The cloth that covered them melted away and their bodies lay against each other, cool and inviting. Gerry felt himself lifted and wafted lower on the pillows until he lay out flat on his back. He felt his nakedness in every pore and every pore was enlarged to contain all the elements of his sexual responses so that he was more exposed, more vulnerable, more erotically sensitive than he had imagined possible. Hands, lips, a questing tongue launched his body on a voyage of sensual discovery. He lifted his arms to take his partner with him but Ernst seemed to elude him. The cloud of bliss in which he was cradled was too fragile to permit him to make an effort. He was adrift in time. His erection stretched to infinity.

It was invincible. It conquered effortlessly. It had finally grown as big as he had always wanted it to be—a yard long, a mile long, without fixed dimensions. It took infinite possession of the superb body and was overwhelmed by what felt like an accumulation of all the orgasms he had ever had, constantly recurring. He held a cock in his hand, flexible but tantalizingly close to rigidity. Had they both come? His whole body bore the imprint of an extraordinary sexual experience but he wasn't absolutely sure of the sequence of events. Had he held this smooth bulky flesh in his mouth? He thought so but couldn't think when it could have happened. As his mind slowly cleared, the experience acquired the fabulous quality of a dream; nothing so supremely thrilling could be real.

"You're amazing, darling," Ernst murmured when they were still. "I've known only one other person who could stay hard after he smoked. Most people have extraordinary sexual sensations without anything actually happening."

Gerry's mind labored heavily to grasp what he was saying. "You mean, you wanted me to smoke the stuff even though it might have made me impotent?"

"Of course, darling. It would have been heavenly just lying here together. You can't imagine. Better than sex, but when there actually *is* sex it becomes almost unbearably beautiful."

"But didn't I make you come?"

"You brought me closer than I've ever been before but you made me feel something much more than just an orgasm. It's indescribable, a sort of orgasm of the soul, as if my giving myself to you were a consummation of everything good in life. If there *had* been any doubt about my needing you, there is none now."

Whatever lingering effects the drug still had, Gerry had placed himself firmly once more in time and his physical surroundings. Ernst's words moved and troubled him. "How many times did I come?" he asked hesitantly.

"Just now at the end."

"Not before?"

"No, darling."

"How long have I been here?"

"A little more than an hour."

Gerry would have guessed ten or fifteen minutes. Except for the way it had ended, it had all been an illusion, a blissful illusion, but if he didn't know how much time had passed, how could he believe that it contained any substance? An orgasm of the soul? A consummation? This was the drug talking, as ephemeral as smoke. He had performed a solitary act; even in giving himself, Ernst had cheated him of his victory. He had absented himself. Gerry could imagine their going on, living a dream of perfect union, until the opium ran out. He gave the side of Ernst's face a wistful kiss. "Do you really need me or do you just think you need me when you're smoking?" he asked.

"Smoking frees you from needing anything, darling. That's one reason I've let myself go back to it. I wanted to free myself from you. I failed. What are you going to do with me now?"

"Let's take a shower and then we'll decide."

"I don't like showers, darling. There's a bidet if you want. I'll have one of the boys give me a bath later."

"That sounds sexy. Maybe we'll have a boy give us both a bath."

"Would you like that, darling?" Ernst asked, his voice brightening. "There's one I'd love to see you with."

"Well, you're not going to. I was joking," he said sharply. "No boys, remember?" He disengaged himself and sprang up, feeling helpless to the point of absurdity. He was determined to renounce off-limits sex and was presumably about to embark on a life with somebody who didn't recognize limits of any kind. He showered, testing his mental and physical responses. He seemed to have returned to normal. Having experienced for the first time the effect opium could have on him, he was beginning to understand the problem he was up against. What had he to offer that would take its place? A saner and more satisfying vision of reality? Try telling that to an addict who was accustomed to living on a different level of consciousness. There was nothing mind-blowing about reality.

Could he follow Ernst into a cloud of smoke? He had spent the last five years trying to shed all his addictions, down to cigarettes, so that he could live freely for the truth in himself. There had been moments of tenderness and human contact with André that were worth much more than a weirdly heightened perception of orgasm. Such moments were the best he could offer Ernst but the drug barred the development of sensibility. That was the best argument he could bring against it and he didn't think it would get him very far. He was going to have to pull Ernst's whole world crashing down around his ears before he could be sure of gaining his full attention. How?

He dried himself thoughtfully and returned to the other room with only a slight headache to show for his hour in the clouds. Ernst sat up as he appeared and folded his legs under him and propped himself on one arm. He held him with his eyes and smiled a little madly and patted the bed to indicate where he wanted him. He was more youthful and spontaneous than Gerry had ever seen him and he was instantly captivated by him. He quickened his pace and sat where Ernst's hand had been. Ernst edged closer and laid his arms on him and rested his head on his shoulder. Gerry was thrown off balance. This often frightening man, with all his power and his minions and his tax-free millions, his complexities and his vices, was giving in to him like a kid. He rubbed his chin against the sleek yellow hair and felt his responsibility growing. All the words he had been preparing, the questions, the conditions, the tentative pledges were all superfluous. Ernst seemed to assume that they both knew what they had been battling for and that they would both accept the consequences once the victor had been declared. Gerry found himself in a situation that seemed to have been already clearly defined without his having been knowingly a partner in its creation. Total surrender left nothing to work with, like entering the villages in Vietnam that Jack had talked about from which all the inhabitants had fled.

He shifted slightly so that Ernst lifted his head and they faced each other. "Are you sure you're glad the dope didn't free you from me?"

"That's not the question, darling. All I know is that it didn't."

"Then how about letting me free you from the dope?"

"Don't let's talk about that, darling."

"I'm sorry but we're going to. We're going to talk about a lot of things." He felt the steely resistance immediately arrayed against him. He took him in his arms and pulled himself up onto the bed and stretched himself out with him. "Do we have to stay in the dark? I want to see you—all of you." Ernst stretched out an arm to a rheostat control and one of the bedside lamps slowly filled the cabin with light. He watched as it washed over the body that was part of the spoils of conquest. "Oh my God," he breathed. He had it all at last. It was tanned a golden honey color and was resplendent with health. It made him think of ski slopes and polo, a finely tuned, leisured body, strong and full of suppressed energy. The slight tonelessness of his handsome face was nowhere reflected in it. He wondered how he kept it in such good condition; he had never seen him do anything more strenuous than walk deliberately across a room. His narrow hips and the strongly defined pelvic area with the hollows running down to his groin on each side of the taut belly constituted the most erotically stimulating anatomical formation he had ever seen. He wanted to see his sex springing up with all of the vitality that the rest of his body conveyed.

He rolled him over onto his stomach and looked at his back. Broad shoulders, a ripple of muscles in the torso as it tapered to a slim waist, the sculptured curve of powerful buttocks. A sensual feast. He rolled him onto his back again and looked thoughtfully into his unseeing eyes. If his conquest was as complete as it seemed, he was faced with so many decisions that he didn't know where to begin. He must teach him first that no subject was taboo. "Don't you see anything wrong with being stoned all the time?" he asked.

"Not all the time," Ernst said with a touch of petulance. "It's something that's been happening only quite recently."

"You agreed not to, according to Solange, when you're traveling, when you can't always trust the personnel. Do you know everybody you have on board?"

"The crew? Of course not. I don't keep them all on when I'm not using the boat. It just makes them lazy. Quite a lot of them come back every year. The new ones are very carefully selected. The captain checks them."

Gerry could see bored impatience in the slight contraction of his brows and hear it in his voice. This wasn't the moment to tell him about his amorphous fears but he wanted a clear picture of how everything was run. "Have you had the captain long?" he asked.

"No. I had one for quite a long time but he retired last year. This one was with the Thurstons. Maria knew about him. She's very helpful about such things."

"She's helpful about a lot of things. Why do you suppose

she gave you the opium when she knows you could get it for yourself?"

"She likes to please me. I suppose it's that awful American expression, brown-nosing."

"What do you know about her?"

"Everything," he said, the ruthless edge coming into his voice. "She's from a very good Franco-Italian family. She's a cousin of André, in fact. No money, like many old European families. Trevor is from a rich family in Cleveland or Denver. I never can keep them straight. He inherited quite a nice little fortune in trust. A few years ago, he managed to break the trust and he hasn't invested wisely. He's been very badly hurt recently in what everybody is calling a recession, although I can't say that I've noticed it. I hope they survive. It's inconvenient having friends without money."

"I see. I go on thinking there must be some reason for her choosing opium to please you. Just for the sake of argument, what if she has a load of it on board? If it's discovered and you're using it, she could say it's yours. She apparently has a good reason for wanting to make a quick killing. Somebody could easily have a million dollars' worth of the stuff on board without anybody even noticing it."

"Really, darling, don't be tiresome." His tone was sharp. "If my friends do things like that, I don't want to know about it."

"I do. It's not tiresome if Maria gets you back on dope. If I talk about it, it is. I'm afraid you're going to find me tiresome quite often."

"I'm sorry, darling." He was immediately conciliatory; he hugged Gerry closer and kissed him briefly on the mouth. "You're too exciting to be tiresome, ever. I love your wanting to know about everything and beginning to control my life. That's what I need, but I'm not very good at discussing things when I'm so deliciously high. Life can be a bore if we pay too much attention to people's foibles."

"If we got rid of the people there's some reason to distrust, maybe we could relax."

"She's planning to get rid of Heinrich for me, darling. She says she can arrange for him to be left behind in Goa."

"What do you mean by that?"

"She knows people there. She's going to have them take him out to that beach where all the hippies are. I've been there. They're all on wild trips. All they'll have to do is take his clothes away from him and let him loose. He'll love it. By the time he gets back, we'll be gone."

Gerry drew back with distaste. Ernst had become a callous child again. "What a lousy trick. How do you think he'd feel when he discovered what you'd done? I thought she was friendly with him. I wish somebody I could trust spoke German. I'd like to talk to him."

"Solange does, of course, but I don't want to get her involved in one of my mistakes. André manages pretty well."

"He does? That's perfect. I'll talk to him with André. I'm sure we can work something out that's fair to him. If he wants trouble—well, we'll see. There won't be any more Heinrichs but I don't want any more Marias either. I know how to manage your life much better than she does."

"I hope so, darling, but I think you'll find that people don't always understand fair treatment. There is sometimes much to be said for a diplomatic stab in the back."

"I'm not naive. From now on, I want it understood by everybody that I have the right to act for you. I'd like Yorgo to tell the captain, in case there's anything I want to talk to him about."

"Very well, but please don't create difficulties. I like everything to run smoothly."

"And you're damn good at it. I want to learn how you do it so I can do my share. That's what it amounts to. I want us to be partners—equal partners. It might not work but there's a chance it will. If we're talking about the same thing, we know it won't work if we try it any other way."

"I'm awfully used to doing everything my own way, darling."

"Exactly. And if something goes wrong, you can always fall back on a pipe. I want you to learn to fall back on me." The boat had begun to sway in an unfamiliar way so that everything in the cabin that wasn't attached moved restlessly. Gerry braced himself in order to keep himself from sliding off the bed. "What would you do if your entire supply of opium suddenly disappeared?"

"Take to drink. Rather heavily, I'm afraid. That's what happened before. It's very bad for me and I am very bad while it lasts."

"That would happen even though I'm here?"

"I'm afraid so, darling. You surely understand we're not talking about a craving for wild strawberries. It's an intoxication, something in the blood that requires careful treatment."

"I understand. I could kill Maria for getting you started again. I want you to cut down. That's not a lot to ask. Solange says if you have only a few pipes at a time, we needn't worry about it."

"You and Solange seem to have been talking a great deal. I'm not sure I like that."

"Who do you think I've had to talk to for the last few days? We've talked about you with love. You damn well better like it. She wants us to have something good together. So do I. We have to start with the goddamn dope."

"I don't see why it makes so much difference to you, darling," Ernst said, placating him once more. "It does no harm physically, like drink. Everybody will tell you that. Your being able to have sex makes it so perfect."

"Perfect if I went in for solitary sex. You're not here when you're on a high. That's what difference it makes. I don't even know if I've ever seen you when you were entirely yourself. How can we talk about having a life together when I'm not sure you know what you're saying? The same goes for sex. If you can't come, how am I supposed to know we're good together physically?"

"I've told you, darling, you do something much more thrilling than giving me an orgasm. When you're actually—"

There was a sudden clatter of water against the glass behind the curtains, as if a powerful hose had been turned on it. Gerry sprang up, startled. He strode to the curtains and drew one back and looked into a wall of water.

"A squall," Ernst said, his voice almost drowned in the thunder of rain. "We must be going through the islands. The Nicobars."

Gerry dropped the curtain and returned to the bed and stretched out again. "Do you like to see me hard?" he demanded.

"Oh, darling, of course. It's incredible."

"Then you can understand why I want to see you get hard for me."

"There's nothing incredible about mine, darling. Why

do you care when we both know that all we want is for you to take me?"

"How do I know when it doesn't show in the one way that makes it possible for men to have sex together? *Together*, you understand?"

"But darling—" Ernst's voice broke. Panic and pain flooded his eyes. Gerry looked into them for an appalled moment; what had he said to inspire such terror? He moved closer and put his arms around him.

"Please, darling. Understand what I'm saying. I can't stand for any part of you to get away from me. Won't you tell me you'll try to cut down?"

There was a touch of indomitable pride in the lift of Ernst's chin but Gerry could sense an obscure agony in him, some torment that was perhaps a precursor of the ordeal that breaking the habit would be for him. "Can we do it gradually?" he asked in a subdued voice.

"Of course, darling. As gradually as you like, even if it's only one less a day." He was making his influence felt, he was accomplishing something. They were getting to each other. Stragglers were returning to the village.

Ernst smiled and the pride with which he carried his head became more pronounced. "We can do better than that. If you stay with me after lunch every day, I think I can get down to five quite quickly. Less than that would be more difficult. The most difficult of all would be after dinner."

"Even if I'm with you?"

"Will you want to be, darling? Don't you like to spend the night with André?"

Gerry could hardly believe his ears. Ernst was mad. "I don't give a damn about André," he burst out. "I don't mean that, of course. I love him but he knows all I've been thinking about is being with you. How can you go on saying things like that? I want to be with you at night most of all."

"At night, darling? I've never been able to sleep in the same bed with anybody but perhaps it will be different with you."

"It better be. I like to cuddle with people. We're definitely going to sleep together."

"Even if you don't like to make love with me?"

"I didn't say that, darling. I'm talking about the dope

making you impotent. I'm alone. It's like being unfaithful. I don't want anything or anybody to come between us."

"What if we had André here with us? Would you like that? Nothing would come between us. I would share what you have with him."

"It's hopeless when you're like this." Gerry groaned with frustration. "I suppose it's really very simple. There's no reason for you to be jealous of me until I can give you an orgasm. I guess everything depends on that. Once we can really make love, you won't want me to make love with other people. Haven't you ever been jealous?"

"I don't think there's ever been anybody to be jealous of. The one Solange told you about—Manfred—he wanted no one but me. I can't be jealous of boys I buy."

"I never thought I'd want to make anybody unhappy, but I do with you. Just for a little while. Just so I'm sure you know who we both are."

"You make me want to know. Surely that is a great deal, don't you think? You must, or none of this would be happening. I keep forgetting that I have nothing to offer you except myself. Is that enough?"

"I keep wondering the same thing about me. What do you give a man who has everything?" Gerry laughed briefly. "Can you imagine what people would say if they could hear us? Here we are, swimming in money, two men who have everything except what we really want and maybe about to get that. We better stop wondering and damn well make sure it's enough. Come here, darling." He moved up over him and they lay with their bodies tucked in against each other. He ran a hand over the yellow hair and looked down into slightly unfocused blue eyes. He felt a deep peace enveloping them and realized that the drumming of the rain had ceased and the boat was no longer swaying. He chuckled softly. "Is any happiness seeping into you, wherever you are in there?"

"Yes. Quite suddenly. I feel as if I'd like you to hold me like this forever. If you feel anything like it, I don't see why we should ever let each other go. Is that because I'm stoned?"

"I hope not but I guess we'll have to wait till you're not, to be sure. Do we start cutting down tonight?"

"I can't tonight, darling. I've already got started. I know what it will be like after dinner."

"All right. We'll forget about tonight. You can be

unfaithful to me again with your damn pipes. I wish I wanted to be unfaithful to you. Shall we say it for the record, darling? Have we fallen in love with each other? Till death us do part and all the rest of it?"

"Of course. I thought you knew that."

"I didn't know it could happen so slowly and cruelly." He spoke with difficulty as his heart suddenly began to pound. Was this the moment he had been preparing for all his life? It would probably take time for him to grasp all that it might mean for him. "We won't hurt each other anymore, not on purpose," he added with the stirring of a faith he could cling to.

"I hope I hurt you less than I hurt myself."

"Thanks for the thought. Right now, you don't look as if you could hurt a flea. So sweet, positively angelic. It's funny. You're handsome in such a classic way and yet you can look like a fiend when you feel like it." He touched the straight nose, the sensual lips, the dimpled chin, and chuckled. "I don't see how you do it. I wish you wouldn't wear makeup."

"Then I won't. I do it because it shocks people so."

"I know. It doesn't shock me. I just think you're too good-looking to spoil it." Gerry lowered his head and their mouths opened and they exchanged their first peaceful tender kiss. His hand strayed over the smooth muscular body, setting off small tremors in it when he touched some sensitive area. He stroked his cock and the whole body responded with a little leap. It remained much as it had been earlier, a bulky cylinder of flesh too rigid to lie between his legs but incapable of taking its own direction. He could feel it stirring and he slid down to it and drew it into his mouth. It swelled to the skilled attentions of his tongue and lips and for a thrilling moment he thought he might be achieving his goal, but then he felt it subsiding slightly again. He relinquished it and laid it out straight and measured it with his eyes. "I love it," he said. "I know it's nerve-racking for somebody to try to give you a hard-on when you don't feel like it. Do you want me to leave it alone?"

"Everything you're doing is divine, darling. Just try not to make me feel you're attempting the impossible. You get me so close, much closer than I've ever been. Maybe when I've cut down, you'll actually make it happen."

"You have to be entirely off it before it really works?"

"That's the way it has been always. Maybe with you it will be different. Like everything else."

"It's awfully damned exciting the way it is. You're a tease." He lifted himself to his knees and straddled Ernst's hips and walked up along his sides and sat on his chest and laughed. "Look how big and hard mine is, darling. I love to show it off to you, now that it's retired from public life. We'll let it do the work for both of us." He dropped forward and shot his legs out behind him and lowered himself onto him. He held himself for a moment so that they were barely touching from toe to forehead, the last aching moment that anything could keep them apart, and then let all his weight go to him. "Oh God. Oh darling. Jesus, I love you." All the frustration and longing and conflict of the last few days gathered into a flood of tears. He clung to him, his teeth clamped on his shoulder, and his body was shaken by sobs. He was held and loved. He was aware of being prepared for union. Their bodies shifted smoothly against each other and were joined. This was real. This was happening in the world he knew. He had performed the act before but there was nothing familiar in it. They were one flesh, one need, one roaring torrent of consummation. His cock was all of him, with the might of multitudes. It seized and overpowered the man he wanted. His chest swelled with pride in its huge prowess. His orgasm was theirs. Ernst was his.

"There was nothing wrong with that, was there?" he murmured against the side of his mouth.

"You have all of me. I've never known anything so complete. You understand, don't you?"

"Yes. I can make us belong to each other."

"You did. Your sublime cock has recreated me to serve you. When you filled me with yourself, I ceased to exist without you."

Gerry laughed unsteadily, awed by the profound communion they had achieved. "We're going to have to redefine fucking. It's a very spiritual activity."

They followed each other into the bathroom and returned to each other in bed. "I don't know about you but this is beginning to feel real to me," Gerry said. "We've actually found each other. You're a beautiful naked guy and you belong to me. I'm glad I haven't had many others that way. It makes it feel so new. My first sex. Should I try to tell you how much I love you?"

"Please do, darling."

"It's probably too soon because it's still working around inside me. I know we belong together. For the first time in my life, I feel sure that everything's going to be right with someone. It's so completely different from anything I've ever known. With you, of all people. It's unbelievable but I believe it now."

"I know, darling. I think we can call it an unlikely occurrence." They laughed and reached for each other's hands. The very fabric of life had altered.

"Is this a good time to talk about plans or would you rather not grapple with hard facts?" Gerry asked, looking into the face that had become the mirror of all his hopes and dreams.

"My mind is always quite clear. I'm not good at arguing or discussing unpleasant subjects when I'm high. I don't think we'll argue about plans. You have only to say what you want and we'll do it."

"Well, we've got to let Solange in on it too. She's waiting to hear if I'm going to become part of the household. I think she'd like us to make it official. She said she'd be willing for me to be the father of your heir if you wanted it."

"I've thought about that. After this afternoon, I think I do. I have no great paternal urge. I'd probably like your son better than my own. It should bring us all so close. That's as it should be. In any case, we can wait for another year or two. I've thought of it as something for when I was forty. She's just your age. There's no hurry unless you two don't want to wait."

Gerry choked on a wild burst of laughter. "I suppose we're all slightly mad. She thinks so. I'm awfully fond of her. One of the nicest things I know about you is that you chose her as a wife."

"It *was* rather clever of me, especially as she's so suitable for you. You're lovely together and we can be reasonably sure that my son's hair will be dark." They gurgled with laughter.

"Our plans seem to be going swimmingly. I told you I'm willing to give up the next six months or a year to finding out what your life is like, unless we strike some ghastly snag that I can't stand. I'd like us to go to New York fairly soon to see my mother. She's waited long enough for me to settle down. She'll be delighted with you."

"I was delighted with her. It's part of our curious destiny. Of course, I was on my best behavior, which is more than I can say at the moment."

"We'll take care of that. I'll let her know right away that we'll be coming soon. She'll be so pleased. It'll make her feel that all the money she's given me hasn't been a waste."

"How rich are you, darling?"

"That's something else we have to talk about. I'm not rich at all. I'm whatever you call it when somebody has no money but what seems to me a very nice income. My mother's kept me for the last five years. I'll be rich soon, I guess. The man who still thinks he's my father has been practically dead for a year. When he goes, I'm to get my share along with my brother and sister. When last heard of, I think we'll be splitting between fifteen and twenty million. Of course, it'll go to my mother first but she's told me she wants me to have the income right away. I'm her spoiled baby."

"That would come to about half a million a year. Hardly poverty, darling."

"Good God. You must be joking. It can't be that much. I've never bothered to figure it out. What would I do with all that?"

"Hire a good tax lawyer to begin with. You could easily end up with only a tenth of it."

"That's about what I have now and I haven't spent much more than a quarter of *that*. Of course, living with you will be more expensive. We'll have to break things down and see where my money should go. Jesus *Christ*." He bounced up and landed on his feet. He stood at the foot of the bed and looked down at Ernst. "I can't believe it. Half a million dollars a *year*? It's not possible."

Ernst laughed with quiet amusement. "Haven't you ever done any arithmetic, darling? You really are extraordinary. You seem so wise and competent and so young at the same time. We needn't worry about your money for now. You can take care of your personal expenses and I won't have the corrupt pleasure of patronizing you. Fancy your not knowing how rich you're going to be."

"It sounds fairly dumb, doesn't it? Well, you see, Americans are brought up to take care of themselves. I was always a working boy until Mum gave me this money. It was sort of like going back to college. Five years. Time to get my masters in something or other. You know about Saigon. When that ended I realized it was time for me to go back and do something with whatever I'd learned. I know there's something in me that wasn't there before. I've been getting ready for you. I haven't bothered to think about money because it can't affect what I do with my life, not basically. I have to do something. I'd be bored out of my wits leading a life of leisure. You've been trained to turn style into substance. You do it beautifully but it's bound to get boring. I don't have to tell you that. Listen—" He broke off and went forward to the curtains and lifted one to make sure the world was still out there. The sky was clear and the great red ball of the sun was dropping to the horizon dead ahead of them. Melancholy touched him and he turned back and made a dive for the bed. He lay on his stomach and threw an arm across Ernst's chest and gloated over him for a long silent moment. "Sex *does* make a difference," he said conclusively. "You're so real to me, now that I can look at all of you and touch you, now that you know my body and say you like it. There's nothing mysterious about you. I don't know why I let you bamboozle me for so long. You're just a fascinating, tough, slightly hysterical, terrifying human being like everybody else. The only thing special about you is your looks and your body. What a relief to know that I'll never find a more beautiful one. How rich are *you?*"

"About four times richer than you will be, darling. Still, you'll have quite enough to hold your head up in polite society."

Gerry impetuously edged in closer to him. "I'm so damned excited. Listen. I haven't had a chance to tell you how impressed I was by the other evening—was it only night before last?—the party in Penang. Anybody who could do that could do almost anything. With all this money, there must be a million things we could do. Four times richer? Two million a year? Jesus. I'm speechless. What're you interested in, aside from the ex-crowned heads of Europe?"

"Don't sneer at the ex-crowned heads of Europe, darling. Some of them can tell you more about history than anybody else, how things really work. My ex-family's expower fascinates me. When I'm very old, I might write a book about it if you'll help me. I'm interested in music and dance and some of the new theater. I adore giving elaborate parties like that for the sake of the spectacle. The people I invite usually interest me less. They are simply a captive audience."

"This is too good to be true. You're saying it. Producing a party isn't much different from producing a show. How about starting a dance company? I'd love to do something like that."

"I've dabbled a bit in that sort of thing. Years ago, when so many old ladies in Paris were keen on Boulez and his crowd, I subsidized a number of concerts. I've even given money to avant-garde theater companies. If I'd gone to bed with the actors I might have felt better rewarded, but actors in avant-garde companies are always hideous. If one had complete control and you were doing it with me, it might be quite interesting. It would have turned life into pure drudgery if I'd done it alone."

"I knew we'd think of something. We'll look into it in the fall. Theater. Dance. It's the sort of thing my father did on a big scale. You heard what Farr said about him."

"I've heard of him, of course."

"Maybe it runs in my blood. More so than Argentinian bulls. Talking about it makes me want to be rich. We can do things together that neither of us could do alone. I've suspected you're an intellectual deep down inside somewhere. God knows I'm not. I'd be good supervising anything to do with decoration. Who says being rich *has* to be boring?" Gerry put a hand in his armpit. "I like your not having any hair there."

"There's not much to begin with. A few wisps."

"You do your legs too, don't you?"

"Yes. Is it like makeup? Should I shop?"

"No. I like it. Your body is like marble. It would look peculiar with hair."

When it was time to get ready for the evening, Gerry could feel the troops gathering in the wings to take over. Paolo. The boy to help with a bath. Yorgo with his portfolio. Until the rule of the drug was broken, if then, he couldn't hope to enjoy the simple intimacy of wandering around a shared room, washing, pulling clothes out of the same closet, any more than he would expect a rich wife to let him help her dress and arrange her hair. The trouble was, he didn't want a rich wife. He wanted the easy masculine camaraderie he had known with Jack. Even if he kicked the habit, Ernst would probably think it a great hardship to bathe himself. Maybe in Argentina they could ride off together across the pampas, if that's what they had in Argentina, and discover the joys of being on their own in natural conditions, as only two men could be. "May I ring for Paolo?" Ernst asked.

"Not till we put our dressing gowns on," he said firmly. "I guess having personal servants, you forget what privacy is. I'm beginning to crave it like opium." He rose and put his dressing gown on and waited for Ernst to wrap himself in his. "I'll go get dressed and come back for you. As soon as we have the pipe under control, I'll move in here with you. You'd better tell them I'll come and go as I please. They mustn't ever try to keep me from you."

"Certainly not, darling. Never. Just a minute." He rose with surprising agility and went to a built-in chest of drawers and fumbled about in the top drawer. "I never know where anything is. That's why I wanted Paolo. Never mind. Here it is." Gerry had moved in close beside him. Ernst turned and held out a massive gold ring. "My father's signet ring. Actually, it's mid-nineteenth-century. It belonged to my great-grandfather. Give me your hand, darling. Such beautiful great things. I think that's what I first fell in love with. I thought so. Your little finger is the only one it fits. There. Nobody but a von Hallers has ever worn it. Now it belongs to the man I belong to. Everything is yours, Gerald."

"If I let myself, I'd burst into tears," Gerry said from an aching throat. "Do you know what you're doing?"

"Of course, darling. Trapping you. Now that I've set my mind on it, nothing will stop me. I want you more than I knew it was possible to want anything in life."

Gerry touched his cheek with his fingertips and gave him a fond little smile. "I'll be right back."

He was aware of people in the next room but he went through with a vague "Hello, everybody," without looking at them and hurried down the passage to his cabin. He hoped André wasn't there. The ring weighed his hand down. He called out as he entered and was greeted by silence. He toppled over onto the bed and lay on his stomach, his hands joined in front of his face. He looked at the heavy ring. It was unbelievable but it was there.

He had become the consort of a von Hallers. He twisted the ring on his finger. A dark stone was set in the massive gold, bearing the crest that was on all Ernst's things. On him. He bowed his head and rested his forehead on his hands.

He tried to swallow the lump in his throat. His eyes misted. He began to tremble. What was it? The sense of doom? He shook his head. That had been dispelled by the afternoon. There were no more mysteries. A handsome and fascinating man awaited him as soon as he had cured him of a troubling habit. He had claimed him and won him. There was no doubt about that. They had offered each other glimpses of what their life could be. He was attempting no more than what a fairly ordinary, reasonably sensitive guy could hope to accomplish. Why did he find the prospects so overwhelming? He ached with the afternoon's experience. He hadn't known that he was filled with so much painful love. His life depended on converting it to joy, joy he could offer to the man who needed him, who held him in an iron grip. Perhaps he could teach him to take him; they would take each other in a perfect equality of physical union. Thinking of his handsome erection created an emptiness of longing in him. He felt a sob gathering in his chest. He inhaled deeply, painfully, and adjusted his breathing to achieve tranquility. Oddly enough, it worked.

He pulled himself up and seemed to leave part of himself impressed on the covers of the bed. His old self? His new self was driven by a compulsion to be with the man he'd just left, to look into his eyes, hear his voice, touch his hand. It bore no resemblance to the sexual cravings he knew so well. He hadn't felt anything like it even with Jack. If he had, he couldn't have borne the unannounced, often protracted separations. It stirred through his whole being, demanding nothing but Ernst's presence. Why was he wasting his time here? He'd washed enough for today. He put on a new outfit, another pair of beautifully tailored tight trousers and a simple tunic with a stand-up collar and a single fastening at the waist so that the chain gleamed on a good deal of bare mahogany chest. He gave his hair a quick comb and was ready.

When he reached Ernst's door, he started to knock but tried the knob. The door opened and he entered. Yorgo looked up from the desk in the small sitting room.

"Hello again," Gerry greeted him. "Do you always leave this door unlocked?"

"No, but the Baron was anxious for you not to be locked out."

"You call him Ernst, don't you?"

"When there's no need for formality."

"OK. We'll call him Ernst. You can call me Gerry, if you don't already. Let's not let everybody in. Do you have a spare key for me?"

"Of course." Yorgo reached into a drawer and rose and brought it to him. "He told me to ask if you have any suggestions to make, anything you're not satisfied with on board."

Gerry's throat knotted again. He was part of the household. He felt Ernst's presence near and a piercing contentment flowed into him. "Everything's perfect." He cleared his throat of a slight hoarseness. "If you have any problems you think I can handle, don't hesitate to come to me."

"He told me I'm to consult you about everything." They exchanged a glance. Yorgo's eyes told him that he accepted the new alignment of power.

"OK. That's fine. Remind me to give you that money you asked about, will you?"

"Why don't I get it now?"

"Would you? It's in the dressing table thing in the top drawer. A sealed envelope under some fancy scarves. Exactly eighteen hundred dollars."

"I'll enter it in the petty cash with Ernst's. You can sign for it. It's the same system we use for him."

"I've never thought of eighteen hundred dollars as petty but I'll try. Fine. Thanks." He smiled and nodded and headed for the bedroom. He had a secretary. He'd never particularly wanted a secretary but he might be useful. He found Paolo sitting by the bed arranging the smoking equipment.

"Good evening," Gerry said. "Are you getting that ready for now?"

The young man smiled in the slightly insinuating way that Gerry had resented on occasion. "Sure. He has a few after his bath."

"Who?"

Paolo's eyes hardened. "The Baron, sir."

"I thought that's who you meant. Well, carry on." Gerry heard water splashing in the bathroom and turned to it with a shrug. Paolo had probably been spoiled by too much familiarity of an intimate nature. Paolo would go. He entered the bathroom. Ernst was in the tub. A beautiful boy wearing nothing but a sarong knelt beside it scrubbing his back. Ernst glanced up and his face lighted with a smile of welcome. Gerry felt as if he'd reached an ultimate destination. There was nowhere else he wanted to go.

"Stunning, darling," Ernst said in his muted voice. The boy glanced up over his shoulder with limpid doe eyes.

Gerry smiled down at Ernst. "I feel as if I'd been gone for hours."

"You have been. The bath soothed me somewhat."

Gerry chuckled. "And the boy?"

"He's very pretty, isn't he? Are you tempted?"

"I'm afraid I would be if he were giving me a bath."

"I'm sure he would be, too. Unlike most of them, he's rather a forward hussy." Ernst emerged from the water with a ripple of muscles and stood unselfconsciously, his body glistening like a rain-washed statue, his sex looking as it had most of the afternoon, bulkily enlarged and tantalizing with potential virility. The boy rose and removed the shower attachment from its hook and turned it on Ernst. Gerry watched, trying not to mind. It would be ridiculous to be jealous of the bath boy or of anybody else, for a fairly basic reason. If Ernst had somebody help him with his bath, he could hardly be expected to remain fully clothed. He turned to have his back rinsed. The boy put a hand on his buttocks and parted them slightly, a service doubtless performed by all bath boys. He completed the rinsing and reached for a towel and began to dry him.

"He always gets a hard-on when he does my back," Ernst said over his shoulder. "Shall we tell him to take his sarong off?"

"No," Gerry said curtly. Why did Ernst go on offering him boys? Did he feel a need to compensate for his own inadequacy? The thought both touched and hurt him—it hurt for Ernst to remain so indifferent to his straying. "Please, darling. Don't do this." His voice was harsh with reproach.

Ernst turned quickly and took the towel and made a dismissive gesture. Gerry was careful to keep his eyes on Ernst as the beautiful youth withdrew. "I'm sorry, darling," Ernst said contritely. "I was only teasing you. You know I didn't mean anything."

"I hope not. We've got to be careful with each other at the beginning. I'm not a saint but I want to be. I'll be your bath boy from now on. It looks like fun." He went to him and took the towel and began to dry the handsome body. The tub made Ernst taller than Gerry and he looked up into his eyes. "You probably have an exaggerated idea about my sex life. I was faithful to my guy in Saigon for almost a year. Before that, I went through long periods of celibacy for three or four years. If I hadn't been so worked up about you, I might not have had an affair with André. Hank got into it because André's been getting so hooked on me that I thought he needed a change. Granted, I've had it in every possible combination known to man so you can't shock me. I just happen to want you. God, do I ever." He let go of one end of the towel and kissed his nipples and dropped down and kissed his cock. He rose, his spirits restored. "If I'm going to be your bath boy, we'll have to allow plenty of extra time. Now, just as an experiment, let's see if you can dry some small part of yourself. Here, for instance." He touched his navel. Ernst smiled into his eyes as if he were mesmerized and did as he was told. Gerry stooped and ran a tongue around it. "Pretty good. You'd better do it again before you drop with exhaustion." Ernst lifted the towel to himself once more, his body beginning to heave with laughter. Gerry tested the area with his finger. "Hey. You're absolutely marvelous. It's as dry as a bone. That's enough for one day. I'll do the rest."

Ernst's laughter broke from him and he climbed out of the tub. "Oh darling. You've trapped me, you know. When it comes to seduction, I have everything to learn from you. I don't know how I dared talk about trapping you."

"Poor boys have to work at it. Lift your arms." He licked drops of water out of his armpits and polished them with the towel. "There. You have the driest armpits in Southeast Asia. Incidentally, Paolo's out there getting the pipes ready. I don't want to keep you."

An impatient look crossed Ernst's face. "Tell him not to bother. You're here. I can do without."

Gerry dropped the towel to his side and stood motionless for a moment looking at him intently while happiness spread through his chest. "Thank you, darling. That's the most seductive thing you've ever said in your life." He leaned forward and kissed his mouth tenderly. "How about a bottle of champers instead? We can put it on my bill."

Ernst unfastened Gerry's tunic and put his hands on his chest. "How about taking off those lovely clothes before they get mussed? Even Sam couldn't make allowances for what's happening to you now."

"That's one measurement he didn't take." They laughed and Gerry squeezed his hand and went to the door and stuck his head out. Paolo was at the closet shifting hangers about. "The Baron says he doesn't want to smoke until later. Would you get us a bottle of champagne, please?" Gerry followed him to the door and bolted it after him. He was out of his clothes in seconds and hung them on a chair and returned to the bathroom. Ernst stood waiting for him, holding the towel in front of himself.

Gerry cupped his chin in his hand and drew him close and their mouths met. He could feel Ernst's partial erection going through various stages, from more to less to more again. The uncertainty was maddening. It failed to achieve completion. He slowly relinquished him with a few final passes of his hands to check for dampness. "That's the way I like to dry you—with my body," he said, hating the drug more than ever.

A knock on the door freed him. He gathered up a towel to cover himself and returned to the bedroom and admitted Paolo with the champagne. "Thanks. Just leave it over there. I'll open it." He remained at the door until Paolo withdrew and then he bolted it again. "Wine is being poured in the bedchamber," he called. He went to the bureau where the bottle stood and unwired the cork. He felt Ernst approaching from behind and the hairs on his arms stirred in anticipation of his touch. He smiled at the bottle.

"This is heaven," Ernst said as he appeared at his side. "You've become all my life so quickly and naturally. Everything about you is right." He moved in close against him and put his hands everywhere Gerry wanted them. They made him feel loved and known and wanted. It was going to be perfect as soon as Ernst was ready for action.

He slowly twisted the cork until it was expelled with a small pop while his body thrilled to the touch of possessive hands. He poured wine into a glass and filled his mouth with it and put an arm around Ernst's neck and joined their mouths and let champagne flow between them. He felt a tremor run through Ernst's body.

"Are you getting desperate for a smoke?"

"No. Not with you here. Not when you do things like that. You mean why I shivered? I'm frightened I can't be what you want me to be. You're so good and kind."

"Are you mine?"

"Yes."

"Then I'll be yours and we'll live happily ever after." He filled both glasses and handed one to Ernst. "I'm going to come just standing here with you." He backed up against the bureau and planted his feet apart and pulled Ernst in between his legs. Ernst held Gerry's erection against himself. "There. Now we know where it is in case of an emergency." He reached out and toyed with the hair on the back of Ernst's neck. "I'm glad you wanted me to take my clothes off. I can't think of ways of getting close enough to you. Having a drink with you holding my cock is nice. Don't be frightened, darling." He thought of his own quite practical fears and wondered if he should be doing something about them. There was no point in telling Ernst until he knew more.

"You're right," Ernst said. "It's too absurd to go on talking about being frightened. You're here to drive all the fears away."

When they had finished the champagne and Ernst had relieved him of his erection, Gerry put his clothes on again and ordered Ernst into his robe before Paolo was summoned for the ceremony of dressing. Ernst waved away the clothes selected for him and Paolo produced trousers and a tunic similar to Gerry's, in black. Ernst selected a single gold chain from the case that was presented to him and put a gold ring on his little finger. Gerry noted what he was doing with pride and amusement; they had become sartorial twins.

They left the stateroom with Yorgo and Paolo in attendance. Gerry felt like one of a royal couple as they proceeded along the passage; he missed the cheering throngs that should have been lining their way as he adjusted to Ernst's deliberate pace. He wanted to see him run and leap and shout with laughter, to give way to the youthful exuberance he felt he had been trained to repress. When he was freed from the drug, would he remain a prisoner of his legend? He felt another urge to knock the props out from under the elaborate structure of his life.

They entered a roomful of old friends, as closely knit as members of a secret society. They were instantly absorbed into it as if there had been a gap that required filling. Gerry felt a lift in the atmosphere. The room buzzed with jocular greetings. André approached and he kissed him.

"Hello, darling. Did you have a nice afternoon?"

"I got caught in the rain." André giggled. "I'll tell you about it later. How about you?"

"Momentous."

The boy's great eyes gazed at him from depths of adoration. "Everything's all right?"

"Everything's wonderful. We'd better leave that till later, too. I'm told you speak German."

"After a fashion. Not very well but I manage."

"Talk to Heinrich when you get a chance, will you, darling? Ask him what his plans are. I'd like to know if he seems nice or a total shit."

"He'll probably think I'm making a pass at him but I'll try. I'm still 'darling'?"

Gerry put a hand on his shoulder and gave it a gentle squeeze. "Of course, darling. Always. Things have changed the way we've expected."

"I'm glad, darling. Truly. I feel almost as if something wonderful had happened to me."

"You're an angel." A small hand slipped into his from behind him and closed on the ring. He swung around and found Solange looking up at him, her eyes sparkling.

"What a blessing." She lifted his hand and glanced down at the ring. "I'm so very happy." She stopped a boy who was passing with drinks and took two glasses and handed one to him. "I know you like whiskey, darling, but champagne is for special occasions. This is the most special one of many years." She toasted him with her eyes over the rim of the glass and drank.

Gerry burst out laughing. "I'm feeling like a blushing bride. Don't make fun of us."

"Not fun, darling. I'm toasting the ring. Nobody has worn it since he's had it. He once told me he would give it to anybody he found who was as true as a brother. He said he expected to be buried with it."

"My goodness." The lump rose in his throat and he took a hasty swallow of wine. "He didn't say anything like that to me. He just gave it to me."

"I've been waiting to see if you would get it. I would've given it to you the day we met."

"Please, darling." He turned away and ran a hand over his eyes and pressed their corners with thumb and forefinger and took a deep breath. He turned back and leaned down to her and kissed her. "Sorry. It's been quite a day. He's promised to start cutting down on the smoking."

"He will, darling. He will do anything for you. That's what the ring means. He has such a very generous nature but it has been twisted by his own folly and bad judgment. You know? It's not too late. You'll give him a new life."

"We'll give each other a new life. And you too, my darling."

"I could use one." She uttered her hearty laughter and nodded over his shoulder. "Look at him. How handsome he is tonight. Shall we go to him?"

She tucked a hand under his arm and they took the few steps to Ernst's side. He was speaking German to Heinrich and the perfidious Maria. Gerry had never seen him so animated. His enormous charm was in full flood, making even the loutish young German show signs of respectful interest. He held out his hands to Solange and Gerry while he finished what he was saying, then switched to English to address Maria. "You must try very hard to win over my Gerald," he said. "He's still displeased with your gifts."

Her bulging eyes rolled over Gerry, not belligerently but with thoughtful examination. "You must remember it was before you joined us, dear lamb. I hoped that was understood and forgotten." She made it a wistful rebuke.

"I wasn't exactly crazy about your plans for our young friend here, either," Gerry pointed out.

"Oh that. It was simply a suggestion. Men probably know how to deal with each other much better than I can. When we get to Ceylon—what was I saying? Oh yes, you as a man will know how to handle it. When we get to Cochin or wherever, you'll be able to convince him that he's no longer wanted. I'm delighted to be out of it."

Gerry noted her slip. What was her connection with

Ceylon? "I may need your help as an interpreter," he suggested disarmingly. He thought of the Oriental on the foredeck. How could he make sure that he was the one he'd seen her with? "Remind me to tell you something about that anonymous note." He watched her odd eyes but they revealed nothing.

"Tell me, darling." She was tolerantly affectionate. "We both have Ernst's interests at heart. What about the note?"

"Nothing that won't keep." If his wild guess about her smuggling was correct, Ernst would find it tiresome if he caught her at it. He held one hand with the other and settled the ring firmly on his finger. "I think I've figured out why it was written." He didn't want to give it the weight of a meaningful look and turned quickly to Yorgo, who was hovering at his side as if he wanted to say something. "Yes?"

"Mr. Farr says his mother should have only clear consommé and plain rice for dinner. Ernst thinks people who want special diets should stay in their cabins. What should I tell him?"

"Oh heavens, give her what she wants tonight. We can't send the poor thing back to her cabin now. Would you put André and Heinrich together at table?"

Yorgo smiled smoothly. "I'm sure Heinrich will make no objections."

Gerry smiled to himself as his secretary departed. He hoped Ernst wouldn't be annoyed at seeing a plate of plain rice served at his sumptuous table. The burdens of being a host. Well, yes, he realized, it could be a burden. Was it worth it? He had a vision of being alone with what he thought of now as his family, with André and a boy for him, relaxing with peanut butter sandwiches if they damn well felt like it. A distant vision but worth working for.

André rejoined him. "Are you going to the film tonight? It's that marvelous Truffaut about making a film. I'm dying to see it again."

"I've read a lot about it. I think Ernst wants to be alone tonight. I'd like to see it."

"Can we go together?"

"Of course, darling. If I'm not with Ernst, I love to be with you. I've been having a dream about putting all the guests ashore except you and maybe Hank to keep you company."

"I'm glad I can stay but you better not count on Hank."

"Oh? What's up?" He'd noticed that Hank seemed to be ignoring both of them.

"I imagine it has to do with what I have to tell you about. He's barely speaking to me."

"That won't do. I'm going to have to knock some sense into you two. Have you been bad?"

André smiled angelically. "I suppose so. Not that he knows anything. He's just jumping to conclusions."

"On this boat, that's the only place to jump." They laughed. "OK, darling. We'll see if we can straighten it out later."

"Lovers' secrets?" Ernst asked, moving in beside them. Gerry slipped an arm around his waist and they looked at each other with startled wonder. They were together.

"André keeps me very busy with his love life," Gerry explained.

"I'm in love with him," André said to Ernst. "I imagine everybody knows that. I like to do everything he does so I'll probably fall in love with you, too. I would have at the beginning if you'd encouraged me. I've never watched two people fall in love before. It's amazing."

Some sense of what had occurred seemed to have touched everybody and gave to the evening an air of watchful gaiety, as if they were waiting to see how openly the lovers would declare themselves. They sat together at dinner but their slight physical intimacies were secretive, their knees pressed together under the table, their hands occasionally brushing against each other. Gerry was pleased, feeling it as a recognition that what they shared was too important to display casually in public. Ernst dazzled, exhibiting an erudition on a wide range of subjects that Gerry had barely glimpsed before. As the meal drew to an end, Gerry was aware of strain slowing him down. There was a tremor in his hand when he lifted his glass, which he began to do frequently. The wine waiter kept it full.

Gerry leaned to him. "Are you all right, darling?" he asked in an anxious undertone.

"I must leave in a minute. It's getting difficult."

"Take it easy. Everybody's finishing." He looked over his shoulder for Paolo and he was beside him immediately, bending down to him. "Get things ready," he instructed. "We'll be right there."

Ernst drained his glass again and it was refilled. He sat

immobile for another few moments while dinner came to a natural conclusion. "Is everybody ready for coffee?" he asked. He rose with Gerry at his side and they made their way out in the general exodus. His pace remained deliberate as they returned to his cabin.

"Paolo has gone ahead?"

"Yes. Everything's OK. You were fascinating at dinner."

Ernst turned his head quickly to Gerry and took his hand. "Thank you for thinking so, darling. I couldn't have got through it without you beside me."

"That's where I'm going to be. It's hard to get used to, isn't it?"

Gerry let them in with his key. They went through to the dimly lighted bedroom where Paolo was waiting with his equipment. Gerry took Ernst's clothes from him and could feel the urgency gripping him again. He screened him from Paolo with his dressing gown for the moment that he was naked. He went to the bathroom and Gerry crouched beside Paolo.

"Show me how to do it," he requested.

"It's very simple." Paolo held the small silver ladle over the flame. "You form it into a ball and ignite it and put it in the pipe." Paolo followed his own directions and handed the pipe to Gerry. He drew on it to watch the gummy substance being consumed but didn't inhale. He handed the pipe back. Paolo concluded, "Scrape the bowl when it's finished. Be careful not to melt too much at a time or you'll waste it."

"Fine." Gerry stood. "You can wait outside. I'll be here for a while. You'll probably be wanted later."

He waited for Paolo to go and bolted the door after him and headed back to the pipes. Ernst emerged from the bathroom and they held out their hands to each other and stood facing each other. Gerry could feel the tremor in the hands he held.

"You're going to prepare the pipes, darling?"

"Yes. I've had a lesson."

"It's very thrilling, smoking with somebody I love."

Gerry gave his lips a quick kiss and let him stretch out on the bed. He found his job more difficult than it looked. He wasted quite a lot on his first tries but by the fourth pipe he had begun to get the hang of it. He prepared a few more and saw Ernst's movements smoothing out and growing lethargic.

"You'd better go now, darling," he said. "I love to have you here but you don't approve. I'll let myself go one last time and forget I'm supposed to stop. It will be heavenly thinking of you and of all we know now. I adore you, my dearest Gerald."

Gerry moved over and sat beside him on the bed and stroked his hair. "I want so much to be with you all night. What time do you start functioning in the morning?"

"About eleven."

"I'll come give you a big good-morning kiss."

"You will spend the night with André?"

"I guess so, unless he has something else up his sleeve. We won't make love. That's all over."

"Are you sure? I think I'm beginning to be jealous."

"I hope so, darling. I want us to be jealous of each other. I wouldn't let André spend the night with you."

"But I don't want him. You do."

"Did, darling. I only want you now. I don't have to force myself to be faithful. There's nothing there anymore with others."

"I want you," Ernst said dreamily.

Gerry gently removed himself from his embrace and rose. He wished Ernst would admit that he didn't care about sex when he was like this instead of pretending that orgasm was a trivial detail. He doubted if much had been going on with Heinrich, even with the assistance of a troupe of whore boys. "I'll leave you now. You can get as zonked as you like without me. I'll send Paolo in to man the pipes. I hope you miss me so much that you'll never let me out of your sight again. Send for me if you want me. Any time. It doesn't matter when."

He found everybody sitting around the saloon having brandy or liqueurs in small glasses. He asked a boy for coffee. Ken was playing the piano. Hank stood behind him, marking the beat with his body. He avoided Gerry's eyes.

Gerry took the coffee that was offered him and wandered into the room. He nodded reassuringly to Solange in reply to her questioning look. André and Sally were sitting together, engaged in their usual cheerful banter. He perched on the arm of André's chair.

"Hello, babies," he greeted them.

André put a hand on his thigh. "Here you are, darling. Have you come to rescue me from this ghastly female?"

"I'll get even with you later for that, you beastly boy."

They joked and laughed. Sally rose. "It must be almost time for the film. I'm going to find somebody who'll grope me madly in the dark. Heinrich, probably."

Gerry looked down at the boy at his side. "Did you have a chance to talk to him?"

"Heinrich? Sure. He says my German's pretty good but I can't understand half what he says."

"What's he like?"

"He was all right once he realized I wasn't flirting with him. I was surprised by how frank he is about doing it for money. He said I wouldn't have to pay. He says Ernst is going to give him money to open a bar."

"A bar, eh? Ernst has never mentioned it. When is this supposed to happen?"

"I don't know. He was a bit vague about it. He seems to think Maria wants him to stay on until something's settled."

"Stay on?" Gerry was silent for a thoughtful moment. Had Maria offered to get rid of him to prove that she could save Ernst the price of a bar or was she keeping him in reserve with the hope that Gerry's tenure would prove brief? She could profit in Ernst's eyes in either case. "Your cousin puzzles me. Did your mother ever tell you why she thinks she's wicked?"

"Oh, I think that's nonsense. She doesn't approve of people chasing their rich friends. That's all it is. That and introducing me to Ernst."

"It might be more than that. No. I'm being unfair. We have things to talk about." People were rising and there was movement toward the cinema. Gerry stood and André followed suit.

"Are we spending the night together?" he asked, his eyes darting about the room distractedly.

"As far as I know, darling, we're still sharing the cabin. I'm planning to move in with Ernst tomorrow. I'll tell you about it."

André's eyes settled on him with a rapturous smile. "That's all I wanted to know. We'll have plenty of time to talk when we go to bed."

When they seated themselves in the back row again, Hank and Ken didn't join them. The lights dimmed and Gerry put his arm around André's shoulders to find out if he'd been truthful with Ernst. He had been. The sexual spark was gone; love remained. He wouldn't risk putting an arm around Hank. When the film ended, André readily agreed to his suggestion that they have a nightcap in their cabin.

Gerry ordered ice and a bottle of whiskey and they went forward along the passage. Gerry had to struggle with himself to stop at their door rather than continue on to Ernst's. He knew he should leave him alone for tonight; if he wasn't already asleep, he would be so lost in an opium fog that a visit would be pointless. Once the door was closed behind them, André's presence made it easier to contemplate a night without the only person in the world he longed to be with. He took a quick glance around to make sure there weren't any messages and started to pull his clothes off. A knock on the door announced the arrival of a pretty boy with the drinks tray. He finished undressing and put on his dressing gown and went to meet André as he came out of the bathroom, naked and carrying his clothes. Gerry took them from him.

"I'm learning how to be a valet from Paolo. I'll take care of these. You can fix us a drink." He disposed of the clothes and brought André his dressing gown and held it while he put it on. "How's that for service? Ernst couldn't hope for better."

André laughed. "It's nice. I'm going to have to get a valet. Why aren't you with him now? Is it all right to ask?"

"Of course. We have a problem. Opium."

"Is that what he's on?"

"Yes. I knew it but I didn't know how serious it is. He's been stoned all day. He was so gone when I got there that I didn't think we were going to make any sense at all. I'll stay with him tomorrow and see if that helps." They carried their drinks to bed and made themselves comfortable, André against the pillows, Gerry propped on an elbow at his knees.

"As much as I hate to think of it, I probably should be hoping for you to be with him all the time," André said. "I mean, I know that's what you want, but for my own sake too. I feel as if this cabin's ours. Even when I'm alone here I feel you with me and it's all I want. That had a lot to do with what happened this afternoon."

"Aha. This afternoon. What about this afternoon?" Gerry shook André's leg and grinned at him while the boy smiled into his drink, looking flustered.

"You'd suppose somebody had offered me a bar from the fuss I'm making about it. Actually I stayed with Hank after you left. We had the pool all to ourselves and I was feeling very good with him. Then the sky covered over with clouds and he wanted to come here. I wasn't sure I wanted him to—well, I've been talking about that all day. I wanted to be with him but I wished we had someplace else to go. We were naked and his cock was the way yours gets when I think you'd better cover it. I could barely keep my hands off it. I admit that. So we wrapped towels around ourselves and were leaving when we ran into the first mate. He offered to show us around again and was looking at me the way he did this morning. I guess Hank didn't like it. He said he wanted a rest and told me to go ahead so I did."

Gerry laughed. "The suspense is killing me. I can't imagine what happened then."

"Don't be horrid." André pouted charmingly. "Hank could've come with me or said he'd rather do it some other time or anything. I didn't particularly want to do the tour but I didn't see why I should let him decide what we did, either. Anyway, it was very interesting, especially down below where the engines are. It's so clean, just like a spaceship on telly. When we came out, it was raining torrents. That beautiful uniform was ruined in seconds, the time it took to run up from one deck to the next. He rushed me into his cabin on the bridge and—well, there he was, stark naked with this stupefying erection. The next thing I knew, he was having me. The towel didn't leave me much time for second thoughts. It was practically rape."

"Or would've been if you'd resisted." Gerry felt a reluctant little pang of envy. Cocks were springing into action all over but he was going to have to wait for the one he wanted.

"I don't see how anybody could've resisted," André said sensibly. "He's much too big to fight. And his cock, darling. Well, as you say, everything in proportion. He wants me to come see him every afternoon at four."

"I don't think we can allow that."

"No?"

"Is it leading to anything?"

"Of course not. He told me how lonely he gets for his wife and kiddies back in Bergen."

"Well, then. Does Hank know about it?"

"Of course not. He's angry because I went off with Axel. Why should he assume anything happened?"

"Axel, is it?" Gerry paused as a thought struck him. "You could help me. I'd like you to ask him some questions for me. You're getting to be my official go-between. I'd just as soon not go to the captain. For one thing, ask him if everything's running as usual on board."

"I can already tell you something about that," André said, looking pleased with himself. "He said they're having trouble with one of the engines. We're going slower than usual."

"Really?" Gerry swirled the ice around in his drink and drained it. Anything abnormal might be significant. It might be in somebody's interest to arrive at Cochin at night rather than during the day, or vice versa. Something to keep in mind. He rose and held out his hand for André's glass. "Let's have another drink." He refilled their glasses and returned André's.

"What is it, darling?" André asked, reacting to his silence.

"I'm going to tell you." He resumed his place on the bed. "Does cousin Maria have any connection with Ceylon?"

"Ceylon? Isn't it called Sri Lanka now? Not that I know of."

"She speaks the language, even if she says she doesn't." He told André about the odd incidents that had aroused his curiosity—Maria's possible encounters with the Oriental who was now a deckhand, the brief episode in the bow that he and Hank had witnessed. "Don't forget the taxi crash. Do you think I'm imagining things?" he concluded.

"Well, you say you and Hank aren't sure what you saw. That's what you were talking about with Axel this morning? Are you sure the man you saw with Maria is the same one you saw on deck?"

"No, that's the trouble, but I'm pretty sure he's the one I bumped into at the bar. Maria was there. That's peculiar enough."

"It's very peculiar." André's beauty was intensified by a look of grave intelligence. "What do you think you should do about it?"

"I don't know. Do you have any ideas? The easiest thing to do would be to ask the captain to have the guy locked up until we get to India. He's the law on board." He found his smuggling theory so convincing that he was almost ready to accept it as fact. "If Maria is in on some smuggling deal, do you think I should interfere?"

"You don't want Ernst mixed up in anything like that."

"Exactly, darling, especially since she's loaded him with the stuff. He must know what he's going to do with it if there's any chance of a customs inspection. That's something else you can find out from your friend Axel. Ask him how carefully we're checked going in and out of port. Ask him about smuggling generally, whether yachts do a lot of it."

"I feel like Mata Hari. It sounds as if I'm going to have to be fucked at considerable length to find out all you want to know."

"I could ask him myself but he'll obviously talk more freely to you. Do you intend to let him have you again anyway?"

"It was pretty thrilling, the way it happened, but it might not be if it's planned. Probably. Just to teach myself once and for all that once is enough."

"OK, then there's more. He said there was something funny about the crew list that he noticed after Hank and I spoke to him. Tell him that Ernst is thinking of asking the captain to muster all hands to look them over and see if he objects. Something's fishy but I don't know what."

"If it's smuggling I can't see Maria in it, somehow. She goes in for dramatic gestures. Smuggling's so common. Maybe she's planning to have Ernst kidnapped and held for ransom. That would be more her style."

"Yeah, that sounds like her. I'm joking but she's the only one of us who might be up to something funny. It's *too* obvious. There's something else but I hardly know myself what I'm driving at. It has to do with how free communication is between the passengers' cabins and the crew's quarters. I mean, suppose I wanted a sailor. How would I go about getting him if I winked at him? What I'd like to know is whether it would be to anybody's interest to have a spy below decks to check on the sailors' movements—for blackmail, for instance, or to run a sort of call-boy service—or if it's all so free and easy that there wouldn't be any point in it. The more I talk about it, the more farfetched it sounds, but I'm trying to figure out some reason for that damn man from Bangkok to be on board. Just get Axel to say a few words on the general subject of passenger-crew relationships and we'll see if we come up with anything."

"I'll probably give him the wrong idea and drive him mad with jealousy. I don't think I'd want that."

Gerry laughed. "Tell him Farr has been asking. Anyway, we have plenty of time to play detective. It's supposed to take five or six days to get to Cochin. How long have we been out? Only about a day and a half? Amazing. Try to talk to Axel in the morning. You can find out if he has anything interesting to tell us and if you don't find him thrilling again, you can drop your Mata Hari act."

"You won't tell Hank, will you?"

"You probably should tell him yourself. He can't think yet that he has any exclusive rights. Let him raise a little hell with you. It would probably do you both good."

André's face lighted up as if he had discovered an enviable secret in himself. "I'd rather like him to raise hell with me," he said.

They had another drink and Gerry told him something about his afternoon without mentioning the sexual problem. They yawned and finished their drinks and slipped under the sheet. They kissed before they turned out the light and lay with their hands clasped, but at a chaste distance from each other. Gerry was grateful for André's simple acceptance of the altered situation.

They went out to the pool early the next morning, too early for Gerry to go see Ernst. It was another glorious day. The sun was a golden globe in a clear pale sky. Nobody was out yet. The yacht cut smoothly through an enormous empty sea of glass. A pristine world was recreated in the golden clarity of the light. The sting of sun in the cool air was invigorating; Gerry slipped off his trunks and dived into the pool. He thought of the darkened forward cabin and he wanted to go to Ernst, pull aside the heavy draperies, coax him out into the fresh promise of morning. No drug could match its restorative power. They were together; they had declared themselves. He could feel love brimming over all through him, spilling out to include everybody around him. It was a beautiful way to feel at the start of a day.

He swam fast, burrowing into the tingling purity of seawater. When he paused for breath, treading water, he saw that Sally had joined them. She and André were splashing about in the shallow end, both naked. The sight stirred him curiously. They looked so sweet together, young and slim and perfectly matched, two beautiful young animals. He felt as dotingly affectionate toward them as if they were his children. He wanted to put his arms around them, hold them, encourage them to find pleasure in each other's bodies. He was turning into a dirty old man, with an unexpected little twitch of heterosexuality as an extra added attraction.

He returned to where he'd dived to retrieve his trunks and they all waved and called to each other before he went aft to the banquette and stretched out in the blazing sun. They soon joined him.

"Here he is," Sally said, pushing André from her. "You can have him back. He's no fun. He won't even let me play with his sweet little thing. I thought it might at least show some signs of life like yours."

"Why are you so mean to her?" Gerry sat up and made a grab for André and pulled him down to him. They wrestled playfully and André's protests were smothered in laughter as Gerry accomplished his purpose. He flipped him over onto his back long enough for Sally to have a good look.

"I say," she exclaimed. "It's not so little, after all. It's absolutely smashing. Why is he so shy of it? I quite like it. I wish I had your magic touch."

André scrambled up into a sitting position and folded his arms in his lap and covered himself. "You see? It works when it wants to," he said, sounding pleased with himself.

"Indeed it does. I'm frightfully impressed. It's super. Thanks, lads. You've made my morning." She gathered up her loose shapeless covering and dropped it over her head.

"Where's Solange?" Gerry asked.

"Sleeping, I shouldn't be surprised. She stayed up all night playing bridge. She and Farr lifted a packet off the Horrockses. Good show, I say." She laughed and cast Gerry a merrily speculative glance and shook back her hair and left.

Gerry sat back, grinning at his beloved friend. "I guess I've underestimated girls. Wasn't it sort of fun getting a hard-on for her? Who knows what it might lead to."

"My chance to go straight." André smiled down at him naughtily. "I must say, it made me feel awfully cocky. Now that we've broken the ice, I might let her play with it as much as she likes." They laughed and lay back side by side.

The interlude had turned Gerry's thoughts to children. Since parenthood had never entered into his picture of himself, he was astonished by how much the prospect pleased him. He would talk to Solange about it and find out if she wanted to wait. To be firmly established at Ernst's side, with an adorable mother for their children thrown in, was more than anybody had the right to hope for.

The stirrings of his body were subdued by the sun and as he watched it climb the sky he knew it was almost time for Ernst. "I'm going to go see the love of my life," he said, giving André's hand a squeeze. He pulled himself up and stood. "Hail, hail, the gang's all here," he announced, looking forward to where a number of the party had gathered around the pool. He put on his trunks. "Isn't this a good time to go look for Axel and do some spying for me? I'd like to know what you can come up with as soon as possible."

He dived into the pool and swam past everybody to the other end. He paused for a beer and to dry off. He felt so alive that he couldn't imagine anybody still lying around in bed. This was the last time he would start a day without Ernst. There wasn't any point in being in rare high spirits if Ernst wasn't sharing them. He finished his beer and stopped at the cabin to pick up the key and went along to the end of the passage and let himself in. There was nobody in the sitting room. He went on to the bedroom. Ernst and his two henchmen were there, Ernst in bed but not exactly lying around. He looked rather like a bedridden but busy executive, surrounded by papers, with Yorgo sitting on a chair beside him, the open portfolio on his knees. Paolo was doing something at the dressing table. The curtains were parted and the room was filled with light.

"Here I am," Gerry announced.

Ernst looked up with a loving smile of welcome. "Thank heavens, darling. I've just told Yorgo to show you all these. They're invitations for the next six months. I've marked the ones that might be amusing. You can look them over and decide. We'll have to tell everybody that we'll be three. It would be much simpler socially if we could just send out a wedding announcement." He gathered everything together while he spoke and handed it all to Yorgo who rose and headed for the door. Paolo followed him and closed the door behind him. The new regime of privacy had been inaugurated. Gerry didn't bother to bolt the door but, feeling the need to further mark his territory, went to the bedside and leaned down to Ernst and gave him a quick kiss.

"Good morning, darling. I'm sweaty. I'm going to take a shower." He went to the bathroom and peeled off his trunks, hoping that Ernst would recognize his right to make himself at home by not following him. Taking a shower need no longer be a sexual event but an ordinary occurrence in their daily life together. He got out of the tub and dried himself and wrung out his trunks and put them on again, making a little grimace at the disagreeable sensation of damp cloth against his skin. He went out and found Ernst up, wearing very smart brief shorts. Gerry had never seen him in anything sporty and was still not used to the splendors of his body—wide shoulders, deep chest, the torso tapering to narrow hips, the statuelike modeling of his muscular abdomen.

"God, you're a stunning-looking man," Gerry said, stopping to survey him. Ernst smiled with pleasure as he approached.

"You brought the sun in with you, darling. I thought it would be nice to get out into it."

"I was hoping you would. You can join the nudists and put us all to shame. I've just been showing Sally André's cock."

"Good heavens. The things that go on behind my back." His smile broadened. "And showing her yours too, I presume. One of the most thrilling things about you is your total sexual authority. I look forward to seeing you exercise it on every possible occasion." They stood facing each other, their eyes studying each other with interest. "You were right about me, as I expect you to be always. I missed you so much that I never want to let you out of my sight. Will you sleep with me from now on?"

"Naturally. I told you we'd have to. I'm going to exercise my sexual authority in our bed. Did you tell Heinrich you'd give him money for a bar?"

"I said something to him about it a month or two ago. Why? Shouldn't I?"

"Of course you should if you said you would. Why didn't you tell me? We've talked about him often enough."

"I think quite honestly I may have forgotten. Certainly not because I wanted to conceal it from you. It wasn't something I discussed with him at any length."

"André thinks that's mainly what he's waiting for."

"Why didn't Maria tell me? How tiresome. I'd like André to be with me when I speak to him so that there won't be any more misunderstanding. We've all spent much too much time worrying about Heinrich. I told you I thought he was harmless."

"You did. You also think Maria's harmless. Maybe she is. I hope so." Their eyes hadn't left each other, probing, watching, learning. Gerry laughed suddenly. "Do you know what we're doing? We're living together. I love it."

Ernst uttered his gentle purring laughter. "In that case, I think we must decide which date to choose as our official anniversary." He moved to Gerry's side and put an arm around his shoulders and walked him toward the bureau. They were old friends. It was a tranquil asexual moment generating deep confidence between them. Gerry had thought it might take them months to achieve anything like it.

Ernst found an engagement book on the bureau and opened it to a crowded page and pointed. Gerry read the notation: *Lunch—hotel barge.* "Should it be the day Yorgo found you?" He flipped over a couple of pages. "Or today, the first day we'll spend twenty-four hours together, beginning now?"

Gerry put his hand with the big ring on Ernst's. "Actually, it should be yesterday, the day I received my seal of office."

"Of course. You're quite right." He picked up a gold pen and circled the date and wrote: *Gerald and Ernst till death us do part.* "You write something, darling."

Gerry took the pen and wrote: *Ernst and Gerald together at last.* The lump formed in his throat but was quickly dissolved by the tranquil glow of happiness that spread through his chest. Their eyes met and marveled at each other. "That makes it pretty official," he said.

Ernst touched the ring. "I was stoned yesterday. I couldn't tell you how happy it made me to give you that."

"Solange explained a bit about it. I almost cried." Their eyes summoned each other and they exchanged a lingering kiss that trembled with controlled passion. Their hands rested lightly on their nearly naked bodies. They were exquisitely balanced between the loving comradeship they were building and the perils of their unresolved erotic demands. Gerry wanted to do nothing to push them one way or the other but rather to preserve the balance while they evolved a few safety devices to catch them when they fell. He felt a corresponding caution in Ernst.

They stepped apart and Ernst picked up some sort of jersey from the end of the bed and slung it around his neck. He looked dashingly young and vital and sexy, almost unrecognizable from the day of *Lunch—hotel barge*. "Shall we go astonish everybody?" he asked.

"You will. Do you feel as good as you look or did you sneak something before I got here?"

"Nothing. I'm going to attempt the impossible. It's not yet noon. Try not to let me come back here before three. Even later if I seem to be all right. Do you really want to stay with me all day and all night?"

"That's what it's all about."

"Yes, I believe it is. That's why I must do my best to see that it isn't a bore for you."

Ernst's arrival turned the casual gathering on the after-deck into a party. He asked for a Bloody Mary and a boy began to circulate among the others with drinks. Mrs. Farr was the first to receive the full force of his charm and was reduced to a blizzard of non sequiturs. Solange was there in one of her gossamer coveralls and the couple kissed affectionately. He exchanged ribald witticisms with Trevor and Farr and left them laughing. Ken and Heinrich formed an unexpected pair beside the pool and he went to them and spoke briefly to the German who brightened visibly. Gerry drifted along in Ernst's wake, drinking beer and tingling with admiration and devotion. Ernst stepped back to him and their eyes lighted up with delight at simply looking at each other and finding each other near. Hank and Maria joined them.

"Where's our beautiful young friend?" Hank asked Gerry, apparently recovered from his sulks. He was becoming increasingly attractive as his tan deepened. Gerry felt the little flutter in the pit of his stomach that Hank could still stir in him.

"Doing something for me, I think. He'll be along. He told me about yesterday. Have you forgiven him?"

"I missed you both last night." He grinned. "Maybe one more than the other but I won't say which. I decided to take your advice. If he doesn't know what he wants, I'm going to try to help him make up his mind."

Gerry chuckled. "You're on your own. I won't be there tonight."

"Well, we wouldn't want him to be alone, would we?" They laughed. While they chatted, André emerged from the saloon with Sally. They both looked taken aback by the festive atmosphere with which they were immediately surrounded and then André's eyes traveled across the gathering until they lighted on Gerry. He headed toward him with an eager smile. His eyes shifted to Hank when he reached them and looked up at him in a way that sent a shiver of vicarious rapture down Gerry's spine. Who could resist the appeal of such extraordinary eyes?"

"Are you speaking to me today?" he asked.

Hank put a hand on his naked shoulder. "You know I am. I was being silly last night. I'm sorry."

André shifted slightly as if taking shelter against Hank's body and looked at Gerry to convey a private message. "Once is enough," he said with conviction. "I'm going to have to be an awful tease if you have any more errands for me."

"I want to hear all about it. Let me get you a drink. What'll it be?"

"I didn't know it was going to be a party. Shall I have champagne?"

"Of course. Beer is for the lower classes." He had only to take a few steps and reach out to a tray for the champagne but André stayed close to his side. He positioned himself so that he and Ernst could look at each other over Maria's shoulder. Talk was lively around them so they could speak privately. "What did you find out?" he asked, handing the glass to André.

"Well, I led into it by saying I'd be buying presents for people and wondered if I'd have to have papers for customs. He says that yachts are pretty carefully checked, particularly in the Mediterranean, but Ernst uses what he called the envelope system. They have envelopes full of cash waiting for the officials who come on board and also for the police on shore so there won't be any trouble with boys or drugs or anything." He nodded at Maria's back and slurred his words slightly. "He says she took a lot off last time with no questions asked."

"Everybody's paid to look the other way?"

"That's the idea. I said it sounded perfect for smuggling, and he agreed but said he couldn't imagine the Baron's guests doing anything like that, and the sailors are much more carefully watched. He seemed amused by the idea of Ernst passing them all in review. He said he was sure they'd meet the Baron's high standards. There're half a dozen older men but they're kept out of sight in the engine room or the kitchen—sorry, the galley—where they won't offend our eyes."

"Did he say if they're Orientals?"

"The plain ones? I think he said they all are."

"Only six? I'm in business. That's perfect, darling. I'll have him point them out to me on my tour. I'll wait till tomorrow morning for that. There's plenty of time."

"There's plenty of time for me to be raped, too. He kept playing with my behind. It was quite exciting at first but then it got to be silly. I dropped a hint that I have a very jealous lover and might not be able to make it this afternoon. About the rest of it, he says that Ernst's policy is for the crew to indulge the passengers' whims so long as it doesn't interfere with their duties. He says they're allowed to bunk up, as he puts it, wherever they want. I wasn't sure exactly what to ask but I think that's more or less what you meant, isn't it? I mean, there's not much point in spying if it's all open and above-board. Is that all you wanted me to find out?"

"I'll take care of the rest. If you don't want him again, avoid him."

"I will. I can't believe what's happened to Ernst. He's absolutely ravishing. You transform everybody."

The party was given an additional lift by food. Blocks of truffled *foie d'oie* made them all groan with gluttony. Bottles of a sensational red Burgundy were consumed. The sea developed a swell and they were rocked gently by the deep. Gerry told Paolo to prepare everything at Ernst's bedside and not to come with them when they left. He and Ernst remained within physical reach of each other, their attention focused more and more on each other. As they flirted the current of desire grew more highly charged between them.

It was well after three when Ernst rose abruptly. Gerry sprang to his feet and turned to Paolo, who had the key ready. Ernst looked tense as they fell into step beside each other. They strode along the passage more briskly than Gerry had ever seen him move. He had the key ready and quickly opened the door.

"Please fix a pipe for me, darling," Ernst said, heading immediately for the bedroom. "I've waited long enough."

"You've been heroic. Everybody was enchanted by you."

The windows were heavily shrouded. The lights were dim. Gerry paused to bolt the door and Ernst stayed with him. They stripped together and went around to the table where the pipes were laid out. Ernst settled onto the bed but didn't stretch out in the smoker's traditional supine position. He turned the lights up and reached for Gerry and held him in front of him and studied him with enthralled eyes. Gerry sensed his hunger for the drug receding slightly. He realized that this was the first time they'd been naked together when Ernst wasn't stoned and his heart accelerated with excitement and curiosity. He had yet to learn the range of his lover's sexual tastes. If his cock had been good enough to get those nutty Hindus worked up into a religious frenzy, maybe it could make Ernst forget the pipes.

For fear that the craving for the drug might break its spell, Gerry leaned sideways to light the spirit lamp and prepare the pipe. When it was ready, he lifted himself onto the bed and knelt upright before Ernst with his hips thrust forward and a hand wandering suggestively along himself, guided by Ernst's eyes. Ernst smoked distractedly, reaching out to him. Gerry felt the sexual charge building up between them again, still undissipated by the drug. He lifted the tray onto the bed and leaned across Ernst to prepare the second pipe, making the most of the tantalizing approaches and withdrawals that this permitted him. He prepared a pipe for himself and smoked with Ernst, flaunting his potency. Ernst's eyes began to glaze but their attention didn't waver; he had found a new addiction.

They both put their spent pipes back on the tray and Ernst's hands and mouth immediately resumed their mesmerized play as if the pipe were an unwanted interruption. Gerry backed away, inciting him, his hands moving over himself again, and performed little sexual charades, striking poses to make an extravagant exhibition of himself.

Instinct told him to stay out of reach; he sensed that physical contact impinged on fantasy and cut off Ernst's active response when he was drugged.

He saw Ernst's sex stirring and his heart leaped up with hope. Was this the exercise of sexual authority that he wanted to watch? He altered techniques and positions and continued his slow voluptuous play. Ernst's sex lengthened and thickened; his hands crept closer to it and he finally held it and began to stroke it. Gerry's heart was hammering in his chest while he willed him to reach a climax. Oh God, let him come, he prayed while he still posed and performed for him, knowing that any break in his activity would shatter whatever fantasy they were enacting. Ernst writhed and moaned and uttered sharp cries.

"Oh yes, God yes. Now," Ernst called to him.

Gerry applied the final pressures and held himself while his ejaculation was flung out onto Ernst's chest. Ernst uttered another tormented shout and his hips leaped up and his own massive ejaculation mingled with Gerry's.

"Oh darling," Gerry cried out ecstatically as he sprang from the bed and ran to the bathroom. He rushed back with a damp washcloth and a towel. He dropped to the edge of the bed and sponged him off and dried him. Only two pipes. They had shared their orgasms. He didn't care how forced and nearly solitary it had been. They had triumphed over the drug. Gerry wouldn't give him time to want more this afternoon. He lifted the tray from the bed and returned it to the table and fell on Ernst and hugged him close.

"Oh, darling, darling, darling," he crooned. He covered his face with kisses. There were tears on his cheeks and he kissed them away. "We've done it, darling. Oh God, what heaven. Sex is better than opium any day. We'll get rid of it soon now, darling."

"You made it happen," Ernst said with difficulty, as if he were in shock. "I didn't think anybody could. You're magnificent. Your cock—I want to see it getting big no matter what makes it happen."

"That's easy. You do. You can make it hard again in no time. It's so heavenly to know that you like it. There. Feel that. Oh God, darling, watch it getting big and hard for you again. Yes, hold it. It'll stay that way as long as you like. Now let's talk about music."

They talked about the guests who were due on board the yacht in the next few months.

They talked about vintage time at the chateau in France. They talked about their trip to New York and about Gerry's company of performing art's. Ernst made a reference to the film that was going to be shown that evening; he had partially financed it.

"There you go again," Gerry exclaimed. "Now you're a film producer. What next?"

"I can be anything for you," Ernst said. "It thrills me to surrender my will completely to you. I want to live the dream I've always had of being governed by a man who is stronger and better than I am. Your power to dominate thrills me."

Gerry had sensed from the beginning the power he could exercise over him. He was being offered it now and he accepted it triumphantly, feeling his life acquiring its final meaning.

"You want me to be a father figure? My cock is beginning to feel quite patriarchal." Ernst's laughter rang out on a light boyish note. Gerry remained still for a moment and gazed at him while a shiver of delight ran down his spine. "I've never heard that before. How lovely. Are you really going to turn into a child? I've seen it in you, of course, and I love it when it doesn't scare me. If I can make you laugh like that, I'll be a very happy father figure."

Later, Gerry summoned Paolo and asked him to bring all his things from the other cabin. He canceled the bath boy and ordered a bottle of champagne and they shared it and the bathroom while they prepared for the evening. He was turning Ernst's life upside down in small ways; more drastic changes would doubtless come later.

After they had greeted the gathering in the main saloon and Gerry had whispered a few encouraging words to Solange about their almost drug-free afternoon, he was approached by Yorgo.

"The captain's very upset," he announced. "He's heard that Ernst is planning to have all the sailors out for an inspection."

"Why is he upset about that?"

"He says it would be a breach of discipline and upset the orderly operation of the ship."

"Really?" Any hint of a conspiracy of concealment aroused his suspicions. Ernst wasn't to be told of the slip up when the crew had come aboard. Ernst wasn't to be allowed to inspect his own men. A normal effort to protect his own interests or was the captain hiding something? "Tell him there's nothing to be upset about," he said to Yorgo. "Tell him a couple of the passengers were joking about the idea. Ernst doesn't know anything about it." Ernst liked things to run smoothly.

Ernst was sufficiently interested in seeing the film to postpone the session with the pipes until afterward. It turned out to be a dramatically effective treatment of a homosexual theme. There was considerable male nudity when the plot called for it but the love scenes were handled with tact and it wasn't remotely pornographic. Ernst stirred as the final credits came up on the screen and they rose and hurried forward to the cabin.

They found everything in readiness for them and Gerry took Ernst's clothes and gave him his dressing gown before settling down to preparing several pipes in quick succession to relieve the tension he had felt accumulating in him. Knowing that they weren't going to be disturbed by Paolo and that he wasn't going to have a door slammed in his face, Gerry felt more tolerant of the drug and was ready to find whatever pleasure in it he could.

He threw off his clothes and joined Ernst on the bed and continued to prepare pipes at a slower pace. He was quickly aware of existing on two planes of consciousness. The real world remained part of him with sufficient clarity so that he had no trouble manipulating the tools involved in preparing the pipes but he found another level of intensified and slightly distorted perception where nothing was quite what it seemed. Their hands touching became a prodigy of eroticism. They looked into each other's eyes for what seemed like an eternity, plumbing each other's souls. What was no more than fondling and caressing became an orgy of sensuality. He understood better Ernst's indifference to orgasm but remained hardily potent. At the sixth or seventh pipe, he snuffed the lamp by mutual consent and they lay at peace in each other's arms.

"It seems mad that we haven't been like this since the beginning," Gerry murmured.

"I know, but at the beginning we might have let it be a one-night stand. I'll feel you beside me all night and know that I'm safe for life."

Gerry awoke with a headache and saw that it was too early to disturb the sleeping form at his side. He slipped out of bed and stole away to the bathroom to prepare for the day. He found his trunks without waking his sleeping lover and went out into blinding sunshine and found a boy to give him a beer. A swim helped clear his head. Opium was powerful stuff. He would have to watch it so that he didn't start looking forward to it as much as Ernst did. Now for business. He was counting on his conducted tour of the yacht to be conclusive. Either something fishy was going on and he should be able to spot it, or there wasn't and he could forget it. His sense of foreboding had been dissipated by the night at Ernst's side but his responsibility had become total.

He found First Mate Torberg in crisp handsome command and assessed him briefly as a bed companion. For such a gleaming, strapping young man, he found him curiously without magnetism. André must have been carried away by sheer bulk. Or perhaps there really was only one man now who could turn him on.

He knew that anything he said would be reported to the captain so his approach was cautious. He asked casually to be shown around; he would decide what to do about the man from Bangkok when he saw him. The tour proceeded uneventfully. There were several elderly Orientals working on the lower decks but his man was not among them.

"My roomboy at the hotel in Bangkok told me his uncle was a member of the crew," Gerry improvised. "I haven't seen him. I suppose he's on a different watch."

"You know him?"

"I saw them together in the street one day. A heavyset man with a moon face. I promised the boy I'd give him a message."

"Ah yes. I know the one you mean." Axel smiled suggestively. "The roomboys of the East. The trouble we will sometimes take for them. Isn't it so? Come with me."

He led the way along an antiseptic passage and opened a metal door and banged his ring on the metal frame of a tier of bunks. Gerry had had time to decide that if he were confronted with the familiar face he would pretend not to know him. He had the feeling that it was important not to reveal his suspicions. Three sleepy impassive Oriental faces peered at them from the bunks. Two of them were very bony. The third was indeed plump-featured but not the one he was looking for.

"No," Gerry said, turning away.

"Perhaps we passed him on the way down," the first mate suggested, closing the door.

"We passed three. I was particularly watching but I didn't spot the one I mean. There must be others, aren't there?" Of course there were. He had seen the man.

"Orientals? Just six on board. Aside from the cabin boys. If we passed three, you've seen them all. Your boy's uncle doubtless changed his mind and sent some member of his family to take his place. It happens often."

Gerry's brain stalled. The sense of foreboding, of being doomed came rushing back. Why was Torberg talking about somebody's uncle? Couldn't he understand that something was wrong? "It doesn't matter," Gerry muttered hastily, remembering that he didn't want to arouse suspicions. A knot of apprehension tightened around his heart. Something was wrong. He hadn't invented the man or the scar beside his eye. Had their chance encounter driven him into hiding? He felt as if he were going crazy. Torberg was quite positive that there were six Orientals in the crew. He had seen a seventh. If he and Hank had seen one of the crew being disposed of, it should have been one of the Orientals to keep the tally straight. Nothing made any sense but something was definitely wrong. A fresh explanation suddenly flashed across his mind.

A chill passed through him that made his hands and feet tingle. He had been so preoccupied with smuggling that he hadn't considered other possibilities. Could anybody want to kill Ernst? One man would be enough for that. "What about stowaways?" he asked Torberg, making an effort to keep his voice even and unconcerned. "Is that ever a problem?"

The first mate laughed. "On a yacht this size? It would be possible of course, but much more difficult than on a regular liner. Are you still worried about what you thought you saw the first night?"

"Not worried." The man's complacency was both reassuring and infuriating. "Still puzzled. It's pretty difficult to worry about anything, leading this sort of life. How many men are there altogether?"

"Thirty, plus the officers. We could do very well with twenty but the Baron is particular about details." The suggestive smile returned. "Do the guests still want to inspect them?"

Gerry forced himself to play along. "A couple of them do. The cabin boys aren't to everybody's taste. Where are we now? I mean, on the chart."

"Ah. I will show you. You've seen everything down here."

They returned to the bridge and he was shown the charts. "That was our position two hours ago," the first mate explained, pointing. "Late tomorrow afternoon, we will sight the southeast coast of Sri Lanka. Our course carries us around here well offshore and the following afternoon we will be in Cochin. The run is taking a little longer than usual, twelve or fifteen hours. We may run into a storm tomorrow evening, but like most tropical storms at this time of the year, it should be short."

"You mean, we would've arrived in Cochin in the morning?"

"Normally. We've been having some engine trouble. Most unusual. As you've seen, the Baron has all the latest equipment. We're as fully automated as a boat can be."

Gerry thanked him and managed a smile and left. He ran down the companionway across from his cabin and hurried forward and knocked at Ernst's door. Yorgo admitted him. "Ernst is shaving," he announced. Gerry went through to the bathroom with a "good morning" for Paolo and found Ernst with a lathered face. They smiled at each other in the mirror and Gerry went to him and kissed the back of his neck.

"You know how to shave. How amazing."

"It's the only thing I can think of that I've never liked anybody to do for me. You ran away. Isn't that against the rules?"

"I was restless and didn't want to disturb you. It won't happen often. I like to watch you sleeping."

"I didn't like waking up alone. That's the first time I've slept all night with somebody in bed with me. I think we suit each other."

"I'm glad we agree about that. I'm going to clear the cabin for a few minutes, darling. I've got to talk to you."

"I'll only be another minute."

Gerry went out and asked Paolo to wait outside and

locked the door behind him. In a moment, Ernst appeared looking radiantly healthy and happy. Gerry took a few quick strides to him and put his hands inside his dressing gown and held him against his bare body and kissed his mouth. He drew back and looked into his eyes. "God, you're so damn precious to me. I've had a shock." He gave him a quick outline of the cause for his concern, about the man from Bangkok and his disappearance. "Either I'm dreaming or that damn man is hiding somewhere. Do you know of anybody who might want to do you harm? I mean, we've talked about blackmail and kidnapping and trying to get money from you but I mean worse than that. Well, do you know anybody who might want to kill you? It sounds crazy on a lovely sunny morning but I've got to think of all the possibilities."

Ernst squeezed his hands and withdrew from his embrace and took a few thoughtful paces away from him. He looked serious but not alarmed. "I suppose there are always madmen who might want to kill anybody, but otherwise no. Once upon a time, before my inheritance was settled, there was reason to believe that somebody might decide to do something desperate. Governments have been known to arrange fatal accidents. All that was long ago. I've led a depraved life, perhaps, but I've never done anything bad to anybody. There may be parents who think I've corrupted their sons but I never have. Their sons have corrupted me. The only irate parent I can think of at the moment is André's mother and I doubt if it would occur to her to murder me. No, darling, assassination has never been one of my fears but it's worth considering. What should we do?"

"I'm going to have an armed sailor patrol the corridor out there and not let anybody through except the four of us. I'll also have a man on watch around the area aft where we spend all our time. That's simple. Is it enough? If I were planning any dirty tricks, I'd wait until we were getting into port so I'd have a chance of getting away. Does that make sense?"

Ernst looked at him tranquilly. "Definitely. You're marvelous, darling. I've never felt safer."

"I hope I'm not missing anything. We're not getting into Cochin until day after tomorrow. A few hours before we're due, I'll have everybody lined up on deck whether the captain likes it or not and checked against the crew list. He won't like it if it turns out that he's fucked up royally. If we don't find that son of a bitch, then maybe I *am* nuts." Would finding him neutralize him or drive him to some desperate act? It was going to be a long nervous wait till Cochin.

Gerry passed on instructions to Yorgo to have the armed guards posted with orders to keep everybody off the passenger deck except the serving boys and the European crew with legitimate duties to perform. "Try not to let it seem like a big deal," Gerry suggested. "You can say that one of Ernst's friends thinks he's getting too lax about security. Just a matter of form."

When he and Ernst joined the others around the pool, there was no sign that anything had ruffled the smooth surface of life on board. A sailor with a gun on his hip patrolled at a discreet distance but nobody appeared to notice him. Gerry hoped he would get over the feeling that they were sitting on a powder keg.

After lunch, when Ernst and he exchanged a glance and rose, he was looking forward to a calming smoke.

"André and I talked to Heinrich," Ernst said as they headed for the owner's cabin.

"Yes, I noticed."

"Do you watch me as constantly as I watch you?"

"I can't take my eyes off you. I'm afraid travel is going to be wasted on me. We might as well stay in one place and let me gaze at you to my heart's content." They laughed and touched hands.

"I told him I'd give him five thousand dollars for his bar and he was eating out of my hand. He wants to leave as soon as we get to Cochin."

"So much for Heinrich. That's very generous of you, darling." Another source of conflict disposed of. He wished he could dispose of the man from Bangkok. "Speaking of watching each other, you cast more than a casual glance at Hank when André got him out of his drawers."

"He's eye-catching, to say the least. Who would have guessed it? You, of course. I'm sure you have an unerring instinct for choosing worthy partners."

"Instincts atrophy from lack of use. I'm glad it was operating when I chose you." They nodded as they passed another armed sailor fifty feet from their door. Gerry breathed a deep sigh of relief as he let them in. The cabin was an easily defended fortress. He intended to keep Ernst in it as much as possible for the next day or two.

Before dinner that evening, Farr proposed putting on a show. "I understand we arrive in India day after tomorrow," he said to Gerry. "Do you think Ernst would like us to do our party turns tomorrow night? Trevor and I have an idea for a comedy routine that has us absolutely screeching with laughter. The last night out is usually when the passengers make fools of themselves. Don't let me interfere with anything more scintillating, such as colored slides of the slums of Calcutta."

Gerry welcomed the suggestion. He had a feeling that he'd need all the entertainment he could get by tomorrow evening. Thoughts of the following morning continued to fill him with alarm. Would his friend from Bangkok be dragged kicking and screaming from some dark corner? Would the captain be outraged by his interference in the yacht's routine? What if all his guesses were wrong and he touched off some eruption from an unexpected quarter? He would see that Ernst stayed safely locked in their cabin until whatever was going to happen had happened. He would also have Hank with him, he decided. Hank would be a comfort in a crisis.

Ernst was easily persuaded to skip the after-dinner film in favor of retiring to their fortress and they remained in bed until late the next morning. They held each other and drowsed their way into full consciousness.

"Hello, darling," Ernst said into his pillow. "That is you, isn't it?"

"It's not Hank, if that's who you're hoping for."

Ernst uttered muffled laughter. "I doubt if he would know how to inflame my imagination the way you do."

If his memory was dependable, Gerry had limited them to seven pipes the day before. Eight maybe? It was great stuff for allaying fears. It also kept their sex life on an odd but even keel. They neither of them cared what happened when they were high. He was going to try to cut them down by a pipe or two today so that in the next day or so they would be down to what Solange said was an acceptable limit. That would give them the rest of the cruise to Bombay to cut it out entirely and discover the wonders of sane sex together. *If* they went on to Bombay. He wasn't going to allow Ernst to leave Cochin until the mystery below decks had been cleared up.

The noon scene on deck was animated by the excitement of entering a new phase of the journey. What had begun to seem like an eternal alternation of timeless days and nights on the empty sea was coming to an end. The prospect of seeing land again was enough to get them all slightly keyed up. The piano tinkled from the saloon where Farr and company were rehearsing, a hauntingly urban sound. After lunch, the sky clouded over and quite a heavy sea began to roll in from the south, rocking the boat sufficiently to make footing uncertain. They all expressed concern for the evening's performance and teetered off to their cabins.

They were still rolling uncomfortably when it was time to dress for the evening and Gerry asked Yorgo to find out from the captain if he expected it to continue. He returned with good news. "He says he's altered course slightly. Everything should be calm in an hour or so. He's staying on the bridge so he won't be down to dinner."

The captain proved to have the elements under control. While they were all having predinner drinks, the boat steadied and they were soon throbbing along on their usual even course. Dinner was even more of a banquet than usual, an extravaganza of the chef's considerable skills, with four wines in addition to champagne. Everybody proposed toasts to everybody else. By the time they were finished, Farr's audience was prepared to cheer.

While coffee was being served, Gerry stepped out onto the afterdeck to make sure that the guard was on duty. He was, but Gerry was startled to see that they were running along quite close to land. He could make out lights at regular intervals along a coastal road and ahead of them a blur of light that looked like a large town. Their altered course. They must have run in close to Ceylon to avoid the heavy sea. He wanted to stay out to see if he would recognize anything but the performance was about to begin. He took another long look, imagining the palm trees lining the road and lush jungle beyond. The most beautiful country he had ever seen. He wished they were stopping. Reluctantly he returned to the party.

Everybody was having after-dinner drinks and Gerry had a whiskey while boys pushed chairs into a row in front of the piano. They all seated themselves and Ken went to the piano and played an overture made up of familiar songs, some of which Gerry recognized as being from Farr's old shows. He had been growing up when Farr was at the height of his Broadway success.

When the overture ended, Farr rose and stood at the piano, assured and in command of his audience. "We're going to start with a number I did when I made my professional debut. I was five at the time. My mother was the star of the show. When I was hurled onto the stage to give the act some class, we were known as 'Daisy Farr and a Little Farr From Home.' It took me years to recover. Very well, Mother." Mrs. Farr bounced up and stood beside him, beaming. Farr looked at her dubiously. "Try not to break any bones. None of these people has paid a penny to see us. It's not an audition. We don't care a straw whether they like us or not." He rolled up his trousers and gave a hitch to his jacket and became a little boy. Ken struck a chord and they broke into a patter song between mother and child. "What will Mummy give him if he's a good little boy?" was a recurring refrain. They performed a soft-shoe routine while they sang. Mrs. Farr was winsome, light-footed and utterly captivating. Farr was hilarious. They loaded it with show-business nostalgia and the applause continued until they did an encore. Mrs. Farr threw kisses to the audience with such enthusiasm that she appeared to be hitting herself in the face. Farr returned her forcibly to her chair.

"We always were a hard act to follow," he said.

The performance continued with a selection of numbers from Farr's shows, interspersed with the actor's acidly witty reminiscences. It was a one-man show of consummate skill and glamour and had gone on for almost an hour when there was an odd metallic ripping sound from somewhere below and the boat gave a slight lurch. Gerry glanced around to see if the others had noticed it but Farr seemed to have their undivided attention. The ripping sound came again and the boat gave a violent leap and the lights went out. There was a scream and the lights came on again. Farr was picking himself up off the floor.

He flung himself against the piano as the boat was seized by convulsions as if it had run up on a rocky road. Glasses crashed. Lamps toppled. The piano strained against the chain that held it to the deck. They all stared at each other, frozen and aghast. There was a wrenching crash of such force that for an instant the hull seemed to be shattering like glass. An enormous silence followed, broken only by a hissing like air escaping from a tire. Life was draining out of the yacht. The distant throbbing of the engines' heart had ceased.

They were suddenly all on their feet crying out and exclaiming and making aimless little rushes in one direction or another. Gerry and Ernst stood slightly apart, motionless, looking into each other's eyes as if they could discover there some explanation for what had happened. From the instant he had heard the ripping sound, there had been no doubt in Gerry's mind that this was the catastrophe he had been trying to avert. As he had feared, danger had struck from an unexpected direction. Ernst looked at him with calm confidence, awaiting guidance. Gerry was gripped by a need for action. He looked around, expecting the portly Oriental to appear suddenly in their midst. He saw Yorgo fending off Maria, who seemed determined to hold him in consultation. Gerry called his name and she immediately stepped back from him.

"Go out and see if that armed guard is still there," Gerry ordered as he hurried to him. "Bring him in. If there're two, so much the better. I want somebody to stay with Ernst until we know what's happening. Don't let anybody else in here except the officers. Where's the captain? Never mind. Get the guard." Paolo stepped up to them and handed Ernst a flat lethal-looking automatic. Gerry nodded. "Good. Is the safety off?"

"Of course, darling," Ernst assured him, dropping it into his pocket.

"Use it if anybody makes a false move."

"I intend to."

Gerry's thoughts grew more ordered. He became aware of a great hubbub on the deck—shouts, whistles, the pounding of feet and sailors flashing past the windows. Everybody in the saloon was talking at once in high excited voices. He saw with relief that Yorgo had found the guard. He came in with the flap of his holster open and his hand on his gun. Yorgo led him to Ernst and gave him orders in Italian. The sailor pulled his gun out and took up a position facing the forward entrances. Yorgo hurried back to the big doors that gave onto the pool and closed and locked them. Gerry breathed more easily. Ernst was safe. Now what?

The captain burst in and charged up to them. "We have struck," he declared in hearty tones as if it were all in the day's work. "There need be no alarm. We must abandon ship immediately."

"Can you explain what has happened?" Ernst asked in his unruffled muted voice.

"There's no danger. We're hard on rock. An error. We have a fire in the engine room. I think it will be controlled but if the cables go we'll have no light. We must hurry. The boats are being lowered. You must all leave immediately."

"And then what?"

"We're only a mile offshore. The night is calm. Everybody will be safe. In the morning, we'll see what can be salvaged."

"In the morning, I'll expect a full report. This is hardly the time for discussion." He turned to Gerry. "We should tell everybody to get whatever they think they can carry."

"No, no," the captain interjected. "Nobody is to go to the cabins. If the fire spreads, there's danger of an explosion. Everybody must remain here until the boats are alongside. That's an order from the captain."

Gerry reached for Ernst and gripped his arm and swung him around to him. "Don't try to make sense of it now. I swear there's more to it than running up on the rocks. Watch the doors. If anybody you don't know comes in, get ready to use that gun. Is Paolo armed?"

"No, but the sailors are."

Gerry glanced around and saw that a second sailor had taken up his position nearby. Both had their guns in their hands. He looked for Yorgo but didn't see him. The others swarmed around the captain, all talking excitedly. He caught André's eye and beckoned to him with his head. Hank appeared at his side. He put his hands on their shoulders. "Stay with Ernst. I'm going out for a minute. I'll be right back." He gave them both a pat and headed for the forward exit. He registered the fact that Maria was missing. Maria and Yorgo.

He came out onto a brightly lighted deck and stopped dead in his tracks, momentarily disoriented. Surely this was where he'd been standing when he'd seen the lights of the road. The dark sea stretched away to a star-filled sky. He ran forward, prepared to encounter the man from Bangkok. If he didn't appear, nothing made sense. Running up on the rocks had nothing to do with a smuggling operation. They were confronted with some huge disaster. He was filled with a sense of failure, of having missed an essential clue.

All the ship's lights were on; no shadows provided mystery. He heard a hubbub of shouts and calls ahead and arrived at a scene of intense activity. At least a dozen men were milling about on the forward deck, handling ropes and tarpaulins. A speedboat hung from the crane and was being slowly lowered over the side. The big open cutter was being uncovered. All the men were young and spare; there was no portly Oriental. Gerry skipped around obstacles and got to the other side. He was shocked by how close they were to land. He could see cars moving along the coastal road and the buildings of a town. The beam of a lighthouse swept over them as he paused. They were headed in the wrong direction.

The first mate was supervising the lowering of the speedboat. Gerry looked down over the rail and saw that a heavy swell surged around them. Sea broke on rocks not far away. From where he stood, he could see several more men lowering the boarding stairs near the pool. Otherwise, the deck was empty. He sprinted aft and reentered the main saloon. Maria and Yorgo were there with several big flat metal cases at their feet. Voices had returned to a conversational level. There was even a suggestion of a party getting underway; two boys were passing drinks.

"They've got one boat nearly in," Gerry reported to Ernst. "No sign of you-know-who. We're very close to land, practically on top of a lighthouse. We're also headed south. How in God's name could this happen?"

"I think you're right, darling. This is no time to wonder. The main thing is that it has. It would be unpleasant if the lights went out. Maria and Yorgo have emptied the safe. Very quick-witted of them, I must say. I had just thought of it when they came back with the cases."

Gerry glanced at the metal containers. "Is that what those are? I'm afraid I wouldn't've thought of it at all. I'm more worried about you than the safe. Getting you across the deck and into a boat could be dangerous. If anybody wants to take a potshot at you, that would be the perfect time. Don't move without these two sailors. I'll have two more posted on the deck above to make sure nobody's hanging around up there." He called to Yorgo and gave him instructions. Yorgo hurried off as the captain returned.

"Ladies and gentlemen. The first boat is waiting. The second will be only another minute. The town where we are is called Galle. There will doubtless be a hotel. I wish you good night on this very regrettable occasion."

"What do you intend to do?" Gerry asked him.

"Please hurry, ladies and gentlemen. I'll remain. As soon as the fire is extinguished, I'll have all your belongings gathered together and sent ashore. In the morning, we can assess the damage."

"OK. I guess that's that." Gerry's eyes moved over Hank and André and settled on Ernst.

"What now? Do women and children go first?"

Ernst gave him an approving little smile. "You go, darling. Take those things. I'll—"

"I'm not going anywhere without you."

"They're our guests, darling. We must share the responsibility for them."

For a moment, Gerry forgot his fears. Even under these circumstances, Ernst hadn't forgotten that they were partners. He leaned forward and gave him a quick kiss. "You're right, darling. I love you."

"Take André and Hank with you. Oh, and Ken, of course." He turned and addressed Maria. "Do you wish to remain the custodian of my treasure? Yorgo will go with you. Everybody else will come with me." He gestured to Paolo, who bent to the cases. Gerry judged that they were heavy from the way he lifted them. There were five of them. Yorgo returned.

"Do you have the men up there?" Gerry asked. Yorgo nodded. "Good. Keep an eye on the cases, will you? Put them in the first boat. You can unlock those doors now. Station the guards beside them." He turned to Ernst. "If we're taking valuables, what about the Cézanne?"

"It might be nice to have it with us in the jungle."

"Will you get it, Hank?" He took Ernst's arm and moved him off to the side as Yorgo opened the doors and the armed sailors stationed themselves beside them. Everybody was on their feet, moving toward them.

"I'm not dressed for boating, Farr," Mrs. Farr's voice rose in protest.

"It's all right, Mother. Cecil B. DeMille is expecting us. He heard we were passing by and asked us to drop in."

"That nice Mr. DeMille? How charming. It might be chilly, Farr. I want my mink."

"No, Mother. Your brave little mink is going down with the ship."

André remained at Gerry's side. Hank joined them with the picture under his arm. "Stay with Ernst, darling," Gerry ordered André. "I'll come get you when we're ready. Come on."

He put a hand on Hank's shoulder and they went out onto the afterdeck. A warm breeze blew in across the sea. "If we had to get shipwrecked, I guess this is a nice night for it. Jesus. We're shipwrecked. I hadn't thought of it like that." He moved out toward the swimming pool until he could see the bridge deck. Two sailors with guns at the ready were stationed at the rail. The passengers were gathering at the head of the boarding stairs. Gerry went to the rail and looked down and saw that getting off wasn't going to be easy. In the lee of the yacht, the sea's swell was still strong enough to lift the speedboat giddily above the landing platform and send it sliding out to the end of the lines that held it. A sailor was struggling to steady it with a boat hook while another grabbed for the cases that Yorgo held out to him. Maria was standing halfway down the stairs, waiting to board. Gerry saw Paolo pass the last case to Yorgo, who managed to transfer it safely to the sailor. "OK, Maria," he called down. "Go ahead. Yorgo, stay down there. We'll be right there." He turned back to Hank. "Right. Watch that picture. Take Ken. I'll get André." Paolo came tripping up onto the deck and headed for the main saloon. Gerry looked at the others. "Trevor, you should go with us. Ernst will take the rest of you. That divides us up evenly." He followed Paolo.

Ernst and André were standing just inside the door, laughing together as if they had forgotten the shipwreck. Paolo was putting a cigarette in the jeweled holder. Gerry took Ernst's hands. "Now listen, darling. Be careful. I'm not going to believe any of this is what it seems until you're safely ashore. When Paolo tells you everybody's on board, get going and don't dawdle. All right? You won't let anything happen to you?"

"I can't, can I, if you say I mustn't." They smiled into

each other's eyes and Gerry gave Ernst's hands a squeeze and released them. "We're lying off a beach. You'll be able to see where we land. Come in beside us. Let's go." He put an arm around André and hurried him out. The others still clustered at the head of the boarding stairs. Gerry peered over the rail and saw that the second boat was waiting to move in. He took a final look up at the bridge deck to make sure the sailors were still there. His eyes fell on the little waiting group—Solange and Sally, the Farrs, Heinrich—and he felt as if he were abandoning his dearest friends. He gave them all a big smile. "OK, everybody. Ernst is staying out of sight till you're in the boat. Watch those steps down there. They look tricky." He gave André a gentle push and followed him down. The boat was still performing its giddy dance, rising, falling away, coming up hard against the stairs. The sailor with the boat hook stood in the bow trying to break the impact. Hank looked up.

"Hurry up," he called. "We're all getting seasick."

André took the last few steps on the double, paused for a second and made a graceful leap for the bow. The sailor held a hand out for him. His feet shot out as he landed and he toppled backward and pitched into the sea. The boat surged in sickeningly against the platform as his head disappeared.

Gerry's heart stopped. He dived after him with murder in his heart. He would kill the captain. He would kill anybody who had done anything to expose the boy to harm.

Light from the yacht sifted down through the water. There was a spine of rock only six or seven feet below the surface. He swam in under the speedboat. It was dark but he could see a pale form sprawled out on rock. With the skull crushed? He choked back a cry of protest and reached André with a powerful thrust of his legs. He gathered the inert body into his arms. Hank swam in beside him and they both held André and shot to the surface. André began to struggle feebly and Gerry uttered a sob of relief. His head was unmarked. A gush of water spewed from his mouth.

"Got him?" Hank panted. He pulled himself up over the side of the boat and reached for André and together they lifted him aboard. Gerry tumbled in after him.

"Is he all right?" he demanded as he pulled himself to his knees. Both he and Hank were breathing heavily.

André's chest heaved. They both held him and lifted him onto a seat and stretched him out on his back. They knelt on the floorboards beside him. His eyes fluttered open and he smiled weakly. "What happened? Did I do something stupid?"

"You're all right, darling," Gerry assured him with another burst of relief. "You almost got killed, that's all. Don't try to talk. Lie there until you're feeling better." Hank kissed his forehead. The others were stumbling around in the heaving boat, trying to look helpful. Gerry glanced up. "He's OK. Everybody better sit down. Tell those guys we can take off."

"Thank God, it's warm," Hank said, crouched solicitously over André.

"Yeah. I could do without these wet clothes." The motor roared into life. Sailors leaped for lines. Gerry looked up and waved to the group at the rail as he was swept away into the night. He and Hank stripped to their Jockey shorts and jostled each other into the seat across from André. The rush of air against them was almost hot. Gerry lifted his arms and stretched to ease his tense nerves. André was safe. His alarm about Ernst was proving to be groundless. If there were a killer at large, he would have struck immediately. The smuggling theory was still plausible, although he couldn't see why it had been necessary to scuttle the yacht. Mystery remained. "Thanks for coming to the rescue," he said to Hank above the roar of the motor.

"I thought an underwater threesome might be sort of fun." Their eyes glittered at each other in the dark and they laughed. Hank put an arm around him and lay his hand on his lap. Gerry breathed deeply.

"Don't, honey. Not now." What did that mean? Not now? Never. He lifted Hank's hand and returned it to him while his own brushed against the hard knotted power contained in his shorts. Hank's arm tightened around him.

"I'll never forget the way you dived in after Andy. You were beautiful."

Gerry felt himself relaxing into the refuge of his body and he pulled himself up and edged away from him. "I was scared shitless. You didn't waste any time yourself."

"The two greatest guys I've ever known. I couldn't let you *both* drown. How're you—"

The motor coughed, backfired and died. The boat settled

into the water and glided for a moment on its own momentum and came to a halt. It rose and fell on the swell, rocking gently.

"What is it? What's the matter?" Gerry called forward. He was instantly on guard, divorced from Hank's lulling presence, his nerves taut and alert.

"Engine trouble," Yorgo replied. "I don't think the captain will have his job long. Ernst has always insisted that these boats be kept in perfect condition."

The starter whirred to no effect. A lighter clicked and a flame sprang up in Maria's face. She had a cigarette in her mouth. The flame went out. The lighter clicked again. Gerry saw that she wasn't holding the flame to the cigarette. It went out. He sprang forward as she lighted it for the third time and snatched it out of her hand. "What're you doing?" he demanded.

"Lighting a cigarette, sweet lamb," she said, blowing smoke at him.

"I say, old bean," Trevor protested lazily. "Can't the old girl smoke if she wants to?"

"Sorry. I'm nervous." He returned the lighter. What had he thought she was doing? Nothing was happening in a way that he could have predicted but he remained convinced that some surprise was still in store for them that would bring everything into focus. A sailor had moved the cases and was lifting the top of the motor housing. Gerry looked astern. *Hephaistion* was gaily lighted and immobile. He listened for the roar of the other speedboat. Ernst couldn't be more than a few minutes behind them. He hoped their shouts for a tow would be heard. He looked forward and judged that they were about halfway between the yacht and shore. He could see the palm trees now and a truck and two cars parked on the road and people walking. The beam of the lighthouse flashed across the sky above them with mocking regularity; nobody could have overlooked its warning. André was sitting up. Gerry dropped down beside him and put his arms around him and kissed him. "Poor darling. How do you feel?"

"OK. My head hurts. Did you save my life on top of everything else?"

"Hank would have if I hadn't. We did it together."

"Hank too? That's nice. What're we going to do now?"

"Hope for Ernst to come pick us up unless they fix the engine." He heard the chug of a motor nearby, seeming to grow nearer, and searched the sea. He saw a dim light off to the south, so dim that he wasn't even sure it was moving. He thought he could make out running lights, red and green, dead astern, but they didn't appear to be moving either. He listened for the roar of the speedboat but heard only the labored chugging of what was probably a small fishing boat, definitely getting nearer. He reached for his wet trousers draped over the seat and pulled them on with difficulty and went forward to Yorgo. The sailor was checking the engine with a flashlight.

"What's the story?" he asked.

"He can't find anything the matter with it."

"There's a boat getting close. Shall we ask for help?"

"I wondered. I expected Ernst by now."

"Me too. They may've been delayed getting Mr. Farr aboard. The lights are still on. They've probably got the fire under control by now." He glanced toward the sound of the chugging motor. The dim light was close enough now, so that he could see it came from a lamp on a short mast. It was headed in their direction. "It doesn't look as if we're going to have to ask for help. They're coming over anyway. Tell this guy to wave the light at them."

Yorgo did so and their signal was answered by a strong beam of light directed at them. Gerry's heart leaped up with instant irrational alarm. The powerful light didn't match the laboring motor. He grabbed the flashlight from the sailor and directed it at the approaching boat. It was a small open battered-looking craft with what looked like a privy in the middle of it, presumably a wheelhouse. Gerry shifted the light slightly and his blood froze. It was impossible. The man from Bangkok was standing in the bow.

The shock of it almost made him drop the light. He fumbled with it and it went out. He made an effort to gather his wits. "Hank," he called sharply. Hank sprang forward and joined him. "That guy in the bow. We've got to keep him off."

"Are you nuts? Don't you see what he's got in his hand?"

"What?" He got a grip on the flashlight again and lifted it and picked out a gun pointed directly at him. He instinctively ducked and Hank grabbed him and dragged him back and pulled him down into the seat beside him.

"Don't try to be a fucking hero. Let's just sit here quietly and see what he wants."

"That's beginning to be ridiculously clear." The boat swung in to within ten feet of them, holding them in the beam of light.

"All armed here. No trouble, please," a voice called out. The boat circled them slowly and bumped up alongside. Two slim figures in sarongs dropped down into the speedboat and began to grapple with the cases. Maria cried out, more a bellow of outrage than a scream.

"Of course," Gerry muttered grimly to himself. The end of the mystery. The plot was revealed. He addressed Hank in an undertone. "Why should we let them get away with this? I know enough judo to take care of those little guys in two seconds."

"And get yourself shot? Don't be an idiot." Hank tightened his grip on him.

"How do we know his damn gun is loaded?" He reached for Hank's ribs where he knew he was ticklish. Hank tried to evade his fingers and his hold relaxed. Gerry wrenched himself free and made a lunge for one of the boarding party. He seized him and lifted him easily and flung him over the side. A shot rang out. The report was so close that it made the soles of his feet tingle. For a second, he thought he'd been hit as he ducked down between the seats.

"No trouble, please," the voice repeated from above him. "One warning enough."

He watched the last of the cases being transferred to the other boat. The Cézanne followed while Gerry's victim was fished from the sea. Gerry hitched himself back to where both Hank and André were straining forward to get their hands on him and pull him into a seat. He let himself go to André.

"OK. It was loaded," he said to Hank with a rueful chuckle.

"Why do you do things like that?" André protested. "What do you think it would do to us if anything happened to you?"

"I'm sorry. I just wanted to see if he meant business. You know who it is, don't you? The man I told you about. The one I saw on the yacht."

"The businessman? Here, in a sarong?"

"Yeah, he has an interesting wardrobe. Now what're they up to?"

One of the boarding party had taken the bowline of the speedboat and was making it fast to the stern of the other boat. The motor, which had been idling, now chugged into action and they were taken in tow with a little jerk. At least, he saw with satisfaction, they were headed for shore. The beam of light remained on them. The man from Bangkok stood clearly visible in the stern, his gun glinting.

Gerry was no longer worried about Ernst's safety. The cases were obviously the primary objective of the operation. Their contents remained the only unknown quantity. Was there something in them that would make the elaborate plot worthwhile? He was pretty sure he had put all the pieces of the story together. It was too beautifully ingenious to include murder or kidnapping. Both speedboats must have been tampered with to make it work; Ernst and his group would be adrift somewhere behind them. The only detail he couldn't understand was what was happening now. Why were they being towed ashore, still covered by a gun? The cases had been removed with such calm finality that it seemed pointless even to hope to recover them. If they were irrevocably gone and nobody was in danger, why not relax and see what happened next? A reasonable thought, but he still wanted to retain his freedom of movement. He might be able to warn Ernst to stay clear if some final little twist of the plot was about to unfold.

He removed his trousers again and hung them over the seat in front of them. "Take care of my clothes, darling. They're all I have. Be a good boy and do whatever you're told. I'll be watching."

"What do you mean? Please don't do anything silly."

"I don't see why I should go anywhere just because that bastard wants me to. I feel like a swim."

"Out *here?* How will you get ashore?"

"It's not far. I can swim almost as fast as we're going now." He looked forward at their captor and his heart began to pound. Holding them could serve no purpose, but his Bangkok friend seemed to have a mind of his own. As he watched, the bow of the speedboat was lifted on a swell and planed forward so that for a moment the man with the gun was blocked from view. The speedboat lost the swell and dropped back to the end of the line. He squeezed André's knee and waited for the bow to rise again. As it did so, he gathered himself together and toppled ungracefully into the sea. He submerged immediately and swam under water until his lungs were bursting. He came up for air, prepared to submerge again if bullets started whizzing around his ears. The boat was still chugging toward the beach. He caught movement out of the corner of his eye and was touched by panic. Had they dropped somebody in to get him back? He turned and saw Hank swimming toward him and burst out laughing. He had known he could count on Hank. It might be scary out here alone. Good old Hank.

"Well, hi there," he called, swimming to meet him. "Fancy running into you here."

"This is a nice place for a midnight swim. What brings you to these parts?" Gerry burst out laughing again. Their bodies brushed against each other while they kept themselves afloat facing each other. "Hearing you laughing like a maniac out here in the dark is one of the nicest things I've ever heard. What's the program?"

"Did anybody seem to mind my leaving?"

"I'm not sure they even noticed. Nobody was shooting at you, if that's what you mean."

"Then we better swim like hell and keep an eye on them. I felt stupid being held prisoner."

"You seem to know what this is all about. I'm lost."

"Oh, I know, all right. I'll tell you later. Let's go." They set off, swimming fast for shore. Gerry kept his ears tuned to the chug of the motor ahead of them. After a few minutes, he heard the tone alter and he slowed and looked ahead. The boat was circling out away from the beach. The distance between it and the dark shape of the speedboat was widening. The tow had been a simple courtesy. It figured. Maria wouldn't want to be left floating around in the middle of nowhere. He caught Hank's foot as he churned ahead and they treaded water, breathing heavily. The speedboat looked as if it were a couple of hundred feet from shore. The dim light of the other boat was moving out to sea. Going to pick up Ernst? This was a very polite hijacking.

"That's the end of it," he said. "We can catch our breath for a minute."

"You're a demon swimmer." Hank moved in close and their arms and legs slid over each other.

"You're no slouch yourself."

"We're a good team." Hank's teeth gleamed whitely in his dark face and he sank. Gerry felt his shorts being removed. The soft night and the velvet flow of water over his body were powerful aphrodisiacs, with perhaps an extra little charge of excitement provided by having been shot at. It felt awfully good to be alive. He wanted Ernst with him. After the drugged eroticism of the last few days, he reveled in the real physical world.

Hank surfaced with a pair of shorts in each hand. He dropped them over his head so that they hung around his neck. "There was a lot of us waiting to be let loose," he reported. He ran a hand over Gerry's buttocks. "God, what an ass."

"You pick the damnedest places to make passes."

"What do you expect when you have a hard-on? It's not easy to ignore it."

"Thank God." He chortled. Fooling around with a guy you'd already been to bed with didn't rank very high on the infidelity scale. "OK. Let's get going. We're supposed to be helping the others get ashore."

They swam hard again, racing each other. When Gerry's breath was laboring, he slowed down and lifted his head and shook water out of his eyes and surveyed the scene. The sailors were standing in the water ahead of them, holding the speedboat a few yards from shore. He could see figures grouped on the beach.

When the water was only waist deep, they stopped and Hank pulled their shorts over his head. "I don't know which is which. I guess this is yours. It feels sort of silky." They put on their underwear and Hank ran a hand over Gerry's behind. "Yeah, it's silky, all right."

Gerry giggled. "I've been breaking rules right and left. That's enough."

"What rules?"

"You know. The rules that say I belong with Ernst, and if you belong with anybody, I guess it's André."

"Yeah. Those rules. We'll see about them."

"Is that you?" André called from the beach. Gerry saw him break away from the group and walk into the water toward them.

"Don't get wet again. We're coming," Gerry called. They walked the last few hundred feet with the water remaining waist deep until they were almost out. Gerry heard the faint chug of a motor and stopped, listening to it getting louder. Was there still a chance of foiling the plot? Should he swim out and tell Ernst's guards to start firing? Too risky. Better let it ride and be thankful nobody had been hurt.

"I thought I heard you laughing out there," André said as they approached him. "I was worried."

"How's your head, darling?"

"Better. I've got a bump." He took Gerry's hand and put it on his damp hair.

"Yeah. It's a wonder you have any head left at all. Feel that, Hank."

Hank stepped up to him and put his arms around him and held him. "He says I belong with you. What do you say, sweetheart?"

"I'd be dead if it weren't for both of you. What can I say?"

Gerry turned from them while they murmured together, and called to Yorgo. "Have they found anything wrong with the motor?" he asked when the secretary appeared.

"We're out of gas. The gauge is stuck at full."

"Naturally. What're we supposed to do now?"

"There were people here a minute ago. They spoke quite good English. I told them we wanted gas and transport and they drove away. Unfortunately, we can't pay for either."

"Everybody's money was in the cases?"

"Money, passports, everything."

"I guess we really *are* shipwrecked. How fascinating." It occurred to Gerry with a surge of mounting euphoria that this was what he'd been hoping for all along—a clean sweep. He and Ernst could start a new life naked, penniless, even without official identities. With any luck, the pipes were gone along with everything else. They would be on their own at last if he could somehow cut them loose from the others, prevent him from reassembling his soft confining world. He heard the chugging motor coming in quite close. He looked out and saw the privylike structure as a dim shape against the sky. "This must be Ernst," he said to Yorgo, suddenly blazing with a need to get to him.

"The same boat?"

"I think so."

"Can you think of anything we can do to stop them?"

"If your people would arrive with gas, we might have a hope. We could at least follow them and see where they go." As he spoke, he saw the indistinct outline of the boat turn broadside to them, revealing red and green running lights in its wake, still several hundred yards offshore. Courtesy was all very well but they were playing it safe this time. The sound of the motor began to recede. "Those are the speedboat lights. I'll go help get them in." He ran down to the sea and plunged in and set out slowly for another long swim. After several minutes, he could make out the low profile of the speedboat and heads bobbing around it. It was approaching at quite a good clip. He closed the gap between them with a burst of speed and came in among three men churning up the water with their efforts to bring the boat in. He grabbed the side where Ernst was sitting.

"Welcome to Ceylon," he said breathlessly. Mrs. Farr shrieked. The others exclaimed with astonished welcome. Ernst put a hand on his.

"Hello, darling. We ran out of petrol. A kindly fisherman gave us a tow. I thought you might send the other boat to look for us."

"We're out of gas too. Nothing happened? You're all right?"

"Of course. Nobody tried to shoot me. They tell me you saved André's life. I wanted to pay the fisherman to take us all the way in but he didn't understand. He just dropped us and went away."

"Don't worry. You've paid him plenty."

"Have I, darling?"

"He took the lot—the cases from the safe, the Cézanne—everything."

"How extraordinary. We've been robbed? Out here? How would he know the things were worth taking?"

"Exactly. I knew something was wrong but I couldn't figure out what it was. That wasn't a fisherman. It was the man on board, the one I kept running into in Bangkok. He made quite a convincing show of shooting me when I tried to stop him."

Ernst's hand tightened on Gerry's. "You're not supposed to take risks, darling. You promised we'd be together. Ought you to be swimming around out here alone? Mightn't there be sharks?"

"There are but when I was here before everybody said they don't eat you. I shouldn't be hanging on here. I'm slowing us down. I have plenty to tell you later. I'll help push."

They gave their hands a squeeze and Gerry dropped back to the sailor who was beating his legs at the stern. He felt the boat pick up speed as he joined in.

When they all stood up a few yards from shore, he saw that the beach had become the scene of considerable activity. Half a dozen cars were pulled up on the road and people were streaming in from the direction of the town, many carrying the flaming palm torches he remembered from before. They were lining up in a wide semicircle gazing silently at the bizarre strangers who had landed in their midst, the women in graceful sarongs and tight bodices, the slim men also in sarongs, most of them barechested. Yorgo was supervising the arrival of two jerricans. The handsome sailors offered glistening arms to transport the passengers to dry land. Mrs. Farr was lifted out with an excited screech. Solange and Sally followed.

"There might be photographers, Farr," Ernst said slyly. "Aren't you afraid of being caught in the arms of a burly beauty?"

"I'll wear an expression of utter loathing and disdain," Farr replied. "Oh dear, what a sweetie."

Gerry went around to Ernst. "No sailor's going to get you." He reached up for him.

Ernst put his hands on his shoulders. "How heavenly to find you running around so gorgeously naked. You look like a native."

"I am. Me black boy. You white boy. Come on." Ernst's heroic body filled his arms with delight but he staggered quickly to the shore and dropped him, laughing. "I'm going to have to go in for weight-lifting if you expect me to carry you over all your thresholds."

Maria swooped down on them. "Here you are at last, my darling lamb," she cried, clutching Ernst's hands. "It's been too ghastly. You have no idea. Watching everything being carried away. A nightmare. I wanted to fling myself on the things and dare them to take me too. Gerald was heroic. He—"

Gerry slipped away. He couldn't listen to her. One more word and he'd really let her have it. He saw that Sally and Solange were making a fuss over André, petting him and feeling his bump. Hank had put on his clothes and they clung sexily to his body. He couldn't imagine his ever having looked buttoned-down. Yorgo approached.

"Word seems to be spreading fast," he said. "Five taxis have turned up. They say the best hotel is the New Oriental. They've brought enough gas for the boats to get back to the *Hephaistion*. They'll fill up there. Paolo is going back to make sure everybody's things are being taken care of properly. Ernst is rather anxious to get his smoking things off. It seems the latest word was that the crew is staying on for the night." They watched as a military-looking jeep stopped on the road and three uniformed men descended from it.

"The army?" Yorgo asked.

"The police, probably. They wear that kind of uniform here."

"They'll get no envelopes tonight."

The three dark smartly uniformed men advanced across the beach, while the townspeople drew back a few paces, and moved about casually with no apparent official mission in mind. They chatted with everybody in slightly singsong English, asking their names and nationalities and what their problem was.

"You wish a hotel, isn't it?" one of them asked Gerry.

"Well, yes. I didn't know whether we could just drive off to a hotel or not. I mean, what's the proper form? I don't think any of us have been shipwrecked in a foreign country before."

"No, it's not usual. I should think if you bring your passports to my office in the morning, we could settle on the proper formalities, is it?"

"That's another difficulty. We don't have any passports. We've been robbed."

"Upon my word. Robbed? Already?"

"Before we got ashore, actually. A boat came along and a man held a gun on us and took everything we had with us, everybody's passports included."

"I say, I say, I say. Armed robbery. We'll have to catch the rogue, isn't it? Well, well, well. Come see me in the morning and we'll sort it all out. You'll stop at the New Oriental? Mrs. Brohier will show you where we are."

André brought Gerry his clothes and he put them on and went to Ernst. "We might as well go. There's nothing more we can do tonight. They seem very casual about our invading their country. I suppose the fun will begin tomorrow."

"Yorgo will take care of everything."

"Yorgo can't issue us passports."

"That's true. Good heavens, what a nuisance this is for everybody. I'm sorry."

"You mean, you didn't plan it as one of your more

spectacular entertainments?" He put an arm around Ernst's shoulder and turned to the others who were all animatedly discussing the details of the robbery. They looked as if they had gathered on the beach for a party, the women elegant in evening dress, the men, except for the three who had been in the sea, crisp and stylish. "Come on, gang," he called out. "The night is young. Let's see what happens next."

They strolled up across the beach surrounded by their retinue of police officers and taxi drivers. The silent townspeople backed away. The taxis were tiny, barely big enough for two passengers. The policemen offered to take somebody in the jeep and Gerry installed Ernst in the front seat and perched on the edge of it with him, trying not to get him wet, feeling an infinite solicitude for him. He wondered how he had managed to remain so cool while they were apart. Now that they had been expelled from their private world, he would never again allow anything to take him from Ernst's side. It was wonderful to know so surely where he belonged. He gave the back of Ernst's neck a small caress. His conscience was clear about his aquatic romp with Hank. Well, almost, he amended truthfully to himself. Some sense of unfinished business remained. Nothing that anybody need worry about, nothing that wouldn't wear itself out.

They waited while everybody squeezed into the toy cars —Hank and André together in one, he noted happily—and swung around in the road and headed back to town in a cavalcade. The taxis were a comedown but at least they still had a police escort. Gerry had the impression that neither Ernst's nor Farr's name had rung a bell with the police. Better and better. He and Ernst might yet become just a couple of guys together. He pressed his shoulder. Ernst lay a hand on his knee.

"All things considered, I imagine we deserve a prize for abandoning ship with such alacrity," Ernst said.

"Now that we have, I'm beginning to wonder if we really had to," Gerry said. "That's part of what I have to tell you."

"You heard the captain give the order, darling."

Gerry winced at the endearment in front of the policemen. Perhaps they would think that all foreigners called each other darling. "I did indeed," he said. "I'll tell you later."

The palm-fringed road quickly became a street of mean one-story buildings. Despite the hour, people were sitting in it. The jeep came to a halt while a reclining cow got reluctantly to its feet and moved aside. They passed a deserted bus station and swung around a field and headed for an arched opening in a massive low wall. The beam of the lighthouse flashed over them from near at hand.

"The fort. Very ancient," one of the policemen said.

They drove through a wall that was more than forty feet thick and turned up a steep incline and came to a halt in front of a big dark square building set directly on the street. An enormous tree towered from the ramparts across from it. Several cows reclined under the tree. The policemen dismounted with a creak of leather and starched cloth. The flotilla of taxis pulled in among the cows and Yorgo spilled out of one, followed by Ken and Heinrich. He hurried across to them.

"This place looks closed," he said.

"It appears that the police are going to open it," Ernst said. "I feel as if we were being taken to jail."

They followed the uniformed men up some steps to a broad bare veranda. A policeman pounded on great double doors. Words were exchanged through them. The doors swung open and a little old man in a sarong stood in the doorway bowing before authority, almost to the floor. Orders were issued. The old man scuttled about flicking switches. Lights came on. Overhead fans began to whirr on the veranda. They entered a vast high-ceilinged room that dwarfed its handsome old furniture. Great arched doors led everywhere. At one end, they led to a dining room. Outdoor furniture was piled up beside the entrance. The only clue that they were in a hotel was a simple white wooden counter visible through one of the great doors. The party gathered, the space and silence making them walk cautiously.

"A cheerful hostelry," Farr commented. It broke the spell. They all began to chat in normal voices.

"Mrs. Brohier will be here in a jiffy," one of the policemen said. "If that's all, we'll take our leave, isn't it? We must confer with the naval authorities. You've given us a busy night." The three saluted and departed.

Yorgo handed Gerry Ernst's leather carryall. It was unusually bulky. "You'd better keep that. As soon as I've arranged about rooms, I'll go back for Paolo."

"What's in it?"

"Bottles," Ernst said. "I thought a drink might come in handy. There's no need for you to carry it, darling. Give it to me."

"Don't be silly. You don't know how to carry anything. What're husbands for?" They smiled into each other's eyes.

A white-haired woman in a simple print frock floated toward them from the inner recesses of the hotel. She moved with an ambling gait as if she were out for a stroll. Her body began with narrow shoulders but billowed out amply in the middle, not heavily but as if she had been inflated. She looked as if she would blow away in a breeze. "Good evening. Who are all these charming people? I'm Mrs. Brohier. I own the hotel." She spoke in a light melodious voice. The accent was English but the lilt was local. They all introduced themselves as she floated among them. "I know you. I've seen you in the cinema. You're a dreadful man," she said to Farr. Her smile was gay and flirtatious. She looked at Hank and André and Gerry. "You lovely boys look as if you'd been for a bathe. You're the most beautiful boy I've ever seen," she said to André. Her nose was beaky but her eyes, magnified by thick spectacles, were filled with melting gentle kindliness. She clasped her hands in front of her in a gesture of girlish delight. "How lovely to have you all here." Gerry fell in love with her on the spot.

"I wonder if I could speak to you about rooms," Yorgo said.

"Yes. Rooms," she said vaguely. "I imagine you'll all want rooms. We'll have to see what we can do about it. Is somebody seeing to your luggage? I have no staff till morning. Who goes with whom? I hope some of you will double up. I have plenty of beds but not many rooms."

"Yorgo and I can go over it with you," Gerry volunteered.

She looked up at him and smiled with instant approval. "Which one are you? You're Gerald? I hoped you might take charge. You look so nice. I'd love to talk to you about rooms."

Gerry burst out laughing. "I'd love to talk to you about almost anything."

"Well, come along then. We mustn't keep everybody waiting." She tucked a hand under his arm and they ambled off with Yorgo in tow. "You *are* wet, you poor dear. Where have you all come from?"

Gerry launched into an explanation while they went to the counter behind which were desks and other signs of business activity. She listened to his tale and commented with lively interest. She opened a ledger and flipped over pages filled with squares and names and numbers while he explained how many they were and who could be put together.

"I see. The boys go with the boys and the girls with the girls. Aren't you all naughty." She bubbled deliciously with laughter. "André is the beautiful one? And we'll put him with Hank? How lovely for Hank." They laughed and giggled together. She was a wonderfully wicked old lady. When they had it all sorted out, she summoned the little old man and gave him keys. She handed Gerry the key for Ernst and himself. "I'll leave you now. Tell this poor old thing if you want anything. I've never seen so many good-looking people all at once." She gave him the smile of a dazzled child and pressed his hand and turned and ambled off. The twin balloons of her behind seemed to drift about under her skirt as if they were about to escape captivity.

Gerry turned to Yorgo with a chuckle. "I think we're in good hands. Will you help herd everybody into their rooms before you go back? Most of you are down here in what she called the new rooms. I'll take the others upstairs. Be sure to tell the captain to let us know as soon as possible if there's any chance of getting off. I doubt it somehow." He hesitated, trying to frame a question without giving his suspicions away. Could he trust Yorgo? It hardly mattered now. "Tell me something. Would you have normally taken those cases off with us or was it Maria's idea?"

"It's difficult to say. It seemed quite sensible at the moment. We didn't know whether we were sinking or about to blow up or what was happening. Actually, I was mostly worried about an explosion. If we sank in shallow water, it would be easy to dive for them. They're waterproof. If I'd had time to think, I probably would've advised Ernst to leave them where they were. I'm afraid I let her rattle me. There was almost a million dollars in cash in one of them."

His mind rocked at the matter-of-fact announcement. "You're kidding. He carries that much with him?"

"Always on the yacht, in case we're caught at sea during some international crisis."

"I see. Thanks. We'd better get everybody settled." There was no need to search further for motive. Why bother with small-time stuff like smuggling? A million dollars in cash. He joined the others while keys were distributed. Ernst was talking to Hank and André and held out a hand to him as he joined them.

"Thank heavens you rescued this child, darling," he said. "I've been wondering what it would have been like for us if you hadn't. It makes me think quite violent thoughts about the captain."

"Me too. That's what makes it really criminal. No matter how carefully it's planned, there's always the chance of somebody getting hurt."

"Planned?"

"You don't suppose it was an accident, do you?" He glanced hastily around. Maria was at a safe distance but might not stay there. "Don't let's talk about it till we go to our room."

"I've asked these two to have a drink with us. Shall we get drunk and celebrate?"

"Celebrate? That's a funny word to use, considering what you've lost."

"We needn't think about that. We're all safe and together. When I think of what might have been, I feel quite sick. Oh yes, most definitely. We must celebrate." They caught each other's eye and Gerry's heart went out to him. Ernst meant it.

"You're a nice guy." He gave Ernst's hand a squeeze.

Yorgo assured everybody that their remaining belongings would be brought ashore during the night and got them moving toward bed. There would be a meeting in the great salon at eleven to discuss their next moves. Gerry and Yorgo agreed to meet at nine to cope with whatever problems confronted them. The group split up at the foot of a flight of stairs that seemed to mount to the sky; Solange and Sally climbed them along with the four would-be drunken celebrants.

"Remember Schloss Fahrstenberg?" Ernst asked his wife when they paused for breath halfway up. "That staircase was three stories high. I used to insist on being roped to a footman before I would go up. They had a very nice selection of footmen."

They went on, laughing and panting. At the top, a high wide corridor stretched before them with closed doors on one side and open windows on the other. They conferred in whispers in order not to disturb other guests, checking keys against the numbers on the doors.

There was an exchange of good-night kisses and the party subdivided further as the girls went along the corridor to their room and Gerry inserted a key in the first door he came to. They all waved a final good-night from opposite ends of the corridor.

The four entered a large room and came to a halt. They were hemmed in by what looked like remnants from a clearance sale at a thirties department store, all lumpish armchairs and awkwardly curved wood and sunburst chintz, but the room retained a Victorian colonial flavor—high ceilings, white shuttered windows, the ungainly old fan slowly whirling above them. A haphazard partition in one corner enclosed the bathroom. A wide opening gave onto another room filled with enormous beds, all heavily draped in mosquito netting. The eye of the lighthouse peered in through the windows at regular intervals.

"Is this for all four of us?" Ernst inquired.

"No. Hank and André are downstairs," Gerry explained.

"What a pity. We could all bounce from bed to bed, festooned in netting."

They had barely had time to take in their surroundings when there was a knock on the door and the old man shuffled in bearing a tray. "The lady sends to masters," he announced. There was an interesting-looking cheese, studded with nuts, and toast and butter and slices of some sort of smoked fish and a bowl of bananas. A bucket of ice and bottles of water and soda completed the array. Gerry disposed of everything on a coffee table surrounded by a ring of crouched and misbegotten chairs and sent the old man on his way. He pulled a bottle of whiskey out of Ernst's carryall and put it beside the ice.

Ernst moved in quickly to the table and poured himself a drink with hands that shook slightly. Gerry noticed it with concern. He peeled off his damp and crumpled clothes, aware of eyes on him, and carried them to the bathroom and threw them into the tub. He hitched a rather meager towel around himself and returned. "You two should do the same," he told Hank and André. "We don't want to spoil all this lovely upholstery. Fix yourselves drinks." He saw that Ernst had gulped down half his and moved toward him. Their eyes met and spoke to each other of private matters. Gerry put a hand on his arm and guided him through the opening to a corner of the other room where they were screened by beds. They held each other close and kissed. "How are you, darling?" he asked.

"Surviving. I needed a drink. I told Paolo to bring the pipes and everything but that was just a precaution. You've cut us down so far that I won't need anything after I've had a few drinks."

"Good. Paolo might take some time. We'll get drunk instead." His fears receded. He could feel reserves of stamina in him. "God knows what's going to happen next but there's nothing to worry about."

"I've never felt so safe. You, and nobody knowing where I am, and those nice youngsters for company if we feel like it."

"I'm amazed by you. I was afraid you'd be horribly upset."

"I was while we were apart. I got frightfully nervous floating around in the dark. I almost jumped overboard myself to look for you. It's quite dreadful being without you."

Gerry kissed him tenderly and stroked his face. "I know. I've decided not to let it happen again, even if it means abandoning a few of our best friends to their fates. We'll be totally selfish and together."

"I need another drink. We'd better go out, darling. There will be very little point to that towel in a moment."

Hank and André were sitting in front of drinks, naked except for their towels. Gerry replenished Ernst's drink and poured one for himself. He sat on the arm of Ernst's chair with a hand on his shoulder. Ernst laid a hand on his thigh. Hank was spreading cheese on toast. Gerry held out a hand for some. "I want to talk," he said. "Are there any secrets you don't want to talk about in front of these two?"

"What sort of secrets, darling?"

"About what happened tonight. About what's been taken."

"Oh, about that there's a small secret but I don't mind their knowing if they promise not to mention it."

"They won't if you ask them not to." He glanced from one to the other and they both nodded.

"OK. Let's begin at the beginning. You had a lot of cash, didn't you?"

"About a million dollars in various currencies."

"Jesus," Hank exclaimed.

"What else?" Gerry prompted.

"In the cases? Jewelry. Solange and I between us had over a half million dollars' worth. I don't know about the others. Farr has some good things but I don't know what he put in the safe."

"Let's make a guess that about seven hundred thousand dollars' worth of baubles would be average when you have guests aboard."

"Minimum," Ernst noted. "Most of you had very little on this trip. You're not exactly maharajas, any of you. Wait till we've had a few birthdays and Christmases together, darling," he added, exerting a small pressure on Gerry's thigh. "You'll be absolutely blinding. Very well. That covers the tangible assets, as they say. Then there's the very intangible secret. I've been conducting business negotiations over the last few months that promise to be highly profitable. Some Hughes people are mixed up in it so there's been the usual cloak-and-dagger nonsense. A month or two ago, just when I was due to leave on this cruise, it looked as if it might come to a head. I almost canceled the cruise—good heavens, think what would have become of me if I had." He again exerted pressure on Gerry's thigh. "I decided that if I had the dossiers with me, I could carry on wherever I was. If they fall into the hands of somebody who understands what they are, I imagine both the Hughes people and myself would be contacted so that we could bid against each other for their possession. Depending on what value the opposition places on them, I would be willing to pay as much as a million dollars to keep them out of their hands. That, of course, is what I wouldn't want anybody to know except you three."

"Is there anything in them that would damage you in any way?" Gerry asked.

"Certainly not. They would simply queer a very nice deal."

"I don't think you need worry about that. You'll be hearing about them soon enough."

"A Maylay bandit couldn't make head nor tail of them."

"I doubt if we're dealing with Maylay bandits. Is that everything? There were five cases."

"Precisely. One for the cash. One for the papers. The third for our valuables. The fourth for the guests'. There was nothing of intrinsic value in the fifth—our passports, documents that are easy to replace, such as insurance policies and so forth, correspondence that I put in the safe simply to get it out of the way."

"That leaves the Cézanne. I know enough about art to know that it's worth well over a million."

"Very much so. Perhaps not so much if it's disposed of clandestinely."

"Let's say it all comes to four million dollars, give or take a few hundred thousand," Gerry recapitulated. "Quite enough to make it worthwhile to run *Hephaistion* on the rocks, even if it's split two or three ways. That's the only thing I was wondering about. It's all clear as crystal now."

"What is, darling?" Ernst asked. He held out his empty glass. Gerry took it and glanced at the others. He had their full attention. There was a silence except for the clink of glass as they all poured fresh drinks. Gerry fixed a generous one for Ernst and settled back against him.

"We'd all assume it was an accident if I hadn't seen what I saw," he said. "The hijacking could've been a coincidence, something that might've happened to any foreigners leaving a luxury yacht at night. Just some fishermen who saw a chance to pick up some loot. Except the head pirate was on board as a deckhand. People were waiting here for him. He knew what he wanted and once he had it he didn't bother with Ernst's boat except to give it a tow. Fishermen would've taken everybody's watches, at least. One of the engines was giving trouble and making us run slow. Better to go slow at first and put on a burst of speed if necessary than to arrive early and have to go around in circles waiting for a rendezvous. Somebody had to be on board to drain the speedboats. Otherwise, we'd've been ashore, guns blazing, before anybody could've got near us. Could it've been worked without smashing us on the rocks? Suppose we'd stopped obligingly offshore and allowed an armed band to come on. They'd have had to shoot their way to the safe, get it open somehow and probably end up dead while they were at it. Am I imagining things? Does anybody think it was an accident?"

"You're suggesting the captain was in on it," Ernst said quietly.

"You're damn right I am. He decided to stay on the bridge and take the wheel. The weather wasn't all that bad. When there's an investigation, he'll say he misread the charts and that'll be that. It might end his seafaring days but he can retire quite comfortably on a million or two. The captain and—who else? Did the captain know enough about your affairs to know it was worth the bother?"

"I've never addressed more than three words at a time to him."

"Right. Nobody would've planned this without having a pretty good idea what was in it for him. That eliminates just about all of us. I mean, we could eliminate the Farrs in any case. Who's left? How about you, darling?" he asked André. "Did you know Ernst carries all these goodies around with him?"

"Me? I've been much too busy with my love life to think about stealing four million dollars."

They all laughed. Gerry shook Ernst's shoulder to prod him into speaking. "OK. Who talked the captain into running up on the rocks?"

"It's quite obvious who you mean but you've been down on her right from the start," Ernst said with an edge in his voice. "Very well. She's been with us a great deal for the past few years. I've often mentioned that I carry enough cash on board to make a run for South America and live quite comfortably for a while if the world blows up while we're at sea. She has eyes. She knows that Solange and I travel with quite a lot of jewelry. The Cézanne was there for everybody to see but it hasn't lived on board. I brought it with us last year for the first time. When Maria told me I was being foolhardy, I said I thought it made the salon look much more distinguished and would probably bring it again. Now that I mention it, I remember she joked about it not long ago—she asked if I was being stubborn about it this season and I said of course. When we were all in New York, she knew I was on the verge of calling off the cruise. When the time came, I told her I'd reconsidered and would take some important business papers with me. She had no way of knowing that they were important enough for me to pay a ransom for them. There. Is that your case against her?"

"That's *your* case against her. Actually, I've just thought of a point in her favor. She didn't suggest taking the picture off. I did. Maybe she had other plans for it and didn't want it to go into the common kitty. *My* case against her is made up of a lot of small details. The first day I met her, she lied about what she'd been doing that morning. She denied knowing Sinhalese when I'd heard her speaking it with her Oriental henchman. She made a slip about when we were getting to Ceylon and changed it to Cochin. Tonight, she signaled from the speedboat. How else do you think they knew which boat to go after? I could mention a couple of other things, but those are the main points."

"Is that why you grabbed her lighter?" Hank asked. "I thought you'd gone nuts."

"She signaled with her lighter?" Ernst inquired. "She wasn't just lighting a cigarette?"

"She had a cigarette in her mouth but she wasn't holding the lighter anywhere near it. She flicked it on three times before I stopped her."

"She does that all the time. She puts a cigarette in her mouth and lights her lighter and then forgets what she's doing. She keeps lighting it and letting it go out. I've teased her about it often. I do think you're inclined to think the worst of her, darling."

Gerry made a sound of exasperation in his throat and hitched himself forward so that Ernst's hand was dislodged from his thigh. If she hadn't signaled, what had brought the hijackers over to them? "You know why I'm not crazy about her," he said sharply. "You really don't mind what we talk about in front of these two? All right. You know how I felt about her supplying the opium. I couldn't understand why she did it but it fits now. She wanted you stoned all the time so you wouldn't pay attention to what was going on around you. By rights, you'd've been stoned tonight and there would've been some justification for her taking over. As it was, she made herself conspicuous. It jarred, with you there in perfect control of yourself and everything else. Yorgo thought so too."

"I've told you I don't like to think ill of my friends." The steely note crept back into Ernst's voice. "Even if you're right, it doesn't sound as if you'd be able to prove it. She's used to managing things for me. It was typical of her to take charge of my possessions while the rest of us were wondering about our own safety. Are we supposed to treat her like a criminal now? You *do* make things difficult, darling."

"Oh, for God's sake. There you go again. Somebody wrecks your yacht and makes off with a fortune and *I* make things difficult by trying to find out who it is." Gerry jumped to his feet in the heat of the moment and stood over Ernst. He didn't give a damn how they treated her, aside from putting her in jail; this was too serious to sweep out of sight for social reasons. "Try to get a few things straight, for heaven's sake. Forget about the money. André was almost killed. It might have been any of us. It's a wonder we got Mrs. Farr off safely—a woman of eighty-something forced to teeter around on slippery decks. People were shooting at each other. I'd call that making fairly serious difficulties. I might even be rude to whoever's responsible."

"Of course, darling. You're perfectly right." His tone was instantly as conciliatory as his words. He reached for Gerry's hand and gave it a tug to bring him down beside him again. Gerry stood his ground, waiting for an apology. "It's probably foolish but I've never liked to confront people with their shortcomings. Life becomes such a bore."

"Shortcomings. That's very good. You say you've never been able to trust anybody. This must be a bore too."

"I was speaking of important things. Since you've come into my life, I already trust André and Hank completely because you make friends in a way I have never seemed able to do. So many things stand in the way. I've accepted Maria's friendly services without having any illusions about her motives. Unless there is proof, how can my behavior toward her change?"

"I have a hideous feeling Gerry's right," André interjected. "I saw her push the picture with her foot after the cases were gone, as if she was afraid they'd leave it."

Gerry nodded. "I thought so. I don't claim to have proof but once the insurance people start investigating the leads I can give them, I'll bet they make mincemeat of her."

"What insurance people, darling?" Ernst asked.

"The insurance people for the yacht. Lloyds or whoever you use. You don't suppose they'll pay off on a thing like this until they make damn sure it wasn't done on purpose?"

"The yacht isn't insured, darling."

"What?" Gerry stared at him aghast. "Not insured? Oh my God." He put the heels of his hands on his forehead and gripped his head. He dropped his hands to his side. "I don't believe it."

"Have you ever tried to insure a private yacht of that size? Regulations. Restrictions. You could never go anywhere without violating some clause or other. I prefer to be my own master. I knew I might lose it. Yachts have a way of getting lost. It's a risk I can afford."

"But everything else. That's all covered, isn't it?"

"The jewelry is insured against everything imaginable. The Cézanne is insured when it's hanging where it belongs —in France. I'm not sure the insurance people would approve of my having taken it to sea, not to mention French customs. That *was* rather breaking the law. Probably the less said about it the better."

"Jesus Christ. Do you know what this means? Nobody's going to take the slightest interest in the whole affair. There might be a little local investigation for the record and that'll be the end of it. Insurance companies are used to jewelry being stolen. Can you imagine them mounting a big offensive to catch my Bangkok friend? He's probably Ceylonese and has already faded into the underbrush. Well, that's it. We might as well forget about it. It's hardly worth asking if Maria knows about your insurance arrangements." The rich were very strange. If you could have everything you wanted, what would give anything value? If you lose a Cézanne, buy another. He thought of being rich himself but found it difficult to stay in tune with Ernst.

"She could hardly help knowing," Ernst said. "The question has often arisen in casual conversation."

"What a perfect setup. She had nothing to risk except all our lives and I must admit it was very well managed from that point of view."

"I'm sorry, darling. I appreciate your caring." Ernst took his hand again. "We can stop seeing Maria if that's what you want, although I still think you're taking a great deal for granted. It seems to me your Bangkok man is the big winner. He has everything. How do you expect Maria to find him again any more easily than anybody else?"

"Because whoever brought him into it must have very firm control of him. He wasn't on the wheel so the captain has to be in it. If not Maria, who could it be? The answer is pretty obvious."

"Yes, I've already thought of that. If I had to choose

between Maria and Yorgo, I'm afraid I'd have to agree with you. He has too much to lose."

"So I assumed. You must tell me what someday."

"I will tell you anything you wish. I simply find it impossible to imagine people we know doing such things for money."

Gerry laughed dispiritedly. He was suddenly bone-weary. The spirit of the chase had sustained him; his conviction that he was in a position to unmask the plotters had made him forget fatigue. Without the apparatus of normal legal procedure to back him up, he had succeeded only in stirring up trouble with Ernst. "You're such an innocent sometimes, darling," he said. "People do all sorts of things for money if they're not rich. Don't you remember what it was like when they were trying to disinherit you? Weren't you ever tempted to do something to win?"

"I fought fire with fire. I was fighting for my rights. Nobody has the right to anything of mine except you."

Their hands gripped each other. Gerry dropped onto the arm of the chair with his legs in against Ernst's. "Thank you." He leaned forward and kissed him, hastily so as not to let it get out of control in front of the others, but with gratitude. "You don't think I'm tiresome or make life a bore?"

"I don't understand why I say such things. It's a tiresome—" He checked himself with a laugh. "There you are. It's a silly habit of speech. You must cure me of it. Please forgive me, darling." His hands moved over Gerry, bringing conflict to an end. One hand slid along his thigh and came to rest between his legs. Fingers stirred invisibly on the stirrings of Gerry's flesh. Small wounds were instantly healed.

Gerry was still amazed by how sensitive he was to Ernst's moods, how easily Ernst could hurt him. All his feelings were on the surface of his skin, as the French said. He was as vulnerable to Ernst's disapproval as a child. Ernst's fingernails traced provocative patterns at the base of his spine and the small reconciliation became an affirmation of their need for each other. He realized that the skimpy towel offered no concealment for rapid expansion. He was about to make a public display of himself. Ernst might like it but there was no need to display himself further to André and Hank. He bundled himself up in the towel and dropped to his knees on the floor and took cover against the table.

"We haven't even finished one bottle," he exclaimed, all alive and glowing again from the moment of loving connection. Learning how to fight was part of the course. He turned back to Ernst and put a hand on his knee. "Come on. I thought we were supposed to get drunk. Nobody's trying." He took his glass and refilled it and started to share out what remained in the bottle between the rest of them.

"No more for me," André demurred. "It's just making my head worse."

"You should probably go to bed," Gerry suggested.

"I don't want to miss anything."

"You won't. There's nothing more." Modestly quiescent again, Gerry sat back against Ernst's chair and hooked an arm over his knees. Ernst caressed his shoulders and played with his hair. Gerry dropped his head back, feeling totally content and at home. He loved and was loved and was filled with strangely painful peace.

"You really don't think anybody, the police or anybody, will do anything about a robbery this size?" Hank asked.

"Oh, they'll write it all down," Gerry replied, lifting his head. "My guess is that the stuff is already on the way out of here—probably on its way to Colombo."

"What's Colombo?"

"The main town, only a couple of hours away. It's a pretty important port. Gems are a big industry here so there's already plenty of well-organized smuggling. The jewelry will probably be unrecognizable by tomorrow evening. The cash will have to be smuggled out too, because of currency controls, but that's no problem."

"You know this country, don't you. It *is* a country? Not part of India?"

"No, a real live country all its own. I spent over a year here, most of it in a Buddhist monastery but a couple of months with a pair of beautiful blond Swedes." He laughed and took a long swallow of his drink. He was finally getting a little drunk. From the way Hank was looking at him, he suspected that Hank was getting a little drunk too. Hank was thinking forbidden thoughts.

"This is the first I've heard of Swedes and monasteries," André said. "Have we decided we're going to treat Maria as if nothing had happened?"

"Who wants to bet that Maria won't be up and away first thing in the morning, regardless of whether or not we can go back on board?" Gerry demanded. "She'll leave a note full of plausible excuses and promise to come back in the evening."

"That *would* be rather damning," Ernst agreed, giving Gerry's ear a tweak. Gerry twisted his head and kissed his hand and pressed it against the side of his face.

"All right. I better give up," André admitted. "My head really hurts."

"Poor darling," Gerry said. "Get a good rest. It's silly to stay up if you're not drinking."

"Can I stay and finish my drink?" Hank asked, looking at Gerry.

Gerry looked up at Ernst. "What about it, darling? Are you going to have another?"

"It might help me sleep. I'm not drunk, am I?"

"Not nearly as drunk as you deserve to be." He rose with André and gave his towel a cautious hitch, feeling Hank's eyes on him. André gave the other two a good-night kiss.

"I'll be fine in the morning. Is it all right if I go down like this?" He held his arms away from his sides, looking defenseless and breathtakingly desirable.

"You'll probably be abducted but you're used to that." Gerry collected his clothes from the bathroom and put an arm around him and conducted him to the door. André let his body go to him when they kissed. Gerry held him with tender protective care.

"I love being with you and Ernst now," André murmured. "I had no idea he could be so sweet."

"He even surprises me sometimes. Get lots of sleep, darling. God knows what we'll be up to tomorrow. Today, actually."

"If we don't go on with the cruise, are you and Ernst apt to go off together?"

"And leave you in the lurch? Don't worry. You're our baby. Unless Hank makes off with you."

"He'd much rather make off with you."

"We don't have to worry about that. Sleep tight, darling." They kissed again and Gerry let him out and returned to the drinkers. They were discussing the possibilities of getting the yacht off the rocks. Gerry resumed his seat on the floor at Ernst's feet. Hank reestablished contact with his eyes; Gerry kept his neutral.

"Watertight compartments. Emergency engines. All sorts of things I know nothing about," Ernst was saying. His speech was getting slightly slurred and Gerry saw that a second bottle had been opened. He smiled up at him and squeezed his knee.

"Watertight compartments. I thought that's what you had for holding your liquor."

Ernst giggled uncharacteristically. "It seems to be slopping over a bit. Wasn't Hank talking about the yacht?"

"Probably. All I can say is that when we were rescuing André, it looked as if there were a lot of very ugly rocks around. I don't see how we could've helped tearing a great hole in the bottom from the way we crashed onto them. We should probably be deciding what we'll do if we have to leave it."

"Why don't you and Hank talk about that while I collect my wits?" Ernst closed his eyes and laughed softly. Gerry smiled at him. This wasn't the bad drunk Ernst had warned him about. He was just getting pleasantly pissed. Gerry made himself comfortable against him and turned back to Hank. "I guess we'll just do what we'd planned to do. We were due in Bombay in a week or so. Ernst has the houseboat in Kashmir all laid on for a couple of weeks. We'll get reorganized and fiddle around until it's time to go there. That'll give time to repair the yacht."

"Fiddling around takes money. My ticket home was in the cabin but all my money, such as it was, was in the safe. I'm in a bind. I can hardly ask Ken for more."

"André is in the same boat, except that I don't think he had any money at all. Don't worry about it. You're even more our guests now than you were before. Isn't that true, darling?" He twisted around to look at Ernst. He was breathing regularly, dead asleep. "Hey," Gerry called, laughing and giving him a shake. Ernst's lips moved and he muttered something and seemed to settle into deeper sleep. "That was quick." He turned to Hank with a smile.

"Passed out. It's not surprising. He's been really knocking it back—two for every one of ours."

"If I'd just lost four million dollars, plus whatever the yacht comes to, I'd have a few drinks myself."

"I'll say."

"Well, we seem to've separated the men from the boys," Gerry said with a chuckle. They looked at each other in silence for a moment. He was struck again by how handsome Hank had become. His tan made his intelligent humorous eyes look bigger. His shapely mouth was strong and passionate. The twitch in his jaw that Gerry hadn't noticed recently was pronounced tonight. It somehow invited a caress although Gerry decided to deny himself the pleasure. He'd been enough of a tease in the sea.

"I've been waiting for some time alone with you," Hank said.

"It looks as if you're going to have it. I'd better put him to bed." He pushed himself up and found that it took a slight effort to get his feet planted steadily. He leaned over and lifted Ernst's arms to his shoulders and got a grip around his waist and pulled him up. He stood leaning against Gerry with an arm around him. He opened his eyes heavily and closed them again.

"Sleepy," he muttered. "Take care of me always, darling."

"Of course." He tightened his hold on him and turned toward the other room and they began a slow steady march in the direction of the beds. He slipped a hand inside his shirt and held him. His guy, to get drunk with and make love to and live for. He smiled to himself as he observed the jut and swing of His Majesty growing more pronounced under the towel. Ernst suddenly stopped, his head lolling against Gerry's.

"Where we going?" he asked fuzzily.

"Bed, darling."

"In that case—" He lifted a hand and ran it down over Gerry's chest and encountered the towel. He pulled it off and let it fall to the floor. His fumbling hand moved on until he found Gerry's hard flesh lifting to meet it. He gripped it. "I thought so," he said with his lips pressed to Gerry's neck. "Beautiful. Hank still here? Show him."

"He knows all about it. Come on." They continued their slow progress. At the first bed they came to Gerry dropped him and lifted his legs and stretched him out on his back. He sat beside him and began to undress him. His hand brushed against something that demanded investigation.

He eased his trousers and shorts down over his hips and found what he was hoping for. Ernst was close to erection. Drunk and exhausted but free of the drug and damn near hard. The handsome cock was beginning to function again. No more pretending, with the help of the pipes, that it didn't matter if they couldn't share the ultimate pleasure. He kissed it and drew it into his mouth and felt little surges in it as it continued to fill out. He swung himself up onto the bed to make love to all of him. Hank would have to wait.

Ernst muttered something and then spoke quite clearly. "You can bring Hank in to bed if you want," he said.

Gerry recoiled with anger. "No," he blurted. "Not even if *you* want it." Before he had finished speaking, a snore escaped Ernst's parted lips. He probably hadn't known what he was saying—words issuing from a muddled dream. He lowered his head to him again to see if he was really out, and felt the erection subsiding. The gentle snore continued. He rolled off into a sitting position. Only three pipes this afternoon. A few too many drinks tonight. Only a small step remained to finding their highs in each other.

He looked around for something to cover himself. He expected to find Hank in an amorous mood and the thought of fending him off abruptly, miraculously, cooled him. The nagging sense of unfinished business was gone; Hank was just a good friend. He rose, keeping his eyes off the body sprawled out on the bed. By the time he had started for the other room, he was in an appropriate condition for seeing a friend. Hank looked up when he entered and he gave him a smile and picked up the towel from the floor. He started to hitch it around himself but decided to let him see how the land lay. He continued toward him.

"Any booze left?" he asked.

Hank hitched his chair away from the table at his approach, dislodging his towel and bringing Gerry to a dead stop. There was no doubt about who and what he wanted.

"There's plenty for you," Hank said, laughing and reaching for him. Gerry was disarmed by his laughter and took the last few steps to him. He stood for a moment with his hands on his shoulders while Hank tried unsuccessfully to arouse him with his mouth and then, to save them both embarrassment, dropped to his knees in front of him. Hank spread his legs and drew him closer. His prodigious virility swung against him like a club.

"We've got to knock it off, honey." Gerry was firm but affectionate. "You see how it is. I told you. I'm sticking to the rules. No cheating, remember?"

"I suppose you think I'm cheating on Andy. I'm not. We're both in love with you. He knows I'll do anything to get you."

"You're both sweet but you're crazy. What about me and Ernst?"

"You know that'll never work. He's from another world. We understand each other. We can have something terrific together. What about when we were swimming? There wasn't any problem then."

"Oh, honey, that was all sorts of things. Being naked and playing in the sea. We'd just had a bit of excitement and I was pretty sure everything was going to be OK—I was really flying. You were just part of it."

"Thanks."

Gerry chuckled. "Well, a pretty big part of it, depending on what we're talking about." Gerry put both hands around the part in question. Hard and unyielding. He spread his fingertips tightly along both sides of it and marveled at its power. From the thick base to the sweeping curve of the head, it was a massive embodiment of the phallic drive that had ruled his life. Hank's arms encircled him and pulled him in against him and he didn't resist him. The fact that Ernst continued to thrust freedom on him made it essential for him to be sure of what he wanted, since he lacked the restraints of guilt.

The avidity of Hank's hands and mouth failed to arouse him. The spark that had been kindled between them at the beginning and had kept him on edge for the last few days had somehow been extinguished; he was prepared to go along with anything Hank wanted to prove it to both of them. Hank's breathing was labored when their mouths broke apart and to test himself further Gerry offered him the skills of his lips and tongue. He was astonished by himself. He had never knowingly stirred a man to passion without being carried along by it. He remained blissfully detached and inviolable. He felt Hank's hips straining up to him.

"Oh Christ, Gerry," he gasped. "You're fantastic. Nobody can do it like you."

Gerry drew back. "Not many guys are so inspiring. Shall I go on?"

"No. We both know what we really want." He dropped forward out of the chair, forcing Gerry back flat on the floor. He knelt over him and reached for a handful of melting butter and applied it to himself.

"Marlon Brando should be so lucky," Gerry said with a choke of laughter, looking up at the glistening shaft that hovered over him. Hank slipped his hand between his legs and ran his fingers between his buttocks. Gerry's body gave an involuntary leap and he uttered a short cry and lay still.

"Yeah. You want it. You can quit pretending. You're getting hard now."

"I'm not unconscious, honey. I like to be fucked. You've got the kind of cock that usually makes me flip. *Something's* bound to happen but this isn't really it. You'll see." He was willing for Hank to take him. He was exulting in his indifference. If the curious block survived Hank's possession of him, he was safe for life. He let himself be rolled onto his stomach and immediately became responsive to the lightest touch to make it easy for both of them.

"Christ, that ass," Hank murmured, moving his hands over it.

Gerry's heart accelerated as Hank took possession of him. Had he carried the test too far? He teetered on the edge of surrender and waited for ecstasy to follow as Hank completed the long thrust into him. It took him a moment to fully grasp that he remained untouched. He let out a crow of exultant laughter. "Oh, honey, you're fabulous. What a cock. Feel mine. How's that for a bum lay? I'm a one-man guy, honey. Who would've believed it? Go ahead. Fuck me if you want. I don't mind. You deserve something for your trouble."

"God damn it. I'm going to make you realize we belong together. Feel that. Feel me in you. It's what we both want. Together. Like this. Oh God, Gerry, I've been going crazy for you."

"You have me now. It's not worth going crazy for, is it?"

"Oh hell. I don't want it if it doesn't make you hard."

"I understand that. I'd feel the same way."

"What's the matter with you all of a sudden? I guess this just isn't our night."

"I'm in love, honey, tonight or any night. That's what you refuse to understand."

"Oh damn." He withdrew slowly and sprang up and went to the bathroom. Gerry rolled over and sat up, smiling to himself, impotent, peaceful and contented. He had survived the test. There was no longer the shadow of a doubt; he was beyond anybody's reach but Ernst's. That was the way he had hoped it would be, the way he intended to keep it. He reached for his precious towel and put it around himself. He stood on his knees and helped himself to another drink. Hank returned, wrapped in his towel again.

"I'm sorry," he growled, keeping his distance and not looking at him. "I guess I got out of line. Why didn't you stop me instead of just lying there and letting me do it?"

"I guess I wasn't absolutely sure I didn't want it too. We know now. I'm sorry if that was the wrong way to find out. Come here and look at me and tell me it's all right."

Hank lifted his head and met his eyes with a hesitant smile. "There's nothing all right about it. We've got something going between us. I can feel it."

"I know what you mean. I've felt it too. It bothered me, even tonight in the boat, but it doesn't anymore. I'm sorry if that leaves you out in the cold."

"One bum try doesn't mean anything. I'll believe it if it's the same next time. There's going to be a next time. I'm sure of that. Can I have a nightcap?"

"I wondered if I was going to be a solitary drunk. Here. Finish the ice." He poured Hank a generous drink and handed it to him as he seated himself in the chair beside him. They lifted their glasses to each other and drank.

"I'm not like Andy," Hank pointed out. "I don't wish you luck with Ernst. I just hope I'm still around to grab you when the time comes."

"Don't hope that. I wouldn't be worth grabbing if anything goes wrong with Ernst."

"It's like that? He'll always have people like Maria around him, you know. You won't like it."

"I think I can get rid of her kind."

Hank shook his head. "You won't. He's not used to doing anything for himself. He needs hangers-on. They make it possible for him to avoid facing unpleasant truths. You'll start out wanting to do everything for him but you'll get fed up when you discover he's using you to dodge the truth, the way he uses everybody. I know. Ken's the same. He's starting something with Heinrich because he doesn't want to face the fact that I've made my declaration of independence. It's all so soft. It almost makes me hate being gay."

"It has nothing to do with being gay, honey. It's money, pure and simple."

"Money *and* being gay. Andy's too young to be spoiled but he'll be the same if we don't watch out. It's not money in his case. Soft. Much softer than a girl. Male soft. I hate it. You're tough. I'm remembering how to be tough. That's why we'd be so terrific together."

In spite of the tendency of his thoughts to run into each other or simply vanish before they led anywhere, Gerry found that he was listening. Hank had touched on something important. "There's plenty of toughness in Ernst," he asserted. "He just hasn't bothered to use it except when he's seriously threatened. That's what comes of leading a purely social life. The challenges are too trivial to make a fuss about. He's ready to change all that. There's a lot there that most people don't see."

"I wouldn't be surprised. He's fascinating and I like him much more than I expected to and it's not difficult to see why you're attracted to him, but he's sick. I don't mean dope or anything obvious. There's something about him that scares me."

"I know. There's something even I don't quite understand. It may be as simple as his never having let himself care about anybody in a big way. I think we're ready to do something about that. I like talking to you, honey."

"Yeah. Everything we do is good. Even bad sex. I'd've killed anybody else who did that to me. You made it all right. You're straight, and you stick your neck out. That's what's good."

"I guess we like each other."

"I'll drink to that."

They both drained their glasses and set them down and smiled at each other for a silent moment, Hank with a speculative lift of his eyebrows, Gerry trying to communicate the genuine affection he felt for him. Hank gave his knee a decisive slap and pushed himself out of the chair with a slight lurch as he straightened. He laughed. "Something the matter with the floor. Be careful." He went to the bathroom and returned with his clothes over his arm. Gerry was on his feet and walked with him to the door. "I'll be standing by in the morning in case you want to go somewhere and get shot. I don't want to miss any of the fun."

"Don't worry. I'd prefer it if there's an alternative target."

Hank faced him again with the speculative lift of his brows. "Shall we defy tradition and not kiss each other good night? All this social kissing gets on my nerves. I want to kiss you until you come."

"You're a big boy. You'll get over it." They gripped each other's arms briefly and Gerry closed the door behind him. He turned back into the room, Hank already forgotten, all his thoughts concentrated on the man he belonged to. The thought of simply lying beside him and watching him sleep peacefully turned the room into a shrine of perfect happiness. He went to the antiquated bathroom and coaxed a feeble stream of water from the rusted shower head, both taps running tepid, and washed as best he could. Who needed gleaming modern plumbing? They had each other. He caught himself grinning into the mirror while he dried himself, and laughed out loud. He completed his preparations for bed by brushing his teeth with his fingers.

He turned out the lights in the sitting room and picked his way through the furniture and found Ernst lying on his back, as he had left him. He stretched out beside him, carefully, so as not to disturb him, and kissed him lightly on the forehead and lay back with a deep sigh of contentment that was almost a sob. The touch of their bodies here and there along the length of them immediately accomplished what Hank had failed to do. He was ready as usual whenever he was wanted. Even his body knew finally where it belonged.

He seemed to contain within himself a distillation of every moment of happiness he had ever known. Love offered everything he had longed for from it. It was an essence, yet seemed to expand to include every aspect of life. He was learning how to treasure and defend it. He wanted to prolong the circumstances that had produced this moment; they were in surroundings that were equally unfamiliar to both of them. Given a few days, they could build something out of it that was uniquely their own. Let everything else go.

He awoke to country sounds—bird cries dominated by the cawing of crows, the rustling of a breeze in a tree—and opened his eyes to bright dappled sunshine. Leafy branches swayed against the windows. They were in a tree house. The clarity of the light suggested early morning. It turned Ernst's head pure gold on the pillow. They had wrapped themselves around each other during the night and he extricated himself slowly without waking his bedmate. His head felt heavy with sleep and a hangover and he wondered why he was making himself get up until he remembered his early appointment with Yorgo. He was immediately oppressed by the burden of reassembling all the elements of the interrupted voyage. Passports, baggage, money, police reports, altered travel arrangements. Jesus. Get rid of everybody, at least for the week or so before they were due in Kashmir. A week to savor and assimilate being together until it was so much a part of them that nothing could shake it.

He found his watch in the sitting room and saw that he could be on time for Yorgo without rushing. He looked around for a bell without success and went to the door to see if he could stir up some service. A row of suitcases was lined up outside, one of which he recognized as his. The matching dark leather ones were extravagantly Ernst's. Nothing as vulgar as Vuitton. Opulent hand-crafted things with no one's initials except his own, plus coronet. He was about to pull them in when a bearer in an immaculate white sarong came hurrying along the corridor.

"Master wishes something, is it?" he inquired.

Gerry gestured around the door for silence and ordered coffee and towels, remembering that the others had gone as wearing apparel. He made a grab for his own bag and brought it in and opened it on a chair. His dressing gown was neatly folded on top. He regretted the arrival of the baggage. The program that was drifting around in his mind would have included outfitting themselves locally and as simply as possible—a couple of sarongs and a shirt for dressy occasions. If two people were in love with each other, essentials were all that mattered. Properly covered, he dragged in all of Ernst's things. There was no point in unpacking until they decided what they were going to do. He would help Ernst find the things he needed later. He was happy to recover his battered toilet case—brushing his teeth was an essential. He did so and fingered the stubble of his beard and decided to leave it for the time being. The Shipwrecked Look. There was a knock on the door and he admitted his coffee. Paolo accompanied it.

"I asked them to let me know when you were up. I'll get the Baron's things straightened out."

Gerry barred his way. "Not now. Later maybe." Paolo represented everything he wanted to get away from for a day or two. "Is there any news?"

"Yorgo is waiting to go over everything with you. We won't be going back to the yacht for a while."

"I'm not surprised. Go on down and stand by. I don't know what the service is like here. Mr. Farr may want some help with his things. We'll manage here. Tell Yorgo I'll be down in five minutes."

"But the Baron—"

"Don't worry. I'll tell the Baron you're acting on my orders," Gerry said, firmly closing the door on him. The ritual of life was waiting to close around them again. Today was going to be crucial. He wanted to make Ernst share his enjoyment of the unexpected and unknown, the luxury of seizing whatever the moment offered. He would have to keep him busy so he wouldn't have time to think about pipes and booze. Everything would be all right as soon as Ernst discovered there was something to be said for reality.

Dressed in shorts and shirt, after checking to see that Ernst was still sleeping, he went downstairs and found that the lower floor, so hermetic and impregnable the night before, was all open and full of light. Great arched doors gave from the long high-ceilinged sitting room onto a veranda furnished with weather-beaten wicker chairs and tables. Across the street, the venerable tree he had noticed on arrival towered from the ramparts, framing a view of a wide bay. Buildings were dotted around its sandy shore. A stream of people passed silently in the street, mostly men in graceful sarongs. He spotted Yorgo sitting at one end of the vast living room, his portfolios on the table in front of him. He went to him and they exchanged greetings and Gerry pulled up a chair and sat across from him. The secretary was looking his usual spruce and dapper self.

"What's the story this morning?" Gerry asked.

"Shall we start with the yacht? It's probably a total loss. There's an engineer at some sort of naval installation here. Divers have been down. The whole bottom is ripped out. She's piled up on a reef and he doesn't think anybody can get her off. He practically came out and said we must've scuttled her on purpose. I've got the name of marine specialists in Colombo and we'll get another opinion, but that's probably it."

"Lovely. And what does the captain say?"

"The captain isn't saying much of anything. He came off early this morning with all his gear, muttering that his responsibilities had ended. He was supposed to make a report to somebody—the Coast Guard, the Navy, whoever's in charge of these waters—and then he was planning to take off. You can hardly blame him. He must be a bit embarrassed. It seems you can't do anything to a captain for making an honest error. Insurance investigators might have other ideas but I suppose Ernst has told you that there wasn't any insurance.

Gerry nodded. "You sound as if you think there's more to it than meets the eye."

"Don't you?"

"Naturally."

"Oh, yes." He opened a portfolio and took out an envelope. "Maria left this for Ernst. Will you take it or shall I keep it for him?"

Gerry glanced at it, impressed with himself for proving to be such an accurate prophet. "She *left* it?"

"Yes. She had the hotel organize a car for her about an hour ago. Heinrich and Mr. Bales went with her. She says she's explained everything in the note. She'll be back this evening."

Gerry uttered resigned laughter. He would try not to say I told you so. "And what do the police say about the theft?"

"They want a list of every article that's missing but they don't sound as if they expected to accomplish much. They say the local fishermen are experienced hands at that sort of thing."

"Except it wasn't a fisherman."

"No? It did seem rather neat, didn't it? Do you know who did it?"

The question came out easily but Gerry decided not to leave any stone unturned. He watched Yorgo's eyes closely as he answered. "I know. I'm just waiting for a final bit of proof," he said, stretching the truth. "People give themselves away when they think nobody suspects anything. It's just a question of knowing what to look for."

"I had the impression you were more or less expecting it."

If he was acting, he was doing it awfully well. Gerry couldn't detect the slightest flicker of hesitation or alarm. He tried again. "You remember that anonymous note I got. I did what it told me to do. I went to see the guy who wrote it."

"You did? It had something to do with this?"

If Yorgo had had anything to do with the taxi crash he would know he had nothing to fear on that score, but he looked genuinely curious. "I saw something that made it all hang together," Gerry said ambiguously. He needed nothing more to convince him that Yorgo was in the clear, but if he was wrong he'd given him something to worry about. "How do we stand with the police? I mean, our passports."

"I'd say they can't wait to get rid of us. We're a problem they don't know how to handle. They want to pay a courtesy call on Ernst to express their official regrets. That's the only formality we'll have to go through. They say we should apply for new passports and report to the immigration people in Colombo. I have all the information."

"You've been busy. Did you get any sleep?"

"From about four to six," he said with the same precision that marked his answers to all questions.

"Is that everything?"

"There's a problem with the crew. They want to get off. We can hardly ask them to stay. It seems there can be sudden storms and nobody wants to make any predictions about what might happen. We're in luck in one respect. All their papers, and money to pay them off with were kept below. We won't have them hanging around our necks. The only trouble is that once they're off, I don't think there'll be anything left on board by day after tomorrow. There's already a flotilla of small boats hanging around waiting for the kill. The crowd on the beach is just standing there, looking out to sea and practically licking their chops. I've spoken to every official in sight and they all say they either haven't the means or the authority to post a guard. The police say they'll sent out extra patrols to catch people bringing stuff ashore but on a coast like this they'd need several regiments to do an effective job. I don't see what we can do about it."

"It's all fairly sickening. Is there much that Ernst would want saved?"

"There's the silver and crystal and some very fine china and a number of valuable objects of one sort or another. Also some rather special wine. We can pack most of that but the rest will be for the vultures."

"So be it. We can't leave the men in danger. Now, about money."

"Yes. I've already been through to Colombo by phone. There'll be ample funds for Ernst at the Hongkong and Shanghai Bank by tomorrow."

"You're a genius." Gerry thought of his blanket invitation to Hank and André. "I want to cable for some petty cash, like ten thousand dollars. Does anybody know if there's a bank here?"

"Several."

They discussed the problem of currency controls. Yorgo knew exactly what he wanted and how to go about it—a small sum here, the rest held in Colombo where it could be converted into travelers' checks. "Has the press been sniffing around?" he asked when that was settled.

"I haven't bothered to check at the desk. Farr and Ernst should draw them but it might take a day or two for them to get onto it."

"Just in case." He borrowed pen and paper from Yorgo and wrote out a cable for his mother: AM ALIVE AND WELL IN PICTURESQUE SRI LANKA. IGNORE PRESS REPORTS TO THE CONTRARY. "Put in the name of this hotel as a return address. Oh, for God's sake. I'm really brilliant. How do I expect you to send cables? I'd better borrow some money from the hotel."

"Are you thinking of staying here?"

"I don't know. It's just an idea. I imagine everybody will be anxious to get to Colombo to do something about passports. You'd better see what you can line up in the way of cars. I'd like you to get off as soon as possible to be our advance man. Take some suites at the Galle Face Hotel. When we see the gang at eleven, we'll ask them what they want to do until we go to Kashmir. I'm sure Ernst will want them to be our guests. If we stay on here, you could get things going for passports for me and Ernst. I'll be damned. I don't even know what nationality he is."

"Swiss. It's a sore subject. He hates Switzerland. I'll have a new passport for him tomorrow."

"I know the number of mine. I'll write it down. Date and place of birth. Parent's names. That's all they need to get started. As a matter of fact, it was issued by the Embassy here. That should simplify matters. We'll get the necessary information from Hank and André too, if they want to stay here with us for a day or two."

"You want me to go as soon as I get everything organized? Generally, Ernst prefers for me to travel with him."

"Well, maybe we'll play it differently this time. I don't know. Don't run off without checking."

"No, of course not."

"I want to see the lady owner and ask for a loan. Are you going to fix up the cars with the management? Let's go." They went together to the counter and were greeted by a dark plump young man who rose from a desk behind it. Gerry asked for the owner. Words were uttered in Sinhalese and a boy in a white sarong appeared at his side.

"Lady is in her bungalow," the plump young man explained.

"I'll be right back," Gerry told Yorgo, having understood enough to know that he was to be taken to her. The boy escorted him to the back of the building where stairs led down to a small crowded tropical garden. The heat was stifling. They followed a path around some palm trees, the boy calling. Mrs. Brohier ambled out from a stand of tattered bananas. She beamed from behind her thick glasses as she saw him.

"Here's Gerald. How nice," she said in her gentle lilting voice. Her smile was girlish and flirtatious. She was wearing a short frock that did nothing to minimize her rotundities. She floated toward him. "I hope you've had a good sleep."

"Good but not enough." A large spotted coach dog ambled in her wake. When he got wind of Gerry he trotted forward and began sniffing at his legs and butting him with his head. He apparently liked what he'd found for he reared up and planted his forepaws on Gerry's shoulders, which brought them more or less face to face. Gerry staggered and almost lost his balance. A wet tongue found his cheek. Gerry laughed and fought the beast off.

"Down, Sacha," his mistress commanded. "You wretched dog. He likes you, Gerald. He's quite intelligent for a dog. Will you call me Nesta? That would be nice. We'll be friends."

The dog stood looking up at him, wagging his tail lazily. "I hope we are. I'm about to ask you to lend me some money."

"You're a devil. So attractive. How much do you want?" The lilt in her voice made a melody of everything she said. Her smile was a playful blessing. Gerry fell in love with her again.

"As I remember, a thousand rupees is about a hundred dollars."

"I think that's about right."

"Well, could you make it two thousand rupees?"

"Of course. Shall we break the law together? I could give you an address in England where you can send dollars. Am I very wicked?"

"I'll bet you are—in more ways than one."

Laughter seemed to bubble from her like water from a spring, continuing while she spoke. "Are you all very famous? The press have been calling. I recognized Mr. Farr, of course, and I've heard of the Baron's family. I didn't realize he was *the* von Hallers."

"The one and only, as far as I know."

"He's led such an interesting life. No children with that lovely wife?"

"Not yet. I think they're scheduled for the next year or two."

"I do hope so. What're you all going to do? I hear the yacht is sinking. The whole town is agog."

"We seem to be stranded. I think most everybody will be going to Colombo." He kept pace with her as she drifted toward a bench under a temple tree in full luminous flower. "I'd sort of like to stay here a little longer."

"Oh dear." She pulled a doleful face. "I have a group coming tonight. There won't be a room to spare. I could put you down here in the bungalow with me but you'd be miserably uncomfortable. I'm afraid we have nothing here as grand as what you're used to."

"I don't care about grand but I can't inconvenience you." They sat under the temple tree. The dog tried to climb onto Gerry's lap. He thumped his back and fended him off.

"Stop it, Sacha," his mistress scolded. "Such a silly fellow. Did you mean you were thinking of staying on alone?"

"No. I hoped Ernst—the Baron—I hoped he'd like the idea. And maybe André, the beautiful one, and his American friend." Why talk about it if there was no place to stay? He had known that circumstances would conspire against his breaking away from the party. "If you have no rooms, I'd better have another think. It's not important. When this happened, it just seemed like a good opportunity to get away from it all for a little while. We don't have to go on anywhere for more than a week. A little time for private problems. You know."

"I think I can guess." She was beaming again, naughty and full of fun. Laughter slowly bubbled from her. "I may've had quite a brilliant idea. What do you think? There's a lovely beach bungalow not far from here. It's just been built by two American boys. Dear friends. They've left me in charge of it and said I could use it when I wanted to get away from the hotel. I'm sure they'd love you to have it. Would you like to look at it?"

"It sounds too good to be true. You say it's near here?"

"Less than ten minutes' drive. We'd be neighbors. I'd like that. You'd better make sure you like it before we say any more about it." She floated to her feet. Gerry rose and they took the path back to the hotel, the dog nipping at Gerry's hand and inviting him to play. The dog, the garden, the marvelous old lady—everything was making him feel good. A few days of this with Ernst would give them a happy past to remember.

"Could you let me have some of that money before we go anywhere?" Gerry reminded her. "I have some cables I want to send."

"Of course, Gerald dear. Two thousand, did you say? You can tell me what that is in dollars." They mounted to the open space behind the counter that was her office. Yorgo was waiting. Gerry already felt as if the secretary belonged to an alien world. Underlings materialized around her. She wandered about giving orders in Sinhalese with an indolent English accent that was easy for Gerry to follow. She went to a big old-fashioned safe with the door hanging open and turned back to Gerry with two bundles of folded notes. "There. Are we ready to go?"

"Just a second." He went around the counter to Yorgo and gave him one of the bundles. "Take care of those cables as soon as possible, will you? That's about a hundred dollars. You can give me the change later. Everything under control?"

"People are beginning to stir. Hank was here a minute ago."

"Tell him to stick around. I'll be back in half an hour." The dog leaped up and performed pirouettes around him as he moved on to join his new friend. Gerry dodged and danced with him. "Sacha, Sacha," he cried, inciting him to riot. The dog went mad, racing around the vast room, sliding on the waxed wooden floor and colliding with the furniture. Mrs. Brohier watched, beaming.

"What a child you are. How nice. Sacha hasn't had such fun since he was a puppy. How're you going to stop him?"

The dog was galloping in circles, barking joyously and charging Gerry on the turns. "We understand each other. Sacha. Stop," Gerry ordered, wagging a finger at him. The dog skidded to a halt in front of him and made a leap for his finger and flopped down onto his stomach, panting.

"Is that the effect you have on people? Does everybody obey when you wag your finger?"

"Oh Lord. Is that the way I strike you?"

"No, not really. You probably don't wag your finger nearly often enough. It doesn't do to give in to people too easily."

"Is that something that's generally known? I'm just beginning to discover it."

"I gave in for years but then I'm a woman. We're supposed to. A widow has a great deal to learn, usually when it's too late to do any good." She tucked a hand under his arm and they crossed the veranda and descended the steps to the street. A white station wagon was drawn up under the great tree. A young man in a white sarong held the door open and they got into it. She gave instructions while the young man moved in behind the wheel. They rolled down the short hill Gerry remembered from the night before and through the thick wall and skirted a playing field where dark youths in crisp British whites were playing cricket. The road forked and they veered off to follow the shore of the deep bay. He saw the lighthouse rising conspicuously at its entrance. The yacht was evidently in the other direction, on the other side of town. They passed market stalls overflowing with fruit and vegetables. They reminded Gerry of practical matters.

"If we stay out here, what'll we do about food?" he asked.

"The boys can manage quite well, I imagine. There's a staff of four or five in residence. You'll find fishermen all around you. They'll probably bring you everything you want right to the door. There isn't much meat but you won't lack for anything else. You've been here before, haven't you?"

"Yes. A couple of years ago. I didn't get this far south —only as far as Hikkaduwa."

"Oh yes. The hippies. You don't look like a hippie, Gerald."

"I'm a man with a past."

"I want to hear all about it. I hope it's lurid. Do you have a mother? You must give me her address so I can write and tell her what a delightful son she has."

"You must be a mother, too, to think of doing that."

"Yes, a boy and a girl but they're far away. I collect sons where I can find them. It's such fun picking ones you like instead of settling for what God's given you. I find I get along particularly well with homosexuals."

"My goodness. We *are* letting the cat out of the bag."

"Oh yes. I find it so reasonable to prefer men. I certainly do." She bubbled with liquid laughter while Gerry guffawed. They reached for each other's hands and held them like children.

"Dear Nesta. We picked the right place to get shipwrecked."

They had left the sea and were running through a jungle landscape with low shabby buildings bordering the road. Bicycle traffic was heavy. Buses careened at them. Bullock carts slowed their progress. They traversed a village teeming with pedestrians and were once more driving along a wide sweep of beach. Primitive log outriggers were pulled up along it. Gerry didn't see any power boats with privies amidships.

"There it is," she said as they passed some thatch-covered huts.

He followed her pointing finger and saw a small peninsula with what appeared to be a great many roofs embedded in a grove of palm trees. "It looks enormous," he said.

"It isn't really. Well, it's hard to say. It's all open. Everybody says it'll blow away in the monsoon but it hasn't so far."

They crossed a bridge over a river that emptied into the sea along one side of the point of land and turned off into a rutted dirt road. They bumped along it to a long white wall that stretched down to the sea. They stopped in front of a latticed gate and the driver honked his horn. Gerry's curiosity had become intense. Something about the place filled him with high expectations; he was already imagining moving in with Ernst. He hoped that it was at least habitable.

The driver honked again and Gerry saw a sudden flurry of activity through the latticework. The gate parted in the middle and both sides opened and they drove through onto a sweep of driveway that led to a long low white house set in clipped green lawns and extravagant tropical foliage. They stopped in front of a massive door that seemed to hang in space; no walls supported it, only open latticework. He saw that the house was, in fact, several houses linked by frames of lattice. It was a Hollywood dream of a tropical planter's residence, or perhaps it had been moved intact from Beverly Hills itself.

"I don't believe it," Gerry exclaimed.

"It's rather lovely, I think."

They climbed out of the car and stood looking around them. The property was densely planted with graceful coconut palms that exploded in fireworks of fronds high above their heads. Beneath them, a multitude of decorative trees and shrubs luxuriated. Gerry spotted the sculptured leaves of breadfruit, glossy temple trees, bursts of bougainvillea blazing with scarlet and orange and purple bloom, jam trees, jacaranda, jack. Several dark lithe young men, naked to the waist in multicolored sarongs of similar pattern (the house uniform?), edged toward them, chattering among themselves.

"Master may come stay for a few days with other masters," Nesta explained to them. "Is everything in order?"

"Yes, lady," they chorused amid the flashing of pearly teeth. One youth glided forward and opened the door and they stepped through to a columned covered terrace, or veranda, facing the sea. A fence ran along a beach little more than a hundred feet from them. Gerry saw another small house built against the wall near it. Handsome outdoor furniture was grouped invitingly around the three sides of the veranda that served as a sort of frame for an inner room furnished with substantial pieces in the manner of a traditional living room though no walls enclosed it, only a succession of arches fitted with louvered doors. The eye moved freely from indoors to out, from garden to sea and through the living room to more garden without making any abrupt transitions. A rough cotton fabric had been used lavishly for upholstery and cushions in the colors Gerry had liked to use as a decorator—hot pinks and oranges and acid greens, all reproduced in the bountiful nature that crowded up to the wooden columns supporting the great expanse of roof. It was, Gerry decided, the most brilliant creation of out-of-doors comfort he had ever seen.

"I'm speechless," he said.

"You see, Gerald?" Nesta pointed out, looking across the water. "We can almost wave to each other." Gerry moved in beside her and followed her gaze. The familiar lighthouse stood at the end of the farthest point across the bay. "You see the lighthouse? Now move in along those low buildings until you get to the big square white one. That's the hotel."

"We can send up flares to each other. Come on, love. Don't be a tease. Could we really move in here?"

"You haven't seen all of it yet. I don't want to rush you into it. That's the guest house," she said, indicating the small building near the beach. "Just a room and bath. As you can see, they've divided everything up into separate buildings. That's a bedroom and bath at each side of the main part. I'll show you. That's all there is."

A few feet of raised walkway separated the bedroom unit from the central section. They entered a comfortable-sized room dominated by a wide four-poster bed, complete with canopy and hangings. The adjoining bathroom was compact but completely equipped, including a bidet. Gerry turned on a tap and hot water flowed from it. His decorator's eye checked towels and sheets and saw that everything was of the best American quality.

"All right. What's the hitch?" he burst out. "There's electricity?"

"Oh yes, it's all hooked up but it breaks down quite often. It's best to have plenty of candles ready."

"It sounds lovely. I assume there's a kitchen. Is there a refrigerator?"

"Oh, they're very proud of the fridge. I think you press a button and ice comes out. Is that possible, Gerald? And the telephone. I don't think there's another house in all Sri Lanka that can compare to it for mod cons."

He threw his arms around her and gave her a big hug. "You're divine. You really think we dare move in without asking permission?"

"How sweet you are when you're excited. Of course. They've said my friends can use it. I wouldn't want to give rowdy parties here but I don't imagine you'll do that."

"That's what's so amazing about you. You don't know anything about us. What're they like—the guys who did all this? Who are they?"

"They work in the cinema. Wigs or hairdressing or

something of the sort, isn't it? I don't quite know. They're charming boys. Jim Hager and Chris. Don't you want to see the other bedroom?"

"Is there anything wrong with it?"

She bubbled with laughter. "It's practically the same as this but usually people want to see everything when they're taking a house."

"I took it the minute we drove in. I want to get back to the hotel and tell everybody." Trust American faggots. Nobody else would create such a fantasy on a remote beach in a country nobody had heard of. Cheers for Jim and Chris. He took her hand and they went back to the car. Four half-naked youths were lined up at the gate, bowing and grinning, as they drove away.

"Be careful of your things," Nesta warned. "They look harmless but they're cunning rogues. Now, let's see. I'd better let you keep the car for the afternoon. You'll want to stock up. I'll tell the driver what shops to take you to. Food's no problem. What do you drink?"

"What can we get?"

"Local spirits. Beer."

"No wine?"

"Oh dear, no. Not since the new government. Hotels are allowed a little. I can let you have a case or two if we pretend you drank it on the premises. I'm not sure it's good enough for you—just ordinary French stuff that we sell at exorbitant prices. What else?"

"There was something everybody had when I was here before. Wasn't it called ganja?" He named the local equivalent of marijuana.

"You *are* wicked, Gerald. You mustn't ask me things like that. Ask the driver when I'm not listening."

"Are you shocked?"

"Oh, I know all you young people are on drugs. It seems rather silly to me. You're somehow not the type."

"There's no type, love. Don't be old-fashioned. Actually, it doesn't mean much to me one way or the other but it makes some people feel good. It's quite harmless."

"Doesn't it make you want to go to something stronger?"

"Not if you're already *on* something stronger."

"I see."

"Anyway, we mustn't have any secrets. If you don't approve, just say so and we won't take the house."

"That's very straight of you, Gerald, I must say. Of course you must have the house. I know I can have complete confidence in you."

"That's saying a lot but I don't think I'll let you down. Honor among thieves, right?"

"Oh dear, you rather have me there." She clapped her hands with sudden girlish delight. "This is all such fun."

By the time they were heading up the hill to the hotel, they had settled all their housekeeping business, including the fact that she would accept no rent. They could tip the boys and leave a small sum to cover the electricity and telephone. All that remained was to convince Ernst that it was a good idea. There was no rush about waking him. It was only a little after ten.

Sacha was sitting at the top of the steps on the veranda and gave him a boisterous greeting. Nesta stood at his side, laughing and saying, "Silly boy, silly boy," while Gerry calmed him.

"If you think everybody's going to want lunch, I'd better go to the kitchen and knock a few heads together," she said. "I'm not proud of my cuisine. Do you suppose lobsters would do?"

"Sure. And could you chill some white wine? That would keep everybody happy. It seems to me we're putting you to a great deal of trouble."

"Not at all. You'll all be my guests. That way, I can seat you where I want you and everybody will have to be polite about the food." She rolled her eyes heavenward and ambled off looking thoroughly pleased with herself.

Gerry headed for the endless stairs to the upper floor but found Hank asking for him at the counter. "Here I am," he announced, moving in beside him.

"Oh, hi. I was checking to find out if I had your message straight. You weren't supposed to go anywhere without me."

"Wait till you see what I've found. Come on. Come have a beer with me. I've been up long enough to deserve one. Do you have a hangover too?"

"It could be worse. I probably should thank you for sending me to bed." He looked at him levelly with an apologetic little smile and the muscle in his jaw twitched.

"Well, we got all that straightened out," Gerry said, leading the way back to the veranda where a few people were sitting with cups and pots in front of them. He ordered the beer from a waiter who seemed slightly taken aback.

"Master wishes beer, sir?"

"The coldest you've got."

"What is this master bit?" Hank asked when the waiter had gone.

"It's crazy, isn't it? It made me uncomfortable at first when I was here before but it means mister more than anything else. How's André?"

"Fine. His head's all better. He was waking up awfully slowly so I left him to it."

"Our chums need their beauty sleep. We're too ruggedly handsome to bother with such nonsense."

"You're looking awfully good for a guy with a hang-over. Have you caught Maria red-handed?"

"Ha. She did just what I said she would. She went off this morning with Ken and Heinrich. The hell with her. We agreed last night to stick together until we go to Kashmir, didn't we?"

"I guess that was the idea. You said we'd be your guests. Guests do what they're told."

"Wait till you see what I've found for us. Well, what the lady who owns the hotel has found for us. She's a dream." The beer was put before them and Gerry filled two glasses and took a long swallow of his. "Oh, thank God. How did I go this long without it? Now then. I've found us a house. As an architect, you'll flip. It's faggot paradise. All the comforts of home and then some, with four or five naked boys running around at our beck and call."

"You beck. I'll call. We can stay in it?"

"For a few days, I thought. We might like it so much that we'll skip Kashmir."

"Shouldn't we be doing something about our passports? I thought we had to go to Colombo for that."

"There's no rush. I've asked Yorgo to go up and start the ball rolling. That'll give them time to cable Washington or whatever they have to do."

"We'll need photographs."

"So we will. You're very practical, honey. We need somebody like you around. So how about it? We can settle down and work on our love lives."

"Mine could do with some work."

"OK? You and André have to back me up. I don't know what Ernst will think of the idea. I don't see how he can object except that it's not what he's used to. No state banquets. No royalties. No limousines. Definitely no Paolo. Just the four of us and sun and sea and the naked boys. I know we'll all love it."

"When you get started on something, you make everybody love it." Hank laughed. "Maybe I'll finally fall in love with Andy."

"In this place, you're bound to. I'm really excited about it. I'd better go up and wake Sleeping Beauty." He drained off his beer and rose.

He met Yorgo coming down the stairs as Gerry was climbing up. "Have you seen Ernst?" he asked.

"No. I understood you didn't want him to be disturbed. The Princess wanted to hear about the yacht."

"Good. Everything under control? Oh, do you have Maria's letter? I'll take it in to Ernst now." Yorgo produced it from his portfolio and Gerry took it and opened their door quietly and closed it behind him. He walked lightly to the room with the beds. Ernst was sprawled out under the sheet, still peacefully asleep. Gerry stood smiling down at him, eager to speak to him and hold him. He'd give him another few minutes while he asked Solange what she thought of his plan. He withdrew on cautious feet and closed Ernst in again and went down the hall to Solange's door.

Sally admitted him. "Cheers," she greeted him perkily, looking boyish in a simple dressing gown. "It's our hero and savior," she called out into a room as ludicrously furnished as the other. Solange appeared from the bathroom already wearing a smart summer dress.

"Good morning, darling," she welcomed him gaily. "I hear you've been making plans for us."

"Nothing very elaborate. I thought everybody would want to go on where they could take care of business. We can't stay here anyway. It's full up. There's the grand old Galle Face in Colombo. I think you'll like it."

"I rather love this. It reminds me of the house I grew up in. You know? Such marvelous bad taste. It's rather ghastly about the yacht, isn't it?"

"It sounds pretty bad."

"Does Ernst know yet?"

"No, but we talked over the possibilities last night. He seemed prepared for the worst. Before I wake him, there's something I want to talk to you about."

"If you two are going to hatch a plot, I'll go splash about in the bath," Sally said.

"Do you mind if I take Ernst away from you a little while?" he asked when they were alone. It sounded outrageous when he put it into words, an intrusive tampering with the foundation of their lives. He couldn't believe he'd actually made love to her. He hurried on to tell her about the house. "It'll just be for a few days so we can be together in completely different circumstances. More like living together in an ordinary everyday way. That's what I want."

She tucked her chin in and smiled up at him. "Did you arrange to have us wrecked?"

"If I'd thought of it, I might have. Do you mind saying you want to go if he'll stay?"

"Of course not, darling. Is everything going well?"

"We're almost finished with dope. Yes, everything's going beautifully."

She reached out and touched the wooden back of a chair. "I'm so glad but don't expect too much right at the start. He's a creature of habit. The house sounds ideal but he might be tiresome if anything goes wrong. He's an impossible houseguest because he's such a perfect host himself. You know? I shouldn't try to advise you but I know him awfully well. If he wants to leave, I wouldn't make a very big point about it."

"He's used to having his way too much. That's the only reason I'd make a point about it."

"Of course, you must be the judge, darling, but I want so much for it to go well for you, for all of us."

"I think this might be the best thing that could've happened to us."

"I understand what you're thinking and you may be right." A troubled little frown settled on her brow. "It's too awful. I want to ask questions that I know I mustn't."

"What about?"

"No. I mustn't. You'd tell me if there were any problems you thought I should know about. I see for myself about the smoking. It's very wonderful. If you could do that, you can do almost anything for him. I shouldn't worry."

"You're being very mysterious." He went to her and took her hands and kissed her lightly on the lips and felt the small sexual current between them begin to flow again. She represented a unique experience in his life; it made him feel that questions of loyalty were involved. "Come on. Tell me what you're thinking about. We promised not to have secrets."

"It's all right to tell each other our own secrets but not other people's."

"Does Ernst have a secret?"

"I don't see how he can have them from you anymore."

"I don't either," he said, wondering. He was aware that she had sidestepped his question and his mind was racing over the last few days, finding nothing that could cause him any serious concern. "Anyway, I didn't ask you to tell me any secrets. You said you wanted to ask me questions."

"Perhaps you've answered them now. We can have a nice long talk after you've had your holiday here. Go tell Ernst about your house."

"I'm dying to. Don't worry. I'm sure everything is perfect." He was as sure of it as he could be sure of anything, despite the curiosity she had stirred in him. She touched the wood of the chair again.

"You'd better wake him. Everybody will be waiting to decide what to do."

"Not Maria. She's already gone."

"Yorgo told me. She'll probably have all our passports ready when we get there."

"What do you mean by that?"

"Just that she's such a manager."

"Yeah. That's one reason why I want to get Ernst to myself. See you downstairs." He gave her lips another light kiss and left. He let himself silently into the room again, tempted to take his clothes off and get into bed and start the day off with Ernst all over again. He reminded himself that Ernst liked to get going very slowly, today probably more so than ever. He adopted a normal gait as he went to him, letting his presence be known, and sat on the edge of the bed and put a hand on his leg. His eyes fluttered open. They focused on him and he smiled dreamily and closed them again.

"You're here, darling. That's good. Am I supposed to wake up?"

"Don't do anything drastic. How do you feel?"

"Not too dreadful. Did I get very drunk?"

"You passed out in a dignified way."

His smile broadened and he opened his eyes again. He sat up and the sheet fell around his waist. His tousled hair made him look young and appealing. "I suppose it could be worse. I don't think I should make any sudden moves for a while. Have you had breakfast?"

"Hours ago. I'll order coffee for you."

Ernst's eyes cleared and grew more wakeful. "You've changed your clothes. Have our things come?"

"Yes, everything's here but not unpacked. For one thing, we can't stay."

"I can't say that breaks my heart. Where are we going?"

"Just a second. I'll order the coffee and tell you everything." He returned to the corridor and found the room-boy and ordered. He collected Maria's letter from the table where he'd dropped it and found Ernst propped up against the pillows. "There's a letter for you. Guess who?"

"You were right?" They exchanged a significant glance. "What does she say?"

"It's addressed to you."

"Me. You. It's all the same. Read it to us."

Gerry opened it and glanced through it. Except for the details, he could have written it for her. Heinrich was worried about being without a passport because of something in his record. She had agreed to go with him and vouch for him. She felt she should do something about her own immediately because of being a naturalized citizen. Ken knew an art dealer he wanted to contact. She would call in the middle of the day to see if she could do anything for anybody before returning that evening. "That saves us some trouble," Gerry commented as he finished reading it aloud. "I'll make sure they tell her when she calls that there're no rooms here tonight. She can stay where she is."

"You won't allow her to come back on board with us?"

"Nobody's going back on board, darling. There doesn't seem to be much hope of getting the yacht off. Yorgo's getting another expert opinion but it doesn't look good."

"What a nuisance for everybody. What are we going to do?"

"When are we due in Kashmir?"

"Yorgo has it all. The twenty-eighth, I think."

"That gives us a good ten days. Better and better. There's a marvelous house here we could have for a week. I thought it'd be much more fun than sitting around in a grand hotel in Colombo or India somewhere."

"Is it big enough for all of us?"

"No, thank God. It's perfect for us and Hank and André if you'd like to keep them with us."

A hint of the panic he'd seen before passed fleetingly across Ernst's face. "Wouldn't that be rather naughty of us—leaving the party to fend for itself while we disappear?"

"I told you I'm going to be selfish from now on. We come first."

"You mean you want to ship Solange off along with everybody else?"

"It's only for a few days, a week at the most. I've already talked to her about it. She understands. It gives us a chance to be alone together for a little while, with the other two for company, like you said. It's beautiful, right on a private beach of its own. You'll love it. It has everything we could possibly want, complete with a staff of four or five pretty boys."

"I've told you what I think of Ceylonese boys."

"Well, I don't think anything at all of Ceylonese boys so that's all right. They're just a decorative touch. The house is the thing. I wouldn't've suggested it if it weren't so perfect." He heard a wheedling note in his voice that set him on edge. Why should he have to wheedle? They were together. Everything they'd done so far had been governed by Ernst. He could at least say he wanted to see the house before he started making objections. "You're too young to be so set in your ways," he added, glad to hear that he was no longer wheedling. "I've set my heart on this. We're not upsetting anybody's plans. Maria did that for us last night."

"I probably haven't been awake long enough to think about it. You know I want to do whatever you want, darling." It sounded like instant surrender but he suspected that Ernst's surrender could pack a punch. There was a knock on the door and he gave his leg a squeeze and went to admit the coffee. It was on a tin tray emblazoned with an ad for a soft drink. He was sure Jim and Chris wouldn't allow anything like it in their house. He took it to Ernst and put it on his lap. "The baronial coffee-pot, darling," he announced.

Ernst laughed with the sense of fun he had been hoping to arouse in him. "We should probably be thankful that there was any hotel here at all," he said sensibly. "Does Paolo have everything—you know, the pipes and all?"

"I didn't ask but I suppose so. We won't need it here. We'll just relax and make love at last and forget about everything else." The expression in Ernst's face puzzled him; it wasn't his withdrawn look nor was there any pain visible in it. He was smiling slightly but his eyes were empty. He didn't look preoccupied so much as resigned, as if he'd come to the end of a road and hadn't found what he expected there. Lost? "Aren't we going to have to do a lot of boring things about money and papers and the police?" he asked.

"No. Yorgo's a whiz. He says you'll have money tomorrow. I want him to go up with the others and get started on our passports. The police aren't going to bother us but the press is after you. That's another reason I thought you'd like to hide out. The house has a telephone so we can keep in touch without telling anybody where we are. What more could we want?"

"You and Yorgo are extraordinary. What else have you arranged?"

"That's all, and nothing's settled until you OK it. That's the way I want it always."

"You're very sweet. Will you make sure nobody feels I'm abandoning them?"

"You'll see for yourself. Nesta's invited us all to lunch. The owner of the hotel. She's a sweetheart. We'll see them all off in style."

"I hope I don't regret this. I've never done anything like it—dropping out of a party I've organized myself." The slightly lost, resigned note continued to prevail. Gerry remained puzzled. "I must make sure Solange agrees."

"Of course. That was the first thing I thought of. Talk to her. I'll leave you to pull yourself together and go make sure Yorgo hasn't hit any snags. Don't expect too much of the bathroom. The water sort of dribbles and it's neither hot nor cold. All that will change when we move into our new house. Have you any idea where I can find a sexy pair of shorts for you and a shirt? That's all you need wear."

"Isn't Paolo there?"

"No. I'm your new valet. How about wearing something of mine? We wouldn't have to bother opening your bags till we move."

"Is this what you really like, doing things on the spur of the moment and without any organization?"

"Just wait and see how well organized I am. I didn't ask to get shipwrecked but we are. We might as well get some fun out of it."

"You do seem to be having fun. It's exciting." He seemed to shake off his melancholy mood and suddenly uttered light boyish laughter that sent a tingle of delight down Gerry's spine. "Am I going to be free for the first time in years? Is that what you're doing, darling?"

Gerry hugged his waist with his hands. He had won. "Let's just get out of here, out of everything that resembles hotel living. This afternoon we'll have a home of our own." He lifted himself and kissed the top of Ernst's golden head and stood. "Make yourself beautiful. I'll put some things out for you."

He went to the next room and unpacked a few of his things and found a small case among Ernst's bags that he thought he recognized; it proved to be a beautifully fitted toilet case. He went back and peered around the side of the doorway. "OK. Everything's in order. If I stay another minute, I'll climb back into bed with you, which would probably be fatal in our delicate conditions. See you downstairs, darling."

He withdrew, congratulating himself on his restraint. He had heard him laugh; that was worth all the sex in the world. He wanted to make him laugh a lot in the next few days.

Everything that he was eager to get away from awaited his attention below. Plans, travel arrangements, hotel bookings. Yorgo had taken care of everything but it was a nuisance to have to hear about it. Cars had been a difficulty but Yorgo had found three that looked as if they'd survive the journey. He had hired a small truck for the luggage and the salvage from the yacht that was now being brought ashore. He had tried to get five or six suites at the Galle Face but had been promised only two. Life was tough. Gerry thought of his footloose days and decided that the discomforts had had their compensations. He saw through the great arched doors that André had joined Hank and as soon as he could get away, he hurried to them.

He ordered more beer as he sat and put a hand on André's knee. "First of all, how are you this morning?"

"I'm fine. It was nothing but a bump on the head."

"Well, try not to look too beautiful. We may use you as an excuse. Hank told you about the house? We might say you don't feel quite up to traveling and we've decided to stay and look after you. Can you manage to look faint every now and then?"

André laughed. "If I do, Sally will probably insist on nursing me."

"Is it OK with Ernst?" Hank asked.

"He didn't make any big objections. He's just worried about the others thinking he's ditching them. A slight illness in the family might make it look as if we don't *want* to stay. God forbid we should enjoy ourselves."

"You're really glad to get off the yacht," Hank said, probing him with his eyes. "What was wrong?"

"I guess I felt it all coming. It's a relief to get it over with."

"Is that all? You're not thinking a change of locale might be a good idea? It usually doesn't work. You must know that."

Gerry met the speculation in Hank's eyes and saw the muscle of his jaw twitch. Hank was shrewd. He should have known that a lover spurned doesn't always lie down and play dead. He wondered if living in the same house with him was such a brilliant idea.

"I can't get over the whole thing with Maria," André interjected, apparently unaware of the undercurrents swirling around him. "It really shocks me. I'm like you. I don't see how I can ever speak to her again."

"I'm glad somebody else feels that," Gerry said, doubly grateful to him, reaching for his beer and switching Hank off. "Nobody seems to care about crookedness and dishonesty anymore. It's too much trouble. I still can't understand that for people like Ernst a few million dollars isn't worth making a fuss about. Maybe the money isn't, really, but the way people behave is."

"That's what I was saying last night," Hank intervened again. "You're tuned into reality. Maybe you'll be sorry."

"What're you two talking about?" André asked innocently.

"Mostly about Ernst," Gerry explained, making light of it. "Hank thinks I have ideas above my station."

"He thinks we're all lost souls, except possibly you. I can't even go mad about him in bed without his thinking it has something to do with the decline of Western civilization." André's angelically innocent smile made the other two laugh. Gerry's eyes lingered briefly on the two chains around the boy's neck. The chunky one was beginning to look as if it belonged on its owner.

They drank beer and Hank seemed content to let them drift into an aimless friendly conversation. Gerry answered questions about the house he had found and about the country in general. Trevor joined them.

"Has Ernst heard from the old girl?" he asked. "She's always been nervy about being a naturalized citizen. Nothing would do but for her to go dashing off at dawn. Something to do with Heinrich, too, I think. She's never believed anybody can manage their own affairs nearly so well as she can. She's sometimes right, of course."

He was followed by Solange and Sally and then the Farrs until they formed a large circle. In the buzz of plans, nobody seemed to care where anybody else was going. Farr let it be known that he was being hounded by the press and that he was anxious to get on to New Delhi where another Embassy was waiting to receive him. André told everybody who asked him that he was feeling fine except for "these funny little dizzy spells" occasionally, but Gerry didn't bother to follow it up; the party had been adjourned until Kashmir. Trevor said that he was waiting to talk it over with the old girl but thought they might wait in Colombo. Something about a cousin who had once shown them a good time there. Very highly placed in official circles. Gerry was so pleased by the dissolution of the close-knit party spirit that he wasn't paying much attention. He suddenly choked on his beer. Was Trevor drunk? Hadn't he been briefed? He had blown Maria's story sky high.

His first impulse was to question Trevor further, to pile up the evidence. For nonexistent insurance investigators? Ernst wasn't in danger. He had better things to do for the time being than play detective. Perhaps what he'd said to Yorgo was true. Perhaps he had only to sit back and let them give themselves away. His wish to expose Maria would be satisfied without sending her to jail. The missing link with Ceylon would damage her further in

Ernst's eyes. He saw their host approaching from across the enormous lounge, accompanied by Paolo, and he rose and hurried to him. He saw that his clothes were a surprisingly good fit.

"Everything's fine, darling," Gerry announced. "Nobody cares what we do. They've all got plans of their own. Did you get a chance to talk to Solange?"

"Yes, she came in to say that she thinks your idea sounds lovely. Nobody can resist you. Is the company assembled?"

"Yes. Trevor's just been telling us what a good time they had when they were here before."

"Really? I had the distinct impression that they'd never been."

"Me too. It seems they have a cousin who's big in the government or something."

"Poor Trevor. He never remembers what she tells him to say. If we asked him if they planned the wreck, he'd probably tell us. I've just found out from Paolo that the opium was stolen too."

"Yours? You mean, from the cabin?"

"Yes. It's not surprising. Several of the cabin boys knew it was there. Again, it's not something I'm likely to report to the police."

"But are you going to be all right? You don't mind?"

"It means that all I have is you. *Am* I going to be all right?"

"Yes, darling," Gerry said with a quick blaze of conviction. He was getting used to saying almost anything in front of an audience but he wished Paolo would go away. He gripped his hands and felt the puzzling resignation in him. There was courage in it, as if he were being marched off to a firing squad after having lost his final hope of a reprieve. "We don't need it. Believe me. We'll make it with each other."

"I can always get more," he said, as if reminding himself that he had the right to be blindfolded. "I think it's very important that you take me soon to wherever it is we're going."

"Do you want to go now?"

"Right after lunch will do. Let everybody go. You can tell Hank and André to go if you want."

"Are you sure you wouldn't like company?" Gerry asked, trying to stir some warmth of life in him.

Ernst offered him a smile that almost made him flinch from the intensity of its unguarded need. "You're more wonderful even than I realized. I can almost believe that a miracle has happened."

"Believe in us. That's all I want." Something had happened. He was perplexed but he could add the smile to the laughter as the promise of total happiness. His arms ached with the longing to hold his love. He released one hand but retained the other and gave it a little shake. "Are you ready to join the merry throng? They'll all be gone soon."

"Keep our two friends with us if you've already spoken to them about it. At least until we see how we all like it."

"That's what I thought. We'll play it by ear."

They adopted a stately pace and joined the group on the veranda. Ernst's arrival had its usual effect. They all sat up more alertly, voices became animated, there were bursts of laughter as he exerted his enormous effortless charm. Gerry heard him order a double Bloody Mary and began to relax.

Yorgo appeared at his shoulder and handed him a sheet of crested stationery. "That's all the information about your money. I've had to make special arrangements because of your not having a passport but I don't think you'll have any difficulty. That's the name of the bank manager here."

"Thanks a lot. You've heard we've found a house here? Get the passport particulars from Hank and André. They'll be staying with us. Don't let me forget to give you our telephone number." Yorgo circulated with his portfolio, giving them all his attention and making notes.

Nesta joined them and Gerry watched her and Ernst become fast friends in moments. There was nothing to worry about. Ernst looked as if he'd already forgotten that he'd said it was important to leave soon. Everything would be fine as soon as they'd taken the measure of their new circumstance and new setting. He had to get over living every moment as if it might alter his whole life.

Lunch was an eternity for him. Everybody seemed to dawdle over their food. They even gave the appearance of enjoying themselves. An old grandfather's clock swung its pendulum at one end of the vast dining room and he watched every minute tick past. At times, he was ready to swear that it was going backward.

The moment finally came when they were all gathered once more on the veranda. Antiquated cars were drawn up at the foot of the steps leading down to the street. Sacha weaved about among their legs, sniffing everybody. There was a great flapping of sarongs as porters piled luggage into the truck on top of heaped-up salvage from the yacht. Extravagant kisses and embraces were exchanged and they all promised to keep in constant touch for the next week.

Solange had a hurried private word with Gerry. "I never really expected him to agree, darling. Your magic touch. Take good care of him. I know you will. Nesta's given Yorgo your phone number so we won't lose each other." They kissed fondly.

"Such a splendid old house. You're lucky to have it," Mrs. Farr assured Gerry as she passed. "We've enjoyed our stay."

There was much slamming of car doors and more flapping of sarongs and the convoy rolled into motion. Silence descended.

"I've had such a good time," Nesta said, breaking it with her sweetly lilting voice. "You're all so nice, but I certainly got the pick of the men. The most beautiful boy. The most handsome man. And you two aren't so bad either." She ended with a roguish glance at Hank and Gerry and bubbled with laughter. "The car's all packed. Your valet assured me that everything's there. I've put in two cases of the white you had at lunch. I might be able to get some more if you stay longer. Oh, it would be such fun if you do."

"You've been very very good to us," Ernst said, taking her hand in both of his. "I'm going to try to think of a present that will be right only for you. You'll come to dinner with us, won't you? She must, mustn't she?" He underlined it by turning to the others. The few words defined the change that had taken place. They were no longer host and guests but equal shareholders in a common venture; they could do something as simple and natural as inviting a friend to dinner. They seconded the invitation.

"I have another of my tiresome groups tomorrow. The next day perhaps? You must be dying to see Gerald's house. I'd gladly come just for the sunset. You don't have to give me dinner."

"I want to. I'm a good cook," André volunteered, claiming a role in the household.

She looked at him with a little gurgle of delight. "You sweet boy. I'd love you to cook for me. Thank you, my darling. Gerald, I want a complete report. If you find the slightest thing wrong, I'll never forgive myself." She looked at each one in turn with a radiant smile, as if checking some precious new possessions, and gave a satisfied little nod and turned and ambled away into the hotel, the twin balloons of her behind floating her through the door. Her driver called up to them from the street.

"Car here, masters." He indicated the white station wagon under the tree.

Gerry held Ernst's arm in a firm grip and moved in close to him and studied him. He still radiated the aura of confident glamour he was able to produce in public. He smiled gently at Gerry. "You're really wonderful with people, darling."

"I was thinking the same about you."

"No. With you, I can make friends in a way I never have. Ordinarily, I probably would have paid no attention to Nesta. She's a complete delight." They started down the steps. Sacha barked behind them.

Gerry turned. "Oh dear. I've forgotten to say good-bye to Sacha." The dog was leaping and prancing on the top step.

"He's not allowed in the street, master," a waiter explained, flicking a napkin at him. Gerry took the few steps up to him and calmed him and patted him on the head. "There. Be a good dog. I'll see you soon." He ran down the steps and gave André and Hank a hug and resumed his place at Ernst's side. "It pays to have friends everywhere," he said. The statement elicited Ernst's clear boyish laughter and another thrill of delight ran down Gerry's spine.

They climbed into the car, Gerry in front with the driver as guide and interpreter. He twisted around in the seat as they started off and surveyed his companions. They looked like people he would enjoy being with. The most handsome man, the most beautiful boy, and Hank wasn't bad either. Hank had his arm up on the back of the seat around André, who was in the middle. He beamed at them. "Is everybody having fun?"

"I am," André said. "Hank practically has his arm

around me in public. It's the last gasp of Western civilization."

"I'm getting ready to throttle you," Hank said amiably, moving his arm around his neck.

"Is it the heat of passion that's scorching me or is it just bloody damn hot?" Ernst inquired.

"It's hot. I didn't realize how hot, once you get away from the hotel." He dropped a hand onto his knee. Ernst put his on it. "Maybe I should take you all out to the house and come back for my chores."

"Nonsense, darling. We're all in this together. What are you planning to use for money?"

"We've got some."

Ernst leaned forward to the other two. "Isn't it nice having somebody to take care of us? Perhaps we should stay here for the rest of our lives and let him provide."

Gerry was touched but told himself that he must get over being astonished whenever Ernst behaved like a human being. That was what this operation was all about. They rounded the playing field and they all exclaimed over the cricket game that was still in progress. Cows lay about on its outskirts.

"Is there a town?" André asked.

"I think this must be it." They veered away from the sea road and entered a long narrow busy street with a row of shabby two-story shops on either side. They inched their way among bicycles and people and bullock carts and drew into an ill-defined square containing an open market under a low wide roof. They parked beside a nondescript fountain or trough with sculptured blue-painted elephants around its base. People ebbed and flowed, looking cheerful and clean. No beggars swarmed around them. This wasn't India. There was nothing beautiful or even strikingly picturesque to be seen nor was there anything notably ugly. Gerry decided that he couldn't be given any very black marks for bringing them here.

"I'll try not to be long or you'll roast," he said to the three in the back seat. A glance at Ernst assured him that he was taking everything, even the heat, in his stride. He turned to the driver. "We must be quick," he said in Sinhalese, doubting if his halting words would have much effect. They got out and Gerry pushed his way in and out of shops under the driver's guidance, causing a flow of goods to start moving toward the car—crates of beer, bottles of local whiskey and gin and brandy, assorted mixes, tomato juice for Ernst, sugar, flour, salt and pepper, ingredients for curries, rice, coffee, and tea. As he remembered, there were few imports. He found some butter but the only other delicacy available was Australian corned beef. He didn't think Ernst would find it a satisfactory substitute for caviar. He had done the shopping for his two Scandinavians and knew the routine, which shops had what, and cut it as short as he could, hoping that the house would be adequately supplied with toilet paper and kitchen cleanser and the like. He would replace everything they used later but his immediate concern was not to let this become too much of a bore for Ernst. He kept the vegetable market for last and purchased several woven baskets before storming it with the driver.

It was the trial he had expected. The aisles were clogged with slowly drifting women in simple cotton saris who didn't seem to know what they were doing there. The heat under the low roof gave him instant claustrophobia. Men shook carrots in his face and shouted and gesticulated energetically at piles of tomatoes. He stopped at the first stall he came to and committed an act of Western aggression, elbowing women out of his way until he was face to face with the vendor who had seized him and was pulling him in as if he were landing a fish. Vegetables were flung into antiquated balances and dumped into his baskets. He found a pineapple and some mangoes and bananas, and fought his way out, dragging the driver behind him. He stood outside, panting and streaming with sweat.

"We want ganja," he said, taking charge of the baskets.

The driver grinned. "It is prohibited, master. How much do you want?"

"To buy how?"

"Four cigarettes one rupee. Very expensive."

"Get me fifty cigarettes. Very much time?"

"Very quick. Right down there. I'll be back before I go."

"Good. Very quick. To car." He handed over money. A dollar and a quarter. They could afford it. The three in the back seat looked as if they hadn't moved a muscle since he had left them. They didn't turn around when he added the vegetables to their provisions.

"We've discovered that if you stay very still, you don't sweat," André explained. "We're having a contest. It helps not to talk, too."

"Did you think I meant it literally when I suggested staying the rest of our lives, darling?" Ernst asked. "I've never seen so many things."

Gerry returned to the front seat and looked back at them and laughed. "You look like a row of dummies. I made it as quick as I could."

"You were heroic to have done it at all," Ernst said appreciatively. "Are you finished?"

"The driver will be here in a second. Who's winning the contest?"

"I am, of course," Ernst said. "I have a natural talent for repose. These two fidget."

They continued their good-natured banter. Gerry felt a comradely harmony between them that hadn't had an opportunity to evolve in the ceremony of life on board the yacht. It flowed through and out of Ernst. He had become one of them. He hoped the driver wouldn't spoil it by getting lost. He couldn't expect them to go through much more of the excruciating heat without tempers beginning to fray. He saw the driver drifting through the crowd and honked the horn. He broke into a trot.

"Come on," Gerry burst out in English as he got in behind the wheel. "Let's get out of here." The driver handed him a small packet wrapped in newspaper.

"Very good quality, master."

"Thanks." He realized that his was the only impatient voice that had been raised so far. He turned and touched Ernst's knee. "I'm sorry. I feel responsible for making you all wait. It won't happen again. If we have more shopping, I'll do it at dawn."

"You were doing it for us, darling," Ernst said with sweet reasonableness. "We have no complaints."

Was Ernst actually going to enjoy the unfamiliar aspects of routine life? In another few minutes, they had turned back onto the sea road and a breeze swept through the car as they put on speed. They all shifted about and tugged at their clothes with relief.

"Wow," Hank exclaimed. "Air. It's beautiful. Where do we go now?"

"To the house. Only another five minutes or so." They

turned inland to pass through the village and then were back on the sea again. Gerry could see the roofs buried in palm trees on the point of land but he said nothing while they all commented on the picturesque fishing boats pulled up along the beach. They crossed the river and turned off the highway and lurched over the rough road toward the long white wall. The driver honked. It was a tense moment for Gerry. Had he been so eager to find a hideaway that he'd looked at it with blind uncritical eyes? The gates swung open. Five half-naked youths were lined up along the drive as they entered and came to a halt amid rolling lawns. The low white house gleamed in its setting of flowering tropical vegetation.

"This is it?" Ernst asked. "Darling, it's quite unbelievable."

"My God," Hank exclaimed.

"How beautiful," André joined in.

"What did I tell you?" Gerry burst out, as pleased as if he'd built it himself. "Just wait." They let themselves out of the car while the staff moved in around them, grinning and chattering. The driver organized a work team to unload the car. Gerry took Ernst's arm and led him to the door hanging in space. They passed through it and entered the seascape composed of the wide expanse of bay, framed by the columns of the veranda and the palm trees beyond. A cool breeze came in off the water. Gerry saw that the columns were in fact palm trunks and immediately grasped the key to the magic of the place. It was an outrageous marriage of the natural and artificial, so artfully blended that the observer was unaware of where one began and the other left off. Furniture was placed where it might have been in an enclosed space with no regard for structural logic, as if in observance of the theatrical convention of the fourth wall. Draperies hung where windows might have been. Arched doors opened onto other arched doors to infinity, confusing the eye with indoor and outdoor views. Over all, the towering palm fronds were a jungle umbrella sheltering the planned and tamed luxuriance of the flora below. The meticulously clipped lawn was the most outrageous joke of all, a lush carpet for Disney elephants to gambol on.

"It's the damnedest thing I've ever seen in my life," Hank commented. "Who could ever've thought it up?"

"I told you who," Gerry reminded him. "Our very own American brethren."

"Oh yes, the faggots, God bless 'em. Long may they reign. I've got to measure it all out. I'll bet it's not much more than a hundred feet long and it looks as if it went on forever. Fabulous."

"I must say, I can't make head nor tail of it," Ernst said. "Is there anyplace to sleep?"

"You probably just walk through an arched door and disappear," Hank suggested.

"That's the general idea," Gerry said. The boys were bringing in baggage. He saw no sign of the provisions so assumed there must be another entrance to the kitchen. "There's a bedroom here and one at the other end. Does it matter who has which? They're supposed to be exactly the same. We have the most stuff so we might as well stay here." He indicated the two bags that were to be taken to the far room and they wandered on along the veranda.

"I feel as if we'd finally reached the ends of the earth," André said with shining eyes. "It's even cool. Imagine going to work in the morning and trying not to go broke before payday. I'm ruined for life."

"We probably all are but don't know it yet," Hank said. "If we stayed here, we'd never find out."

They sat at the first grouping of furniture where there was room for all of them—curious high-backed wicker chairs and a low divan strewn with cushions that Gerry guessed was a bed with its legs cut off. Bamboo blinds were lowered between the columns and big-leaved potted plants brought the garden onto the veranda around them. Gerry pulled off his sweat-soaked shirt.

"This calls for a gin sling or whatever they drink in Maugham," he said. "Does anybody have any objections?" He waved to one of the boys who was putting the last of the bags into the nearby room. He noticed that they had put on shirts in honor of their arrival. "What's your name?" he asked as the boy responded to his signal.

"Hector, master," the boy replied with a flash of white teeth.

"OK, Hector. Can you bring us drinks or should we fix our own?"

"I make, master. Gin and passion fruit? Other masters like it."

"Passion fruit sounds like just the thing. I know I got some. There's plenty of ice?"

"Much ice, master. I go and come?" He went.

"I'd better check supplies and make sure we don't start using things that aren't ours."

"Can I take over in the kitchen?" André volunteered. "I really like to cook."

"Somebody's supposed to do it but it'll probably be local. You can supply the Tour d'Argent flourishes." He reached for Ernst's carryall. "I mustn't let you start missing Paolo. You're supposed to wave at me when you want anything."

Ernst's smile was almost sheepish as he pulled the bag away from him. "Paolo wouldn't be suitable to roughing it in the jungle. Anyway, Hector is much prettier. I'm going to have a cigarette and I'm not going to use that damned holder." He lighted a cigarette and blew smoke in Gerry's face. "I'm really quite clever with my hands."

Gerry was entranced by him. He wanted to go to bed with him while he was in a mood to bring laughter into their lovemaking. It was time to dispel some of the emotional intensity that the drug had built up between them. Relaxed enjoyment of each other was what they needed for the long haul. He reached for his hand and didn't relinquish it when Hector returned with a tray of drinks. He had seen men holding hands here. Nobody thought anything of it.

They were all thirsty and were quickly ready for another round. Gerry and André followed Hector to the kitchen after they had ordered more. It ran along the back of the "indoor" living room and was spacious, well planned and gleamingly up-to-date. André was delighted with it. Hector assured them that the only provisions the other masters had left were locked up and that nothing was needed for the house.

"Then you can tell the driver not to wait. We won't be going out again today."

"You wish fresh fish tonight, master? You give rupees. We buy. Very good."

Gerry gave him some money and went with André to look at the second bedroom.

"What a gorgeous bed," André exclaimed. "We can play house in it. The whole place is a dream."

"How's everything going, darling? I feel as if I hadn't had a chance to talk to you for weeks."

"You mean with Hank? Everything's heavenly in bed and we fight the rest of the time. No, not really. I like him a lot but he'll never be you. He probably thinks the same thing about me."

"Don't be silly. There's no law that says you have to fall in love with each other but I wish you'd leave me out of it."

"You know how it is with me, darling. I had a beautiful time with you and I knew it wouldn't last. I think Hank's out to get you."

"I doubt it. I may've been leading him on in a way—well, I guess I had a little thing about him, but we got that straight last night. You're obviously having a nice affair with him. You might not find another guy like him for a long time."

"I know. I'm really looking forward to being here—all of us being together like this. He'll have a chance to see how things are with you and Ernst. The amazing thing for me is—I don't see how you managed it—it amazes me that I can't imagine making love with you now. Or anybody else, for that matter. Hank's made me really his in that way."

"That's saying a lot for Hank, darling. Hold on to it."

"If Hank holds on to me." He laughed and Gerry put a hand on his shoulder and they returned to the veranda. Hank had shed his shirt and was settled down on the divan among the cushions.

Gerry returned to the chair beside Ernst. "The chef has inspected his kitchen," he said.

"I can't wait to show off for you." André moved in beside Hank and put his hands on his thighs. "You say Gerry's advice is always right. He says I should hold on to you."

Hank's eyes shot to Gerry. Gerry hastily shifted his. Hank looked back at André. "Not out here," he said and they all laughed.

"Shall we have another round and cross it off as a deliciously drunken afternoon?" Ernst suggested. Gerry was all in favor. He became aware of the sun glinting in his eyes through the bamboo blind and saw that it was rapidly descending the sky in front of them, across the wide bay. He rose and wandered along the veranda to where the blinds remained rolled up, offering a view of the lower sky from under the deep overhang of the roof.

"I can see what Nesta meant about the sunset," he called to the others. "We're facing due west. Except for the lighthouse and the hotel, there's nothing between us and Africa."

"I'm glad sombody knows some geography," Hank said. "I had no idea Africa was anywhere around here."

"It's right over there, only a few thousand miles away. The Indian Ocean is lapping on our beach."

"I hope you can't see the yacht," Ernst said.

"No. It's around a point to the north." Long strips of ragged clouds stretched along the horizon. The sky above was clear. As the sun sank toward them they began to catch its rays and light up. "You all better come here. It looks as if it's going to be spectacular."

They moved to chairs that had obviously been placed to offer an unobstructed view of the show. A big glass-topped table was conveniently placed for their drinks. Gerry began to study the site in detail. At one side just beyond the long white wall, a wooded hill rose steeply above them. Farther along where it met the sea, rock had been gouged out of the hillside as if it had been quarried, leaving a bare cliff. On the other side, where the river bordered the property, there were massive rock outcroppings that had been thickly planted, creating a jungle rockery. He saw more handsome wicker furniture sitting about out there, luring them to another living area. Although the whole place didn't consist of much more than an acre, he had the feeling that they had barely enough time to discover all its wonders. A domain of endless vistas.

He returned his attention to the sky and watched enthralled as the sun passed behind the bands of cloud and transformed them into massed armies with flying banners, charging cavalry, landscapes of towers and palaces, galleons under full sail. The blinding ball of fire turned red as it touched the rim of the sea and was slowly drowned. Great streaks and swirls of color were flung up into the sky and the bay was covered with a saffron slick. Gerry had the impression that his head was reverberating with crashing chords, as if the display had been accompanied by sound effects. A profound silence enveloped them as color faded from the sky.

"Maybe not as impressive as your show at Penang," he said to Ernst, "but not bad for a poor country like this."

"It's rather an ostentatious way to call our attention to the fact that the day has ended."

"And the night has just begun. Shall we go get fixed up for it? It's almost time for drinks."

"Which drinks are those?" Hank asked. "Post-presunset drinks or pre-postsunset drinks? Did I get that right? I must be sober."

"I'd better check the boys about their hours. Is dinner at nine OK with everybody?"

"I doubt if we'll be leading a very formal social life," Ernst said. "Why don't we eat when they're ready to feed us?"

Gerry was grateful once again for his sweet reasonableness. "That sounds sensible. Let's leave it up to the chef." He turned to André. "Why don't you talk it over with them and decide what you're going to cook? We'll follow your orders."

"I'm going to get a chance to be boss? I like it here."

They stood and the two couples drifted off in opposite directions. It was getting dark fast. By the time Gerry and Ernst had followed the veranda around to the short walkway that led to their room, several boys had taken over the area where they'd been, wielding brooms and snapping on lights. Gerry found switches for the ceiling fan and the lights, and closed the bedroom door behind them and turned to Ernst with a contented sigh. "I *enjoy* myself so much when I'm with you," he said. "Aside from wanting to lay hands on you."

"Here I am. Aren't you a bit surprised?"

"I was amazed until I decided I shouldn't be," he said. "You're not a nut case. It was a reasonable suggestion. We're together. What could be more normal than one of us going along with something the other wants?"

"I count on you for everything, Gerald dearest." Ernst's smile became youthfully vulnerable and slightly wistful. "Even the impossible."

"When are you going to stop being enigmatic?" There was nothing puzzling about two people wanting each other. It was time for their bodies to find simple pleasure with each other. "Those are my clothes. I want them back," Gerry said playfully. He unbuttoned the shirt and removed it. His hands dropped down over the front of the shorts and for an ecstatic moment remained motionless. He wanted to let out a shout of joy but kept it down to a growl of satisfaction. Ernst was a man again. A vigorous erection sprang into Gerry's hands as he stripped him. His eyes gloated on it but he was careful not to act as if there were anything special about it. Their real lovemaking was finally beginning. When he wasn't stoned, Ernst got hard like everybody else. What had he expected? "God, what a guy. All those chiseled muscles. I'm almost embarrassed to let you see me. I'm such a string bean. Nothing but cock."

"Since I can't take my eyes off it, the rest of you hardly matters."

They laughed as Gerry got out of his clothes. Their cocks swung about and touched while they made erratic progress toward the bed with their mouths joined and their bodies all over each other. Gerry exulted in every sturdy phallic contact. They tumbled onto the bed and Gerry caught a glimpse of the incredulity in Ernst's face before he moved down to celebrate his restored potency.

"Yes, darling," Ernst urged. "Quickly. I'm about to come."

Gerry felt ecstasy swelling the hard flesh and stirring all of Ernst's body and he responded with a surge of lust that launched him toward orgasm. He heard brief cries as his tongue and lips found the rhythm of shared desire. He felt a slight slackening of tension in the flesh his mouth was mastering and he performed the prodigies that had never failed him in the past. He willed his mouth to be the ultimate sex machine and his eyes misted with frustration as rigidity continued to slacken. Ernst tugged at his hair. Without abandoning his efforts completely, he drew back enough to speak. "I'm doing something wrong. Tell me."

"I have."

Gerry heard an edge of bitterness in the reply. He chose to ignore it. He took a deep breath and relinquished the dwindling cock and lifted himself to his knees to display himself in the way Ernst liked, smiling down to demonstrate that there was nothing to worry about. A momentary failure could happen to anyone. "Do you want to see what you do to me?"

"Yes, darling. There you are. So sublimely hard all the time."

"It feels awfully good like that. If it won't get hard for anybody else, you're fairly important to me. You might almost say essential." Ernst flung himself forward and pressed his face against Gerry's erection. "God, darling. I'll come if we don't watch out. I don't want that until I find out how to do everything the way you like it."

Ernst's lips moved against him. "I have no secrets except for things you don't want to know. I've tried to tell you."

"Tell me what? Don't you like me to suck your cock?"

"You can't make me come. I hoped it might work but I was wrong." He dropped back with the look of bleak resignation. He was facing the firing squad. A chill passed over the surface of Gerry's skin.

"But darling, if I can't do it right, I won't."

"You do it thrillingly but something goes wrong. Don't you understand?"

He didn't. He wouldn't. His mind refused to find any meaning in what Ernst was saying. "I understand we haven't really made love yet. What happened when we were smoking doesn't count. Everything's all right now. We can do anything you like."

"I want to watch you with others."

Gerry's scalp crawled. "But I've told you. I can't be with anybody but you."

Ernst began to stroke his own cock. "Why did you bring Hank and André? You want them. I want to see you with them."

Gerry's stomach churned. He felt as if he were spinning into a void. He toppled over onto his back and covered his face with his hands. A sob rose in his chest and he choked it back. Their life together depended on his retaining control. Ernst had offered him truth; he couldn't fail him now. He waited until he felt confident of his voice and finally spoke. "It's not just the opium? Is that what you're saying?" His throat ached. His mouth was dry. He could hardly force himself to put it into words. "You're—you're impotent always?"

"No, not always. The things that excite me have the usual effect. I'm not impotent now. I'm thinking of you with Hank."

Gerry rubbed his face with his hands and let them drop to his side. Ernst had stroked himself erect. Everything was clear at last. All the insistence on Gerry's freedom of choice, the cryptic references to "the miracle" or "the impossible" that had intrigued him as part of Ernst's slightly grandiloquent style, all pointed to the sad calamity of his twisted libido. André had warned him. Ernst didn't want him alone. He felt his spirit wither and he struggled against despair. There must be some new equilibrium they would find once he had adjusted to the fact that their love was crippled.

"You won't see me with Hank," he said, watching Ernst's hand moving on himself. As long as he stayed hard, there was a chance of getting back to each other. "He wanted me last night. I knew it was finished but I let him do it to make sure."

"You let him have you? That's all I'm talking about. To be with you when those things happen."

"But they won't happen. He made *me* impotent. It's all in the mind. You know that." He lifted himself and turned toward him and propped himself on one elbow. He looked down at the moving hand. It was in the mind. If he approached it as a problem that they could talk about freely and solve together, surely they could work their way through it. They had to. His dream depended on it. "You're still hard. This is the longest I've seen you stay like that. It's wonderful. I want to watch you make yourself come."

"Yes. Watch me, darling. Don't go on pretending to yourself that I have no special tastes. We can enjoy them together. You have no inhibitions. In the first few days I knew you, you had had Solange and André and Hank and heaven knows how many roomboys. How could it be otherwise with that sublime cock? I couldn't deny you any right it claims. Of course it's all in the mind, darling. My mind is full of your great cock conquering an army of lovers. I don't want them for myself. I want them for you. We'll always be together. That is my fidelity. You see? I stay hard just talking about it."

Gerry saw it and felt that something in him would break if he were finally forced to accept the fact that they couldn't find their happiness in each other. His own erection had subsided at the shock of Ernst's self-revelation. He dropped back and threw his arm over his face to shut out the world. The chill had penetrated deep into him. He felt cold and dead. Ernst went on and he listened. Was this a cry for help from the soul?

"I talk about special tastes but I don't think they're really very special. There are words for all of it. It's part of every language. Voyeur. Partouse. Gang bang. Many people prefer group sex. The only thing that is a little special about me is that I don't like to be touched when I'm approaching orgasm. Something is cut off. Can you explain why that happens?"

Hope still cast a ray of light into his black despair. He pulled himself up again so that he was lying against Ernst's side with his arms around his shoulders. He kissed his mouth. "Oh darling, I can't explain anything. I'd have to know your whole life's history before I could begin but I've guessed some of it. Fantasy plays a big part in sex for you. When you were stoned I fed your fantasies. The real physical part probably gets in the way. If that's what it is, there must be a way we can learn how to handle it."

"The easiest way would be for you to indulge your natural inclinations for my delight."

"But they're not natural. Not anymore. When I was a kid in New York I was practically a pro. I performed at parties. I learned how horribly empty sex can be. After that, I always hoped for more than sex but I was too silly to get it. I let every new trick distract me from things that might have mattered. We've both missed what we really wanted. We have it now. I'm not going to let us lose it."

"There's no reason why we should. You can take me whenever you want me. I don't have to have an orgasm when you're there."

"Maybe not while it's actually happening, but before or after. We've got to learn how we can make you come with me."

"I've told you, darling. It would always be with you. It didn't matter when I was smoking, but of course I want sex like everybody else when I'm not."

"All right. You said smoking was like a sickness but we got you over it. This may not be a sickness but it's a threat to us. Habit has an awful lot to do with sex. I used to think I couldn't be the active one—you know, couldn't fuck a guy. It made me impotent whenever anybody wanted it. That certainly changed. Let's start from scratch. We both know how to masturbate. Let's jerk off together. I won't touch you. Let's see what that leads to. Now that I know, we can play all the games you want."

"I'm not talking about games. I'm talking about sharing the pleasure you can find with others."

"My only pleasure is with you. All my life—at least, as long as I've made any sense at all—I've hoped for somebody I'd *want* to be faithful to, not because of being afraid of getting caught, but because of wanting and needing to be. I'm so bored with that little hankering in the cock for something new. It's OK for kids but I've had it. I want the big experience of two people opening everything out to each other and living for each other and caring for each other so much that they can't be bothered to look at anybody else. I want you."

"I want you in your unique glory. To see you display yourself to others and know that you're mine—that's my need."

"And if everybody makes me impotent but you? That'll throw a monkey wrench into your gang bangs. Just a minute." He sat up and slid over to the side of the bed and stood. His eyes ran around the room and lighted on the small package wrapped in newspaper. He had bought it in case they ran into some sort of withdrawal crisis. He sighed as he went to it, feeling bruised and battered inside but clinging to hope. He pulled out a cigarette and sniffed its pungent odor. The locals claimed that it was good for every ailment known to man as well as acting as a powerful aphrodisiac. They both needed something now. He was afraid to leave the issue unresolved, even more afraid to precipitate another failure. He couldn't stand witnessing Ernst's humiliation. He had never felt so unsure of himself in his life, although he was very sure that the point he was making was vital to their future.

There would be other Hanks who would intrigue him if he was ready to be intrigued. He would surrender again to all the weaknesses he had struggled against and overcome—the trivialization of passion, the dulling of sensuality by overindulgence, the quest for momentary sensation that ended by making life meaningless. He felt some spiritual muscle stiffening in him that caused a physical ache in his chest and abdomen. He mustn't give in. He would offer Ernst sympathy and understanding by helping him redirect his needs into the satisfactions that only two people could find together. It was all in the mind.

He put the cigarette in his mouth and lighted it and

took a deep drag. His head reeled and his senses seemed to jangle into some strange new alignment. "My God," he exclaimed. "This is powerful stuff." He went back to the bed and offered it to Ernst. He took it, sniffing.

"What is it? The local hash? I've had it. It's rather coarse. It just gives you a silly high." He spoke with a touch of the petulance that infuriated Gerry.

"I didn't expect it to be the choice of connoisseurs. I thought it might give us a new slant on things."

Ernst inhaled and held the smoke and, after a moment, smiled. He exhaled without releasing any smoke. "It's rather nice, much better than what I had before. How clever of you to find it, darling."

Gerry lay on his stomach beside him again and turned his hand so he could take another puff. His head began to float and his limbs became oddly heavy. Ernst's proximity and his unexpected pleasure sent a charge to his groin. He shifted his hips to accommodate growth and watched Ernst's smile spread while he held his second drag. They both laughed for no discernible reason.

"Where were we?" Gerry began to stroke Ernst's hair. It was beautiful stuff, pure gold, and slipped through his fingers without his feeling it. "There's a lot to explain before we get zonked. I've been stupid. Maybe you tried to tell me about this and I wouldn't listen. Will *you* listen? You've got to understand why we have to do everything we can to change it." They continued to share the cigarette in alternate puffs.

"I'm willing for it to change. I want what you want. You know that."

"You've got to understand how important it is for me. If having others with us would make us closer, I'd be all in favor but it wouldn't work like that."

"How do you know unless we try?" Ernst asked, expelling air. Their faces were very close. By looking into his eyes, Gerry felt as if he could show him his mind.

"I've tried everything and ended up with nothing, least of all self-respect. You make me feel as if I could be worth something." Gerry felt as if he'd taken a long time to say very little. He tried again. "Once upon a time, I made love with my mother. Not in any big way—just her mouth on my cock. I can't say it ruined my life—it wouldn't be fair to her—but it took me a long time to understand what it *did* do to me. It made me feel that there weren't any rules. I felt free to do anything I liked without thinking about right or wrong. Maybe there isn't any right or wrong except in terms of what you do to others, but that's the part I didn't take into consideration. It took me until this year with Jack to understand completely. He made the rules and I followed them and I was happier than I'd ever been. That's what I want with you—to live through you, and for you to live through me. If you give me beautiful boys, I'll be trapped again in a life where nothing matters. We'd lose each other. It would destroy me. You too, I think. There isn't all that much time left. We've got to help each other escape from what the past has done to us." Ernst lay motionless on his back holding the stub of the cigarette. Gerry looked down over the powerful body at his side and his eyes were held by his cock, taut and well filled out and smoothly aggressive. His brain seemed to take a long time to grasp the fact that it was erect.

With one swift movement, he disposed of the butt in an ashtray and seized his hand and folded it around the exciting cock and set it in motion. He slid away from him and was somehow on his feet, although there seemed to be a cushion of air between them and the floor.

He moved according to some plan although he wasn't quite sure what it was. Time kept slipping cogs. He found himself with a towel over his shoulder. He pulled on a pair of shorts. His erection looked grotesquely big jutting out from the open fly. He was a pornographic pinup boy. He swallowed a fit of the giggles.

He got the jar of lubricant from Ernst's toilet case and put it on the bedside table. He dipped a hand into it and applied it to himself in long slow strokes. He kept his eyes averted, as if he were preparing himself for an imaginary lover. He heard Ernst gasp and cry out and he raised his eyes. Pools of milky fluid were scattered across his chest and shoulders. He lifted himself quickly over him and wiped him with the towel and rolled him over and entered him with one long thrust and had an immediate orgasm.

He gripped him close and began to drive slowly into him with undiminished vigor. "Was that the impossible?" he gasped. He had a sensation of almost unbearable ecstasy with the tremors of his orgasm still racing through his loins. "You came with me."

"Yes. Alone with you. My God, darling. Your cock. You're a god."

"Am I? I made you come. I'm going to come again. You're going to give me everything my big cock wants. I want you to worship it and keep it for yourself."

"How can I? It was more enormous than I've ever seen it. It was ready to take a host of worshipers. It can't be curbed or tamed."

"Sweet Jesus. Feel what's happening now. It doesn't feel tamed to—" He broke off with a shout and made Ernst's body the instrument of his satisfaction and was shaken by a conqueror's orgasm. He moved in him again and the conquered body responded to his bidding. "You're almost hard again," he murmured.

"Yes, darling. You're my divine husband. An insatiable god. I'm serving you as I want everybody to serve you."

"I'll make you want to be the only one."

"You don't understand addiction. Addicts always want to proselytize, like members of a cult."

"OK. You organize a cult but first you're going to be the apprentice high priest. Maybe for a long time."

When Gerry returned from the bathroom, he dutifully gave his attention to the luggage while Ernst lay on the bed and watched. The high was passing. He tried to sort out his thoughts while he organized Ernst's belongings. He felt physically as well as spiritually battered—the cigarette had given him a headache—but a deep sense of fulfillment sustained him. Patience and an effort of the imagination and an arrogance that was quite foreign to him would be required, but he had broken the pattern of Ernst's desires. He hadn't succeeded in giving him a second orgasm but there was nothing troubling about that; once was enough for lots of people. Apparently Ernst had lost, or had never had, confidence in his ability to make love satisfactorily. Gerry was sure he could get him over that. Ernst's readiness to pledge fidelity, if not demand it, matched his own. He felt as if he'd made his way through a labyrinth. From now on, he would know where he was going.

"I'm a lazy valet," he said, breaking a silence. He went to Ernst and sat on the bed beside him and looked into the clear blue of his eyes. His handsome face was composed and looked more relaxed than Gerry had ever seen it. A clean-cut Aryan Superman, with not a complex to ruffle the surface of his wholesome good looks. He leaned over and kissed him. "I've got out your dressing gown and some things you can use here. There's no point in unpacking much. What're you thinking about?"

"Nothing that could be called thought, darling. Watching you. I love to see you fooling about with my things. Wondering if anybody could be as good as you seem."

"I'd call that a thought. A very nice one. Aren't you ready for a drink?"

"It must be that time. Do you have more hash? You think of everything. We might have a few joints after dinner. We can share it with the others."

The others were already having drinks on the veranda when Gerry and Ernst appeared. They were all greeting each other when the telephone rang. Gerry had spotted it on a table in the inner room and went to answer it. Yorgo was on the line, reporting that everybody was happily installed at the Galle Face in Colombo.

"The Horrockses are with you?" Gerry asked.

"Yes. I don't think they're planning to go anywhere. The Farrs are going to Delhi tomorrow. He's being given some sort of special diplomatic papers. Heinrich is going to Bombay with Ken as soon as they can get away. Have you done anything about your passport photographs?"

"No. I'll see if we can take care of it in the morning."

"Good. I'm coming down tomorrow with the marine engineers. Maybe I can collect them then."

"OK. If we get them, I'll leave them at the hotel for you. Any news of the police?"

"Nothing of any importance. They've done the usual—special alert at the airport and so forth. The only thing that could be easily identified is the picture and I knew Ernst didn't want me to mention it. I've started things moving through our private channels. He'll probably be able to buy it back in the course of time. Do you want me to come see you tomorrow?"

"There's no need to. Just a second." He put his hand over the instrument and called to Ernst through an archway. "It's Yorgo. Do you want me to tell him anything?" Ernst waved a dismissive hand. "That's all. Give our love to Solange. Tell her we'll call tomorrow." He hung up, pleased. He had preserved the privacy of their sanctuary for another day. Yorgo's voice reminded him of how hemmed in they'd been, of what a burden traveling with a dozen people could be even in the most luxurious conditions. They would never have felt free enough on the yacht to risk the dangers of this afternoon's confrontation. It was behind them now. They deserved a few days of simple relaxation.

He picked up the phone again and rang the hotel and was put through to Nesta. She gurgled with pleasure when she heard his voice. "Gerald? How nice to know you're so close. Are you calling to make a complaint?"

He assured her that they had none and asked about having their pictures taken. She started to tell him where to go in Main Street but broke off. "Never mind. You'll need the car. I'll send it in the morning. Not too early? About 10:30? The driver knows where to take you."

"It's not inconvenient?"

"Nothing's inconvenient for you, Gerald. Perhaps you'll come have a drink with me before lunch. You're all charmers. I liked the Baron enormously." They said good night and Gerry hung up.

He went out to the others as a round of drinks was being served. "I ordered a whiskey for you, darling. Is that right?" Ernst said.

"Sure. It's the local stuff. I remember liking it."

Hector had been replaced by Rana. Rana, they all agreed when he was out of earshot, was a dish, lovely-looking in an androgynous, Western rather than Oriental way. He had looked at Gerry with a charming smile when he'd offered him his drink, unlike the others' mechanical flashing of teeth.

"He has a real body," Hank commented. "The others look as if there's nothing but sticks under their sarongs."

"Look who's thinking about what's under their sarongs," André teased him with a lover's familiarity. "We're eating in little less than an hour. They all seemed to think nine was reasonable. I have to go attend my casseroles—I mean, pots—in a little while. The boy in the kitchen knows what he's doing. Dayendra. Is that a name? It sounds like a flower. He says they all have regular shifts but don't pay much attention to them when masters are here. I'm getting to rather like being a master." André was in high spirits and made them all laugh at his adventures in the kitchen. Rana remained within view, ready to replenish glasses at a signal. A gentle breeze brought cool air from the sea. Gerry didn't think even Ernst could have any serious complaints.

"You'll have to eat the minute I tell you to," André announced as nine approached. "I have to get used to the oven." He went off for a moment and returned to summon them to table in a bustle of happy self-importance.

They followed the veranda around the corner at the far end where massive antique dining-room furniture was set about in a room without walls. The table was inviting with smart modern cutlery and place mats. *House and Garden* in the jungle. When they had seated themselves, André supervised the presentation of a model soufflé. They all applauded its perfection and he beamed angelically. It was the auspicious beginning of an excellent meal, followed by a poached fish with hollandaise sauce. With the simple ingredients available, André had created a mini-banquet.

"You're a pretty good kid to have around," Hank admitted when the meal had been completed with flambéd bananas. They held hands on top of the table and exchanged a long loving look. Gerry looked at the chains and wondered if André was getting close to losing one.

"This wine really is quite dreadful," Ernst said, looking at his glass with astonishment as if he'd just noticed what he'd been drinking.

Gerry laughed. "Blame André. It's French. We're lucky to have any at all."

"Did Yorgo say anything about the wine on board?" Ernst asked.

"Yes. He took some off. We've probably broken every law in the land."

"Several lands. It was bonded. I suppose he knows what he's doing."

Gerry liked his taking an interest at last in the fate of his possessions; he wasn't completely anesthetized by money. Perhaps he might begin to want to identify the perpetrator of the crime.

They carried wine to the area they now referred to as Maugham Corner, amid the big-leafed plants, and Rana served them coffee. At Ernst's suggestion, Gerry brought out several joints and lighted one and they passed it from hand to hand. It was André's first experience with a drug and he began to giggle a great deal. Time played its tricks on Gerry. His sense of place remained unimpaired but he felt as if an invisible layer of cotton insulated him from his surroundings. It took him a long time to lift the cigarette to his lips and an equally long time to find the hand that was waiting to receive it. They finished the wine and ordered long iced drinks. The light was dim in their corner. The leaves cast mysterious shadows on the blinds. Gerry was aware of lighting another joint and then perhaps another, although he wasn't sure that it wasn't only the memory of the last one he had lighted. Their voices drifted into the night in disjointed conversation and bursts of laughter. They signaled for more drinks.

"I feel like doing the most outrageous things," André said with a giggle. He sank back into the divan, pulling Hank down with him, and they became one form in constant undulating movement. Small whispered cries and giggles escaped from it.

"You're charming. Don't stop," Ernst said approvingly.

"They don't look as if they had any intention of stopping." Gerry was seized by a paroxysm of laughter.

"Don't you want to join them, darling?" Ernst murmured at his side.

Gerry wasn't shocked by the suggestion although he thought perhaps he ought to be. It didn't matter. He wanted to stay with Ernst. His aroused sex strained against his shorts and he expected to be in bed with him soon, although this thought too carried with it an uncertainty he couldn't fathom. Was anything wrong? Ernst was looking at him lovingly. They were together.

They drained their glasses and signaled for more. Gerry made some lucid remarks about the effects of the ganja but noticed that Ernst looked amused. "Am I saying something funny?"

"Very funny, darling. It's one of the effects you're not aware of."

"You may be right. I thought I was being terribly interesting. Of course, it takes a superior intelligence to follow the subtlety of my thought."

The form on the divan subdivided and became two as Hank slowly sat up. "Jesus," he said in a dazed voice. "We'd better go to bed. Where are we?"

"In the land of your dreams," Gerry told him.

"Are you still here? Hey, Andy. We better get out of here. I think we've disgraced ourselves." They pulled themselves to their feet, their clothes in considerable disarray, and bowed unsteadily. "Gentlemen. We wish you a very good night." They put their arms around each other and lurched slowly off along the veranda.

Another joint suddenly appeared on the table in front of Gerry. "Hey, there's another one. Did you just put it here?"

"No, darling. You've been handing them out."

"Funny. It wasn't here a minute ago. We better finish it off." He lighted it and took a drag and handed it to Ernst. Rana appeared beside them with fresh drinks.

"Like other masters," he said with a winning smile. "Many pegs. Much ganja. Masters play together. Very jolly."

"Are you intimate with the other masters?" Ernst asked.

"I not understand, master."

"Do you play with them?"

"Oh yes, master. Blow jobs. Other masters give ten rupees for blow job, isn't it?" The phrase dropped from his lips as innocently as if he didn't know what it meant.

"I'm sure it is," Ernst said with a purr of laughter. Rana was standing at his side. He took his hand and the boy let him hold it as if he expected it. He took a step forward and turned to Ernst as if offering himself for inspection. His face had a serene composure that wasn't marred by any hint of suggestiveness. "You're really quite beautiful, Rana. How old are you?"

"Old, master?"

"How many years have you lived?"

"Age twenty, master."

"We're not keeping you up too late?"

"Oh no, master. Not late. One-half after eleven. I wait for masters bed."

"Have you noticed his hands, darling? They're extraordinary."

Gerry tried to focus on the extremities in question. He saw long graceful dark fingers resting on Ernst's palm. He was watching and listening to a dream. The exchange seemed to have some special meaning for the two engaged in it. Ernst struck him as being amazingly rational and authoritative. He smoked and drank, letting himself drift under his guidance. He was smashed; it was the only thing he was absolutely sure of. They continued to converse in snatches while the boy glided about performing inexplicable chores. It was too much trouble to try to follow what they were saying.

"Yes, I think so," he heard Ernst say, presumably in reply to some question he had missed. He wondered if he had been asleep. Rana was standing at Ernst's side again, their hands joined. "Rana is going to lead me through the perilous night, darling." Ernst rose with what impressed Gerry as great dignity and put his hand on the boy's shoulder.

"There's no need. I'm here." Gerry started to rise and settled back, deciding to give it some thought.

Ernst laughed. "I'll send him back for you."

Gerry concentrated on getting out of the chair. When he felt his feet under him, he started walking rapidly backward but caught himself and managed to reverse. He selected as his target the lighted bedroom door and made cautious progress toward it, remembering to make allowances for the walkway that led across to it. He had lost track of Rana but saw Ernst getting undressed. He made the last few feet across the walkway safely and closed the door and fell against it and fumbled with the key. He turned victoriously. Ernst was standing naked with a splendid hard-on. The boy stood nearby, still clothed.

"I've locked us in," he explained, going to Ernst to take charge of him. He wasn't sure he wanted the boy to see him like this.

"Rana and I have erections. What about you, darling?"

"What do you expect with you like this?" He forgot the boy while he kissed Ernst and let him find it for himself. He laughed at the marvelous sense of release as it swung out free from his shorts.

Ernst stepped aside and turned to the boy. "You see? What did I tell you?"

"Very big, master," Rana said, gazing at Gerry serenely. "Other masters big. This master most big."

Gerry threw off his shirt. "What's going on?" He tried to keep Ernst at his side but almost fell as he eluded him. He remembered. This was what Ernst wanted. He had the feeling that some agreement was being violated but he couldn't remember what it was and let it go. If he could give Ernst pleasure, what difference did it make? Rana dropped down in front of him and lowered his shorts and briefs to his ankles almost without his feeling it. He stepped out of them. Lips moved on him as lightly as the touch of a butterfly's wings, sending delicious little shivers of pleasure coursing through him. He glanced toward the bed. Ernst was settled on the far side at the head, half reclining. His eyes were on them, his hand moving on himself. He looked expectant, like somebody waiting for a show to begin, and Gerry laughed. He leaned over cautiously and urged the boy up. Rana stood in front of him, his eyes meltingly direct and trustful, a sweetly hesitant smile on his lips. Gerry reached out to touch his shirt and was surprised to find him so close. He gave it a tug.

"Naked, master?"

"Of course." If they were going to put on a show, he wanted to make it a good one. Rana's clothes dropped off. Gerry blinked. He had dreamed up a beautiful body constructed with delicate refinement. The dream didn't make much of the cock but it was shapely and was obviously not motivated only by money. Gerry felt so densely insulated from everything around him that he was astonished to find a cool supple body pressed against him. He moved his hands over it, discovering that it was real and felt as lovely as it looked. "You're beautiful," he said. "Shall I kiss you?"

"Oh yes. Please, master." They kissed and started for the bed. Everything about the boy was exquisite, the way he moved against him and the touch of his lips and hands. Gerry felt as if he had captured some shy wild woodland creature. He reminded himself that he was holding a boy who was being paid for his services. They slid down around each other onto the bed. Gerry welcomed its support and began to feel more sure of himself. Rana dedicated himself to their bodies' pleasure with delicate ingenuity. His movements were those of a dancer, slow and sinuous, flowing from one position to another. He handled Gerry's cock like a ritualistic instrument, holding it lightly and guiding it over himself. Nothing jarred.

The butterfly touch of his lips was a sensual marvel but threatened to put Gerry to sleep. He stirred himself to participate and was briefly aware of Ernst's rapidly moving hand. He had a smooth effortless orgasm without expecting it and roused himself again to offer the boy the services of his mouth. He sank back gratefully at last and caught a glimpse of Ernst's handsome back disappearing into the bathroom before he plunged into unconsciousness.

He awoke to the raucous din of crows and, in the distance, a full-throated chant interspersed with wild shouts, an odd savage sound that suggested a native uprising. He remembered where he was. He was holding Ernst's morning erection, the first he had had with him. He smiled and gave it a squeeze and released it and rolled away from him. His own lay heavily on him, despite what felt like a fairly disastrous hangover. He pulled himself up out of bed and went unsteadily to the bathroom and began his usual morning routine. He was almost finished and his head was clearing when he remembered how the evening had ended. He froze into immobility and felt his cheeks burning. Had it really happened?

His memory was like a dream. He and the boy and Ernst? Anger flared up in him. Ernst had taken advantage of his stupor and disregarded everything he had said for the sake of his kinky pleasure. He was shocked by his own acquiescence. He had surely acquired enough strength of character for it to operate when he was smashed. No more ganja.

He was able to move again and finished in the bathroom while his resentment grew, although pity would have been more appropriate. Jerking yourself off while watching others enjoy themselves was a pitiable satisfaction. He had pledged himself to taking care of Ernst. Anger wouldn't do any good. He had to help him.

He passed the bed where Ernst still lay inert and went to the bureau where he had left his watch. 9:30. Early for Ernst but he remembered that Nesta was sending the car. He went to the door and opened it and peered around it. Rana was sweeping the veranda nearby. He called his name and he turned and his face brightened. He propped his broom against a column and approached.

"Are our friends awake?" Gerry asked.

"Yes, master. Breakfast now." He met Gerry's eyes directly and with gentle friendliness. Something about his smile acknowledged their intimacy without self-consciousness or embarrassment. Seeing him in the sober light of morning, Gerry understood better his weakness. His face was not only lovely but had great quiet charm. He ordered a light breakfast for both of them and closed the door and returned to the bed. He sat on the edge of it and touched Ernst's leg.

"Is it time to wake up, darling?" he asked from the depths of the pillow without stirring.

"I'm afraid so. We have to have our pictures taken."

Ernst uttered muffled laughter. "You were beautiful last night."

"We'd better not go into that until we've had some breakfast." Gerry kept his voice light and noncommittal.

Ernst heaved himself about and sat up and moved in against his back and rested his head on his shoulder. His hands moved around over his chest and down to his sex. "You're not angry, are you?"

"I don't want to be. Ashamed of myself more than anything else."

"Why should you be, darling?" He caressed his sex. Gerry tried to hold it between his legs but it lengthened and hardened and, when Ernst extricated it, rose under its own power. "You must accept the fact that you're a phenomenon and act accordingly."

"Because I've got a big cock? It's not enough."

"Perhaps not, but there is so much more." His hands had learned where Gerry liked to be caressed.

"Maybe that's what we should talk about." He found it difficult to hold out against him. He reached behind him for Ernst's erection and felt it dwindling in his hand. Fair enough. Morning erections didn't count. "How are you, darling? No hangover?"

"A hangover? I don't think so. Let me go to the bathroom, darling. I'll be right back."

Gerry watched his handsome back disappearing into the bathroom. The last image he retained from last night. Had Ernst made himself come? He supposed so. Sad and lonely. Genuine pity knotted his throat—anger was gone—but he didn't want to pity him. He wanted him whole.

He lifted his legs onto the bed and pulled the sheet up around his waist and punched the pillows and sat back against them. In a moment Ernst returned looking stunningly fresh and alert, and climbed over him and dropped down beside him with his head on his chest. He pulled the sheet back and began to do exciting things with his mouth. Gerry put a hand on his head.

"We'd better wait, darling. Breakfast will be here any minute."

"I think I'll have breakfast right here." They laughed and Ernst continued.

"Then hurry. I'm awfully close." As he spoke, there was a knock on the door and Ernst rolled onto his back and reached for the sheet. As he did so, Gerry saw that he hadn't been aroused. He adjusted the sheet around him and called out to admit Rana with a tray. The boy stood at the foot of the bed and smiled at them serenely.

"I'm so glad it's you," Ernst greeted him. "Good morning."

"Just put it over there on the table. We'll take care of everything." Gerry watched him as he followed instructions and felt an unwanted little hook of connection with him. The boy set down the tray and turned back to them.

"Nothing more, masters?"

"Of course. We've got something here for you." Ernst gave the sheet a quick flip but Gerry was holding it securely around him.

"Don't, darling," he said sharply, trying to keep his voice down. He didn't want to hurt the boy's feelings.

"Don't be silly. You can't object after last night."

"I go now, masters?" Rana asked.

"No. Don't forget what I told you. Take your clothes off." Ernst reared up superbly onto his knees. His erection looked more powerful than it had ever been. Gerry lifted himself to it. Let the boy watch. Perhaps that was all Ernst needed. Having an audience was a small price to pay for working their way through this together. In a moment, he felt the power diminishing.

"It's heavenly, but I told you. With him, darling," Ernst urged.

He dropped back, shocked with disappointment. Lips were instantly on him and he remembered their exquisite touch. He had never been able to accept pleasure without offering it in return. Hostility to Ernst crackled through him like an electric current. He hated him for finding pleasure in what seemed to him their degradation. He pulled himself up abruptly and seized the boy and toppled him onto the bed. His body was as delicately beautiful as it had been in his dream. He attacked it with his teeth. The boy cried out ecstatically and his body thrashed about as Gerry goaded him to a frenzy of excitement.

"Oh, master," he cried. "Master makes it happen now."

Gerry received his ejaculation in his mouth and swallowed it and straightened on his knees and turned to Ernst and began to masturbate with him. The boy slid up around him and tried to take him with his mouth. Gerry held his head and let his tongue dart over him as an accompaniment to his hand while he brought himself to a climax. Ernst's eyes were fixed on them and he let out a cry and fell back as the first jet of his orgasm leaped from him. Gerry was ready and pulled the boy's head back and flung his sperm out over Ernst's body. He scrambled out of bed, lifting the boy with him.

"There. Go, Rana. Quickly," he muttered. He went to the bathroom and gathered up a towel and washcloth for Ernst. The boy was gone when he returned and he washed and dried him and threw the things back into the bathroom. He went to the tray and picked up the glasses of fruit juice and took one to him. He stood over him and drank. He felt sick and exhausted. He drained the glass and looked at him. "We did it together. That's better than last night," he said flatly.

"You're so thrilling with a beautiful boy like Rana."

He took Ernst's glass and went back to the tray and mixed a cup of coffee and hot milk and took it to him. "I hated you while it was happening. It's got to stop. You know that."

"But darling—"

"Haven't you ever tried to do anything about it?" Gerry cut in. "We know it's nothing physical. Haven't you ever wanted to talk to a psychiatrist?"

"To be told things I know already? That I was brought up by a possessive mother who taught me to hate my father so that all my sexual urges were directed toward men? My mother didn't make love to me. I didn't think I was a law unto myself. I was devoured by guilt until I saw other boys doing it. Not actively participating relieved my guilt. That may not be all of it but it will do. The pattern was set by the time I was eighteen. I'm not conscious of guilt with you but I presume it is there. You say sex is habit. Do you expect to wipe out the habits of twenty years in one night?"

"No. I don't know what I expect." He turned back to the tray and poured himself a cup of coffee with a slightly shaking hand. He had to make a stand and he searched for words that wouldn't be unkind or downright insulting. He carried the cup to the bed and sat beside him.

"You said you would be impotent with anybody but me," Ernst pointed out gently. "You were wrong, weren't you?"

"I'm not so sure. You made me hard just now. I got hard last night thinking about going to bed with you. I remember that much. I don't think Rana had much to do with it."

"But if I have that effect on you, why shouldn't we share it with others? Why did you hate me?"

"Because you want me to do things that make me disgusted with myself."

"I would never want to share you with anybody you don't like. Do you mean *I* disgust you?"

"No," Gerry protested. He looked him levelly in the eye. "Nothing people do for sex disgusts me. Some things I like and others I don't and that's the end of it. No, I'm thinking about doing things I wouldn't want to share with you. That's the danger. I never would've dreamed of anything with Rana but now, after the way we just treated him, I want to be alone with him for a little while to make sure I haven't hurt him. You've made me want to have him—fuck him. I could tell that's what he wants."

"You wouldn't require my presence to make that possible?" Ernst asked with a glint of humor in his eyes. Gerry laughed briefly in spite of the residue of hostility that remained in him.

"All right. Let's say I was wrong about being impotent with others. I *was* with Hank, but that may've been because I was already over it. That doesn't change what I'm saying. I *want* to be impotent with everybody but you. I will be if you give me a chance. If you go on throwing boys at me, I know what'll happen. If I see somebody I want, I'll want him for myself. I honestly don't like performing anymore, especially with you. I'm so longing for you not to want me to."

"What are we going to do, darling?" Ernst sounded more deeply troubled than he had up till now. "It seems to me you could compromise in some way since I have no choice."

"But you have. Oh God, can't we forget about sex for a while?" Gerry burst out. "Can't we wait until we both want it so much that it's bound to work for you? I've had too many bodies. I've found you. I want you to be my whole life."

"You *are* my life, darling. Perhaps that is the difficulty. I want you to live for me."

"Then help me make it right for us. Don't you know how sublime it would be if we could give each other everything, just the two of us? We've had it twice, three times I guess, more or less. I suppose this morning was because Rana was here, but still, we had it together. It'll happen more easily and naturally once you know it can. I'm sure of it. Won't you wait and see?"

"Even if you're right, I will still want to see you with beautiful boys. I've tried to explain. It's part of the way I feel about you."

"Maybe later, when it's good with us, I'll feel differently about it. I'm willing to do anything except to feel that we're losing each other. Just give us a little time. That's all I'm asking."

"You don't have to ask, darling. You have only to tell me."

"I thought I had yesterday. I guess I didn't make it clear how important it is to me." He continued to be stunned by how docile and open to reason Ernst was. He had to stop getting so worked up about things. One houseboy wasn't going to destroy all that they'd found in each other. He had made his stand and Ernst had accepted it. They had demonstrated their faith in each other. The anguish that remained was due to his hangover as much as anything else. He leaned forward and kissed Ernst's lips. "We should be getting ready for our pictures. You look superb. I haven't dared look at myself but I feel as if I should wear a veil. Maybe a medicinal beer will pull me through."

Hank and André were dressed and ready when Gerry and Ernst went out to the veranda and they all joked about having been stoned. Gerry and Hank decided that beer was their only salvation and they were having some when Hector announced that the car had arrived. The sun was blazing but there was a pleasant breeze off the sea and the palms provided pools of shade. Once they were on the road, the temperature climbed.

"These damn clothes," Gerry complained. "This silk shirt feels like a fur coat. Remind me to get us all sarongs. The natives aren't crazy."

"Did you hear the fishermen chanting?" André asked.

"Is that what it was? I thought they were coming after us with their spears."

"We could see them across the river from our room. They were pulling in their nets on the beach right up here. It was fascinating. Two teams of men hauling in ropes in time to the chanting. I want to sketch them. Will somebody buy me some sketching paper?" André's enthusiasm was infectious and lifted Gerry's spirits. There was more to life than sex.

"I'll buy you a bale of sketching paper," he said expansively. He told the driver to slow down as they approached the stretch of beach. A crowd of nearly naked men were milling about. Boats were pulled up. Coils of nets lay beside them. It was a busily picturesque scene.

"If you like sketching naked men, you'll have a field day," Hank said as they drove on. "I wouldn't mind doing some sketching myself. Let's have a competition. Ernst and Gerry can be the judges."

"I can't think of anything more likely to introduce strife into our happy home," Ernst said. "Gerry and I can fight over who should win and the loser will hate us all. It's pure genius."

He said it jokingly but Gerry thought he detected a bite in it. Was it a warning that he had a will of his own, despite his conciliatory words? He warned himself against being hypersensitive, but better that than to go on blundering as he had in the past.

The photographer made short work of the picture-taking and told them they could collect the prints in an hour. The heat made them undiscriminating shoppers. Gerry picked up the first sarongs he saw and André refused to look for drawing paper but settled for a pad and a few pencils that he insisted would do perfectly. They fled the town for the relative comfort of Nesta's veranda and had cheerful drinks with her while waiting for the pictures. They confirmed the dinner invitation for the following night before she sent them off again in her car. They returned to the house amid gales of laughter over their pictures. They all agreed that Gerry's was the most hideous.

They changed to sarongs and found that they had a tendency to fall off, which led to further laughter. A lesson from Neville, yet another personable boy, revealed that the cloth should have been stitched into tubes to conform to the local style. They ended up looking bunchy around the middle but decent. More drinks and a simple lunch passed the time agreeably. Gerry kept a close eye on Ernst.

Solange's warning about cutting him off from everything he knew was firmly lodged in Gerry's mind. Ernst might adapt more easily to his stand within the framework of his familiar busy social life. He had seized on the house with such high hopes that he was surprised at how ready he was to reconsider. He was treading perilous ground and had to be prepared to revise their plans from one minute to the next.

In spite of himself, thoughts of Maria and the theft continued to nag at the back of his mind. By not telling the police that the chief culprit had been on the yacht, he was withholding the only significant clue but it didn't seem to lead anywhere. Wait and see. At the slightest sign of restlessness in Ernst, he would be the first to suggest moving on.

They were leaving the table to have coffee in Maugham Corner when the telephone rang. Gerry answered it. It was Yorgo to say that he had collected their photographs. He also reported that the marine engineers were at work. "They've been diving since this morning. They hope to have a preliminary report tomorrow or next day. If Ernst needs money, tell him it's in his account in Colombo. I'm leaving a checkbook with Mrs. Brohier."

They had nothing else to say to each other and Gerry hung up. He found his housemates all laughing and teasing André in Maugham Corner because his sarong had fallen off in front of Neville. They were finishing coffee and talking about spending the afternoon on the beach when Nesta's driver appeared with two telegrams for Gerry. "Lady send them," he explained.

One was strangely bulky. Gerry opened the other. It was from his mother, short and to the point: FATHER DIED TWO WEEKS AGO. LAWYERS CONTACTING YOU. PLEASE CALL WHEN POSSIBLE. ALL LOVE DARLING.

Gerry stared at it for a moment, thinking of the man he had been taught to think of as his father. He was briefly saddened, but they had never been close; when he had learned the truth of his parentage, he had ceased to keep any special place for him in his thoughts. He opened the other and unfolded two long pages that he saw were composed in verbose legalese. He skimmed through them, picking up the gist of it. He was to receive the income from six million dollars. There were intricacies about some special trust that he didn't attempt to fathom. The principal was to pass to him on his mother's death. (He offered up a little prayer.) Fifty thousand dollars was immediately available to him pending etc., etc. He took a deep breath and handed the cables to Ernst. He was aware of the others watching him. He tapped his forehead with his fingers.

"I guess I'll get used to it," he said. "I'm filthy rich."

"No bad news?" Hank asked with quick concern. "You look—"

"I'm trying to look properly solemn for my supposed father's death. Poor guy. He was OK but he's been more or less dead for over a year."

"Have you inherited a lot of money?" André asked with awe.

"An awful lot, darling. I'm a very good catch if anybody's interested." He looked at Ernst. He was carefully studying the long legal cable. He looked up with lively interest in his eyes.

"This looks very orderly. I'll put you in touch with my people in Zurich if you like, darling. They've been very clever about taxes for some of my friends. They can go over it with the New York firm."

"But fifty thousand dollars a month or whatever it is. Why shouldn't I pay taxes?"

"Your mother has handled it very carefully so that you will pay as little as possible. She apparently prefers for you to have the money, rather than the government."

"Yes, I suppose I've got to consider that. After all, it's really hers."

"Did you say fifty thousand a *month?*" Hank growled with something like resentment in his voice. "Christ."

Gerry looked at him and met an odd defiance in his eyes. It was a dangerously intimate and challenging look. Gerry's heart skipped a beat. "It's less than that," he said hastily. "I was pulling a nice round figure out of the air. Anyway, it's enough so that nobody can make me feel like a kept boy, not even Ernst." He saw Hank flush and wanted to bite his tongue. He'd forgotten about Ken.

"What is it in francs?" André asked. Before anybody could answer, he let out an excited shout and sprang up and ran out from under the roof. "Look. Come here," he called excitedly.

They were all on their feet to follow him. Hank barred Gerry's way. "What did you mean by that?" he demanded in a tense undertone.

"About being a kept boy? Nothing. Believe me. Ernst's being so rich makes it something I think about."

"OK. I believe you. You're not a bitch." Their eyes were locked together. The hunger in Hank's made Gerry's waver. He was still a force to reckon with. He touched his shoulder and they joined the others.

André was pointing up at the steep densely wooded hillside. "There. I just saw one," he cried.

A monkey catapulted out of a tree halfway up the hill and landed in a treetop below. Three others followed. They looked quite big, with long white-tipped tails. There was a great commotion in the thick foliage, as if there were many of them. They could hear them grunting at each other. André was skipping about with delight. They exclaimed together and laughed as the monkeys continued to swing up and down the hillside with great daring leaps. The trees grew motionless again, as if the exercise period were over.

"How marvelous," André exclaimed, his eyes shining like a schoolboy's. "We really are living in the jungle. Do you suppose there'll be elephants?"

"If there aren't, I'll see that the boys get some," Gerry said. "You're beautiful, darling."

"That was great fun," Ernst said. "We must watch for them."

Stimulated by the monkeys, they decided to go for a swim. Gerry fetched trunks for Ernst and himself and they spread out through the property, taking possession of it. They explored the guest house and found another comfortable bedroom and well-equipped bath. Deck chairs were stacked in it and they took them out and set them up on a brick-paved terrace inside the fence that ran along the beach. Having just put them on, they all took their trunks off to lie in the sun. A few small fishing boats were drifting about not far off shore but the beach appeared to be private enough for them not to cause a public scandal. They began to notice the wild life around them.

Gerry spotted a dinosaur lumbering along the fence. It was a rather small dinosaur, three or four feet long, but it could have served as a model for the real thing. Hank identified a flash of dazzling blue as a kingfisher. Neat little black magpies with yellow Oriental markings around their eyes strolled across the lawn grubbing for insects. A pattern of white markings on the underside of their wings transformed them into harlequins when they took off. A pair of comic jungle crows approached unconcernedly, smoky purple and russet, complacent-looking birds that seemed to have only a tentative grasp on the art of flying. They stood for long moments on the ground eyeing a branch a foot or two above their heads, shifting their feet and flexing their muscles. When they had gathered up their courage, they leaped for the perch, balanced precariously for a moment and plummeted to earth. When they had repeated the performance several times, their human audience was rocking helplessly in the deck chairs.

"What was up with you and Hank?" Ernst asked when the other two had gone through a gate onto the beach, holding their trunks over themselves.

"I can't get away with much, can I?" Gerry laughed, following André's breathtaking behind with his eyes. "It was pretty tactless, making that crack about not being a kept boy anymore. He's sensitive about having let Ken pay his way. I had to explain that I was talking about us."

"I'm very pleased about the money, darling. I know how important your independence is to you. In your case, it wouldn't make any difference if you were a pauper, but it's good for me that I can't bully you with money. It may not sound very romantic, but there are usually difficulties if people aren't on an equal footing financially."

"If you can call us equal."

"Above a certain level, the rich are all equal, darling. You are definitely one of the rich."

"I suppose I am." He removed his eyes from André's behind and looked at Ernst. What he was saying took their future for granted and he was grateful to him for it. "As I said, I suppose I'll get used to it. For the moment it doesn't seem to change anything. I'm still helplessly in love with you, still only thinking about making our own life together, as if we were a couple of kids without a penny between us. At times, I still wish that was the way it was. How romantic can you get?"

"We'll make our life, darling. The pennies won't get in the way, not with you to guide us. I'm very glad we're here. It was important for us to have these few days together."

Gerry had longed for him to say it. He almost leaped out of his chair with joy. He leaned forward and seized his hand and beamed at him. "Do you mean it, darling?"

"When you smile at me like that, I want to fling myself at your feet. Of course I mean it. It was the best thing you could possibly have done for us."

"Oh God, I'm so glad." He bent over and kissed his hand and burst out laughing. The relief of having Ernst's approval was so intense that it obliterated the agonies and strife they'd been through here. He had been right; sexual problems would work themselves out naturally. He looked at him, feeling as if his eyes must be brimming with an unleashed flood of love. "Oh darling, you don't know how happy you've made me."

"You're an extraordinary creature," Ernst said, studying him thoughtfully. "I tremble in awe of you. How good you are. You make it very difficult for me to feel worthy of you."

"You couldn't possibly be. If you were, I probably wouldn't love you. I'm depraved. Let's call Solange this evening and tell her how depraved we are."

"Yes, I'd like to have a natter and hear all the gossip."

"If she sounds as if she's missing us too much, we can always go join her."

"Of course, but we're having Nesta for dinner tomorrow. I *am* fond of her. We'll have another day or two and then we'll see."

"That's what I thought. Come on, darling. I'll race you across the bay and back. The way I feel, I could make it easily. The sea here is rather like tepid tea but you can't have everything."

In their room, showering and getting ready for the evening, Gerry felt as if they were finally settling down together. When they touched, it was soothing rather than passionate, a recognition of each other without inciting a physical expression of their growing mutual dependence. It had been like that with Jack when they weren't actually in bed, as if they had been together a long time and knew there were many years to come. No distractions kept them from getting to the sunset on time. During their telephone conversation, Solange sounded busy and cheerful.

The evening went smoothly. They toasted Gerry's good fortune at dinner. Hank's eyes were on him frequently and Gerry was careful not to let his own meet them. Rana was in attendance again and Gerry had a chance after dinner to tell him that they'd realized they might fight over him if they continued to indulge themselves. "Maybe you and I can get together some time. Would you like that?"

"Oh yes, master."

"So would I. I doubt if I can manage it but we'll see." It was an empty gesture, but he thought the boy was pleased.

Ernst had a few joints but the others abstained. They all agreed that they were ready for an early night. When the time came, Gerry felt relieved of the pressure of passion. He lay beside Ernst in bed without holding him or pressing himself against him. He was content to wait for a signal if he wanted him. They kissed good night gently and Gerry turned the light out.

"How beautiful to have you beside me all night," Ernst said. "I've missed a great deal in life."

"It's bliss. I have everything I want right here, darling." They held hands and slept. He let Ernst sleep late and joined Hank and André at the guest house. Hank made André practice his swimming. Gerry kept his distance. When André said he had to go to the house to check about lunch and the dinner he was planning for Nesta, Gerry made an excuse of getting beer to go with him. He didn't want to get caught alone with Hank. His eyes made him nervous.

He found Hector taking Ernst his breakfast and relieved him of the tray. Ernst was sitting up in bed, combed and alert and wearing his dressing gown.

"They've switched roomboys on me," he greeted him. "I needn't have got all dressed up. Am I missing any zoological wonders?"

"The birds are still falling out of the trees. It's mostly lizards today. A chameleon turned red when he looked at me. I should find out what that means."

"I'm afraid I'm not up on chameleons, except that you can't count on them. No monkeys?"

"Not yet. We're watching for them."

"They're waiting for me, the dears. Have you been up long?"

"An hour or so. I told you I loved you before I left. Didn't you hear me?"

"I did, darling. It set me drifting off into sweet dreams."

The day was off to a beautiful start. No enigmas. All easy and open and clear between them. They had put sex in its place. When it happened it would be like this, natural and relaxed.

The day passed without any intrusions from the outside world except for a call from Nesta at lunchtime to say that the bank manager had called. There was money waiting for Gerry. Did he want the car? He decided to let it go till next morning. Who needed money?

Nesta arrived, all gurgling laughter and girlish flirtatiousness. She gracefully underlined her awareness of the links that joined the two couples with hints and smiles and flattering references to how well suited they were to each other. She was a delight and Gerry was reminded of how much he had liked from the beginning to have his relationships recognized in public.

André outdid himself with his own superb version of a *bouillabaisse*, complete with *aioli*, and a cake-and-fruit-and-nut concoction that they all moaned over. Nesta insisted that she had never eaten such good food and after they had had some local brandy with their coffee, she excused herself for not being able to stay later.

"You all seem to be having such a good time together. It's lovely. Thank you for including me and forgive an old lady her early hours." She departed, leaving them in great good humor.

They stayed up till well past midnight, caught up in the party spirit. Ernst was the first to suggest bed. He took Gerry's hand and caressed it insinuatingly. "Are you ready, darling?" he murmured.

Gerry was immediately on his feet, scarcely allowing himself to believe what the hand had told him. "OK, gang. The old folks are leaving you. You can stay up all night."

"I'm exhausted," André said. "I feel as if I've given birth."

Gerry and Ernst thanked him again and said good night to Hank and left. As Gerry closed their bedroom door behind them, he warned himself not to push things. Let Ernst take the initiative. The way he had held his hand might have been only a momentary expression of affection. He turned to him and his heart leaped up with excitement. Ernst was looking at him with desire in his eyes.

"What a wonderful day it's been," Gerry exclaimed, wanting to rush to him but keeping his distance.

"It has been, darling. Too good for anything to spoil it. I've been waiting for you all evening."

"Have you? I wish I could think of something original to say but I've been waiting for you, too." Their eyes held and they smiled as Gerry took the few steps to him. Their hands lifted to each other and their mouths met. Their kiss was deep and long and unequivocal; Ernst wanted him. Gerry didn't let his hands betray his eagerness. He warned himself again not to try to force it. He drew back and they smiled at each other. "Don't you think we could do without these clothes?"

Their eyes searched each other with mounting urgency as they stripped. They stood naked together and their hard flesh met. They dropped onto the bed into each other's arms and stretched out with their bodies clinging to each other. "Darling. My dearest darling. Oh God," Gerry whispered against Ernst's ear. "Your body is so thrilling. I want to feel every inch of it against me."

Ernst nudged him up so that he was lying out full length on top of him. "There, darling. Let all your weight go to me." Gerry did so their hard cocks pressed against each other. He prayed for Ernst's to stay that way. "It feels so good," he whispered. "I hope we never come."

"I feel as if it might happen very easily."

"Do you? Do you want to watch me and do it for yourself?"

"Can you do us both together? I want to see you."

Gerry lifted himself to his knees, straddling Ernst, and gathered their cocks into both hands and held them together and moved his hands up and down on them. "Like this?"

"Yes, darling. It's heavenly." He covered Gerry's hands with his and held them in a tight grip and began to move his hips. "Look, darling. Our cocks together. Hold them. Make mine as big as yours. Oh God. Make us come."

"Yes. Now. Our cocks are the same. Mine is yours and yours is mine. Watch me make us come."

Gerry felt and saw flesh dwindling. His mind balked at accepting the evidence of his senses. He lifted his eyes to Ernst, trying to keep dismay out of them. "Quickly, darling. Tell me. What should I do?"

Ernst gave his head a slight shake. "It's no use." His face was suddenly bleak with the familiar resignation.

Gerry pitched forward away from him, choking on the frustration of defeat. A sob broke from him. Uncontrollable tears flooded his eyes. "Oh no," he sobbed. He pounded the pillow with his fists. "No. No. No. I'm sorry. It's nothing. I know it's nothing. It doesn't matter."

"I'm sorry, darling."

"Why should you be? What difference does it make? You were almost there. What did—" He was overcome again. His shoulders heaved. Tears soaked the pillow.

"Almost, darling." Ernst put his hand on his head. Gerry seized it and covered it with kisses and pressed his eyes against it to stop the tears.

"I love you so." He reached out and held Ernst's flaccid sex. "Your beautiful cock. I adore it. Why doesn't it love me?"

"This is the way it happens. Something stops. You're the only person who has ever given me an erection without doing anything. That's why I hoped."

"We're not going to stop hoping. Anyway, it's not hoping. It's knowing. I want it so damn—" His voice broke. His sobs became dry and wracking. He had to get himself under control; he was making it a horror for both of them. It was only a sexual frustration, not a great tragedy. Ernst wanted and needed him. He mustn't let that change.

"It isn't very pleasant for me," Ernst said in an expressionless voice. "We could save ourselves this torture."

"Sure. By bringing on the dancing boys," he said with tearful reproach. His sobs subsided. Anger was conquering self-pity. "All right. I'll be your whore, but not yet. It's too soon." It was a cry of surrender. He flung himself over onto his back and felt all hope dying in him.

"Don't you think you might be making the wrong approach?" Ernst continued quietly. "If you would let us have sex as I'm accustomed to, I would probably end by wanting only you. I would be so proud of showing you off as my lover. I would love for people to see you taking me. You would help me overcome my guilt and perhaps whatever is wrong would pass."

A shudder passed through Gerry. He was proposing something that he had done hundreds of times in the past and he hated being reminded of it. He had gone too far to hold out against him. He would end as debauched as Ernst wanted him to be. "Today was so wonderful," he said with a sob quivering in his voice. "I felt so close to you without sex."

"I was wrong to think that things might happen differently."

"Please go on thinking so for a little while. I'll never make a scene like this again. It caught me unaware. If it turns out you're right about yourself I'll accept whatever you say. Let's leave tomorrow, darling."

"If you're ready to."

"Today was good but I don't want either of us to get bored. I've tried to change too much too quickly. Solange sounded as if she's having fun. Let's go join her. We still haven't settled down. I'm sure that's part of it too." He sat up and looked down into Ernst's eyes. They were gentle with love. They would never let each other go. He put a hand on his chest. "I'm truly, truly sorry. There was nothing to make such a fuss about. We'll work everything out. It must be getting late. We should go to sleep."

They took turns in the bathroom and lay together in bed again and held each other and kissed tenderly. Gerry turned the light out. In a few minutes, he heard the rhythm of Ernst's breathing alter as he drifted off to sleep. He was shaken by a long shuddering sigh of relief and the tears flowed again, silently and from the depths of him.

For long minutes he thought sleep was overtaking him, but each time he was jolted awake by the knowledge of his defeat and his mind labored into action again. A pledge of celibacy? Why not, if what they had without sex was worth preserving? Ernst would think him insane and perhaps he was. Insanely in love. Was he right to suggest leaving tomorrow? There was nothing left here but apprehension and wariness. The questions repeated themselves in weary succession until the strain of keeping still became an added goad. He didn't want to disturb Ernst's sleep. He gave up and let himself cautiously out of bed and fumbled around in the dark for his sarong. He could see through the louvered door that the veranda lights were out. He opened the door with care and closed it behind him soundlessly and headed with barefooted stealth toward Maugham Corner. He stopped dead in his tracks as he saw a cigarette glowing in the dark. He had a brief fright and then recognized Hank silhouetted by dim light from somewhere. He had an instant to consider turning back before Hank spoke.

"Hi," he said in an undertone.

Gerry advanced slowly to him. He was sitting on the divan with his feet up. "What're you doing here?" Gerry asked, barely above a whisper. "Where's André?"

"Resting on his laurels, I guess. I couldn't sleep."

"Me neither." Gerry sat on the other end of the divan so that they could talk without raising their voices, but he was careful not to get close enough to touch. Hank too was wearing only a sarong.

"I guess wishing *can* make it so. I was sure as hell wishing you'd come out."

"What for?"

"I'll let you work that out for yourself."

"Please, honey. I'm too shook up already to get started on that again."

"You too?"

"The course of true love never runs smooth."

"If there is such a thing."

"Is life making you cynical?"

"I've been finishing the brandy. That might have something to do with it. I hope you can afford it."

"What is this about money? You seemed peculiar when that telegram came. What's the matter?"

"Can't you guess? It puts you in Ernst's class. What you're doing begins to make sense. You're no longer the guy who flashed his cock at me. Money makes a difference."

"Maybe it does, but I don't feel it yet. If I had it to do all over again, I'd still flash my cock at you."

"Thanks, but I might not follow it up. I don't want to marry a millionaire."

"What about Ken?"

"Exactly. It's what you said about not feeling like a kept boy. His money put me in my place. That's no good."

"No. We agree about that." Gerry could feel it happening without either of them making a move; they were being almost palpably drawn to each other. A physical collision seemed inevitable. Nonsense, he told himself with an impatient little shake of his head. You couldn't *feel* something like that. You could imagine and want it, nothing more. He was reacting in an embarrassingly predictable way. Under the circumstances, Hank's uncomplicated male strength was appealing. If Hank wanted somebody, he could do something about it. It was as simple as that. He adjusted the folds of his sarong to hide what was happening. He wasn't as invulnerable as he had been in the hotel room. Ernst had turned everything upside down. "We may be leaving tomorrow," he said in a neutral undertone.

"All of us?"

"What do you say? Do you like it here? We've brought in enough stuff to last a week. The house is for free. In Colombo we'll just be in a city in a big hotel. I don't know. We might go up for a day or two and come back for you. Do you want to stay?"

"I might be able to relax if you aren't here."

"Good. It's not fair to André if that's what I'm doing to you."

"That's what you do to me, even now that you're rich. I don't know what it would be like here without you. Let's drink to the unknown. There's only one glass." He hitched himself around to bring it within reach. Gerry took it quickly so that their fingers barely touched, and drank. He returned it and Hank's hand closed on his. Somehow the glass was gone and their sarongs were in a tangle around their feet. They were naked in each other's arms, Hank pinning him down. His lips brushed against Gerry's as he spoke. "It's wonderful to feel you like this again. You don't know what it did to me seeing it just hanging there. I told you there'd be a next time."

Their tongues met and their mouths opened and their bodies thrust in hard against each other in the inevitable collision. The thought crossed Gerry's mind to take him to bed with Ernst and he instantly rejected it. Not Hank. There was something too personal between them to share. He struggled away from him and sat up. "We've got to get away from here. Let's go to the guest house and try to make sense."

"God yes. You're making sense already."

They sprang up and snatched up their sarongs and strode out across the lawn. The moon was just coming over the house, nearly full, and silvering the edges of the palm fronds into a spiky network of light above them. It cast a nimbus of silver light around everything. Hank's cock had a metallic sheen and lifted at an indomitable angle; nothing would subdue it but having what he wanted.

They entered the room holding each other and Gerry found the bedside light and they pitched onto the bed, reaching for one another. Their mouths opened to each other again and they resumed the interrupted kiss while their bodies moved slowly against each other. Their mouths parted and they looked gravely into each other's eyes.

"That's very comforting," Gerry said. "I need comfort."

"I want to give you everything you need. What happened to the rules?"

"There aren't any. Ernst would like to see us like this. He wanted to watch us making love."

Hank grimaced. "Jesus. I hope you told him I wouldn't."

"I told him I wouldn't. I didn't know if you wanted me enough to have me any way you could get me."

"Just about, but not that. Not with Ernst. That would really spook me. Not with Andy anymore, either."

"Of course not. None of us wants it. He told me you're the only person he can imagine being with now."

"Yeah, I know he feels that way. He knows all I've been thinking about is having this again with you."

"Poor baby. I should think he'd hate me."

"No. He understands, even though you got him over it. Why don't you get me over it?"

"I sound like a disease." He smiled hesitantly, uncertain how to handle him. He didn't want his love, only his affection and sexual confidence and passion. He put his hand on his chest and toyed with the scattering of hairs on it. "Maybe we'll get you over it tonight. It's taking me a little time to realize that this is actually happening. I've got to get used to the fact that I'm letting it."

"You don't have any choice. You want me with every inch of this fantastic cock. Sitting out there, alone, I was so sure we both wanted it that I almost went in to get you. I want everything about you. When you and Andy talk about being in love, I'm not sure I know what you mean. I'm not even sure I want to but I sure as hell know what I *do* want. I want you. I want you with me. I want us to live together and have the great life I know we could have. Jesus, Gerry, don't you feel how good it could be?"

The muscle in his jaw twitched. Gerry stroked it with his fingers. "I know exactly how good it could be, honey. I happen to be in love and I know what it means to me and how much I need it, but pretend Ernst doesn't exist. I could easily talk myself into thinking we had a chance together, but sooner or later I'd fall in love with somebody else. It's something that's in me that has to come out. That wouldn't be much fun for either of us."

"I'm willing to take my chances. It might be later, rather than sooner. Oh God, sweetheart. Maybe I am in love with you. Being with you now is the most wonderful thing that ever happened to me. I don't know why we're talking about it. I want to show you." He moved down and ran his tongue along Gerry's cock. "I haven't really had this the way I've wanted to."

"Move around, honey. There. I want the same thing." He wanted to make love to potency. He laid his face against Hank's hard flesh and moved his hands over it, feeling its weight and massive solidity. He teased and toyed with it, fascinated that nothing he did made it falter. It grew so rigid that it became almost immovable. He knew that Hank was on the edge of orgasm as his eyes and hands and mouth dwelled on his hard unfailing virility. He made Hank moan and gasp with anticipation and relented finally and they erupted into each other's mouths. Their bodies were convulsed with the release. They lay curled around each other with their heads resting on each other's flanks.

"God, what a cock," Gerry murmured after a silence.

"I've wanted that from the moment I saw you at that party in Penang. Needless to say, I've never tried anything like it. Was I good for you?"

"God, honey. I was ready to come the minute you started but I couldn't get enough of you."

"I've never known anybody who could do the things you do. You could give us all lessons."

They laughed and sat up and leaned against each other and kissed. "Are you sleepy yet?" Gerry asked.

"After that? With you? I want you more now than I did when we started."

"André's not apt to come looking for you?"

"Don't worry. We're very male-female oriented. I do the chasing in our family."

"So it would appear." This was the beginning, a rehearsal for the life Ernst wished for them, a life of compromise and second best. Relieved of frustration, all his thoughts and hopes and desires turned back to him, but his presence wouldn't make it any better—or worse. There wouldn't be many as good as Hank but he wasn't really part of the picture anyway. He was pre-Ernst, in a sense, and had a claim on Gerry's attention. There would be no claims in the future. Bodies. At least he could use his body to help Hank sort out his feelings. He wasn't pleased that he was so glad to do so, but Ernst wanted a whore.

They knelt facing each other, their knees touching, while he restored Hank's erection with caressing hands. Hank reached for him to reciprocate but Gerry pushed his hands away. "I'm doing fine. I want to see." He watched flesh swelling and lengthening until it lifted heavily and stood. His own repeated the process. "My God," he exclaimed. "It gets so hard."

"Doesn't everybody?"

"I guess so, but when yours gets hard it feels like a battering ram."

Hank laughed. "You said that before. It makes me feel like Superman. I want to take you with it."

"I hope so." He felt his wanting it so much was the ultimate infidelity but that, too, he would have to get used to. He lay out on his back and looked at him. He was a beautiful guy. "There's some suntan oil over there. Check the bottles. The oil, not the lotion."

Hank rose and went to the dressing table where they'd left all their beach things. Gerry watched him moving with supreme confidence in the durability of his erection, taking his time to select the bottle and return to bed. He spread his legs and Hank kneeled between them and began to prepare himself. He lifted a cupped hand and Hank poured some oil in it and he applied it between his buttocks.

"I guess I should get a towel," Hank said.

"Don't bother."

"I meant—"

Gerry laughed. "I know what you meant." He lifted his legs and dropped them over Hank's shoulders. "There. Take me, honey."

"Oh my God, Gerry. I can suck your cock, too."
"What's the good of its being so long if you don't?" He cried out as he was entered and filled. "Oh Christ. Oh God, it's good. Oh, Hank honey. Fuck me. I want it." He thought of Ernst and abandoned himself to his body's pleasure.
They went to shower together, groggy with their ecstatic exertions. They soaped each other and touched each other's bodies everywhere with grateful wonder at the excitement they had found in each other. Their fondling of one another became purposeful. Hank stepped up to him and gripped his head with his hands and plunged his tongue into his mouth and bit his lips. He pulled back.
"Jesus," he muttered. "I think I want you again."
"Who's stopping you?"
Hank's eyes dropped. "God Almighty. Look at us."
Gerry chuckled. "It's beginning to be a familiar sight." He soaped them both and turned and joined them and they sank to their knees. Hank took him again on the floor.
When they were upright and under the shower once more, Hank looked at him with dazed eyes, the muscle in his jaw twitching. "Aren't you beginning to feel it? It's so damn right. We belong together."
"We have terrific sex together, honey. The fact remains, I'm leaving tomorrow with Ernst."
"Goddammit, I won't let you. Are you going to tell him about this?"
"Will you let him watch us fucking?"
"No."
"Then what's the point of telling him?"
"But Christ, darling, I *can't*. Don't you understand? It's too damn queer for me. I feel too much about you to put on a show with you."
"I understand perfectly. I haven't said I like the idea. Unfortunate though it may be, I'm in love with him. That's what he wants. That's what I'm going to give him."
"But it's not like you. You're decent. You can't give in to a guy who's sick."
"Sicknesses can be cured. If you're in love with somebody, you do what you can for them. You don't want to know about love. You're probably right."
"I don't know, but I'm honest enough to say so. I know I'd do anything to be with you except that."
"That's it. We have our limits with each other. In love,

there can't be any limits. Maybe there can't be too much honesty either. I'm not sure but I'm undoubtedly going to find out. Come on, honey." He turned the water off and led Hank out of the shower and handed him a towel. They dried themselves in silence. He was moved by the pain and anger in Hank's face but this wasn't a time for tenderness.

"I can't let you do this to yourself," Hank growled at last. "What would happen if I agreed to what you want?"

"God knows but I don't think it would make us fall in love with each other. Don't be an idiot. Stay out of it. Everybody warned me not to get tied up with Ernst. It's my turn to warn everybody not to get tied up with me. I'm going to have my hands full trying to be whatever Ernst wants me to be and keep my head above water. You've helped a lot. There's nothing like good clean sex to clear the mind. Maybe you'll find the same thing."

"I just don't understand you. It's not like you."

"It's like me when I'm in love with Ernst. Don't worry. I don't think I'll let him do anything too bad to me. That wouldn't help either of us." He hung their towels up and put an arm around him and took him back to the bedroom and their sarongs. He tidied up and smoothed the bed. There were a few damp marks on the sheet but they looked innocent. Probably honest sweat. He put the cover over them.

"Shit," Hank said behind him. "On top of everything else, I'm your fucking guest. With everything that's happened, I can't even do what I want to do. Will you lend me enough money so that I can come after you if I have to?"

Gerry turned to him. "I'll leave plenty but don't use it for that. You and André have a good time. It's lucky I suggested leaving to Ernst earlier. We couldn't be together here after this. In a couple of days, everything will've simmered down and we'll have a jolly time in Kashmir."

"Damn Ernst. I still want to get you away from him. I'd like to kill the bastard."

"I'd just as soon you didn't do that. You're speaking of the man I love. I may do it myself." They hitched their sarongs carelessly around themselves and Gerry smiled. "It *is* convenient how these things fall off when you want them to."

"It's been wonderful. I've never known anything like it."

"If we ever want a good fuck, we'll know who to call. OK, honey?" They paused at the door and kissed lightly and Gerry turned the light out as they left.

It was dark out. The moon was down. The sky looked as if it were paling in the east. They crossed the lawn toward the house. "It must be almost four," Gerry said, resuming an undertone. "I hope our boyfriends have been sleeping soundly." They stepped up onto the veranda and touched each other's shoulders and whispered good-nights and parted.

Gerry got into bed with great care and stretched out on his back beside Ernst without stirring him. He felt almost as if Hank were still with him. His body was impregnated with the feel of him but otherwise he seemed remarkably intact, as if he had reenacted some scene from the past without significance for now. It wouldn't have been the same if Ernst had been there. He would have felt as degraded as he had with Rana. Strange. Why did the presence of someone you loved turn a simple experience into an outrage? If he could figure out the answer to that one, perhaps he could go along with anything Ernst might suggest.

It was hopeless, but he snatched at hope wherever he could find it. Oh God, let him learn to make love with me, he prayed. Hope made it possible for him to sleep.

He was up promptly and had breakfast outside so as not to wake Ernst and was waiting when Nesta's car arrived, sleepy but smiling to himself at thoughts of Hank. If he were unattached, he could easily imagine settling down with him. Nothing heavy. Simple and honest and fun. They would get bored with each other in the long run, something he couldn't imagine ever happening with Ernst. Ernst. The love and the torment of his life.

He went to the bank and withdrew all the money that was waiting for him. It was such a bundle that he had it wrapped in newspaper. He went to see Nesta to tell her of their plans and arrange to hire her car and driver for the trip. He told her that they might be back.

"Oh, please do. I couldn't bear to think I'll never see you again, Gerald."

"You will. I love it here. Now that I know you're here, I'll be back, if not this time then soon. I'll get that check off to England from Colombo." They kissed each other on both cheeks and parted.

When he returned to the house, he called Solange to tell her they were coming and woke Ernst with his breakfast. He longed to get into bed with him to get rid of the lingering feel of Hank on him, but knew that he mustn't unless Ernst asked him to.

"Did you get a good sleep, darling?" Ernst asked as he set the tray down beside him.

"Fine." He intended to tell him about Hank but not till after they were gone. It was something he felt they had to discuss for whatever guidance it might offer for the future. "I have the car laid on for after lunch. Solange is pleased we're coming."

"You really want to leave?"

"Don't you think we might as well?"

"Are you terribly upset about last night?"

"No." He smoothed back a lock of Ernst's hair and looked into his eyes and encountered such unguarded pleading devotion that his own eyes wavered and almost fell. He couldn't lie to him, even by omission. He sat. "I told you how sorry I was about the way I behaved. I was being ridiculous. There's nothing upsetting about us, only things we have to work out together, things that I have to learn how to handle. Hank and I had sex together last night after you went to sleep."

An almost imperceptible spasm crossed Ernst's face and was gone in the time it took Gerry to blink. "I thought he made you impotent," he said composedly.

"I was wrong. He doesn't."

"I see. How very strange. I want to kill you and myself. Is that what jealousy does to you?"

"That sounds like it." Gerry's heart began to beat uncomfortably. If Ernst would hold out his arms to him, the incident would be effaced. He was familiar enough with jealousy to know that that wasn't likely to happen. "I thought I had carte blanche," he said, thrilled in spite of himself that he could make him jealous.

"I've offered you complete freedom but I thought it was understood that whatever we do we will do together."

"We understand that, but how many other people will? Hank won't do it front of you. I asked him."

"And you left the decision to him. Is he so important to you?"

"Oh darling, nobody's important to me but you. I like

sex with him, yes, but I'll never have sex again if you say the word. I've told you that."

"Yes, and its rather absurd. It solves nothing. Where was André when this was going on?"

"Asleep, as far as I know. Not with us, if that's what you mean. I couldn't sleep and I went out and Hank was there and it happened. You'd just told me I should let you have it your way and I wanted to find out if I could. At least, that was part of it. Mostly, I wanted him, since I can't have you the way I want you."

"I gather it was a successful experiment."

"Yes. While I was with him, I realized that I'm willing to do anything to be with you. Some father figure I've turned out to be. I'm in love with you, darling." He looked into his eyes again. They were devoted, but thoughtful. He wanted to shake him to make him say what he was thinking. This wasn't the time for thought but for laying everything out in the open in front of them.

"You mustn't hurt me like this. It does terrible things to me," Ernst said. "If these things happen, do you have to tell me about them?"

"Yes, but I can easily keep them from happening. At least, I can now. I don't know what it'll be like after you shove a few pretty boys at me. It's against everything I believe in. That's why I've begged you to wait. We've got to give ourselves a chance for *us* to work things out. If we can't, then I'll do anything you say."

"Do you have any sort of timetable in mind?"

"Of course not, but a matter of a few weeks rather than days. Is that too long to make things right for a lifetime?"

"In the meantime, do you intend to go on having sex with Hank?"

"No. Never again, now that I know. I honestly didn't think you'd care. I admit I was glad to keep him to myself, but that can't happen again because there'll never be anybody else I'll get to know without you. We're finding out everything about each other, aren't we?" He risked a slight smile. "I can't help being a bit pleased that you're jealous. I never thought you would be."

"To tell the truth, neither did I. I'm quite sick about it. You're right. We have to leave. I couldn't stay here with Hank now."

"Are you finished with the tray? Can I take it away and

kiss you and tell you I don't want anybody in the world but you?"

"You can take off your clothes and show me."

"God yes, darling." He leaped up with happy relief. "That's what I want. I want you to hold me and make me feel you want me and that I belong to you."

Hank and André didn't come in from the beach until nearly lunchtime and by then Ernst had had a Bloody Mary and dealt with them both with his customary charm. Hank's eyes when he looked at Gerry were more affectionate but less intense than they had been for the last couple of days. He and André seemed unusually happy together, perhaps in anticipation of having the house to themselves. Gerry turned the bundle of money over to him after removing a small sum for the trip.

"For God's sake, hide it away somewhere safe. Nesta says the boys can't be trusted."

"Is it enough to retire on?"

"You don't have to spend it all. We'll do our accounts when you get to Colombo."

"You're a wonderful guy." He lowered his voice. "I'll never forget last night."

Gerry gave him a wink and a smile. They had lunch and the boys loaded the bags into the car. Gerry tipped them, with something extra for Rana. Hank and André stood in the drive and waved as they drove away. Gerry took Ernst's hand and squeezed it.

"You were very nice to Hank, darling. I'm glad."

"I'll feel better not seeing him for a few days. The fact that you had already had him makes it somehow less distasteful."

"It's the only reason it happened." Miraculously, Gerry found that each new day made their odd situation easier to live with. It was beginning to feel almost normal. Their lovemaking this morning had been full of gentle rewards, even though Ernst's erection had been only partial and brief. His adoration of Gerry's body was deeply moving after the simple sexual excitement with Hank. He was learning to accept limitations and was able to hope again that if they both approached their physical union without the tension of high expectations, Ernst would function again.

They skirted the town and passed the playing field and

after another mile or two, left the huddle of buildings behind and came out into the open with jungle on one side and a long sweep of palm-fringed beach on the other. They rounded a curve and the *Hephaistion* lay before them amid visible reefs. Gerry's first thought was that it must have taken considerable skill to get through them. If they'd hit head-on, the result would have been quite different, perhaps less disastrous. The yacht lay with a slight list, sleek but crippled and desolate. They drove past in silence until another curve spared them further distress.

"Oh dear," Gerry said. "I hope that wasn't too painful for you."

"I was telling myself how much worse it would be if it had been ours. I can let things go that you haven't been a part of."

Gerry stroked his hand. "What a nice thing to think, darling. Have you any idea what we'll do if it turns out to be a total loss?"

"With the summer? How can I when we haven't discussed it? First, I must call off all the people I've invited. You wanted to do that anyway."

"I guess I did."

"So it has all worked out for the best. We start again with a clean slate."

"Shall we go to New York for a month or so?"

"You should, darling, if only for business. Let's see. toward the end of April? That's a pleasant time to be there. Being without Yorgo makes me feel marvelously irresponsible. He would never let me go to New York on such short notice. People might not have time to arrange parties. I'm tempted to get rid of everybody and just live with you. And Solange, of course."

"Oh, definitely Solange."

They had the whole world to consider in terms of their summer plans and they discussed many possibilities without coming to any conclusions. The road, following the coast, was beautiful. They passed through Hikkaduwa and Gerry spotted familiar landmarks.

"There. That's where we used to go in the evening. The house is right back in there."

"Were you happy?"

"We had a good time. I haven't ever been happy until now. No, that's not true. I was happy a lot of the time with Jack but there was something so unreal about it. It was a bit unreal on the yacht, too. The last few days have showed me what being really happy is, in spite of the way I behaved last night."

"And the two boys you were with—I take it you lived with them in the generally accepted sense of the expression."

"Oh, very much so. Cocks all over the place. But there was a difference, darling. I wasn't in love with them."

"Were they in love with each other or with you—or didn't love enter into it?"

"With each other. That's why I got them both," Gerry admitted, wondering if he should go on telling the truth always.

"So you see, people make all sorts of arrangements. I'm not quite the monster you make me seem."

"I know. It's amazing what people do. I wonder if it's possible to think of anything new and different. Give me a little time. Something may come to me."

Ernst laughed. Gerry heard the clear boyish note in it and the thrill of joy it always produced ran down his spine. If they could laugh at it, anything was possible. He would get all the kinks out of Ernst yet.

Their talk moved on to other matters. They pointed out sights to each other along the road. Temples. The remains of cremations. They saw an elephant being bathed in a river and stopped the car to watch. They reached the vast old hotel on the edge of Colombo as the sun was lowering toward the sea. By the time the bags were being unloaded, the staff had gathered on the steps to greet them. Gerry watched Ernst resume his public persona, the stately pace, the air of royalty acknowledging his subjects. Yorgo appeared and took charge. The manager stepped forward and made a little speech of welcome. There was a great deal of bowing and sarongs swirled around them as bearers scurried for the luggage. Ernst had returned to his everyday life and Gerry was his consort.

They were escorted to an elevator and rose a few floors to the top where another escort was waiting to lead them down a wide corridor to their rooms. They were vast, a vast living room overlooking the sea, two vast bedrooms, two vast bathrooms, all done up in stupefying Oriental style, fit for maharajas. Paolo was there, ready to direct the army that came trooping in with the luggage. Gerry felt their life slipping from his control again. Why had they left their beautiful house so soon? Because Ernst was used to grandeur and he didn't want to change too much too soon. Stick to essentials; the frills didn't matter. Ernst was in his element.

"Is Solange somewhere near?" he asked Yorgo.

"Right next door. A similar suite. She expects you for drinks before dinner. She hasn't any plans for this evening." Yorgo held the inevitable portfolio.

"As I remember, there are no plans to make here. What's left of the party?"

"Just the Horrockses. Ken and Heinrich were able to get away this morning. Ken said he'd write and sent regrets for Kashmir. I arranged for the payment to Heinrich. The report came from the marine specialists. It's hopeless. They can't do anything before the monsoon and there won't be anything worth salvaging afterward. I have other news."

"Good heavens. Can't we have something to calm our nerves after our hazardous drive through the jungle? We were practically trampled by elephants." He smiled at Gerry and took his hand and led him to a grouping of golden thrones and sofas. They sat.

"There's champagne," Yorgo said.

"That's better. Let's open it before we have any more of your delightful news."

"I had to ransack the cellar to find something you'd drink."

"He doesn't know about Nesta's wine." Ernst bulged his eyes at Gerry and they laughed. Paolo appeared with a bottle in a bucket of ice and poured. They took the glasses and lifted them to each other and drank. "Ah, that's more like it," Ernst said approvingly. "All right. The news."

Yorgo took a throne. "We've had a cable from the agent in Paris. Contact has already been made about the Hughes papers."

"They don't waste any time." Ernst's eyes moved to Gerry and he looked at him thoughtfully. "As you predicted, darling."

"Does that mean what I think it means?" Gerry asked.

"It would appear so. This is very disagreeable. I can't believe anybody would have the effrontery to act so quickly, without an interval to pretend to be in some doubt about the papers' value. Why the Paris man? It suggests a very intimate knowledge of my affairs."

"Which our friend has?"

"It surprises me but it's possible."

It was the vindication Gerry had been waiting for but he felt no inclination to gloat. He was too pleased to be sharing this with Ernst, to be establishing additional areas of confidence between them to give much thought to Maria's villainy. "It would be rather marvelous if you could get them back, wouldn't it?" he said.

"Yes, at my price. It will be interesting to see how much the opposition thinks they're worth." He turned to Yorgo. "The cable came today?"

"About an hour ago." Yorgo opened his portfolio and placed a telegram form in front of Ernst, who glanced at it and waved it away. "It's very guarded. He wants you to call to give him instructions. Placing an overseas call here is a major undertaking. It would be easier to wire him to call you. Tomorrow at about this time should be convenient."

Ernst turned back to Gerry. "What do you think, darling? Can we be here then?"

His courtesy was touching. Gerry tried to convey his appreciation with his eyes. "We can surely arrange to be. It's fairly important." Gerry thought of the future. This was a taste of what it would be like when they were doing the things they had talked about—business discussions, asking each other's advice, deferring to each other, feeling the wonderfully close communication that Ernst was creating now, with an occasional glass of champagne thrown in to make it festive. He couldn't wait.

"Is that all, darling? Do we have no further burdens to lay on Yorgo's not particularly broad shoulders?"

"The yacht sounds like a lost cause. You want to cancel your guests."

"Of course. Thank you, darling. Get out the list and we'll go over it in the morning. Also the list of people I like in New York and the list of people I saw last time." He laughed. "We'll have to make sure your mother is on both of them. The first list is largely made up of gorgeous young men. I'll be interested to see how many of them you know."

"Oh Lord, it's so long since I've been there. There'll be a whole new crop by now. That's one thing about New York. There's never a shortage."

"Good heavens," Ernst exclaimed. "Makin. I met a raving beauty called Makin. Do you suppose there's any connection with you?"

"It's an unusual name. It could be my half brother. Was he circulating in telltale haunts?"

"Circulating so fast that one could barely get one's hand on him."

"How lovely if I have a gay half brother. That *would* be fun. Was his name Nathan or Joel? I'm not sure which is which but both were stunning."

"No, that doesn't ring a bell. I remember. They called him Nat. Nat Makin. I suppose that's for Nathan. I think the whole thing is beginning to sound like fun. I'm so glad you suggested it. We'll keep some time to be serious and talk to people about our ideas. There must be masses of brilliant young groups who are waiting to be subsidized by two attractive millionaires."

It was doubtless the champagne that was bringing on an attack of euphoria but Gerry was suddenly bursting with boundless confidence. Money made their reality elusive but they were getting close to it, closer now, surprisingly, than at the house. He emptied the bottle into their glasses. "Well, here's to New York," he said exuberantly. "I'm really excited all of a sudden. We're going to do things."

Yorgo rose without Ernst or Gerry paying any attention to him. Their eyes were on each other. "I'll take care of the cable," he said.

"Tell Paolo to get on with the unpacking, if that's what he's doing," Ernst said, still looking at Gerry. "Ask him to put our dressing gowns and toilet things in the other room. We'll sleep there, don't you agree? The room where our clothes are can be the dressing room."

"That makes sense. It might make sense to have another bottle of this, if there is one."

"There's another on ice. I'll tell Paolo." Yorgo withdrew.

Gerry sat back, grinning. Ernst was even beginning to understand about privacy. He had tactfully excluded Paolo from their bedroom. "Why are we looking at each other like this?"

"Because we like it, I imagine. I can't think of anything I would rather look at. I see new things in you all the time. I'm suddenly seeing the man I'm going to live with for the rest of my life."

"I'm feeling the same thing. It's pretty marvelous, isn't it? Suddenly is the word. Suddenly it's not just being in love as if every minute were all of it. Suddenly it's beginning to build for the future. Do you suppose it's the champagne?" They continued to look at each other, chuckling, while Paolo set down another bottle. Gerry waved him away and poured for them. When Paolo was gone, their laughter subsided, followed by a glow of contentment that seemed to emanate from them and contain them. They drank.

"Shall we take the bottle to the bedroom and shower and change and go see Solange?" Ernst suggested.

"Our minds are running along the same track. Let's go."

"Hold your hands up, darling." Gerry did so. Ernst looked at them. "Yes, I like to see the ring there. It's very reassuring."

"Oh, I'm yours for life. There's no doubt about that." They rose and moved to each other and held each other lightly and kissed. Gerry picked up the ice bucket and Ernst carried their glasses and they crossed the vast room to the only slightly smaller bedroom. "Don't go far. I won't know where to look for you." He set the wine down and turned back to Ernst and recovered his glass. "Listen, darling, if Maria is still around, we'd better have a little talk. Are you convinced now that she's the culprit?"

"It's fairly damning. Who else could it be?"

"Who else, indeed? What are we going to do about it?" Everything was too good between them for any subject to turn unpleasant now.

"I'm going to give very careful instructions to my Paris agent. He's very shrewd and very clever. Somebody might make a slip somewhere. I would like to catch her." The ruthless note that Gerry had almost forgotten crept into Ernst's voice. Love hadn't put him to sleep.

"I would, too, but what do we do in the meantime? What if she's around this evening?"

"What if she is, darling?"

"Well, how are we supposed to behave? I don't see how we can even be polite to her."

"What else can we do? We're civilized people. We have to conform to a certain social code regardless of our suspicions."

"I don't agree with you. I don't think it's civilized not

to make any distinctions. Everybody's so sloppy. Social codes are just an excuse to be even sloppier. It's so much easier to go on smiling. God forbid anybody should make waves."

"There's something to be said for making life easier in small ways. My being rude to Maria isn't going to change her. I can't be responsible for the way people behave."

"But you *are* responsible, darling. By accepting her, you expose all your friends to her. Think what might've happened to André, for God's sake."

"What would you have me do, darling? Refuse to receive her because of what we think she's done?"

"Something like that."

"She would simply deny it and if she's the actress I think she is, put on a magnificent display of outrage at my even suggesting it. It's so tiresome of you—" He checked himself. The petulant note had broken into his voice. He shook his head and smiled. "There's that word again. I'm sorry, darling, but you must admit it's a problem. Think of the unpleasantness."

"I don't mind unpleasantness when it's a question of standing up for what's right. I admit not having any proof makes it difficult. I'd just refuse to see her again and let her wonder why."

"You could, but I've allowed her to be a friend. She is also my guest. When this trip is over, we'll simply drift apart. I don't see any other way to deal with her. I intend to do everything I can to trip her up."

"OK, darling." He was willing to concede the point. They had achieved the equality of being able to argue. Ernst had corrected his slip. There were no unpleasant subjects anymore. "Let's try to avoid her when we don't have to be with her."

They finished the bottle and bathed, at ease with each other, and put on dressing gowns to visit Paolo in their dressing room to pick out something to wear.

"Why don't you go?" Ernst suggested to the valet. "There's no need for you to trail about with me this evening."

"Very well. I've put everything you'll need in your case." He indicated the carryall and left.

"You prefer us to be alone, don't you?" Ernst asked almost shyly, as if he were making a daring play for his approbation.

Gerry laughed and squeezed his arm. "I should hope so." He dropped his dressing gown to put on his clothes. "What about security, darling? Now that we're out of the jungle, is it all right for you to wander around without anybody looking after you?"

"I'm sure Yorgo has taken care of everything necessary here. There is always a check of everybody staying on the same floor when I'm in a hotel. The bodyguards are waiting in India."

"These are things I have to learn about. I trust you not to be careless."

They dressed, Ernst looking rather austere with only the few chains and baubles he had worn ashore after the shipwreck, and went next door. Solange greeted them delightedly but they had hardly had time to kiss before they were followed by the Horrockses. Maria's welcome was overwhelming. She clasped them to her in extravagant embraces. Her eyes rolled and bulged. Gerry realized that he would probably have to slap her in order for his coolness to register with her.

"My precious lambs. How wicked of you to desert us. I'll forgive you now that you're with us again. What have you done with my adorable André? Has he quite recovered? Poor lamb. I'm giving a dinner party for you tomorrow. I've found some charming young men who're traveling together. Dutch and Belgian, all very good-looking. They're dying to meet you. One of them is related to Queen Juliana. I thought that would interest you, Ernst darling."

"I'm not sure we'll be free," Gerry interjected.

"Why ever not, darling?" Ernst asked, looking at him blankly. Gerry tried to signal with his eyes, to no avail. "You don't know Maria's finds. They're always worth having a look at."

"Well, maybe we can work it out," he agreed grudgingly.

A hotel waiter served drinks. Yorgo was there but not Sally. Perhaps Ernst had a point. A few good-looking young men would doubtless be preferable to concentrated doses of Maria. "Are you having a good time?" he asked her. "You said you'd never been here, didn't you?"

"I did. I'm too absurd. This place keeps changing its name. I muddle it with the Seychelles. It's the Seychelles I've never been to."

She pulled it off very well, no matter how farfetched it was as an explanation. He let her monopolize Ernst and drifted toward Solange, who was laughing with Trevor. Their eyes met and she moved toward him as he approached. He kissed her again.

"It's nice to be with you. Where's Sally?"

"When you said you were coming, I sent her to Kandy. She has relatives there she's been wanting to see. This seemed a good time. She'll be back tomorrow. If you'd failed me, I was going to have a big night on the town with Yorgo." She was particularly vivacious and full of fun, looking lovely in a beautifully cut, loosely flowing long gown.

"Not with the Horrockses?"

"They wanted to take me to dinner with somebody but I begged off."

"You mean—good heavens, I hardly dare say it—we're going to be *alone* tonight?"

"Do you suppose we'll be able to think of anything to say to each other?" She uttered hearty laughter. "It's time I caught up with my two men. You know? You both look very sure and settled. It went well?"

"If I told you about it, it might not sound so, but I think it did. I found out what you wouldn't tell me. At least, I guess I did. There's absolutely nothing now I don't know."

She tucked her chin in and looked up at him and the mischief drained out of her melancholy eyes. "It's still the same?"

"So it seems."

"Can you accept it?"

"I may have to eventually. Not without a fight."

"I prayed for a miracle for you, darling."

"Yes, he hoped for a miracle, too. It may yet happen. It won't be a miracle, just love and care and trying to understand it. Little things have happened already. If I'm lucky, I may find the key to it. That's what it is, really. It's like a locked door. There's no reason why it can't be unlocked."

"Do you think it was very bad of me not to warn you?"

"How could you? Patterns change all the time. I wasn't sure I was able to have a girl but I did. I want her again." Their eyes suddenly probed deep into each other. Their breath caught. Their faces grew still.

"Tonight?" The word dropped from Solange's motionless lips.

"With him?"

"Can we?"

"Why not?" They took deep breaths and their hands briefly reached for each other.

"Do you think it will unlock the door?" she asked in a normal voice.

"Not necessarily. Anything might. I like the idea better than anything else he might want. If we're together all the time, it could easily happen anyway."

"He'd insist on it if you're to be the father of his heir."

"That's what I figured. I've wondered how he was planning to be the father."

"Heaven knows, darling. The fascinating thing about living with him is that nothing is predictable. You know?" The mischief sprang into her eyes. They laughed and he put his arm around her waist as they turned back to the others.

Yorgo left with the Horrockses and Gerry and the von Hallers had dinner at a table set up in front of the open doors that led onto a balcony. The restless sea surged below them, stretching to an invisible horizon. It was like being on the yacht, but somehow more peaceful. They talked about New York and their theatrical plans. Solange joined in with enthusiasm. They whittled away at the summer, adding London and Paris to their itinerary for serious exploration of the artistic scene, until only a few weeks were left for warm-weather leisure. They decided to set Gerry's income aside for whatever project they settled on and let Ernst take care of living expenses. Gerry felt a sense of family building up between them. He embraced it and wanted to embrace them, recognizing it as what he'd wanted. They had found their reality. Money was an essential part of it, but money to be used creatively, not for idleness.

"He's transforming our lives, darling," Solange said with shining eyes. "He said he was going to."

"If you are both happy, I'm sure I will be," Ernst said.

After coffee, while the waiters were clearing the table, Solange left them and returned wearing a white negligee that made her look very dark and glamorous. She was barefoot.

"Are you trying to seduce us, my darling?" Ernst asked.

"Of course. Women never stop."

"This is turning into the most wonderful evening of my life," Gerry said. "Wouldn't you be more comfortable in a dressing gown, darling? I'll get them. Don't say anything interesting till I come back." He went next door and undressed, modestly leaving his brief Jockey shorts on. They would go eventually but he was too content to rush it. He wanted to go to bed with them both; giving physical expression to the solidarity they were creating between them had become right and necessary. Everything was going to work itself out.

He took Ernst's dressing gown to him and they left the table, carrying glasses and bottles with them while Ernst changed, and settled in a more comfortable corner of the room. Solange curled up on a sofa. Gerry sat beside her. Ernst enthroned himself in front of them.

"I don't think we've ever had an evening like this in our lives," Solange said with a contented sigh.

"I want lots more," Gerry said, looking at Ernst. "What about you, darling? Do you want to fill the room with royalty?"

"I'm with the only two people in the world I love," he said simply. "It's not my fault I didn't find you sooner."

"I think it's lucky you didn't," Solange said. "I've always been afraid you'd fall in love with a boy, somebody like André who wouldn't have been a match for you. You're both the perfect age, with enough experience to know what you want and what's important in life. You know? The only time to fall in love is when you're very very young and still believe in living happily ever after, or much later when you've knocked around and made all your mistakes and learned how to avoid them."

"You're probably right," Gerry agreed. "I wasn't ready to fall in love until the last year or two. I've regretted my wasted life but if it was getting me ready for this, I wouldn't change a minute of it."

They were off again, talking about life and love and a future in which they would be too busy accomplishing things to have time for the hectic social activities that had kept the von Hallers scurrying from continent to continent for fifteen years. They agreed that there would always be time for the château in Burgundy and Ernst wanted to make a side trip to Argentina to show Gerry his ranch and decide if that too was to be retained as a permanent retreat. Gerry had been prepared for a year of aimless wandering. He could almost bless Maria for the wrecked yacht. Time flew. When Gerry thought of looking at his watch, it was almost one.

"Is it getting to be time for bed?" Solange asked later as he was filling their glasses with the last of the wine.

"Almost 1:30," Gerry said, "but I could go on forever." She moved a hand to his lap and caressed his sex. He had wondered how they would make the transition to love-making; he should have guessed that after fifteen years with Ernst she would know the right moves to make. Ernst was watching her. Gerry was quickly stirred into erection and she very deliberately opened his dressing gown. He threw it off and lifted his hips and peeled off his shorts. She leaned over him and opened her mouth on him and made his body leap with the play of her tongue. He pushed her negligee back from her shoulders and she freed one arm and then the other. She lay her head on his chest and he fondled her sweet soft breasts while she trailed her fingers along his erection. He looked up and met Ernst's eyes. He was smiling with gentle approval.

"How beautiful you are together," he said. "Shouldn't you go to bed?" He rose and dropped his dressing gown and stood in front of them, naked and erect.

"God, you're magnificent," Gerry exclaimed. He rose, bringing Solange up with him. She held her negligée in front of her but didn't cover her breasts. They moved toward the bedroom. Gerry put his arms around them and hugged them.

"What a perfect way to end the evening," he said. He knew he mustn't divert his attention to Ernst but holding him made it difficult to imagine letting go of him in favor of Solange. He wished that all three of them could coil themselves into some gloriously explosive whole. There were two wide beds in the room. She lay down on the first they came to, well over on one side, leaving room for Ernst. She was still partially covered by the negligée. He forced himself to close his mind to Ernst. She lifted her arms to him as he dropped down over her on his hands and knees. She put her hands on his chest and slid up to him, her mouth lingering on him everywhere. He gathered her slight body in to him and knew that it was going to be different from the first time. She was giving free rein to her desire. They kissed and she devoured his mouth. She lay back in his arms and held his head on her breasts. He sucked them and felt the nipples contract and harden further. She writhed against him and stroked herself with his cock and held his balls in both hands.

"Oh Gerry darling," she whispered. "I want you in me."

He tipped her onto her back and she lifted her legs and held his cock and lowered it to herself. She crooned and cried out for him as he began a long slow thrust into her. She made it an act of supreme virility for him; he could feel her abandoning herself to him and to the hard flesh that was filling her. She locked her legs around his hips and pulled him deep into her. He lowered himself onto her and her legs fell away and she gave herself up to him.

"Give me a baby," she whispered like a prayer. She aroused in him an unfamiliar procreative lust. He was going to be a father. He rocked her with his long drives and soon felt her orgasms beginning. She sobbed softly and seemed to melt under him. Her body was his and he was filling it with his life. She was becoming his girl, his mistress, his wife. She claimed him with the gift of herself and he assented with his body.

His cock seemed to grow in her; he felt as if his approaching orgasm would be too great for her to contain. He became aware of Ernst again. He was propped up beside them, his hand moving rapidly on himself. As he glanced at him, he saw the set of his face alter. His lips parted and his eyes clouded. He was approaching a climax too. Gerry took a deep labored breath and wrenched himself from Solange and grappled Ernst over onto her. He saw her reach for him and then he covered her. He uttered a great shout and his body was convulsed with orgasm. Gerry fell back and was delivered of his own.

They lay in silence until Gerry became aware of moisture trickling down his ribs. He sprang up and hurried to the bathroom. His mind was a haze of amazement and delight. Ernst had consummated his marriage. If there was a baby, it would be his. He had reclaimed his wife in the only way that people could make the ultimate claim on each other—with their bodies. When he returned, they were lying side by side on their backs. At his approach they both lifted an arm to him and he knelt on the bed beside them, holding their hands. Their eyes bathed him in love. He had never seen Ernst looking so deeply satisfied and at peace.

"How do you like being married?" he asked.

"You're becoming sort of a god," Solange said. "You know? Ordering the universe."

Gerry laughed. "It wasn't easy—stopping midstream, as it were. Did you think I'd gone mad?"

"For a second, I was horrified and then this beautiful man was there."

Ernst turned his head to her. "I hope you get pregnant easily. I'm not sure Gerald could manage it again."

"Come on, big daddy." Gerry gave his hand a little tug. "We'd better go to bed unless you want us all to sleep together."

"I think that would be carrying it too far." He sat up and leaned down to Solange and kissed her. "Please be pregnant, darling."

"I am. I feel it already. Thank you, darling."

He rose and Gerry dropped over her and took his turn to kiss her. "You *are* thrilling," she murmured. "I hope it happens again."

"It will if I have any say in the matter. For a minute, I felt married to you. Well, I *am*. I wanted so much to give you a baby. Maybe the next one can be mine."

They said good night and Ernst and Gerry put on their dressing gowns in the next room and returned to their suite. The minute the door was closed behind them, Gerry put his arms around Ernst and they kissed at length. "That's what I've been waiting for all evening." Gerry took his hand and headed for bed. "I hope you know now that you can come when somebody's touching you."

"It was very extraordinary. I liked it. I liked having her, even though it lasted only a second. Perhaps I will try it again."

"You must. We'll do it often. She's a very sexy lady. I'm sure she'd do anything to make it good for you."

"I can hardly make a habit of having sex with my wife, darling. It would be grotesque."

Gerry let out a shout of laughter. "I adore you. Anyway, we've found something that suits all of us. I don't mind her being with us. She's family. It's hard for me to concentrate on her when you're there but I can think of things we could try. She's ready for anything. I know that."

The next day was busy for both of them. They had to get their passports, appear before immigration authorities, organize their finances. Their official identities were restored. Gerry had to go through the ordeal of signing nine thousand dollars' worth of traveler's checks. He had never had so much money in his pocket in his life. Waiting in stifling offices made Ernst testy.

"I've never waited like this before," he complained petulantly. "You say to be patient but why should I be? These people are paid to do their jobs."

"Don't forget, our cases are pretty special. We've been in the country illegally. I think everything is going remarkably smoothly."

"You Americans. You have such abject respect for authority. These people are used to being ordered about."

They doubtless were but Gerry didn't see why they should be. They got back to the hotel in the late afternoon without having had a major blow-up. Chilled champagne helped to soothe Ernst's nerves. Gerry completed the day's business by remembering to ask Yorgo to cable his people in Bombay to return the money he'd had sent there. Yorgo reported that the call from Paris had been delayed till tomorrow. They bathed and dressed and went next door to see Solange. Sally was back and they had a happy reunion. It was soon time to go down to the hotel bar where Maria was expecting them for predinner drinks.

They found her and Trevor surrounded by her young men. There were five of them, ranging from attractive to handsome, well formed and mannerly, about Hank's age. Gerry watched Ernst conquer them immediately with his charm. They had heard of him and were obviously impressed by meeting him, offering him names of mutual friends and acquaintances. They were all in the travel business and were on their way home from Bali. Singly, there was nothing about any of them to indicate their sexual leanings but as a group, their side remarks, their quick glances, their jokes hinting at great intimacy marked them as kindred spirits. Maria was pimping. If Ernst didn't want dope, there were always young men. Anything to retain a hold over him. His disapproval of her stiffened into loathing.

He had nothing against the young men. The handsome one sitting next to Ernst was Hugo. The others were Curt and Philip and Carl and Jan. Gerry decided that the latter, the least obviously good-looking, was the one he would try to detach from the others if he were on the loose. He had a pert and winning face with a voluptuous mouth. He was blond. His open shirt revealed a smooth hairless boyish chest. He had nice hands and his tight pants contained a promising bulge of genitalia. He was a clown and began to direct his foolery at Gerry. After their eyes had met several times, it became clear that he was detachable. Gerry found him attractive in every way except the essential one; he wasn't aroused by him. Jan was a couple of weeks too late. Having ascertained this basic fact, he was able to enjoy his fun and flirtatiousness but offered him no encouragement with his eyes. Poor Ernst. He had picked a very inadequate performer.

The hotel's outdoor restaurant was richly appointed and dinner passed agreeably. Maria seated Ernst beside her with the handsome Hugo on his other side, and let the rest of them more or less fend for themselves. Gerry dodged an attempt by Jan to sit beside him and ended up between Trevor and Solange. Ernst looked as if he were enjoying himself, pleasing Gerry by not paying too much attention to Maria. He noticed Hugo glance at him several times while Ernst was speaking, as if he were the subject of the conversation. He smiled across the table at them. It was wonderful to be in this sort of gathering and feel totally sure that nobody could come between them.

After dinner, they returned to the bar for coffee and more drinks. Trevor and Gerry and Solange trailed behind while Trevor finished a story. When they joined the others, Jan had his arm around an empty chair.

"This is for you," he said to Gerry. "I don't see how you can refuse to take it without being beastly to me."

Gerry laughed and sat beside him. "I wouldn't dream of being beastly to you."

"Please don't be. I'm trying so hard to make a good impression on you. I gather you and Ernst are a pair."

"Very much so. Where did Maria find you all?"

"Out by the pool. She said she was traveling with Ernst so we sort of let down our hair with her. She told us about the yacht and everything. You've had quite a time."

"Wild. Are you staying here long?"

"No. We're leaving tomorrow evening. That doesn't give me much time to make the kind of impression I want to make." He smiled merrily and winked and pressed his knee against Gerry's. "Ernst has asked us up to your suite for drinks later. This bar is closing soon."

"Oh well then, you can go right on making an impression. You're doing fine." He remained unstirred, although he enjoyed looking at his admirer. He found it quite astonishing that anybody so attractive didn't actively tempt him. Anyway, Jan knew he was with Ernst so his play for him was probably just to keep in practice.

They sat until they were the only ones left in the bar and the waiters were looking restless. Solange leaned across the table to Gerry. "Sally's had a long day. We're going up." He rose with her and they kissed and smiled into each other's eyes and said good night. All the other men rose and the girls departed. Gerry registered for the first time that Yorgo wasn't with them. He had always been a fixture at their gatherings. He wondered if his absence had any significance.

"I'm sorry there's no glamorous entertainment I can offer," Maria said when they had all seated themselves again. "As you've probably discovered for yourselves, Colombo tucks itself up for the night very early. You'll all have to entertain yourselves." She said the last with laughing innuendo and a suggestive glance around the table. Gerry loathed her for intruding so blatantly on their personal lives. A real madam. She rose and put a hand on Ernst's shoulder. "Don't get up. Trevor and I must be out early in the morning. We'll see you later at the pool. I'm so glad I could bring you all together." She moved around beside Gerry. "Gerry lamb, you're quite the hit of the evening. People have been talking. What an utter charmer." She and Trevor left amid a chorus of thank-yous.

Ernst looked at Gerry with a smile full of secret hints. "I've asked them to send up everything we could possibly want. Shall we go up when we've finished these drinks?"

"I don't think we're welcome here anymore." Gerry wouldn't have issued invitations without consulting Ernst but it was probably a small matter and one that they'd had no occasion to discuss. The company was pleasant and a few more drinks wouldn't do them any harm. He was already a bit sloshed and suspected that the others were too.

An array of bottles and several buckets of ice awaited them in their grandiose living room. Privacy permitted a quick shift in the atmosphere. As Gerry made drinks for everybody, shoveling ice into glasses with a slightly erratic hand, he was aware of kisses exchanged, of hands straying. Ernst had settled on a sofa flanked by Hugo and Philip. Their hands were moving intimately on each other as they talked. Gerry didn't like it but was confident that Ernst wouldn't let it go farther.

"Are any of you with anyone in particular or are you all unattached?" he asked Jan, who remained faithfully at his side.

"Hugo and Philip are together but you wouldn't know it once they get started. The same as you and Ernst, I assume."

"You'd better not assume anything. Anyway, we're just starting off on life's rocky road. It's too soon to issue statements." He made their drinks last and handed Jan a glass. Jan took it and put his hand on Gerry's neck and drew his mouth to him and kissed him with delicious lingering thoroughness. Gerry returned the kiss enjoying it more than he wanted to. He drew back and smiled at him. "You've got a very kissable mouth. I've been looking at it all evening."

"You're the most attractive guy I've met in ages. I fool around a lot but I mean that. Philip thinks so too." Gerry seated himself in a chair slightly removed from Ernst. Jan perched on the arm, facing him.

"You do think I'm attractive, don't you?"

"Very." He put his hand on his knee reassuringly. Jan lifted it and put it on his crotch. It felt hard and bulky. Gerry smiled and exerted a slight pressure. "*Unusually* attractive, but you see, there's Ernst."

"Oh, I know that. I don't expect you to be swept off your feet. Just a nice little extramarital frisson."

Gerry laughed and removed his hand. "OK. If you'll settle for that, it's a deal."

"If this is supposed to be an orgy, why don't we start it?"

"Is that what it's supposed to be?"

"Well, of course. I mean, isn't it? Ernst said we could stay all night if we wanted."

"I see." His spirit was torn by a great wrench of anguish. He had begged for time.

"We've all heard of Ernst's parties. We understood from Maria that they still go on."

Anger tightened Gerry's chest but he urged himself to stay cool. He tried to keep a smile fixed on his face. Jan reached for his shirt and started to unbutton it. Gerry held his hand when it got to his trousers. "I told you not to assume anything." His voice sounded as calm as he had hoped it would.

"Are you shy? Shall I start?"

"You felt as if you were pretty well started."

"Shall I show you?"

"Go ahead." Gerry wondered how long he could play along with it. He hated himself for giving his consent. Jan rose and put his drink on a table and looked down at Gerry with merry eyes. He removed his shirt and tossed it aside. He kicked off his sandals and stripped, looking at him teasingly all the while.

"Jan's got his clothes off again," somebody called out and there was general laughter. Jan straightened and swayed his hips. He had a slim delectable peaches-and-cream body and a cock about the equal of Ernst's, made more arresting by his slight build. It pointed at Gerry from a small cloud of golden curls. Gerry was aware of the temptation to touch it but he remained motionless in his chair, his stomach knotted with anger and grief.

"Now it's your turn." Another blond, Curt or Carl, also naked, moved in behind Jan as he spoke and put his arms around him. Hands moved over the delectable body and closed on his cock.

"I knew I'd get you eventually," the newcomer said. "What a big cock you have, Grandma."

Jan writhed against him lasciviously and dropped his head back and kissed his neck. "Later, Carl sweetie. We'll have each other when the competition gets heavier. Right now, I'm trying to make an impression on this fascinating American." He looked at Gerry from under lowered lids. His face had acquired a glutted look, as if he were surfeited with his own sexuality, slightly obscene but exciting. Gerry hated Ernst for ignoring his pleas. He hated the thought of the familiar outcry if he displayed his cock. His star turn. He was sick of it. Above all, he hated the possibility of his enjoying any part of it.

"Is my cock big enough for you?" Jan asked, still swaying his body against Carl.

"Very much so."

"Is yours big enough for me? That's what I want to find out. I like them *big*."

"Unless you have unusually extravagant requirements, I think I'd get by."

"How thrilling. What're we waiting for?" He broke from Carl's embrace and leaned over and slid his hands up Gerry's thighs. Gerry seized them. His heart was beating rapidly. He was going to have to make the kind of scene Ernst couldn't bear. Steel seemed to have entered his will. He stood and held Jan's cock briefly. It felt as good as it looked.

"Nice," he said. "I like you but this is a mistake. I want you to put your clothes on and go." He turned to the others and raised his voice. "OK, everybody. That's enough. Pull yourselves together. The party's over."

There was an outburst of startled protest. Ernst looked at him without moving. His shirt and slacks were open and Hugo was holding his erection. "Whatever has possessed you?" he demanded coldly. "They're our guests."

"They're your guests but this is *our* room. I want them to leave." Ernst's eyes turned hard and remote. Gerry's heart pounded. Ernst pushed his dwindling erection into his trousers and zipped them and stood up.

"I won't have this. I wish them to stay."

"If they do they're apt to get hurt."

"No, no," somebody said. "Let's have no trouble. We're leaving."

Gerry was aware of good-looking bodies being returned to cover as he and Ernst stared at each other in a clash of wills. Hugo was the first one ready and he politely wished them good night. Ernst turned to him. "I apologize for this American's boorish behavior," he said in a voice as corrosive as acid. Gerry wanted to hit him. He felt sick. He turned away blindly and found himself standing beside Jan, who was buttoning his shirt.

"I'm sorry," he said. "I hope you understand."

"Of course. You're in love. It's rather old-fashioned of you, but sweet. Here's my card. Come see me in Amsterdam. I can still feel your hand on my cock. Heavenly."

Gerry took the card and nodded and tried to smile. They

were all hurrying each other to the door. There was a final flurry of good-nights and silence as the door closed behind them, filling the silence with hostility.

"I'm appalled by you," Ernst said, "I don't know why I didn't go with them."

"Maybe because it's no fun if I'm not there to wave my cock around. Isn't that what you said?" His heart was pounding so violently that he had trouble drawing breath to speak. "I'd better warn you that if you ever refer to me again as 'this American' I'll slap you winding."

"Of course. Americans like to hit people to prove their manhood. I have no intention of learning to live with boorish American manners."

"Now listen." He breathed deeply, trying to get a grip on himself. He found his glass still in his hand and drained it. He went to the drinks table and splashed more whiskey into it and took another swallow. Better. He could look at Ernst without cringing at the coldness in his eyes. "We have something important to talk about. We'd better not get started on manners. Or maybe it *does* have something to do with manners. Good manners to me is consideration of others. Did you ask me if I wanted those guys to come up for drinks?"

"I thought you believed in spontaneity in your social life. If you didn't want them you could have said so. You wanted your blond. It was very exciting to watch. He wasn't the only one who wanted you. It was beginning to be a quite exciting sex party. You've destroyed the pleasures you might have given me."

"Yes, dammit. There aren't going to be any sex parties. We might as well get that straight once and for all. It's OK for a bunch of guys like that. Who cares what Hugo and Jan and the others do together? When it's with two people who love each other, it's cheap and ugly. If that's the best we can do with love, we don't deserve it. It wouldn't last long anyway. I've listened to everything you've said and tried to believe there was some way of adapting but there isn't. Letting Maria organize our sex lives, for God's sake. Jesus Christ, I could kill her. That's another thing. We're not going to see her again. She's not satisfied with what she's already gotten out of you. She'll go on worming her way into your favor and taking you for everything she can get. Look what she's done to us this evening. She's the cunt of the universe."

"Your language is charming." He turned from him with a look of distaste and sat on the sofa.

"Fuck my language. Listen to what I'm saying. I'm going to save us from things you don't seem to understand anything about. I sometimes think you're the biggest innocent on the face of the earth. Either that, or you've forgotten there's something called decency."

"I'm cheap and ugly. I disgust you. I don't know what decency is. I've always considered name-calling beneath me. It's too easy. Let me simply say that your extraordinary cock seems to have given you delusions of grandeur. You presume to tell me whom I should know and accept socially. You never hesitate to cause trouble. Five perfectly presentable young men were finding pleasure in something that gives me pleasure. Five, not one of them finding it disgusting. You insult them and me by ordering them out. You don't even know how to deal with petty officials. You waste my day because you don't understand that money gives us certain privileges. I've made every allowance for you but you don't seem to learn anything."

"You've made allowances for me?" Gerry was speechless while his mind seemed to do a somersault. Anger, perhaps fueled by drink, had carried him this far. As anger abated, he realized that he might as well not have said anything. Ernst was as inaccessible as he had been at times in the beginning, shut away in his private impregnable world. He couldn't reach him now unless he could coax him out again, win him back even if he ended by hurting him. Hurting him might make him listen.

He looked at him and gave his head an incredulous little shake. He went to a chair near him and sat. "You poor shit. I find an impotent drug addict and I offer him all the love that's in me. I've discovered that there's an awful lot. I helped you through the dope. I'm ready to help you through the impotency. I've showed you that you can give Solange a baby. What allowances have you had to make for me?"

"You use a certain word a great deal. I've tried to put up with it. My sexual responses are selective, like everybody else's. Some people have intercourse with animals. Very well. The prospect would make me impotent. Some people are impotent if they're in bed with more than one person. I'm impotent if I'm with only one. Which is the more impotent? You can't frighten me with a word."

"I'm not trying to but you sound perfectly satisfied with the way things are."

"Why shouldn't I be?"

"For the love of God, darling, because of everything I'm saying. I could've gone to bed with Jan but I hated you for my even being tempted by him. I would've really hated you after it was over. OK, I'm talking about a momentary hate; but after it happened often enough, it wouldn't be momentary. It would start eating into me while I asked myself why I was denying myself the thing I really need—to love one person completely, with all of myself. Once I was convinced it couldn't be you, we'd be finished."

"There is very little point in discussing our sexual preferences. They are what they are."

"They aren't. We've gone over all that. You know what's happened just in the last few days. You said I couldn't make you come by myself but I did, even when you were stoned. Last night with Solange was beautiful. We can have that. We agreed to give ourselves a little time but the first chance that comes along to have a gang bang, thanks to Maria, you can't wait."

"Maria happens to know my preferences but we could have found those boys on our own. At least one of them clearly pleased you. Why wait, when it's bound to happen eventually?"

"It's not. I won't allow it. I thought maybe I could but I can't."

"You're saying that I'm not to be allowed a sex life."

"I'm saying that you won't want it any more than I do after we've been together a little longer. It's too basic to play around with."

"I don't see that this conversation is leading anywhere." He rose, looking composed and hermetically closed away within himself. "The fact remains that you behaved in a way that I would never permit in anybody I choose to know. You don't apologize but continue to try to justify yourself. I've allowed myself to be deceived by you. I should have taken the difference in our backgrounds into consideration. You Americans are barbarians. I wanted to believe that you were an exception. I should have known that anybody who would make love with his mother was an unbalanced and dangerous neurotic."

"You son of a bitch." Gerry sprang up and hit him hard with the flat of his hand. He felt the jolt in his arm and his chest gave a great heave of release. He would beat him to a pulp if that was the only way to get through to him. "Don't you dare talk about my mother and American barbarians and our different backgrounds. I'll hit you again if you don't start making sense." Appalled, he watched Ernst sink to the sofa and for a moment thought he might have done him some serious harm. He seemed to shrink as he huddled down on the cushion. His eyes were odd, darting about but glazed, as if he couldn't see. He spoke in a voice Gerry had never heard before, breaking into a childish babble.

"Go. I can't allow myself to be hurt like this. I can't bear it. You have no right. I've staked everything on you. I don't want you here. Leave."

He wasn't physically damaged; he seemed to be having a mental collapse. Terror seized Gerry; he wanted to put his arms around him but was terrified of aggravating his condition. Perhaps lucidity and reason would pull him around. "I'm not going anywhere. If you think I'm a dangerous neurotic, you'd better pay attention to me. We're in this for life, remember? You asked me to take over. That's what I'm doing. First of all, we'd better get back to what started all this. Asking people to leave when they're committing obscenities in the living room is not barbaric behavior."

Ernst remained huddled on the sofa, babbling incoherently. "I have nothing to say. I can't bear it. I will not be persecuted. I have never allowed anybody to rule my life. I won't have it. I want you to leave me."

"I will, goddammit, if you don't snap out of it. We love each other. That didn't stop fifteen minutes ago. You've got to see this for what it is—unfortunate maybe, but nothing more. I'll even listen to you if you tell me I should've handled it differently, not that it matters much since it won't happen again. You're acting as if I'd driven you mad."

"You struck me. Nobody has ever dared strike me. It's something I can never forgive. I don't wish to be here with you."

"That's tough luck, isn't it? We took this place together. I'm staying. You can go if you want to."

"Very well. You oblige me to go next door and disturb Solange. You like to throw people out in the middle of the night."

Gerry stepped quickly to the sofa and dropped down beside him and put his arms around him. He was prepared for him to put up a struggle but he remained inert in his embrace. "Oh darling. Please. Don't do this. You've spoken to me as if I were a stranger. This American. You act as if everything we've told each other doesn't mean anything. This is Gerald. I belong to you. We belong to each other. We have a problem but people in love always do. We've said all there is to say about it. All we can do now is wait and see how we can work it out. I'll agree that I behaved shockingly if you want me to. I don't like hitting you but it seemed like the only way I could get you back. That's all that matters—us together, living for each other."

"Unfortunately, I find that you're not a person I wish to live for." The steel had returned to Ernst's voice. Gerry felt as if a knife had been plunged into him. For the first time, he knew that he was faced with the possibility of losing him. His mind reeled. His arms dropped away from him. He rose uncertainly and reached the support of a chair and turned back to him. Ernst had straightened. Gerry got a grip on himself again.

"I'm not going to let you say things like that when you're upset. Perhaps I'd better leave."

"I assure you that it would be better for both of us."

"There're two bedrooms. If you don't want to be with me, can't we both just go to bed and sleep it off?"

"If you stay, I'll go next door. It's quite simple." The venom he managed to crowd into the few words dealt Gerry another blow. He looked at him and wondered if the things in him that had troubled him—the spoiled self-indulgence, the addictiveness, the ruthlessness—were the whole man and all the qualities he loved were only superficial social decorations. Perhaps he *should* hate him. The enormity of the thought made him want to fall on his knees before him and beg him to remain the person who embodied all his hopes and dreams.

"As you say, it's the middle of the night," Gerry said, amazed that he was actually considering leaving. "I don't quite know where to go."

"Go back to your seaside bungalow. Go back to Hank." His contempt was withering and stung Gerry to renewed anger.

"Now that you mention it, why not? He wants to get me away from you. He has a big cock that works. He can fuck me and make us both come. He wouldn't allow me to make a public spectacle of myself. I'm beginning to think that all that counts for more than I realized."

"Perhaps you'll be kind enough to return my ring before you go."

"No. I won't." His voice caught on a sob. His eyes filled. It wasn't over. He wouldn't let it end. They needed each other. He'd just get out for a little while before either of them said something unforgivable. He struggled for control and brushed a hand across his eyes. "You've given *yourself* to me, not just the ring. Nothing has happened that can change that. Get a good sleep, darling. I'll call you in the morning." He turned quickly and made a rush for the door, not sure that he could make it.

Once in the corridor, he had trouble with his feet. He stumbled and almost fell. He leaned against the wall and tears overflowed and streamed down his face. He was grateful that they were silent. His body ached for Ernst's. Physical separation was more painful than all the lacerating words. Ernst must feel it too. The thought of his pain intensified Gerry's. They had gone beyond being able to comfort each other now but they would need each other tomorrow. He knew Ernst hadn't meant the things he had said. He was so vulnerable that he lashed out in self-protection. They had to be apart until Ernst no longer felt threatened and their need for each other could reassert itself.

Where could he go? He had no intention of doing anything that would delay reconciliation. No sulks and waiting to be wooed back; he would make himself available as soon as they talked in the morning. Could he make it all the way back to Galle? It was almost two, not the best time for summoning up strength of character. He had the feeling that Ernst would be impressed if he did something decisive, made a show of independence. If he didn't go somewhere, there would be no impact in his coming back. He was supposed to be the dominating male. Dominating males flew off in rages. They didn't mope spinelessly outside a closed door. Where could he go except Galle?

When he felt that he had shed all the tears that were in him, he went downstairs and found that there were cars for hire outside. Everything he owned was upstairs where it belonged but the beautiful, sleepy-looking girl behind the desk seemed to find it reasonable for him to want to drive to Galle in the middle of the night and agreed to put it on his bill.

Starting out gave him a sense of purpose. He was able to turn his thoughts to his destination. He wouldn't tell anybody what had happened. Hank would only try to make the rupture final. He would pretend that he had come back to get them. They were due to rejoin the party in the next day or two anyway. Some party. He'd meant what he'd said about Maria. He could no longer be civil to her. That was going to be more difficult for Ernst to take than anything else, but Solange would back him up when she knew about the part Maria had played in the hijacking. The thought of losing Ernst because of Maria made his chest and stomach knot up. He wouldn't, of course. If necessary, he would pay her to leave. Hangers-on could be bought.

His nerves remained undependable. At moments he felt that he was arriving at some semblance of calm and then a stray thought of Ernst would set him off again. Tears welled up from an inexhaustible supply. He thought of the total contentment of lying beside Ernst in bed and wanted to shout with anguish. He tried to remember every word he had said during the fight. Very little of it had been bad. His speech about Hank. By then Ernst had been so cut off that he might not have taken it in.

He almost told the driver to turn around and go back. He couldn't let Ernst go through this sort of torment. He reminded himself of the things Ernst had said. They had to be apart. They had to suffer in order to learn how much they needed each other. Ernst was probably asleep. He would feel his absence in the morning and would be longing for his return. Gerry was resolved not to indulge in recriminations. People didn't know what they were saying when they were angry. He had made a stand that was essential for their future. If Ernst wouldn't accept it, there was no hope for them anyway. That was the point to hold on to. He gripped the ring until it hurt.

Only a few more hours. He would try to get some sleep himself. It would be time to call before he knew it and this nightmare would be over. The road stretched away to infinity ahead of them. They would never get there.

He sat up with a start and realized that he must have been dozing. He blinked and peered out and saw that they were swinging around the Galle playing field and heading into the shore road. He was almost there. He gave the driver instructions and sat back with a peculiarly soothing sense of being home. He was going to have to think of some reason for arriving at this ungodly hour. It was getting on toward five but still dark.

They pulled up in front of the gates and the driver blinked his lights. Gerry got out and tried the handles. Locked. He called all the boys' names, keeping his voice low. He hoped to get in without waking Hank and André. He saw movement and a light flashed on in his face.

"Master," a voice exclaimed. "Very early."

"Let the car in, will you?" The gates swung open. The car followed him in. He saw that he had been admitted by Dayendra, the kitchen boy. "Can you give the driver a bed?" he asked as the boy closed the gates behind them. "He may want something to eat. Don't tell the other masters I'm here. I don't want to be disturbed." He went to the driver, who was getting out of the car. "The boy will take care of you. You can get some sleep. I won't be going back until this afternoon."

He went to their room and locked himself in and threw off his clothes. He was glad he'd come. He could feel Ernst's presence here. They would be together again this evening. He lay down and eased the ache of longing for him by hugging a pillow against himself and slept.

He awoke suddenly, his heart pounding with anxiety. He sat up and swung his legs over the side of the bed and stretched, trying to free his body from the grip of fear. There was nothing to be frightened about. It was almost ten. He could call Ernst. He felt like hell but that was to be expected. All the drinking, the drive, getting to bed at dawn. His memory of the evening was blurred, suggesting that he'd been drunker than he'd realized. They'd had a drunken row, something that happened to everybody. Driving down here had probably been a drunken overreaction to a minor incident. He warned himself not to get upset if he couldn't get through to Ernst immediately. He might sleep late. It would probably be better, he decided, to talk to Solange first and find out what she knew.

He pulled himself to his feet and went to the bathroom and rinsed out his mouth and combed his hair with his fingers. He found the sarongs hanging in the closet where he'd left them in case they came back. He put on the one Ernst had worn and gave the ring a few turns for courage. He unlocked the door and opened it cautiously. As far as he could see, the coast was clear. He crossed to the inner room where the telephone was. The house didn't score very high when it came to privacy. He felt uncomfortably exposed. He stood just inside an archway and looked out toward the beach. Hank and André were lying in deckchairs near the guest house, safely out of the way for the time being. Seeing them made him feel better. He took the phone to a corner where he couldn't be seen by them and called the hotel in Colombo and asked for Solange. In a moment, she was on the line and his heart leaped into his throat.

"Oh God, darling. Thank God I've got you. How is everything?"

"Are you all right? Where are you? I've been so worried." Her voice sounded agitated.

"I'm back in Galle. How's Ernst?"

"Very bad. I've never seen him like this. He came to me after you left. He took many pills. If I hadn't been here, he might have taken too many. He didn't know what he was doing."

"Oh God. I'll come right back. I shouldn't have left. I can be there before lunch."

"Wait, darling. We must think very carefully. Is the stand you've taken important to you?"

"Do you know what happened?"

"He said enough for me to guess the rest. Those boys were ready for one of his parties and you wouldn't allow it? You said you knew everything. Didn't you know that's what he likes?"

"Yes. I've even told him that I'd go along with him if nothing else works. He agreed to wait."

"Is it so important that you'd leave him because of it?"

"But, darling, you must understand. I'd lose him anyway if I accepted it. I've tried to imagine what it would be like, loving him and having other people to please him. Last night I knew it couldn't work. Don't you agree?"

"I'm not sure how it would be for a man. For a woman, of course, it would be impossible."

"It's impossible for me. At least until I'm sure we can't make it right together. Then I'd try it his way, though I'd know it couldn't last long. I've found out with him what I want my life to be."

"My poor darling. I'm so sorry, but if that's the case I don't think you should come back yet. You know how much I want you with us, so you can trust me. I know him. You must make him ask you to come back. If you don't, he'll think he's won and will make you suffer until you've given way to him in everything. I think I know what you want. It's not that."

"No. Have you talked to him this morning? Do you think he *will* ask me?" He could hardly get the words out. His grip tightened on the instrument as he steeled himself for her reply.

"I don't know, darling. This is all so new. Nobody has had such a hold on him before. He's frightened of it now and will try to break it. With enough drink or dope or pills, he might succeed. I think our lives will be too horrible to contemplate if he does."

"Don't let him, darling. Please don't let him." His voice broke. His eyes filled with tears. "I love him so much. You know that. Don't you think I should come and try to reason with him again?"

"You know that's one thing not even you can do. He said last night that he would never see you again, but in the condition he was in, that doesn't mean anything. He seemed very nearly mad. You were right to leave. You would've only made it worse. This morning, he seems better, more calm, but he refuses to speak of you. He was up quite early. Maria's with him now."

"Oh God." He was doomed. She would find a way to cut him off forever. "I'm going to try to take your advice, but please tell him that I'm waiting. Tell him there's nothing we can't solve together. Tell him I believe in him. Yorgo has this number, but take it for yourself. Call me as soon as you know what he's thinking. I've never been so miserable in my life."

"I hurt for you, my darling. I want you back. I can't

bear to think of life without you. There was suddenly light after all the years of drifting in the dark. I won't let him let you go."

"That's what I want to hear. Fix it for us, darling. We'll be so happy together." He gave her the phone number and they said good-bye and hung up. He moved cautiously until he saw that Hank and André were still sitting in the sun and then hurried back to his room. Solange would make everything right. Hope buoyed him and enabled him to drift back to sleep, assuring himself that Solange meant more to Ernst than Maria.

Again he returned to consciousness with a rush, filled with dread. It was just after 12:30. Had Solange called? He sprang up and once more checked carefully before emerging. He saw Hank and André's heads bobbing about in the sea. He crossed to the phone and made his call and asked for Solange. The Baron and his party had checked out.

His mind circled the fact. A strange blankness replaced emotion. Maria, of course. Maria standing by in the hour of need, dispensing pills and drink and opium as required to keep Ernst from knowing what he was doing, taking Solange by surprise so that she had no time to intervene. He felt everything that had sustained him die.

He was still standing, holding the telephone, but he no longer felt any connection with his surroundings. He asked for Mrs. Horrocks. She had also checked out. Did the hotel know where the Baron had gone? He had left a forwarding address in Paris. Gerry put the telephone down carefully and stood looking at nothing. Neville moved into his vision, circling the dining table. He tried his voice by saying his name. It worked. Neville came to him.

"Have you been here all morning?" he asked.

"Yes, master. Me and Hector."

"Has the telephone rung in the last hour or two?"

"No, master. Not after master make call." The phone rang as the boy was speaking. Gerry turned back to it and answered.

"Is that you, Gerald?" Nesta's voice was charmingly unmistakable. "You're back? How lovely. I've been quite puzzled. Somebody left a suitcase for you a little while ago. I told the man you were in Colombo but he said he'd just come from there. Now that I know you're here I'll send it right out."

"Thanks."

"Am I going to see you?"

"Of course. I'll call you later." He hung up. His suitcase. The message was clear. He'd been sent packing. He returned to his room and lay down on his back and looked at the ceiling, waiting for something in him to crack. He felt cold and dead. The scales might eventually fall from his eyes. He might see Ernst as a heartless, unforgiving, weak and evil man who could cause him only endless anguish, but thinking of him in that way didn't help now. He felt as if everything in him had been canceled out. It was appalling, worse than any grief he could imagine. There was nothing left to put together a life with.

He heard laughter and thought he recognized Hank's. Could Hank bring him back to life? He wanted to feel some human warmth. He had told Hank that if anything went wrong with Ernst, he wouldn't be worth having; he felt as if he had been right. At least Hank wanted him. He might give him some reason for moving, for getting from here to there, wherever there might be.

After some minutes, when the collapse he had expected, even craved, had failed to occur, he sat up. There weren't going to be any tears. He wished he could howl with despair but he didn't feel anything left in him that was capable of despair. He wanted to touch Hank, to feel his arms around him. It was the only thing he could think of that might make some mark on the appalling blank within him.

He rose and threw open his door and went out. Hank and André were approaching along the veranda, wearing their sarongs. They stopped dead in their tracks when they saw him and looked briefly stunned before letting out shouts of welcome. They hurried to him. Gerry's eyes were caught by the chain around Hank's neck.

The shock hit him in the pit of his stomach. Something was still going on in him after all. He bent over quickly and pretended to swat at a fly on his leg while he made sure that his face could follow instructions. He straightened with a grin and reached out to them both and fingered their chains.

"Something's been going on in my absence," he said. "How marvelous." They smiled radiantly at him and each other, and moved closer together until their hands were touching.

"I finally broke down and gave it to him yesterday," André explained. "We're no longer living in sin." Gerry stepped up to him and gave him a tender kiss on the lips. He turned to Hank and forced himself to meet his eyes and gave him a more guarded kiss.

"I'm so pleased," he said, meaning it as much as he could mean anything. The shock had passed. He knew that he couldn't have hoped for anything from Hank. "Every now and then, something goes right in the world. I hope you're as happy as larks. I won't say forever—it might be bad luck—but for a long long time."

They bombarded him with questions about when he'd come and what he was doing here. Gerry realized that Ernst's departure made it impossible to keep their breach a secret. He postponed talking about it by asking if they hadn't seen the car in the driveway. They hadn't. He was explaining that he'd kept it in case he wanted to go right back when Hector appeared with his bag. He gestured it into his room.

"I don't think I'm following all this," Hank said. "What are you doing with your suitcase?"

"I haven't explained it all yet. Have you made any laws about not having a drink before lunch? I need one."

"I'll go get them started and see that there's enough for lunch," André said, very much in charge. "Hank wants to say something to you anyway. If I come back and find you in bed together, I'll murder you both." He departed with happy laughter. Gerry and Hank sat.

"I just didn't want you to think I'm crazy after all the things I said to you the other night," Hank began with straightforward candor.

"I told you sex might help you think straight." That was the sort of thing the living said to each other in an effort to connect. "I'm glad it did."

"You accomplished what I guess you intended. I realized that even after that fantastic time together, I wasn't really getting through to you. It made me start thinking about how much Andy and I have together. I told him what had happened and he was wonderful about it. Then it just sort of went on from there. He began to make sense about living together and finally agreed to go back to the States with me. When I was sure that you weren't still gnawing away at me, I asked him for the chain. All of a sudden, we knew we were in love with each other. I know what it means now."

"Wonderful, honey. I want to give you a wedding present. You're going to have to make plans. There've been some changes."

"I had the feeling there was something in the air. You're being sweet to us but something's wrong, isn't it?"

"Quite a lot. I'll—"

André returned. "I told them to make us those passionate gin things. Did I give you time enough?"

"Gerry is just about to tell us some news. We'd better shut up and listen."

Gerry looked down at the ring. "OK. The great love of my life hasn't lasted very long." He heard André make a stricken sound and hurried on. "That's all I want any of us to say about it. Please. I don't think I'm going to break down but I might and I don't want to. I just found out that Ernst has left. I don't know where but I suspect Kashmir is out. For me, in any case. I left last night with nothing but the clothes I was wearing. That bag has followed me. No room for misunderstanding there. That's all. Let's talk about music."

"Oh darling, I can't stand this for you," André said. "I'm sorry. I won't say any more."

"I've already said more than I should about how I felt," Hank said. "OK. Let's talk about what we're going to do. Andy and I have already decided we want to get going as soon as possible. We wondered if we could beg out of Kashmir. This makes it simpler for us. We'll go straight to Paris so he can see his mother and then we'll go to Texas and turn him into a cowboy. Of course, there's a little question of money. If you don't lend us some, we aren't going anywhere."

"I won't. That's my first decision as a rich man. I'm never going to lend anybody anything. I'm going to give you a present to help you get started. I'll give you five thousand now and have five more waiting for you when you get home. If you want to get going, why not go in the car after lunch? You'll be my guests in Colombo. It'll take you a day to get your papers straight. Yorgo said your embassies are expecting you. If I were you, I wouldn't fool around any longer. Get started on the important things in life."

"But what about you?" André asked. "What are you going to do?"

"I don't know." He realized that somewhere in the back of his mind he had seen himself picking up Ernst's scent and following him, letting him know through Solange that he was near and readily available. They had talked enough about Paris for him to feel sure that he would have no trouble finding him there. He suddenly rejected the possibility. Ernst had made the breach irreconcilable. All the choices had been made last night without his knowing it. He worked the heavy ring off his little finger and held it in his fist. "I'm more or less on my way to New York but I'm not quite sure of the timing."

"Don't be dumb," Hank said. "Come with us. We'll all go together."

Gerry looked from one to the other, from the stalwart honesty of Hank's dark good looks to the eager beauty of André's radiant face and the temptation to stay with them was almost irresistible, but he knew that it wouldn't be fair to them. There remained a volatility in their closely intertwined relationship that could be destructive until their discovery of each other was tested and sure. "You go on," he replied firmly. "I want to see Nesta again. I'll probably have to come up before you go to help you get the money business straightened out. You can call when you've found out about planes and things. I don't think I want to go to Paris. We'll all meet up again in the States."

"Oh please," André begged. "It'll be so much more fun if we're all together."

"No, babies. You're finally making sense with each other. That's going to keep you both busy. I honestly want to be on my own." He said it with such cold finality that the subject was dropped.

When lunch was ready, Gerry made a quick detour to his room to drop the ring. He passed Rana and nodded to him as if he'd never seen him before. He wished the world would begin to function around him again so that he could recapture some sense of identity in relation to it.

Hank and André were in loving good spirits and appeared to be undaunted by Gerry's blank detachment. He had only to smile mechanically and make an occasional comment to keep lunch happy for them. Some pocket of hope still functioned in him, fabricating a farfetched dénouement in which Ernst arrived to beg him to return. It could happen. Solange might make an effective last-minute plea just as they were about to board their plane. They had left the hotel shortly after noon. Time to drive to the airport. Time for Solange to overcome his resistance. Time for Ernst to grasp the extent of his loss. Somebody, perhaps Solange herself, could get here by midafternoon. He didn't really believe in it but the scenario repeated itself with variations while he smiled.

When talk turned to Hank's resumption of work and the possibilities awaiting André in the States, Gerry found his interest more immediately engaged. He reminded Hank of his hopes of starting a firm of his own and offered to go into financial partnership with him. If André found an opportunity to get into dress design, he too might want financial backing. Getting used to spending large sums of money gave Gerry something practical to think about. He wanted them to go, in a bleak detached way. Being totally alone might jolt him back into an awareness of living. Suffering was better than nothing.

"You better get off by four," Gerry told them when they had finished the meal. "It's no fun driving at night here."

"We don't have much packing to do," André said. "I don't *want* to go. I can't stand leaving you here."

"Don't worry. I'll be along tomorrow or the next day, as soon as you know what you're doing."

"It's exciting talking about being in the States with you. You promise to come see us soon?"

"Sure, darling. I'll give you a month or two to settle down and then I'll be along. We'll all go into business together." He gave the beautiful boy a hug and something seemed to slip into place; a sense of returning from a great distance stirred in him.

They brought their bags out and again went over everything they'd discussed about money and tickets and their reunion in Texas. They hugged each other a great deal and wandered out to the car together while the boys bustled around them. The gates swung open, car doors slammed, Gerry stood in the drive and waved without seeing them as the car started forward.

He turned back to the house and drifted through space to the edge of the veranda facing the sea. He stood looking out, feeling his solitude. The peaceful beauty of the vista was poignant and painful. Ernst had looked at it. He was returning to life and everything in him was beginning to hurt but he felt a steadying strength in himself. He had learned that he could love. He had been faithful to an ideal. He was prepared to suffer again for a complete union with his unknown Beloved. He didn't regret his choice; gain balanced loss. He was finally whole and able to offer his wholeness to another.

He was rich. He was still young enough and apparently attractive. He could go to Amsterdam and see Jan. Big deal. He could look up Nat Makin in New York. His gay half brother. Blood was thicker than water. Maybe Walter had left them something in common. Hank and André would be waiting in Texas to welcome him.

Except for the human incapacity to recognize and seize happiness, sexual incompatibility, the clash of temperament, the overweening demands of ego, the blind insatiable human cry of "I want, I want," there was nothing now to stand in the way of his fulfillment in the only way he had ever glimpsed it—in the love that two men could offer each other. A bird fell out of a nearby bush. He smiled, although his vision was blurred.

Rana appeared beside him. "Master wishes a peg?" he asked.

He gave his head a little shake and turned to Rana and put a hand on his shoulder. "That's an idea. Maybe several pegs and then—it looks as if we can have our time together after all. Do you still want that?"

"Yes, master. Very."

"Good. Several large pegs and then we'll see what you can do for a broken heart."

"Yes, master. Very glad. Very jolly."

"That's the spirit, Rana. Very glad and jolly." He moved away from the boy, rubbing the finger where the ring had been.